STARSIGHT

VOLUME 1

MINNETTE MEADOR

Stonegarden.net Publishing
http://www.stonegarden.net

Reading from a different angle.

Starsight Volume 1 Copyright © 2008 Minnette Meador

ISBN: 1-60076-056-2

StoneGarden.net Publishing
3851 Cottonwood Dr.
Danville, CA 94506

First StoneGarden.net Publishing paperback printing:
March 2008

Visit StoneGarden.net Publishing on the web at
http://www.stonegarden.net.

Cover art and design by Derrick Freeland

To Matt for his inspiration and unconditional love
To Derrick, Devon and Paul for their never wavering encouragement
To Patrick for always being there

STARSIGHT, VOLUME I
TABLE OF CONTENTS

ACKNOWLEDGEMENTS

As always, creativity does not happen without support from loving family, good friends, or kind strangers. There are simply too many people who have encouraged, inspired, and helped over the years it has taken to complete this story to name them all here. Below are but a few brave souls who listened patiently, made suggestions, held me when I cried, or kicked me in the butt. I could not have done this without them.

Matt Meador
Paul Powell
Derrick Freeland
Devon Freeland
Gina Freeland
Jared Meador
Patrick Smith
Roland Smith
Shirley Howard
Dawn Hummel
Steph Bremner
Kris Stamp
Jenny Carress
Piers Anthony
Spider Robinson

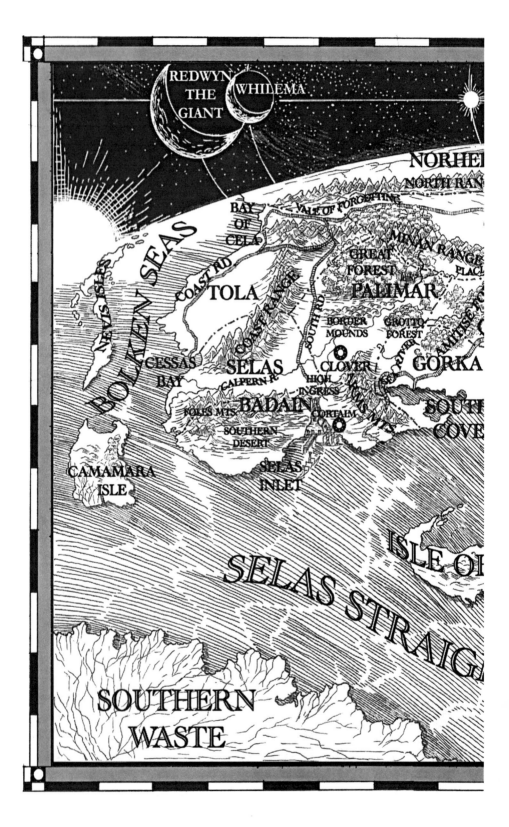

ETHOS EVAS VENTUS HYDOR LEUKO
LENTAS LOGATI ERAZE

RN LANDS Mt. CATSON
GE KEEP
WEST-EAST RD.
THRAIN BAY CALISAE
HIGH OF
CLIFFS EMPIRE

ETHOSIAN SEAS

QUITAIN

WEATEN
BAY

DRU

WELCOME
HARBOR

HT ISLE
OF
MATHISMA

ASSEMBLAGE HOME
SANCTUM BRIDGE
SANCTUM

CAST OF CHARACTERS
(In Order of Appearance)

TRENARA - Second Trial Starguider to Joshan

HAIDEN BAILS - Sergeant of the Gate Guard & the First Prince's weapons instructor

JOSHAN JENHADA KANAINE - First Prince, Heir to the emperor's throne

JENHADA THORINGALE KANAINE - Emperor of the Eight Provinces - Keeper of Mathisma - Joshan's father

PRAVIUS - Councilor of Justice - Advisor to Emperor Jenhada

ENA - Trenara's aide

SALDORIAN - Jenhada's consort - Joshan's mother

VANDERLINDEN - One-eyed sea captain - Master of the Village

WERT - Van's friend from the Village

MATI FORESONS - Innkeeper at Foresons Lodge

PAP - Barman from "Pap's Pub" in the Village

SARK DUMONTAIRE - A mercenary from the Village

SHAWN - One of Van's lieutenants

BORIC - One of Van's lieutenants

TIGE - She is one of Sark's lieutenants

JONA - A private in the Elite Corps

THIELS - A lieutenant in the Elite Corps

ANNO - One of Pravius's northern guards

KIT - One of Pravius's northern guards

MOLLY - Madame of The House

DONNALLY - Sark's first lieutenant

DOTTIE - Saldorian's lady - Joshan's nursemaid

BALINAR - Sirdar's captain

TAM - Vanderlinden's First Mate

TAK - Clurichaune from The Grotto

THE DALIGON - Sirdar's Champion

LEOGAN - Soldier from Felos

SIRDAR - Lord of Badain

SAL CARRIMAN - Imperial sail maker

DEINOS - A reptilian creature serving Sirdar

WITEN - Prelate of Assemblage

GRANDOR - Keep of the Books, Mathisma

ACON - Witen's servant

PALARINE - Provost Elect of Assemblage

THE CRYSTAL OF HEALING - Assemblage's *Power*

THORINGALE - Joshan's grandfather

NINIA - Vanderlinden's mother

NOCINE - Prince of the North

NORSK - King of the North

KRIKOS - Goddess of Life

VENTUS - Goddess of the Wind

STARSIGHT – VOLUME I
BOOK I – THE BOY

CHAPTER ONE
THE STARGUIDER

Age crept through her certainty like a malignancy, leaving the guider feeling old and sick inside, as she stared up at the menacing black wall. She couldn't hold it back—her magic was simply too weak. Trenara stood alone, trembling as the darkness towered above her. It was so long, it faded into distance on either side of her frail form; and so tall, it fused into black clouds high above her head as a deafening thunder pounded the sky and scattered lightning blinded her.

She stood between the wall and the world. The shadow rushed forward, eating away at everything so quickly there was no time to respond. When she could do nothing else, Trenara howled up in frustration, her tiny fists quivering with fury, her mouth silent in the roar of the ruin. There was nothing she could do to stop it from shattering the Imperium, not even a hope she could grasp in her tiny fingers. When the world surrendered, a feeble shaft of light opened the blackness for a fleeting instant and showed her once again the only promise against destruction: a frightened child—and a broken wand. The starguider screamed.

*****

Trenara came out of the dream with a start and sat up. Scanning the room, she thought she had heard a scream and then realized it must have been her own. Her vocal chords still ached as she touched her throat uncertainly, scowling at the early morning. The guider's nightgown was soaked with sweat, and clumps of waist-long gray hair clung to her forehead and neck. She threw her legs over the side of the bed and buried her face in her hands, shaking uncontrollably for a moment. Taking a deep breath to stop the tremors, Trenara got up to cross to her dressing room.

She tried to dislodge the dream that haunted her as she dressed, but her trembling hands were making the simple action of buttoning her undershirt almost impossible. She dressed as quickly as she could. Her aide Ena had laid out food and tea on the table, but Trenara ignored it, as she tied her hair into a loose knot at the back of her head and stepped to the balcony to try to calm her shattered senses in the morning breeze.

Far below, she could see the tide was in and the ships, so very few it seemed, were moored haphazardly to the docks. She frowned at the harbor, wondering why it seemed so empty. *The captain would be furious if he were alive*, Trenara thought. Blue and black sea scalards flew in large flocks as they screamed and darted in the salty air. The pound of the surf and the hiss of the tide were very faint as they drifted up the castle wall. The sound helped to soothe her mangled nerves.

The nightmare was approaching the realm of *vision*, she knew, but of what she didn't know, and the thought unsettled her. It felt as if the gods were meddling again, directing her, forcing her toward something. But, as always, she didn't know what. They had done this to her many times, for as long as she could remember. The guider told no one, of course; it wasn't something you shared. This time the *visions* were frightening, confusing and involved not only herself, but also a child she loved— Joshan. Trenara shivered, returned to the room to grab her satchel, and left in a black mood.

*****

"No, no, lad!" Haiden brought his quarterstaff up and pounded it into the ground. He wiped sweat from his brow with the back of his hand and spat into the dust at his feet. "Put your back into it, not your arms. I've seen you fight better with your nurse."

Joshan, perhaps half the size of the grizzly older man and a fraction of his age, circled around, and adjusted his grip; this man was notorious for his speed and trickery. The boy's tunic was streaked with sweat and his face red with exertion. With energy he didn't feel, Joshan again lunged at Haiden uselessly.

"That's better, lad." The sergeant gave him a half crooked smile and switched the staff to his other hand. "Now, let's see what you can do with some real fighting." He crouched low and readied his attack.

Joshan put up his stave and massaged his side. "A moment, Haiden. Let me catch my breath."

"Your breath, is it? Well, if you think your enemy will give you time to catch your breath, think again." He gave a vicious cry and charged.

In the same instant Joshan dived for the ground. The tip of Haiden's staff just missed the prince's ear and Joshan pushed his staff across the sergeant's legs. Haiden didn't have time to stop before winding his burly limbs around the shaft and stumbling headlong into the dusty courtyard. He spun around, spitting out dirt and glared at the young prince with a mute smile. Joshan was beside himself with laughter.

"You'll be sore a week for that!" Haiden hauled himself up and ran after the boy, who stopped his laughter only long enough to skirt a battle dummy.

"You should be proud, sergeant." Joshan wiped his eyes, which glistened darkly in the morning light. "I've only done what you taught me."

"I'll teach you a thing or three when I get my hands on you. Now hold still."

Haiden feinted to the left, causing the boy to move a little too quickly to the right, and then he had him. Weak with laughter, they went down in a tangle of arms and legs and dust. Over and over they rolled, almost ending under the hooves of two very frightened eechas tethered nearby. The creatures arched their high backs, and a shudder sent the long fur rippling as they skirted the two and shrieked their displeasure.

Guards gathered to watch the play. Though the boy was barely ten and the guard close to sixty, they were admired by everyone who knew them. Their laughter mingled in a delightful harmony of youthful giggle and aged guffaw.

A voice ripped through the courtyard with a sudden, sharp edge that broke the noisy revelry. "Haiden!" Both turned to see the regal figure of Jenhada glaring down at them from a balcony, and smiles dissolved. Haiden and the others fell to one knee and bent their heads.

The emperor clutched a heavy cloak around once strong shoulders as if to ward off chill, although the air was quite warm and approaching the torridness of high season. Deep lines etched his face, and his eyes were shadows under a course mane of graying hair.

"It seems, sergeant, you would have better things to do with your time than this foolery." His voice was edged with a contempt that sent shivers through Haiden's spine; but in it, too, was the underlying fatigue of sleepless nights. The emperor's illness showed in the lines around his mouth, the furrows in his formerly smooth brow, and in those restless eyes. "You will see to it this does not happen again. Failing this, I will find my son another trainer. What brawling you do with your men, is your business. The prince is mine. Do I make myself clear?"

"Yes, sire." Haiden nodded once humbly.

Jenhada snorted an acknowledgement and exchanged a glance with Councilor Pravius who stood at his back. The man returned the look with a nod of approval. "Isn't it time for your lessons?" The emperor barely glanced at Joshan as he pulled the collar up around his neck. "That is, if that *magician* of yours hasn't forgotten again. Get yourself cleaned up and at least somewhat presentable. You are not a beggar. I will not have you looking like one!"

"Yes, father." Joshan lowered his eyes so his father would not see the anger. The blush of embarrassment turned his face scarlet to the ears.

Jenhada leaned on his cane and limped off without another word, as the bent figure of Pravius glared at Joshan. The prince thought for a fleeting moment the councilor's face had changed; it was hard and cruel, a side of Pravius Joshan had never seen before. When he blinked, the expression had faded and the man was once again the tiny, pale figure with massive sad eyes Joshan had known since he could remember. Pravius spared the prince a languid nod before turning to catch up with the emperor.

Haiden got up and brushed dust from his clothes, looking after Jenhada. The crowd disbanded in silence as Joshan straightened his tunic and retrieved his staff. "I'm sorry, Haiden," he said. "Father's been very sick lately. I don't know what comes over him sometimes."

"I know, lad. I've known your da a long time." Grabbing the prince's shoulders, he pushed him gently toward the entrance. "But off with you. I got work to do and Trenara will have my hide if you're late."

"Tomorrow, then." Joshan ran for his quarters, throwing his staff to a guard.

*****

Joshan had just arrived at Fourth Gate when he saw his mentor's beautiful white eecha charging down the road at full gallop, the stallion's flat face and long ears rippling in the wind. There was no mistaking the Starguider Trenara, even at that distance. Her tall, slim figure was held straight in the saddle, a magnificent silver mane of wayward hair flowing behind her like a tempest, despite feeble attempts to tame it. Piercing azure blue eyes shone from a face that seemed ageless, despite soft lines and the mantle of gray around it. Her beauty was still striking, and she often turned heads, even at fifty-two seasons.

Trenara was wearing blue today, a sign she was in a pensive mood. Joshan had been with the guider on a daily basis for so long, knowing her moods had become second nature to the boy. *No stories today*, he thought dismally. He wished he could stay with Haiden, but knew better. It was going to be another day of rote lessons and boring recitals.

Trenara spotted the lad and gave him a curt nod, catching the flash in the young eyes. Joshan had the oval shape of his mother's face and the dark coloring of his father, but the eyes, not the mother's nor even the father's, shone brown-black in the mid-morning light and were distinctly his own.

The black and white eecha he was straddling reared as Trenara approached, spooked by the crystal scepter tucked in her robes. The animal jostled him on the high saddle until Joshan got her under control. "Where to today, guider?" he asked cheerfully, undaunted by the guider's mood.

"The High Cliffs, I should think." Trenara shaded her eyes to measure the sun. "But I'd like to stop in the forest first." She dug her heels into her eecha and did not look back to see if Joshan followed.

As they emerged from the thick archway of Fourth Gate, a huge open plaza spread out before them, alive with marching guards, fighting men and women, and soldiers doing what they did best—marshalling together in perfectly formed straight columns. Joshan glanced at them longingly, again wishing he could stay. There hadn't been a war in the provinces in nearly thirty seasons, but the Guards still recruited, trained, and prepared though the numbers had dwindled to less than a fraction of their old force. The massive military grounds looked strangely deserted.

On the other side of great courtyard, beyond the training fields, barracks, and medical facilities loomed an enormous steel reinforced wall; Third Gate. The large entrance was always open at this time of day. A squad of Elite, the emperor's personal guard, stood at attention on either side like vivid blue standards, bright against the aging stone blocks. The village of Keepton could be seen through the gate, the bustling market at the height of its trade. Between the noise of the shouting guards on one side and the crying vendors selling their wares on the other, Joshan and Trenara had to cover their ears as they passed through the echoing tunnel.

Trenara was thankful to be leaving the Keep, as the wet weather had trapped them in the castle for nearly a month. She glanced up at the pale blue sky, the wisps of grey-white clouds floating delicately above their heads and the mayhem of humanity parting for them as they moved through the first of two villages sheltered in the immense fortress. In earlier times, an escort of several guards would have been required for them to leave the castle. *Thank the gods they don't do that anymore,* she thought as they moved through the milling crowd. The Imperium had enjoyed thirty seasons of peace and the countryside was safe again, not to mention the fact that most people would think twice about attacking a Starguider.

As they made their way through the streets of the village, she saw several uniformed men, but they seemed out of place. Trenara didn't think much of it until they reached Second Gate. She knew many of the guards personally and had for years; but at each of the three gates leading to the countryside, these men seemed to be strangers to her now. The guider eyed a few of them suspiciously, knowing they were not from Thrain.

They were dark, swarthy men who leered at them. Her eyesight wasn't good without the spectacles she habitually left behind, and they all looked alike to her, so she passed it off as fancy. However, as they approached First Gate, Trenara noticed where once there had been a full complement of guards, there seemed to be a minimal crew. Odd, since she knew Haiden kept the gates fully manned at all times. She would talk to the emperor about it next time she saw him, but wondered again when that would be.

Her mind wandered to Jenhada. The emperor hadn't called her in several months, and she missed the dinners they usually shared to discuss the Imperium, both the Empire and Assemblage. Trenara knew of his illness, of course, his lack of sleep and the blinding headaches. When she tried to reach him, she was refused by the Elite, stating the emperor would call at need. Trenara thought she was getting sensitive in her old age. After all, the emperor was a busy man and she had her books, her studies, and Joshan to look after.

"What are you thinking, guider?" Joshan asked, seeing his mentor scowling.

"Oh, nothing, lad," she replied pensively as they approached the tunnel to First Gate. "Let's get going."

"Good enough!" Without warning, Joshan spurred his eecha into a full dash down the long passageway and disappeared in a cloud of dust before Trenara could call. The guider tapped her mount irritably.

"Come along, Gliding. We better catch the young idiot before he breaks his neck." She goaded him into a gallop, the stones echoing the hoof beats like drum rolls.

Some leagues from the Keep, after a grueling race through rutted fields and hidden sands surrounding the fortress walls, the guider caught the spirited rider. Joshan had slowed his mare to a trot and was casually taking in the sights and sounds of the beautiful high season day.

"A marvelous morning, don't you think?" he ventured, as the guider rode up beside him.

"Don't give me that. You're fortunate you didn't break your neck, charging off like that. Your father would roast me alive if anything were to happen to you. I'll thank you not to risk your neck along with mine. Though both are probably worth little, I still value them!"

Joshan gave her one of those special, disarming smiles. "Please don't scold me, not today. This one feels special somehow. I promise I won't do it again."

"I doubt that. But it is a lovely day and there *is* something rather special I wanted to show you."

Joshan regarded her wide-eyed and stood up in the stirrups. "What?" Trenara's "something specials" were really to be marveled.

Trenara chuckled. "Well, you're going to have to behave yourself. That eecha of yours is too large for you as it is. How Haiden ever talked me into it, I'll never know. At the very least, you could cause her a fall and possibly break her leg, not to mention your own. Then where would you be?"

Joshan sat back in the saddle and patted the mare's neck affectionately. "Not Whirl. She's very sure footed and Haiden says she seems to have more sense than me."

"That I won't contest," she said flatly. "Come on. We've a lot of trail to cover, so step it up." They left the main road and proceeded to the forest that lined it. Once through the trees they picked up a well-used path and followed in silence.

Something is gnawing Trenara, Joshan thought. He decided not to dwell on it, though he did wonder what the starguider had in store for him. He knew when he woke this day was going to be exceptional. He didn't want anything to spoil it. Unfortunately, Trenara did not share the lad's enthusiasm. The dreams still haunted her, awakening something she hadn't felt in seasons. Even Andelian, the crystal scepter tucked in her robes, felt colder somehow today. She began to feel ancient.

They finally reached a moss-blanketed clearing in the trees, where they went through the hour or so of voice training. Joshan hit the notes exactly as Trenara had taught him, each one perfect in his high voice. The boy's talents had always been uncanny, almost genius. It was the main reason the prince was chosen to train for Assemblage. His mastery of the musical notes that amplified the *power* with their resonance was unsurpassed by anyone of his age, or very possibly, anyone this side of *second trial.* He had been a phenomenon almost since birth.

Not just with the control notes. The boy had a talent for spoken manipulation as well, which usually came only after many seasons of training for any other guider. When very young, Joshan found if he pitched his voice in a certain way, his nurse would do almost anything. That all ended, of course, when Trenara took over his training. She was immune to his pranks, and he was usually punished severely when he tried to manipulate her. Without knowing it, he could have seriously hurt or even killed someone. It was for this reason Trenara had been selected to train the prince. Her voice and techniques were equally uncanny. On the few occasions when they sang together, everyone within earshot had to stop to listen. The sound was exquisite.

After the lessons, they remounted to travel to the High Cliffs. This was a long journey as the climb was taxing on the animals, so they had to be rested often. Neither the guider nor her pupil minded, however. Despite their differences, they enjoyed each other's company.

On long journeys, Trenara usually told wonderful stories as they rode. If asked, she would take you to ancient times, long before the Crystal of Healing fell from the heavens, or Assemblage and the Empire governed the world. Back to Kerillian the Prophet, and his travels through the old provinces. Sometimes, she spoke quietly of the dark times: tales of monsters, wars, and brave deeds. Trenara would often talk about Assemblage itself, its greatness, and its failings. She would speak longingly of Mathisma, the Assemblage home nestled in an island fortress far over the Ethosian Sea to the east. Or she'd tell you about the Starguiders, their queer, enigmatic ways and the music of *power*, always with a bemused smile.

If you were very, very good, the guider would sing the histories, her contralto voice so pure it would take you to another world entirely. At times Joshan would join her in his favorites, his high voice adding complicated harmonies and intricate melodies. This was always the best time for both of them.

Her tales were not limited to the *power*. They included the history of the provinces, the empire, and the grand (and not so grand) deeds of Joshan's ancestors, the long line of emperors and empresses that preceded him. The prince felt he learned more from these ancient stories than from any books, and Trenara silently agreed.

The eechas plodded along the trail, their hoof beats dulled by the soft ground, as green-filtered sunrays danced solemnly around them. The trees chattered with life and the fragrance of the afternoon had an intoxicating appeal. It caused the guider's mood to soften, and the prince's to mellow. Each was once again immersed in the friendship they had grown to love.

"What tale shall it be today, lad?" Trenara asked cheerfully.

Joshan thought for a moment, but hesitated to ask for what he really wanted. The guider was in such a wonderful mood, it might be the perfect time; or then again, the worst.

"Come, come, out with it. The story of Cessas and the Crystal? The Sea Tarsian and the Princess? The…"

"Well, I had thought, perhaps the story of… of Sirdar, ma'am."

Trenara pulled her reins and shot Joshan a stern look. "Sirdar?" Narrowing her eyes, she didn't speak at once, looking the boy over carefully.

This was too much for Joshan, who stared down at his hands. "That is… of course, you don't have to if you don't want to."

"Hmmm." Trenara clicked to her eecha and continued down the path with Joshan riding in tortured silence beside her.

"It's a dark story," the guider said at length, gazing at the trail, "and to be honest, one I should have told you before this. I suppose now would be as good a time as any." She settled into the saddle and Joshan didn't say a word.

"It was almost thirty seasons ago when the signs came… signs that something was wrong.

"It was a good season." Trenara sighed, an old memory sparking a small smile. "One of the finest, as I recall. Your father was at his peak in those days; young, headstrong and untried, yet brave and wise when the empire needed him to be. The young man who had been simply Prince Jenhada had become Emperor Jenhada Thoringale Kanaine." She paused for a moment, staring off into the woods.

"The first reports came from Badain in the south; reports that a large flying lizard had destroyed several small villages and was terrorizing the populace. The scholars consulted their books and discovered that the monster could only be a flying tarsian. It was an ancient reptile, a creature bent on the destruction of anything living. But tarsians had been extinct for centuries. The emperor sent soldiers, of course, and passed it off as an isolated incident. Unfortunately, it wasn't. More villages burned, more lives were lost, more soldiers sent, never to return.

"Then other creatures began to appear... some of them so strange and unfamiliar we had a hard time believing they could possibly exist. That is, until we saw them with our own eyes," she continued gravely. "There was the sasaran, a perversion of a beast that walked like a man, had immense black horns, hoofed feet, and a wicked temper. The laminia, creatures who lived on the blood of the helpless. The Mourna... the Assemblage Bane. Its voice drew the unsuspecting guider to do the bidding of its master. It appeared as an enormous black bird..." The drone of her voice stopped as a memory sent shivers through her. "There were others." Her eyes stayed fixed on the path ahead. "Gruesome to see—dangerous to cross.

"A seditious starguider named Balinar took the Crystal of Healing from Sanctum where it had been safe for millennia. He escaped to Badain, where he became captain to the master who had summoned him.

"A terrible fear weakened the Imperium. Without the Crystal, the *power* was erratic and often lethal. Assemblage was crippled, and the name of Sirdar spread like fire as his forces marched toward Thrain. The horde blackened the land and the hearts of men as they advanced. Faithful men succumbed to his spell daily, taking up his banner and joining his ranks—hundreds of thousands of them. Edicts poured into the Keep proclaiming Sirdar master, threatening complete annihilation if the emperor did not throw open his gates and surrender.

"By the end of Meridian, the enemy crossed the borders of Thrain, driving a multitude of refugees before them that filled the Keep to overflowing. Sirdar's army stood like a massive wave at our gates. No assault could move them, or tricks deter them. Finally, we could do nothing more than quake behind Thrain's last defense. After a long siege, the emperor and his armies marched out to meet them.

"While the battle raged at The Keep hundreds of leagues away, Sirdar stayed at his fortress in Badain, afraid to move from its protection until his victory was assured. Assemblage sent its strongest men and women to face him. A hundred Starguiders marched on the castle at Mt. Cortaim." Trenara lowered her head and tears filled her eyes. "We believe most were lost to Sirdar's creatures or destroyed by the blackest magic. What few remained charged his fortress and there passed out of knowledge.

"No one knows what happened that day in Badain. All we know is the darkness was soon abated, the creatures drew back from our borders, and the land cleared of foe. The war, which had raged at the Keep's gates, ended all at once when the enemy fled in terror. Many were trampled by their own eechas and more killed by our advancing armies. The rest were captured and eventually sent back to their homes, most uncertain why they waged war to begin with. Sirdar's power over them had been complete.

"None of the Assemblage who traveled to Badain ever returned, and like a miracle, the Crystal of Healing was found back in its place of honor at Sanctum. By what device, no one knows." She stopped for a moment and turned her head away.

"There are many conjectures as to what happened in the south. The only thing we are reasonably certain of was that Sirdar and Balinar were destroyed. When reports came in later, it was found that Mt. Cortaim, where Sirdar kept his headquarters, was nothing more than a pile of rubble and melted rock. No one could have survived. We searched, of course, but there was nothing to find. Safeguards were put into place in Badain and the emperor ordered that no starguider be allowed to set foot in the province again.

"That was the end of it. It took seasons to heal, but the reasons for Sirdar's rise and the cause of his fall are lost in a mountain of fused glass. I suppose the mysteries will never be solved." She grew still then.

The afternoon began to fade to early dusk and the forest was quiet. Joshan glanced at the furrowed brow of his mentor and put a small hand on hers as it rested on the saddle. "It's over now," he whispered.

"Yes—over. It brings back memories just as soon forgotten." She remained silent for some time and finally breathed deeply to shake the feelings. "Enough of this gloom," she said at length, throwing him a glorious smile. "What say we see who has the fastest eecha?"

Joshan grinned broadly. "I'll wager we beat you by twenty spans, at least," he said, hastily adjusting his reins.

"And I'll wager a month's lessons we leave you behind by at least a league."

"You're going to miss me for a whole month. To the ridge?"

"As you wish."

They went thundering down the path in a spray of mud and grass. Despite the prince's best efforts, Trenara won the race and Joshan heartily vowed to beat her one day, to which the guider chuckled. She knew it would not be far in the future, having won this one by no more than a hand's breadth by what she considered luck—with possibly a dash of treachery.

When they reached the High Cliffs, it was approaching dusk. After a light supper, they sat on the edge of the towering rock face that fell thousands of spans below their dangling feet, the Keep to the left and the Ethosian Sea to the right. The sun was a giant red disc hanging lazily on the western horizon, with endless drifts of red and purple clouds billowing across the evening sky. The star Ethos shone like a fiery beacon on the eastern horizon, and the two watched the spectacle of sunset in silence.

"You see the star?" the guider asked at length, pointing to the flickering brilliance as it rose from the sea.

"She always rises before the moons, doesn't she? Why is it Ethos seems larger than the other stars and so much brighter?" Joshan threw pebbles into the chasm under his feet and watched as they bounced off the cliff face below.

"It's closer to our world than the other stars, so it only appears larger." Trenara pointed to the large rosy moon starting its climb. "Both moons, Redwyn and Whilema, would seem like stars if you could stand on Ethos. As would our own world, I'd venture. Though the star is nearer, it is still some billion, billion leagues away."

The boy whistled softly. "I can't even imagine a distance that far."

The guider laughed. "You will, if you pay attention to your lessons. When we reach Mathisma, you'll learn under more knowledgeable teachers than I. Astronomy has never been one of my strengths."

The boy regarded the darkening sky. "When will I reach *first trial*, Trenara?" he asked dreamily.

"Oh, not for many seasons—at least three or four. After that, you will travel to the island and learn so much more of your craft."

"If I ever get to Mathisma."

Trenara shot up an eyebrow. "Now what's that supposed to mean?"

Joshan shook out of his reverie and looked at the guider with a wistful smile. "I don't know. Sometimes I get the impression… well I just can't seem to picture myself studying in the Learning Halls of Assemblage." He turned to regard the Keep and put his chin in his hands. "Just a feeling, I guess."

"More like wishful thinking, if you ask me," she replied, throwing a stone down the cliff face. "You've never been overly fond of book learning."

"Can you blame me? All cooped up with a bunch of dusty old books?"

"Dusty old—scoundrel! You are beginning to sound like Vanderlinden," Trenara exclaimed, but Joshan gave her a sad nod.

"That does sound like the captain, doesn't it? I miss him sometimes."

Trenara's eyes dulled for a moment. "As do I, my boy. He was a good friend." She drew a deep breath. "But once you get to Mathisma, I think you'll enjoy it."

Joshan gave her a half smile. "We'll see."

He jumped up and hung from the limb of a nearby tree. "Guider, tell me more about the stars."

Trenara rose stiffly and brushed the dirt from her robes. "Not just now. I had something entirely different in mind."

Joshan loosened his grip on the limb and dropped to the ground, the excitement making his eyes twinkle. "What?"

"Come on. Let's go back to the clearing. It'll be safer there."

They walked through the few sparse trees that outlined the cliffs and came into a large clearing blanketed by wild green grasses and night-dark flowers. Trenara went to the eechas, threw her cloak over Gliding, and then put her satchel on the saddle horn. She drew her *via* Andelian from her robes and returned to Joshan. The crystal rod caught the early moonlight and colors flashed brightly in the segmented orb at its top.

"Sit there," she said, indicating a small boulder at one end of the glade. Joshan stared at her wide-eyed with anticipation and silently did her bidding, as the guider stepped to the center to survey the grass and trees surrounding them. When she seemed satisfied, she turned to the boy and winked.

"I thought you might like to see what the *power* can do."

"Oh, yes, please," Joshan exclaimed, clapping his hands.

"Very well, then. But first, tell me how it works."

The prince was disappointed by the delay, but said, "The *power* comes from the star Ethos, then into the Crystal of Healing which lies in Sanctum on Mathisma, and then to one of the Assemblage *via*s where it's amplified with the musical notes." The words tumbled out like spilled water, but he added more slowly, "Uh, your *via* is Andelian."

Trenara scowled. "Well, basically correct, though sketchy at best. I'll forgive your curt reply since I know you've learned more than this in all your seasons of training." A guilty look flashed over his young face, but it was soon replaced by excitement, and the chide was quickly forgotten.

"Now…" Trenara began and lifted her arms to allow the sleeves of her robe to fall back.

The clearing was dark. The sun had taken its last yawn at the sky and nestled beyond the horizon to the west, while the larger of the two moons, Redwyn the Giant, rose stiffly from his slumber in the east and cast a ruby hue over the night. Whilema would soon slip from the waves of the Ethosian Sea and try to drown her brother's light. Though a great deal smaller, the moon was several times more brilliant. Their battle for the dominion of the night would begin. Neither moon was full that night, allowing the milliard of stars to litter the sky like a thrown handful of magic dust. A night fowl shrieked, a rodent screamed, and then all was very still.

Trenara faced the east with Andelian held high. She closed her eyes and a barely audible chant chimed on the air, the crystal rod beginning to take on an almost imperceptible glow. A single exquisite musical note came from her throat: low, resonating, and perfect. There was a sudden hiss of wind that whipped the guider's robes around her, and then a blaze of white radiance that flashed through the glade and settled into a frosty glow around the guider's tall form.

She took a deep breath to ease the tension in her limbs and then sang another high note that floated a long time on the air. It focused the swirling light until she glowed like a white flame. Ecstasy enfolded her face as the *power* took hold and a radiant expression chased the age and wrinkles away, leaving not a woman, but an ethereal spirit, a shining goddess. When she lowered her eyes to Joshan, they glowed with white-hot fire that painted the young boy's face with awe.

Trenara's smile was glorious.

"You like magic, don't you?" the guider asked, her voice dulcet and reverberating. Joshan nodded mutely. "Then, let's see if we can conjure some."

She pointed her scepter just to the right of Joshan's ear and began her song, so beautiful the boy's heart skipped a beat. A beam of light escaped the orb with a crackle and stopped where she intended, leaving a white spot no larger than a coin. The beam returned, but the spot remained and began to dance merrily in the darkness to the rhythm of her music. Joshan held his breath and heard a soft tinkling, like suspended glass in the wind.

The air began to fill with tiny dancing lights as Trenara struck fire again and again, until the sound of their music blended with her singing. It became a chorus of delightful bells.

Joshan's intoxication with the lights grew as he jumped from the rock and began to chase the elusive pseudo stars. They evaded his every move, teasing him mercilessly as they glided between splayed fingers, around his head or through his legs. Trenara's laughter echoed through the clearing in rippling waves that shook the leaves of the nearby trees.

The lights seemed to be strangely attracted to the boy as they gathered around him like so many moths to a flame. The guider hadn't given it much thought, however. Ethotic starmoths were an independent lot with likes and dislikes of their own. She remembered vaguely hearing they preferred children to adults. Something about being attracted to purity of heart or that strange, enigmatic quality that youngsters had, which seemed to harden with age.

After the frantic chase, Joshan sat heavily on the grass and Trenara decided to end the chaos. They had a long, hard ride ahead and she didn't relish the thought of carrying a sleeping prince back to the Keep. Off in the distance she caught the faint sound of horns coming up the cliff walls. The gates would be closed soon.

She lifted her scepter once more and spoke to the starmoths gently. "Come, children, time to go." Waving Andelian twice, Trenara sang to the wind and one by one, the lights were extinguished. Joshan held out his hands, watching the failing stars sadly, as they brushed his palms in farewell and then sighed when they were gone.

Andelian lost her sheen at once, and Trenara put the *via* back in her robes. Exhausted, she sat next to the prince and put her arm around his small shoulders. "Well, lad, what did you think?" Joshan was speechless for a moment, but then took the guider's hand and kissed it.

"Oh, Trenara, that was the most wonderful, the most spectacular… I've never seen anything like it. They are—delightful." Joshan felt it inadequate, but could think of nothing better.

"Perhaps, but the moths can be the devil's own when they want to be, especially to those they don't like." She smiled at an old memory and rose stiffly.

"I'm glad you enjoyed them… and they you. But we need to go. We'll barely make it back before they close the gates." She went to Gliding and donned her cloak, throwing the satchel over her shoulder. She turned to Joshan. "Are you coming?"

"In a moment, guider. I just wanted…" His voice was cut off as a strong gust of wind swept from the east, so powerful it threw Trenara into her eecha. Joshan's eyes widened in terror, and his feet became anchored to the ground. He stood as still as stone, although Trenara was having trouble keeping upright. His mouth hung open at an odd angle, moving as though he were trying to speak, but couldn't.

"No!" Trenara screamed against the wind. "Not now!" Fear ripped through the guider when she realized what was happening. She cursed the gods for choosing a time when she was unprepared. She had seen *first trial* several times, but each time the same foreboding took her. *Will the child survive the trial? Will my own power be enough?* And, strangely… *is the child old enough?* Never in her experience had the *power* taken one so young.

She struggled to get to the boy and pulled the still warm Andelian from its place. Joshan went to his knees as Trenara reached him, some silent demand having been given. The guider raised the scepter high above her head. As she placed her free hand on Joshan's brow, anger welled inside her at this unfortunate turn of events. Here, in the middle of the woods, leagues away from another living soul, there was nothing to help her but her *via* and her courage. She hoped they would be enough.

This time the notes she sang were very low, like the sound of distant thunder on a rising storm, a deep solemn song drowned by the *power's* wind. The notes bolted to the heavens and a faint echo answered. The *power* came as a mist from the sky and quickly turned to a torrent of glistening light as it drifted into the scepter she held tightly in her hand. Joshan paled and his breathing became shallow as the *power* took him.

Trenara's body stiffened, her breath became labored and fear threatened to consume her; and would have, had it not been for the overwhelming force suddenly thrust into her hands. The fire spread to her arms, her middle, her legs. With a jolt of clarity, it took over her mind in a single instant. She felt suddenly young and strong, certain of her abilities, and absolutely trusting of the *power* that engulfed her.

The guider fought desperately for the boy's consciousness, which seemed to slip away like sand through her fingers, and just as desperately not to harm the young mind as she entered its fringes. With every awareness, Trenara could feel Joshan's terror deepening to insanity and she struggled to hold him.

All the seasons of training and experience came to this one moment, this brief second in time. If she failed now, the child would die. When the guider had control of the white energy around them, she whispered gently into his ear, "Joshan, don't fight it. Let the *power* touch you. You'll feel pain—terrible, terrible pain—but I promise it will pass quickly. Remember your training. Let it touch you."

The light around them blazed, but Joshan's eyes were dull and vacant. "Trust me," Trenara rasped. "If you don't let the fire touch you, you'll die. You must master it. There's no other choice. Let it touch you." Slowly, almost unseen, a dim light began to grow in Joshan's eyes. "Yes!" Trenara exclaimed, trying to control her own use of the *power* now. "You must sing, Joshan. I can't help you." The drone of the wind swept her words away like dust.

Joshan could feel the presence of the *power* now and was suddenly unafraid. Exhilaration lit his mind with fire; a joy that few mortals could know filled him with ecstasy. He could hear every sound, feel each vibration on the air as though he were somehow linked with the life surrounding him. From the spider clinging desperately to the blade of grass at his feet, to the ancient trees that bowed low to the wind, he felt entangled with them, as if their awareness were his.

Joshan was no longer the child of ten seasons, full of wonder and awe. In an instant, he was beyond mortal flesh, beyond the primitive sight of man, into a new awareness that shouted at him madly and made mortality a small thing—very small. He was ultimate, alive, free.

Then, by degrees, the light began to change. It swirled around them, sparkling with the moon's brilliance reflected on its white beauty, when the fringes became tainted a pale blue. The blue deepened at an accelerated rate, alarming the guider so much she nearly dropped her *via*. *Second trial*, by the color, but that wasn't possible.

The blue veil pulsated, undulating around the two, while the trees watched and the world stood still for a breathless moment. With the abruptness of a lightning bolt, the blue became a shower of green flame, pouring down on them in a torrent, engulfing them with energy Trenara had never known. *Third trial!*

"Joshan, you must sing!" Trenara's demand grated on the boy's mind like a slap in the face. He opened his mouth, but no sound came out, and a wave of terror swept through him. Joshan strained to move the notes to the outside, but they died in his throat. The color of the flame deepened and became as dense as smoke. He felt the danger. He knew he would die and the guider with him, if he did not sing to end the *power*.

Visions came so suddenly to his mind, they made him sick with their intensity: his father's death, a vague shadow of a woman who could bring him triumph or terrible defeat, an annihilation of the empire more horrible than any imagining, a golden sword and then a black one, shot with red and Trenara—*Trenara?*

The *power* blackened. A scream pierced his mind. The pain was intolerable. *It burns! It burns!*

Then the final *vision* came and his destiny opened like a gaping wound. Joshan knew what his purpose was, knew what it would mean for the world, and it almost drove him mad. The horror shook his tiny body like an earthquake. He couldn't breathe, couldn't think, couldn't form the words. Trenara's thoughts reached out to him as a burst of fire in the darkness.

SING BEFORE WE BOTH PERISH!

A note of absolute perfection flowed from the boy's throat, controlled and sustained with such skill, the *power* began to fall away from them in vast, vibrating waves. Then another note, even more beautiful than the first, reverberated on the air with a command that made Trenara gasp. She had never heard anything more stunning, the voice of the gods. The notes grew to a crescendo that echoed down the cliffs and out to the sea taking the deadly light with them.

The *power* disappeared in a spark of brilliance, and the wind settled to a gentle evening breeze around them. The glimmer was gone and the glade was once again silent. Joshan fell unconscious into Trenara's arms, as she wept openly and clutched him to her chest.

After what seemed like hours, she put the scepter back in her robes with a trembling hand, and lay the boy on the ground, the springy turf cushioning her knees when she nearly dropped him. The mentor was weary to the bone and had to fight to keep unconsciousness from robbing her of this experience.

Trenara stared down at the sleeping child, finding it difficult to believe he could be breathing. Joshan should have died in such a conflict. They both should have died. The guider had never seen anything like this—the greatest contest and the longest possession by the *power* at *first trial*. If it *was first trial* she witnessed. The boy had *seen*. The green hue had shown that, but *seeing* wasn't possible until *third trial*. Trenara herself had not reached that pinnacle, though she had been a starguider for almost forty seasons.

Joshan moaned and tossed fitfully on the grass. Trenara struggled to her feet, pushing back the fearful implications that haunted her, to let a deeper, more maternal instinct take over. A light rain began to fall. With an effort, Trenara removed her cloak from the silent eecha and stumbled to throw it over the prostrate boy. Joshan cried out in his sleep; convulsions began to contort his body.

The guider reached into her satchel and removed a vial of imaka. She parted Joshan's lips gently and poured a few drops on the fevered tongue. The liquid worked quickly, changing the pale in his cheeks and stilling the torrents that twisted his small body. Joshan slept peacefully then, and Trenara knew the worst was over.

She wrapped her arms around the sleeping child and closed her eyes to let exhaustion take her, gratefully surrendering to sleep. The night quietly surrounded them, hiding their secret, immune to all experience.

CHAPTER TWO
METAMORPHOSIS

When Trenara finally opened her eyes, the sun had risen well above the sea, a yellow ball misted by early morning fog. Staring at the sky, Trenara felt the age in her neck and noted dismally that the grass and her robe were both soaked with rain. The previous night felt like a bad dream. Trenara lifted her head groggily, squinted at the sun, and looked at the morning suspiciously, trying to reassure herself the night had been more than the ravings of a doddering mind. The sudden ache of loss in her middle told her otherwise.

She sat up stiffly and yawned, stretching her back to remove the knots put there by the stony ground, and reached back to shake Joshan. "Come on, lad…" She whirled around and grabbed an empty cloak. "Joshan?" she called, but the only reply was a flock of birds that scuttled out of a tree and her own voice bouncing off the cliffs mockingly.

She stood with what speed she could and swept up the cloak and satchel. Cupping her hands, Trenara called again. The silence that followed tied her stomach in knots. Somewhere in that nebulous area Assemblage called a guider's *sense*, uneasiness sifted through her awareness. It took her a long time to calm her heart. Something had happened in the night beyond the boy's *first trial*. Something she couldn't wrap her wits around. It terrified her.

The guider's eyes rested on the cliffs as old memories came up to trouble her. She had seen more than one death at the hands of the *power*. Innocent lives swept away because they lacked the courage to face their own strengths—and weaknesses. It was the price they all paid for the gift. Sometimes the cost was very high. The guider never thought for a moment Joshan would not be strong enough for the *trial*. He had always been so special, so talented. But in retrospect, she hadn't thought it possible for the others either.

Trenara went to the edge of the precipice, taking some moments to brace her nerves before looking down. There was nothing but smooth, straight stones and the cavernous distance to the sea below. She let out a grateful breath, realizing the cliffs had not taken the boy. The guider studied the clearing, searching for any sign, but it was exactly as it had been the night before, as if nothing had happened here. The eechas were idly chewing the grass, the packs neatly arranged in anticipation of travel. As the early morning fog started to lift, the trees cast muted shadows against the clearing. Something *had* changed. She could feel it like an ache in her heart.

Trenara threw the packs on Whirl's back and mounted Gliding in one fluid motion. The only chance she had of finding Joshan lay in her scepter and her abilities. She silently thanked Ethos for her studies of the *locare*, the gift of finding, and hoped it would be enough. The guider lifted Whirl's reins to pull her after them, but the eecha dug her hooves into the turf and would not budge.

Trenara cursed. Gliding had been bred on Mathisma, but Whirl, though a sturdy beast of fine breeding, was unaccustomed to the strange emanations that began to radiate from Andelian. Letting out an irritated breath, the guider realized the mare must have endured it the night before because of the boy—strange, but there was no time to wonder about it now.

The eecha's eyes went wide with fear as she reared, almost pulling the guider from her mount. It crossed Trenara's mind to use the *power* to calm the animal, but thought better of it, knowing it would take time she didn't have. In the end, she let the eecha go. Whirl galloped madly out of the glade, giving the guider little time to snatch her pack from the eecha's saddle. The animal bolted through the glade and disappeared into the woods with Joshan's bundle still tied to her saddle, instinctively heading for home.

The guider sang a few soft notes to the scepter making it hum in her hands. "Sweet Ethos," she prayed, "please guide me now." As if in response, Gliding reared expectantly and charged off into the woods, spraying mud and grass behind him.

For leagues they ran, the guider clinging to the neck of the eecha, her cheeks burning from the friction of the coarse mane, fearful that a branch or bush would catapult her from the saddle. Trenara was an excellent rider, but Gliding was running at break-neck speed and it was all she could do to hang on. The guider had to rely solely on the eecha's swiftness and the ability of her *via* now.

They rode higher and higher into the mountains, passing the landscape so swiftly it was nothing more than a blur of greens and browns. Trepidation slowed time to a crawl for Trenara. She became increasingly anxious as each league passed. Doubt began to creep into her mind and she questioned her scepter's ability. Joshan could not have traveled this far in the time allowed him, yet on and on they ran.

Without warning Gliding stopped, almost throwing Trenara headlong into a patch of bristle berries that rose in a thorny wall before them. She regained her balance awkwardly, gave the eecha a colorful curse, and carefully slid off the saddle. Wincing in pain, Trenara rubbed her backside.

They had entered another large clearing. Beyond the trees, she could see a wide, spectacular vista of the sea and the lands of Thrain in all directions. She hadn't been there in a very long time. It stood at the very top of the High Cliffs, open to the brilliant blue sky, the world a hazy distance below her.

The guider sat on a rock and massaged her neck, looking around and wondering why Gliding had stopped. As she scrutinized the clearing, something caught her eye lying in the shade of the trees. It was large, long, and shadow-dappled by the light through the branches. She squinted to try to make out what it was, but only succeeded in giving herself a headache. Trenara owned a pair of spectacles, but was vain about wearing them. As usual, she had left them behind. At that moment, she regretted it very much.

She took a long, deep breath and scowled at whatever it was before collecting enough daring to investigate. Her guider's *sense* was telling her nothing, which irritated her to the core. Taking Andelian out and wrapping her hand tightly around it, she crossed cautiously to the other side of the clearing. When she was half way, she stopped abruptly and blinked, when she finally made out what that something was.

It was a young man, naked, lying flat on his back with his hands at his sides, his eyes closed and his chest moving up and down very slowly. He had long, black hair that fell in delicate curls to his shoulders; his face was finely chiseled with a strong, straight nose, high cheekbones and perfectly formed lips, and he appeared to be about eighteen to twenty seasons. He seemed very tall and slim, but the muscles were well defined. There was something on his arm, but she couldn't make it out. Taking two tentative steps forward, she peered at it carefully.

The guider let out an audible gasp and fell back. On the left shoulder, in vivid reds and darkest blacks was the imperial crest. This symbol had been tattooed on every child of every emperor since the beginning of time—the fine, ancient design was elegant and unmistakable. In addition, on the same arm was a long jagged red scar that ran from the shoulder to nearly the elbow. A scar she had seen countless times and knew belonged to only one person in the world. Trenara sank to her knees; her face paled. She tried without success to come to terms with what it was she was seeing.

It was Joshan… the realization hit against her guider's sense with such force it shook her to the core. Trenara knew it down to her toes. He was no longer a child, but a full-grown man at the apex of his youth. Her heart labored in her chest as she gazed at this enigma. At first, her mind told her it wasn't real, it couldn't be… it had to be an illusion. She crawled to the prostrate form and reached out to touch him. Her hand felt warm flesh, a distant heartbeat, and certainty. He was very real. All she could do was sit back and gape at him in wonder.

Her mind reeled as thousands of questions coursed through her head. Something of recognition flashed for a moment and then was gone. A thing read or heard, but she couldn't bring it back.

What happened? She asked herself a thousand times, but there was never an answer. *This is way beyond anything the* power *can do.* She had seen and performed many feats of *power* in her fifty-two seasons, but this was—what? *Impossible? Miraculous? Extraordinary?* What or who could possibly do something like this? A shiver ran through her. There *was* a power once—but she put it out of her mind, knowing that wasn't likely… *or was it?* A chill ran through the guider making her giddy for a moment.

Maybe Joshan could tell her, she thought, as she reached out to shake him. But she pulled her hand back; another alarming thought made her hesitate. *What if he doesn't know? What would happen if he were to wake to this nightmare so soon after* first trial?

Trenara didn't have to guess; she already knew. His mind would shatter completely. He would quietly manifest a deep depression and then slowly fall into madness.

Assemblage called it *detachment*, which was a very nice word for a very nasty disease. All pre-guiders manifested some symptoms of *detachment*, but one in every thousand quickly deteriorated. Some so swiftly, it could happen in a matter of moments. The sight of these rare occurrences was startling. Trenara had been fortunate; none of her students had gone through it.

She had studied for five seasons on Mathisma to earn her starguider status. Four of those seasons were to prepare for this. It was the primary role of a guider—not a teacher, a councilor, or a mentor, but someone who could lead a young mind through the emotional maze that was the *power* and have it come out on the other end intact. Without thinking about it, the guider's training took over and she knew what she had to do.

Trenara positioned herself behind Joshan's head, closed her eyes, and focused her attention on his mind. She took a deep cleansing breath, and then very gently put her hands over his eyes as she spoke softly into his ear. "Joshan? It's Trenara. Wake up." She could feel his breathing increase slowly and a faint flicker of movement in his head. "That's it. It's time to wake up."

"Trenara?" It was so soft she barely heard it. "Where are you?"

The intonations of her voice were automatic as she controlled the resonance of each syllable. "I'm here, lad. You need to wake up now—but slowly."

She felt his lashes tickle the inside of her hands and then a sudden intake of breath. "Where am I?" he said trying to reach up for her hands.

"No," she commanded, pitching her voice to stop the hands before they discovered the secret. He wasn't ready yet. "Lay perfectly still, Joshan. I need you to completely trust me."

"I feel... I feel strange," he replied, putting his hands back down at his sides. "What's wrong with my voice? It sounds so…"

"I know. Don't worry about that right now. It's very important you do exactly as I tell you. Do you understand?"

"Yes." His voice trembled and she could feel the waves of fear that began to course through his body.

"Don't be afraid, Joshan. I'm with you. Do you feel my hands on your eyes?"
"Yes."

"Good. Now I need you to do the calming exercises. Do you remember them?"
"Yes."

"I'm going to sing the *leea-anu-ema-cha*. Do you remember what to do?"
"No."

His trembling was increasing. Trenara had to hold her hands over his eyes very tightly and force her voice to reverberate perfectly. "Shhh. That's all right. I'll sing down to *cha*. On the first note, you need to take in a deep breath until it has stopped. On the next, you'll exhale until it stops. Repeat the same for the last two. Can you do that?"

"Y… yes."

She sang the first stunning low note, and a very faint blue light enveloped them. "*Leea…*" Joshan took a deep breath, and Trenara continued the note until his lungs were full. Some of the trembling subsided. "*Anu…*" The second note had such resonance Joshan could feel the vibration through Trenara hands. As he exhaled slowly, the terror began to melt. "*Ema…*" He inhaled again and could feel the warmth of Trenara's hands on his face and the euphoric touch of the *power* through her fingers. It felt soothing to have them there. The shaking had almost stopped, and his heart began to slow down. "*Cha…*" He felt very comfortable; panic retreated for the moment. Trenara could feel his emotions relax.

"Something's happened," she said, toning her voice to make him as calm as possible. "You're not hurt or damaged in any way."

She could feel Joshan's head nod slightly beneath her hands. "All right," he whispered, some of the panic returning.

"Before I take my hands away, you need to tell me the last thing you remember." There was a long pause and for a moment, Trenara thought he hadn't heard her.

"*Visions*," he finally whispered.

"Can you tell me about them?"

"No." The reply was weak. "They were clear to me last night, as clear as your voice is now," he said, taking in another deep breath as she had taught him. "It was important—it was so important, but now I can't see them." She could hear the alarm rising.

"Well, don't worry; it's not important right now. You need to be completely calm for me. Deep breath in—and out." They both pulled in more air and let is out slowly.

"Do you know where you are?" she asked.

"In the clearing where we were last night," he said with hesitation.

"No, Joshan. We are at the top of the High Cliffs."

"What? How…"

"It doesn't matter. Focus on calming your body. Relax each muscle one by one. Start with your feet and work your way up. When you're ready, tell me." Joshan took several more breaths and relaxed under her hands.

"I'm all right, Trenara."

"Good. Now I'm going to tell you what has happened, and I want you to be calm. Can you do that?"

"Yes." His responses were getting stronger.

She paused for the moment trying to find the right words. "Last night something happened after your *first trial*. When I woke this morning, you were gone. I found you here at the top of the High Cliffs. You are unhurt, but your body has… changed." He instinctively raised his hands to touch his chest. "No, Joshan, not yet," she said gently and he put his hands back. "You have grown older, perhaps eight or ten seasons. Your body is now that of a young man." She could feel his trembling return.

"What?"

"Stay calm. It appears your body has aged by eight to ten seasons," she said, trying to keep his mind from breaking. "But, that doesn't matter right now. I want you to feel my hands on your face and focus on staying calm. I'm going to take my hands away, but I want you to keep your eyes closed for me. Will you do that?"

He took in a deep shaky breath. "Yes."

She took her hands away. "I'm going to help you sit, but I want you to keep your eyes closed, all right?" She helped him sit up, took her cloak off her shoulders, and wrapped it tenderly around him. She faced him cross-legged on the grass. "You can open your eyes, Joshan," she said. He opened them immediately, and Trenara had to fight not to gasp. His eyes were very dark now: deep, thoughtful, old, and wise beyond his seasons.

He stared at Trenara a long time before he looked down at his hands. There was a moment of stillness and then a dark shadow crept across his face. Joshan focused on those hands, those stranger's hands, long-fingered, large, and strong. He began to tremble.

"No, no, no," he cried softly beginning to breathe rapidly.

Trenara folded her fingers over his. "Look at me." He raised very frightened eyes to her. "I'm here and I won't leave you. One more time, the breathing exercises."

It took almost an hour, sitting there across from one another, the guider holding his fragile sanity in her small hands and skillfully calming the panic that could have killed him. At length, when the crisis was over and the crippling fear had left the echoes of his voice, Trenara looked at his face long and hard, trying to fathom whom this enigma could be… where he could have come from… what she should do next. She was utterly exhausted.

"What's happened to me?" Joshan finally asked softly.

Trenara shook her head. "I seem to recall something like this in a book or a song. I can't remember where." She met Joshan's eyes squarely. "What I'm trying to say in plain words, my boy, is… I simply don't know. Is there anything else you can tell me about last night?"

Joshan's face mirrored the shadows around him as he scowled at the glade. "Something happened during the… the *trial* last night. When the *power* touched me, the pain was… so horrible." His voice trembled.

"I'm sorry," Trenara said, putting a hand on his shoulder.

"It's all right, because when it finally did pass, I felt wonderful—so strong and as light as the wind. I could hear and see everything, even with my eyes closed. I've never felt like that before." Then his eyes clouded with pain. "Then images began to form in my head. Strange, vague. Images of people I've known, or will know—events that seemed familiar, but weren't. Places I know but have never been. Argh!" he cried.

"You saw the future—or maybe the past," Trenara replied. "Sometimes we're not certain which."

"Then you knew this would…"

"No, lad, I didn't know. To my knowledge, no one has ever *seen* at *first trial*. I knew only by the green color. That comes with *third trial*, not *first*." She shook her head and half smiled. "Perhaps you're unique. I've always said so. Tell me what you saw."

"That's just the point," Joshan replied bitterly. "I don't remember. It's as though my memory has been ripped from me."

"I can only imagine what you must be going through," she said, pitching the resonance of her voice to help steady him. "I'll do what I can, but I'm not the Provost." *Hell, I'm not even third trial,* she thought dismally, but kept her emotions under control. "I think Saminee can help you, but we need to get to Mathisma, so better minds than mine can ponder this. We'll make arrangements as soon as we get back." Trenara stood and stretched her back, letting the glowing sun soak into her bones.

"It's a long journey to Mathisma, and we won't solve the mysteries of the universe in one sitting. Rest assured you're not alone. We'll find the answers together. In the meantime," she said crossing to Gliding, "we have other more pressing matters to concern us." Trenara lightened her voice with an effort and managed a confident smile. "The foremost of which is my empty belly. I feel as if I haven't eaten in days. Fetch some water, will you? You'll find a creek just through those trees." Trenara threw the water sack to Joshan, who ran to the stream to fill it. His ability to adapt had always been exceptional and now seemed almost miraculous. It was an attribute the guider envied and had previously credited to youth. She was not so sure now—about anything.

The guider stared after the boy and thought long and hard about what she would do. *What happened?* She asked herself again and pushed it to the back of her mind, knowing those answers would have to come later.

Then her mouth fell open with a gasp. *Dear gods, how the hell am I going to explain this?* Joshan wasn't just another pre-guider fresh out of *first trial*; he was heir to the throne of the Empire, First Prince, and probably one of the most important people in the Imperium. She couldn't just saunter up to the gate and say, *Hello, we had a little problem in the woods today.* To begin with, who would believe her?

To make matters worse, Jenhada's illness had effectively put a wedge in the strong friendship the guider had enjoyed with him for many seasons. It hurt her deeply and Trenara missed their talks, but she had buried herself in the boy's training to try to compensate for the loss. This was going to be very difficult.

The guider took a deep shaky breath. She had to approach this carefully and try not to frighten the prince. Trenara needed help and hated the fact she was the only guider between Thrain and Mathisma. It would take a month to get to the island. *Well, one step at a time*, she thought, as Joshan returned and sat down to eat the last of their provisions.

"We have to return to the Keep by nightfall," said Trenara after they had finished. "It will be difficult to explain your transformation to the emperor. Night will not improve his mood any. He's been very… well, let me say strange of late and leave it at that. I don't relish the task."

"My father's illness is no mystery to me," Joshan replied pensively, helping the guider pick up remnants. "I've seen it grow worse for months now. The physicians say they don't know how to heal him."

"Healers heal," Trenara replied irritably, "physicians bleed people to death."

Joshan smiled, remembering her scorn for them. "Perhaps with my new *power*, I might be able to help him."

"Now, don't get cocky, son. Remember, you're new to this."

"Maybe," Joshan replied, but as though the thought triggered a panic, he turned his head sharply. His eyes narrowed and his face darkened.

"Trenara," he hissed, "do you… feel that?" Trenara's brow furrowed at the prince.

"Something's wrong…" The dark expression turned to horror as he looked wildly at the guider. "Quickly, guider!" Joshan raced toward Gliding and jumped into the saddle, pulling a bewildered Trenara behind him. "Fly, Gliding." The eecha kicked up his front hooves and shrieked loudly, causing flocks of birds to abandon their perch in the trees. The giant beast bolted from the glade, deserting the pack behind him.

CHAPTER THREE
THE KEEP

They flew through the mountains of Thrain with speed Trenara didn't think possible. Some energy was on the boy, but all the guider could think of was the ache in her belly and the hurt in her behind. She wanted an end to this day, a platter of food and a soft bed, but knew all those things were going to be a long time coming. She settled herself behind Joshan, clinging to the boy for life and shivering without her cloak.

She had to scream over the noisy wind in her ears. "What are you feeling—what does it mean?"

Joshan's head was bent almost to the neck of the eecha. "I don't know. Whatever it is, something is terribly wrong and we have to get to the Keep. I'm afraid it may be too late already." The prince adjusted the cloak around his shoulders and glanced hastily back at Trenara. "Don't worry, guider," he said to the chagrin on her face. She grunted an acknowledgement and clung tightly to Joshan's back.

After many leagues and a long silence, Joshan slowed Gliding to give him a rest. The last remnants of mountain fell under their feet as they stood on the edge of the forest. They looked out at the foothills that lay before them like dark green seas, shadowed by a sinking sun. The prince lifted his hand above the dark eyes to shield the glare as he searched the terrain. When he lowered his hand, a sunray sparkled brightly on something he held there, dazzling Trenara's eyes.

"What have you got in your hand?"

Joshan shot her a puzzled look and then opened his fist. He pulled up on the reins so sharply Gliding reared and almost threw them. The eecha recovered his footing and lowered his head gratefully into the grass. "By the gods!" Joshan exclaimed.

"Let me see."

He held his palm toward the guider. The light was not good in the darkening forest, but Trenara managed to see what lay on the young man's palm. Embedded in the flesh, in fine lines below his fingers, were close to fifty tiny crystals, each about the size of a grain.

"It's on both hands," Joshan said to Trenara's silence. The guider's memory raged again, but she still couldn't place where she had heard of such a thing, although she knew it appeared to be made of the same crystal as her scepter. "Another mystery, guider?"

Trenara saw a dark sadness in Joshan's eyes that disturbed her. "I've never seen anything like this. My best guess would be it has something to do with your *via*, although it brings back something else. I wish I knew what."

Joshan resigned himself to this new information with a curt nod. "Well, it doesn't hurt. In fact, until you mentioned it, I had no idea it was there." He goaded Gliding into a trot. "Maybe I'll find the answer to this when we reach Mathisma."

"Perhaps." Trenara felt the prince would have his answer long before then.

*****

Assemblage had designed the Keep almost a thousand seasons before, when they were in their fledgling stage. Built into the High Cliffs on either side, and running east for fifteen leagues to the sea, it housed the emperor and his councils, two small towns, The Village between the first and second gates and Keepton between the second and third. Between the third and fourth were military barracks, training facilities along with medical houses. Beyond Fourth Gate was the castle where the imperial family, the guards, the councils, and their servants lived.

The walls had served from the beginning as a shelter from the Imperium's enemies. During the war with Sirdar, the Keep was subjected to six months of siege, but the structure withstood everything his soldiers could devise to bring it down. The catacombs wound far into the mountains and were kept stocked with supplies. The caverns were so numerous and long, even the oldest of workers didn't know how many or how far. During the siege, the people had barely touched the reserves. They could have lasted another six seasons.

As a rule, the sight of the high First Gate would have been cheering, but now the towering wall seemed dark and forbidding as Trenara and Joshan approached. It was still daylight, yet the gates were closed—something neither of them had ever seen. The only thing that would close those gates before sunset was war. The thought was a chilling one. The sun was slowly setting, painting the wall a bloody red.

"Hail, Guard," Joshan called uncertainly, staring up at the man posted on the rampart above the gates. "What is your post and to whom do you do duty?"

"My post is First Keeper, Third Class, and my duty is to my Lord, Jenhada, and his prince Joshan," was the reply, although inaccurate. "What is your business and to whom do you pay homage?"

Trenara touched Joshan's arm before he could respond. "You better let me handle this. If you tell him you're First Prince, there will be no end to this night."

"You do not speak the hail correctly," she called to the guard. "Have you forgotten or has your duty changed?"

The guard bristled. "I have not forgotten, and I'll be damned if I'll let my duty be questioned by a stranger. It is by decree the hail was changed. Now, state your business, or I will let the dogs out for their evening meal."

"Touchy little fellow, isn't he?" the guider muttered. "I am Trenara, the starguider and this is… a young friend. My business is with the emperor and then with my bed. Let us pass." This last statement was a command from someone who was no stranger to obedience.

Her reply created a stir among the guards along the wall, and several faces appeared from behind the stone parapet. Along with the faces, Trenara saw several weapons glinting in the torchlight. The air was thick with suspicion. She felt as if she had just entered a foreign country and not her home of many seasons.

The first keeper was very slow to reply. "Trenara, you are expected. Enter." The guard again did not reply correctly, leaving out, "*and be welcomed.*" The gates swung open with a sluggish grate. Joshan nudged the eecha into the black tunnel where the previous morning he had raced. It seemed an eternity since then.

"Careful, Trenara," Joshan hissed, trying to adjust his eyes in the gloom. "When my mother's name is left out of the hail, and by decree, there is something very wrong." Trenara merely scowled at the darkness, her hand wrapped around Andelian for comfort. The light at the end of the tunnel shone brightly and Gliding skittered toward it.

"Hold!" echoed a familiar voice as the two approached the arch of light. "Hold and be counted." As Joshan and Trenara emerged, they were surrounded on all sides by a score of archers, each with his or her bow tense in their fingers. Behind the archers were stout soldiers with swords. All the faces were dark with fury.

Trenara looked around, her eyes steely. "This is hardly a greeting among friends, Haiden. Have you lost your mind?" Anger was beginning to overcome her better judgment and with an effort, she calmed herself. This was not the time to demonstrate her infamous temper.

"If you are a friend." Haiden stood with his hands planted firmly on his hips, eyeing the guider. "Where's the prince?"

Trenara saw grief in the old eyes and then scanned all of their faces. It was as if they expected Joshan to be gone. "He's safe, Haiden," she said softly, the trained inflections in her voice meant to soothe. Many of the men and women seemed to relax at the sound, but they held their ground. "In good time you will hear the whole story and feel silly you were so suspicious."

"That remains to be seen," Haiden shot back, not having any of the woman's tricks. They had a very long history. Something in the sergeant's stature changed as he looked for the first time at the guider's companion. "I know you," he said slowly. "State your name."

Trenara stayed Joshan's voice with a touch. "I will explain everything in more private surroundings, sergeant."

Haiden ignored her, took two steps toward Joshan, and then squinted up at him. He opened his mouth to speak, but recognition made him gasp instead. "Great gods!" he hissed.

Trenara brought herself up to her full height and clenched her fists before Haiden could say another word. "Let us pass!"

"Yes… yes," Haiden stammered. "Back to your posts—all of you."

A little disoriented, the archers lowered their weapons, and the guards sheathed their swords. They saluted their sergeant and scrambled back to their stations.

Trenara and Joshan slid from Gliding and with soft words spoken in the eecha's ear, she gave the stallion to a gate squire. Out of the corner of her eye, she caught sight of two dark men breaking from the ranks, hurriedly making for the castle.

Haiden stood still for a moment and stared at Joshan. Trenara had to roughly take the guard's elbow and lead him toward the guardhouse before he could bend his knee to the prince. Once inside the relative safety of the small building, Trenara let out a shaky breath.

"What devilry is this?" Haiden exclaimed when he finally found his voice. "It is you, yes?"

"You have good eyes." Trenara set down her satchel and fell down onto a stool by the fire.

"What? For the boy I raised from a pup?"

"We need food, and the boy needs clothes." She warmed her hands next to the fire with a sigh. "We could use some drink, as well." When Haiden did not move, the guider became irritable. "Man, have you lost your manners as well as your senses?"

Haiden broke from his trance and shot the guider an uncomfortable look. "Sorry." After some scrounging, he placed leftover meat, fresh bread and a tall pitcher of whillen beer on the table and Trenara sat down to eat. "It's been a strange day, but this is the corker," Haiden said shaking his head. "What's happened to you, lad?"

"Never mind that," Joshan said leaning on the table anxiously. "What's going on here?"

"Don't rightly know." A deep grief puckered Haiden's eyes and etched the lines in his face like stencils. "When the decree came down, I… I don't know rightly what I thought. I did his bidding, him being emperor, but I sent one of my crew up to see what she could and report back. I… she… Well, she came back with strange tales." He looked up at Joshan. "Sorry, but there's no way to put this nicely—your da's gone mad, like he's been possessed. Saying there's treason everywhere." He took another deep breath for courage. "The Lady, well, I mean, Saldorian's… I mean your mother's not… that is to say, he had no right…" He sank his head, unable to continue.

"What are you saying? What's happened to my mother, Haiden?"

"It's rumored that your father has taken her Ladyship and locked her up. For treason is what they're saying."

"What?"

"It ain't right. She's the finest lady in the land, if you ask me. And they say…" He stopped to look up at the young man. "Well, they say you're dead. The guider here was supposed to be arrested. Warrant came down no more than an hour ago, saying she's accused of treason—and murder. That's why you was greeted the way you was," he said to Trenara. "If I hadn't of recognized the prince…" but his voice trailed off into the shaking of his head.

"Why would anyone think Joshan is dead?"

"I don't know," Haiden replied helplessly. "I wish I did."

"I must get to the Keep at once," cried Joshan as he turned for the door.

"Stop," Trenara called without rising. "You won't get very far dressed like that." The shortened cloak that barely covered him looked comical. He pulled the cloak more tightly around his body and scowled.

"Haiden, get me clothes. Rags, anything, but get them now," he said. Haiden left the station at a quick run.

"What do you think you're going to do?" Trenara asked quietly, mindful of the disease that could push this unfortunate child over the edge at any moment.

Joshan ran a shaky hand through the mop of long, dark hair and moved frantically about the room like a caged beast. "I don't know. I can't just sit here."

"You can't rush brashly to your father in your condition either. Use your head… and sit down! You're giving me a headache." Joshan sat heavily, not entirely under his own power. "Now, feed yourself, while I think." Trenara stared thoughtfully at the embers in the hearth, while the prince toyed with his food.

After a sullen silence, Haiden came back with a bundle under his arm and laid it on the table, properly bowing to the prince this time. "Something's brewing in the castle. There's a clamor rising," he said breathlessly.

Joshan grabbed the bundle, stripped off the wet cloak unceremoniously, and dressed. As he tossed the worn cloak into a corner, a shadow fell on his heart, the sudden fear making him dizzy and nauseous. "Trenara…" he whispered.

Trenara only nodded. "I feel it, too, lad."

"So, what do we do?"

Trenara shook her head and thought for a very long time. *What do we do?* She had the uneasy feeling that somewhere along the line, a power greater than hers had taken over their lives—good or evil, she didn't know which. "Haiden, can you get us into the castle without detection?" Trenara asked at length.

Haiden screwed up his face in concentration and looked away for a moment. "I think I can, though it ain't going to be easy. The guards are thicker than flies, and edgy. Likely to shoot at us first, then ask questions."

"We have to reach Jenhada and explain what's happened before things get worse."

They donned heavy, dark cloaks and slipped into the night silently, retrieving Gliding from the steward and Haiden's eecha from the stables. A damp drizzle began to settle on the pavement as the gathering clouds darkened the stone roads, making the companions' journey through the maze of streets miserable, but smooth. They were able to avoid the guards, and made it to Third Gate without incident, but getting passage to the castle was not going to be a simple matter.

After Haiden had a long argument with the gatekeeper, an evil-looking fellow with an ugly disposition and a long scar across one cheek, Trenara was about at wit's end. As she and Joshan hid in the shadows, it took every ounce of strength she possessed to keep from blasting the man where he stood. Joshan was amazed at the restraint Trenara was showing. He had known this woman of quick temper to take less abuse and deal out more punishment. Trenara was not used to having her authority questioned.

Finally, when arguments would not prevail and threats became ineffective, Haiden joined the others and they went into a small tavern down the street to recoup and put the animals up for the night at the inn's stables. There were few visitors, so the roadhouse was quiet.

"Curse the bastard," Trenara raged when they were well out of earshot of the barman and settled at a table. She stroked Andelian angrily. "Remind me to pulverize that upstart."

"I could take you to my place," Haiden ventured. "Then in the morning we could try again."

Trenara shook her head. "They know we're friends, Haiden. They'll be watching your place. Besides, as soon as you let us go, two of your guards left the ranks, heading for the castle. Unless I'm mistaken, I think you're in this as thick as we are. I'm sorry."

Haiden shrugged and smiled at the guider. "Wouldn't be the first time." He scratched his head thoughtfully. "There's got to be a way in around the gates. West hall entrance?"

"Too far away and we'd still have to get past Fourth Gate. Catacombs?"

Haiden looked up at her doubtfully. "You been in them lately? You'd need a map and a guide. We'd get lost sure."

An idea struck Joshan. "Hang me if I'm not a fool," he cried. "I should have thought of this before. There is a way into the castle that I don't think anyone knows about—several, actually. There are old tunnels that run into Keepton. Old waste tunnels or heating ducts, I think. I used one just a few days ago to hide from my nurse."

Trenara smiled brightly at him. "Could be just the thing. Show me." But, as they rushed out the door, all three froze in surprise. Dozens of councilor guards with torches, spears, or long blades surrounded the dwelling. These men weren't the gate guards, but the same swarthy men Trenara had seen the previous morning. With a clarity that sent a rapid flush of fire through her, she realized who these men were. Northerners. Men from the Northern Wastes.

The provinces had warred with these people for over six hundred seasons, had defeated them, scattered them, only sixty seasons before. How she could have missed that they were in the Keep was unbelievable. And yet she had… they all had. Trenara's lips began to tremble, as a veil seemed to lift from her mind… as if she were waking into a frozen, deadly morning. Things became all at once painfully clear against her raw nerves. She knew these men were the enemy. They had blindly let them through the gates, to the heart of the Imperium.

"Stand ready!" a man shouted from the group. Swords were raised, and a dark figure detached itself from behind the soldiers. "In the name of Emperor Jenhada

Thoringale Kanaine, you are under arrest. You are to be taken to the hold, where you will be charged with high treason and tried before his majesty tomorrow."

"What mischief is this, Pravius?" Trenara raged, her voice trembling. "What treason have we committed? I have my rights!"

The councilor stopped a few paces from her, malice protruding from his face like a mask. It astounded Trenara. She had never seen him like this. "Here, you have no rights." Pravius clutched the decree with white knuckles and his mouth was a hard line as narrow as his eyes. "But for the benefit of those who would call you friend," he continued, smoothing his voice as he shot concerned eyes at Haiden, "I will tell you and let them judge."

His baleful green eyes became languid, sad… compelling. "You have spirited away the first prince from those who would protect him. You have murdered him. Why, only the gods would know. And, with the aid of the witch Saldorian, the emperor's faithless wife, you have devised a way to drive our emperor mad with your poisons. It is these crimes you will answer for tomorrow."

Trenara realized she was in the presence of genius. She hadn't heard anyone control his voice like that in seasons; shaping the words and the lilt with such mastery, even she began to believe it. It held a power she hadn't experienced in three decades, an experience she had spent a lifetime trying to extinguish from her memory. As she looked back into those weak, drooping eyes, eyes she had known for years, she shuddered. This man was a stranger now… a powerful stranger. They were in grave danger.

Pravius turned and signaled the guards to take them. The men stepped forward and raised their weapons fearfully. They knew well the power of a starguider. This was too much for Trenara. She reached into her robes, feeling the warmth and security of Andelian as she wrapped her hand around the scepter. Pravius twisted around and made a covert gesture only she could see. A sudden searing pain shot through the guider's arm. She screamed and fell to her knees. Joshan was at her side instantly and found her hand that had touched Andelian was badly burned. He looked up to see Pravius smiling down at them.

"Can you stand?" Joshan whispered to the guider.

"Yes," she winced, "I think so." She struggled to her feet.

Joshan's hand sent a wave of relief through the guider's side, like a draught of imaka. She looked up at him, confused. The pain was excruciating, and she had to lean heavily on the prince. The guards forced Joshan away and pulled his hands behind his back to bind him. Haiden was struggling; it took four of them to tie his wrists together. When they came to Trenara, however, Pravius motioned them aside. He stood close to the guider, his breath clouding the night air.

"Your wand, magician," he said, holding out his hand.

Trenara narrowed her eyes. "You'll have to kill me if you want it," she hissed through her pain.

"That would give me great pleasure, but would not serve my purpose." The guards held Trenara's arms until she screamed and her knees buckled in pain. Pravius reached under her robes and tore Andelian from its place. He grimaced at the touch of the crystal and quickly wrapped the scepter in a cloth. "Take them away," he said and turned to leave.

"Rot in hell, Pravius." The guards jerked Trenara's arms behind her back and bound her hands. The councilor turned his head and merely smiled. His robes whirled as he strode to the gates, followed by two of his northerners. Trenara fell unconscious to the ground, for the first time in thirty seasons, powerless.

CHAPTER FOUR
THE HOLD

"You try anything, mate," the man said into Joshan's ear, "and I have my lad there cut the guider's throat. You grasp what I'm saying to you, boy?" Trenara lay unconscious over the shoulder of a very large northern brute. She was seriously injured, but the man carried her like a sack of grain. Joshan watched helplessly as they placed a wooden yoke around Haiden's neck. Knowing his friends were both in danger, he nodded once angrily, but said nothing. "Good boy," the man said, hefting a similar yoke over Joshan's head. "This won't hurt a bit."

Joshan just glared at the men as they locked the device in place and then chained his hands on either side of it. They were shoved through the streets by the northerners. Several times they fell on the uneven stones, badly jarring their backs, their hands useless. The wooden yokes left their necks bruised and bleeding. The northerners just laughed as the two righted themselves and lifted the heavy burdens off the cobbled pavement to stand again. Haiden cursed at them, but the leader lifted Trenara's head by the hair and played a knife across her throat. The old guard remained quiet after that, but fumed as the men pushed them toward the castle.

Once in the hold, the guards took off the yokes and chains. As Joshan was rubbing his wrists, he caught something out of the corner of his eye, which even the guard who was holding him didn't catch. As quick as lightning, Haiden had pulled Trenara's satchel out of the guard's pocket and tucked it into his tunic before anyone could see. Joshan had almost missed it himself, and he was looking right at his old trainer. Before he could respond, they were pushed down a long stone hallway to a cell, where the councilor's guards threw Trenara unceremoniously onto the floor and then shoved the companions in after her. Before either of them could turn around, the door was slammed and the lock tumbled into place. They were left in complete darkness.

"Lad," Haiden called when the guards had finally moved on. "Are you all right?"

"I'm fine," he said quietly as he tried to find Trenara in the gloom. When he came to her prostrate form, he managed to get her rearranged into a more comfortable position and then examined her arm. He could feel with his fingers that it was badly crushed. Joshan gasped and dropped the arm as if it were white-hot. For a swift second, Joshan could *see* inside her. He could feel the coursing of her blood, the swift movement of her heart and the muscles of her body contracting. It was frightening, but at the same time, exhilarating. It terrified him.

He tentatively touched her again and the feeling rose through his body so quickly, it made his stomach churn. All at once, a wave of euphoria coursed through him, as Trenara's life force seemed to merge with his own. As Joshan concentrated, letting the sensations run their course, he felt a brief pang of pleasure run through him that made him shudder, the physical fervor something foreign to him. He had always loved Trenara, but this feeling was deeper, primal—salacious. He was at a loss to comprehend it. Something else caught his attention. Something darker—something beyond the broken arm. He could feel it deep inside her… an element that was perverse and wrong in her blood. Trenara was dying.

Joshan licked his lips and took a deep breath, trying desperately to make his heart stop pounding. All at once, he became very calm, as an emotional wave washed over him, taking away the panic. It was as if there was a quiet presence in the cell with him, a presence that was guiding him, telling him what to do. He lifted his hands, and for the first time, he saw the crystals in his palms pulsating from white to blue to green, over and over again in an ecstasy of color. Flashes of scintillation rushed through his body, making his ears ring and his eyes water. The feeling was a revelation as the *power* took control. He stared down at Trenara, now knowing exactly what he had to do, as if he had done it a thousand times before.

"Haiden?" The old guard just looked across at him, his eyes glowing in the strange light. "Trenara's badly hurt. I need you to hold her down. No matter what happens, keep her there. Can you do that?" Haiden nodded once, moved to kneel at her side, and placed his hands on her shoulder and leg. Joshan lowered his head and let the *power* take him.

*****

When the guider finally regained her senses, a dank, repulsive stench accosted her nose. With an effort, she forced herself to breathe. It was the smell of human misery and the ground was thick with it, slick and wet as if it contained centuries of suffering. Trenara opened her eyes, but there was nothing to see. The black swarmed around her, and she became nauseous. For an instant, she feared blindness, but as her eyes grew accustomed to the dark, vague outlines and shadows began to appear. She moved her head slightly. Even with that, the pain was intense. It constricted her body as agony took hold, and she began to sob.

"Quickly, Haiden, bring me the satchel. Trenara's awake." Hearing Joshan's voice did much to ease her pain. "Lie still now. You're hurt," he said. There was an odd quiet to his voice, and she wished she could see his face, but it was only a vague outline.

Haiden brought the pack and Joshan removed a crystal flask. The imaka seemed to carry its own light, giving them a fleeting glimpse of goodness. Fear gripped Trenara as she reached for her robe with her good arm. Joshan stopped it with a gentle touch that sent an odd sense of energy though her arm, lessening the pain. "It's gone, Trenara. I'm sorry," he said.

The guider relaxed heavily into the stones. "Then it wasn't a dream."

"No." Joshan lifted her head. "Here, take this. It will ease the pain." He held the vessel to Trenara's lips and let a few drops fall on her tongue. The pain was instantly mollified as the liquid worked into the guider's body, easing the stiffness and sending a rapid flow of relief through her. Her arm still ached, but she was able to sit with Joshan's help.

"The arm is no longer badly damaged, but will be cold and painful for a while." Joshan replaced the vial in the bag. "It will pass with time. The imaka is a wonderful healer." The prince sat down with his back to the stone wall and closed his eyes.

Haiden threw a cloak around Trenara's shoulders. "Begging your pardon, but the lad's being modest. It wasn't the imaka. It was him, sure as I'm sitting here. If I hadn't seen it with my own eyes, I'd call myself a liar."

Trenara gave him a puzzled look. "What are you talking about?"

"Well, it's like this. You were hurt bad. He says we have to help you and I tell him it's not possible without some aid, since you were fevered and twisting like the very devil. Sorry, guider, but you were dying. I knew it then, I know it now. He tells me to hold you down and not let up. I got you down and held you—not a simple thing either, you twisting and screaming and all. He covered you with a cloak, laid his hands on you and then he sang."

Haiden stopped for a moment and shook his head. "It was glorious, that sound. And, right away, you settled down. Then a light came from his hands," he whispered, looking at his own, "a pure white light that circled around him like smoke. The prince looked so quiet in that light. His eyes glowed, his face turned bright, and although you might not believe it, he looked like he was all dressed in silver, shining like a star.

"Then he turned to me and asked if I was ready. Well, I didn't know ready for what, but I nodded and the prince closed his eyes and started to sing again, only different this time. I don't rightly know what the words were, but they made me feel young again—it was really something to hear. Then you took to twisting and screaming again, and I was hard put to hold you.

"His singing got louder and the room got brighter. I was afraid the guards would hear, but there was nothing I could do about it. Then the prince looks down at you and sings a note so loud it set my ears ringing. You twisted so hard it threw me back. Then up, right out of your chest comes a puff of smoke, as red as blood. Then it just disappears." He snapped his fingers. "Just like that.

"Then you calmed right down and slept. The lights were gone and it left the place pretty dark, I can tell you." Haiden glanced at Joshan sitting against the wall with his eyes closed. "He stumbled. I almost didn't catch him, it was that quick. Then he lay in my arms—weeping. Almost broke my heart seeing him like that. Didn't rightly know what to do, so I smoothed his hair, like when he was a little boy. Anyway, he calmed right down." He shook his graying head. "If I hadn't of seen it with my own eyes, I'd call myself a liar." Haiden grew very still.

The cell seemed to grow lighter with the end of the story, but when Trenara looked up, she noticed a small window facing east. Dawn was approaching over the sea. She began to rise, gauging the speed with which her body would respond. "Here, guider," beckoned Haiden. "You shouldn't be exerting yourself." He helped Trenara to her feet and turned over an empty pail for her to sit on.

Trenara felt extremely weak, but even now, the pain was subsiding like a bad memory. She looked around the cell and noted, except for the high window and small cell door, it was nothing more than four blank walls. *We have to get out of this place and soon*, she thought grimly. She couldn't imagine what was happening on the outside, but knew that the night could have only made things worse. They had to get to Jenhada. Trenara's eyes fell on the satchel lying at her feet. "Odd," she mused, "why didn't they take that?"

Haiden looked at his hands awkwardly. "Well… uh, they just didn't."

"Now who's being modest?" Joshan said from across the cell.

"I thought you was asleep, you young ruffian."

Joshan stretched and stood to get the stiffness out of his back. "Trenara, you should have seen it. Our man here seems to have more resources than I thought possible, which is stretching a bit. A finer display of the art of pick pocketing I have never seen."

"It wasn't thievery, I can tell you," the guard replied. "'Sides, you pick up a thing or two when you're on the field."

Trenara picked up the satchel and poured the contents into her lap. "However you recovered it, I think we might have a chance now." In addition to the vial of imaka and various other personal items, there was a stone container with a tight lid on it. "This," she said, holding up the jar, "contains an acid that should corrode the metal in those bars. I was taking it to be refilled, so I'm afraid there's not much left. At least it may aid in weakening them, if nothing else."

Haiden brightened markedly. "Now, here's a magic I understand," he said, taking the jar from the guider's hand. "Begging your pardon." He removed the lid gingerly and sniffed. "Aaahh. It's a fine mixture. Tavelson, we called it in Tola," he said. "If you'll allow me."

The guider gave him a mute bow. "By all means."

Haiden busied himself at the door, applying the tavelson carefully to hinges. Joshan joined Trenara on the stones and examined her arm.

"Last night…" Trenara began.

"Yes, last night…" Joshan stopped and stared at the growing light from the window. Dark circles hollowed his eyes and the frown lines around his mouth gave it a sardonic tenseness. He seemed to be struggling with something as he blinked at the advancing light. The guider caught the strangeness in him now. Something in those eyes had changed. They seemed darker, older, and oddly grim, as if they held a terrible secret.

"When Pravius…"

"Pravius!" snarled Trenara. "I'll fry his bones, if I get my hands on him."

Joshan raised a hand. "Peace, my friend. That would be a task, let me assure you." He looked at the guider a long moment. "Trenara, I don't think that man *is* Pravius."

Trenara scowled at him. "You noticed."

He looked up at her sharply. "You knew?"

"I realized it last night. I just wish I knew who he is."

"Whoever he is, he has incredible power—an evil thing, corrupt and wrong, somehow. Pravius is no guider, at least not in my memory. He has served my family well for seasons. I can't believe any man could come to such evil within a few months, nor to this kind of power."

The crevices in Trenara's face made her look older as she spoke. "You're right. I don't know Pravius well, but have never thought him evil, although perhaps not always as clever as many of the others." Trenara folded her arms and reflected on the events of the previous night. "Perhaps if we can escape, answers will come." She looked down at her hands. "To this and other questions."

"The healing?" Joshan asked.

"You know my concerns?"

Joshan stood up and paced, doubt beginning to creep into his face. "When I healed you last night it was as though some instinct told me what to do. It was like I wasn't there at all." He shook his head. "You haven't heard of this either, have you?"

"No, I haven't." Joshan sat as if he'd been struck and Trenara looked at him pleadingly. "Starguiders hold a special *power* and a very real responsibility to the Imperium. When you reach *first trial*, you are taken to Mathisma to receive your *via* and to learn your craft. Many seasons are spent in study and rigorous practice. Then and only then, are you able to control the *power*. I have never seen any of my students control it before they received their *via*—until last night." She looked at Joshan as if weighing her words. "Without the *via*, there is no *power*. Without Andelian," her voice cracked, "I'm just another old woman."

Joshan regarded her sadly. "And the healing?"

"Yes… the healing…" She paused to think. "Healings are rare—healers are rare. There is perhaps a handful throughout the world. Oh, I don't mean those 'physicians' that call themselves healers; they're fortunate not to kill more than they cure. But the real healers, that's another matter entirely. Perhaps one is born to that purpose every twenty seasons. No healer, to my knowledge, has ever cured anyone without the assistance of at least some herb or medicinal to aid her and her *via*, of course. The imaka is not a cure for anything, except perhaps fatigue and pain. What you did last night has not been done since the Crystal of Healing came to us; and then, the only acts that depict such a thing are legends—myths." She looked down and shook her head. "I'm sorry, lad. I wish I could give you answers."

"Begging your pardon," Haiden said urgently, "but we got company." He quickly corked the jar of tavelson. Joshan and Trenara sprang to his side, and Haiden handed the jar to the guider. "Three of them by the sound," he said, wiping his brow, "two guards and one other."

"It appears you have good ears as well as good eyes, Haiden," said Trenara.

"I'm afraid I didn't get more than a couple of drops on, guider. Sorry."

"It's alright, we can try again later… I hope." Trenara said tucking the bottle into a pocket in her robes.

A familiar dread gripped Joshan as he pulled in a sharp breath. "Pravius is with them," he said.

"There's more now, maybe six… or seven… hard telling," said Haiden. "They got chains from the sounds of it."

"Well, we know Pravius doesn't trust our strength," Trenara mused. "I've never been fond of chains. I'm getting too old for this sort of thing." She looked at Joshan and smiled. "We will have to see what we can do to placate an old woman's whims, eh?"

Joshan raised a brow, knowing a battle was eminent.

Haiden rubbed his knuckles greedily. "I got a whim or two myself, your lordship. A couple of them boys and me got some things to discuss, if you take my meaning."

Joshan looked from one to the other. "Well, we haven't exactly an army, but I think we can stir enough of a fuss to give us a fighting chance." He looked through the bars. "Keep your wits about you. Pravius is powerful and dangerous."

Now they could all hear the group coming noisily down the cellblock. They formed a triangle around the door, Trenara at the center, furthest from the door, Joshan to the left and Haiden to the right. They heard the gathering stop outside the cell and the jingling of keys. They breathed deeply and prepared to leap at whatever came through the door.

What came, however, was so unexpected it devastated their plan instantly. A flash of blinding light burst into the room like the firing of a sun, burning their eyes, and doubling them over. The guards took them easily.

CHAPTER FIVE
FLIGHT TO FREEDOM

Hands appeared from nowhere and gripped their arms tightly. Joshan was pushed to his knees, and his arms were yanked savagely behind his back. When his vision cleared, the pseudo-Pravius stood over him, smiling down judiciously.

Again, Trenara noted the touch of genius in the way this man carried himself, the tone of his voice and the smooth way he transitioned from the benign, sad-eyed councilor to the aggressive, self-assured master of manipulation. Trenara guessed his personal guards were the only ones who saw this side of him on a daily basis. The guider was amazed she hadn't seen through this before and it frightened her. If he was showing this side of himself to them now, it didn't bode well for their future, or the future of the empire.

Pieces were beginning to fall rapidly into place for her. From Pravius's position in the Council of Justice, he could easily infiltrate any part of the Keep he wished. The councilor possessed keys, pass codes, and almost the highest immunity sanction granted. The only ones higher were held by the Chancellors of Justice and Trade and the emperor himself. The thought sent tremors through the guider, as her mind wandered to Jenhada's recent illness and the fabricated accusations against herself and Saldorian, the Emperor's Consort.

"I trust you have spent the night well," he was saying. He had his arms folded over the red robe of judgment, the insignia depicting the shield and scales glowing red-gold in the dim torchlight. He paced before the three as they were held to their knees. Haiden had apparently fought in his blindness, for a deep bloody gash glistened on his left cheek where someone had struck him. He strained at his three holders. Trenara was breathing heavily as Pravius reached for her arm, but she pulled it away before he could touch it.

"You heal quickly." Trenara returned the gaze, but said nothing.

The councilor scanned the prisoners. "I come to bring you solace and what do I receive in return—hostility." He clicked his tongue and shook his head. His tone was suddenly concerned and real, sending shivers through Trenara. "The city is ready to tear you apart for the murder of their prince, and except for my intervention, you would have died horribly hours ago." He turned and smiled. "You should be grateful." Haiden struggled against his captors, receiving another blow to the back of his head for his troubles. He cried out and almost lost consciousness.

"Why, the whole of the empire is relieved at your capture. The prince was a well-loved child." He grinned at Joshan as his eyes sparkled with malice and his voice changed once again. "But none as grateful as the emperor's consort," he said cruelly, quietly, so only Joshan could hear, mere inches from his upturned face. "Her gratitude was… most enjoyable."

Joshan jumped at the man so suddenly, the guards lost their grips. He grabbed the front of Pravius's robes, twisted him around, and rammed his face against the wall. The guards seized him at once, one thrusting the hilt of his blade into the prince's stomach and the other knocking him to the ground. They lifted him to his knees and twisted his arms behind him until he cried out.

Pravius took a handful of Joshan's hair and pulled his head back, as he wiped blood from the corner of his mouth. "I have been ordered not to harm you," he hissed, "but someone needs to teach you manners, boy." A glint came into those terrible eyes when he let Joshan loose and motioned to a wall. "Hold him there."

The guards wrestled him to the wall, each taking an arm, and pinned him against the stones until they bit into his back. Pravius drew a scepter from his sleeve, and Joshan took in a startled breath when he recognized Andelian. Trenara's gasp was quiet and agonized. The gloved hands showed the devil's reluctance to touch the scepter as he toyed with it. "I see you recognize the witch's wand. It is capable of a trick or two... in the right hands." He signaled the other guards. "Bring them here. I think an objectivity lesson would be good for all of them."

The guards pushed their prisoners to the wall and held them there with swords at their throats. Trenara noted the councilor's guards were enjoying this sport. They seemed more interested in what Pravius was doing than in their respective prisoners. An idea struck and she waited.

"His shirt," Pravius said.

They ripped the front of Joshan's tunic open, exposing his chest and shoulders. The tattoo shone out even in the torchlight and Haiden gasped. Pravius turned his head to the guards and a chuckle escaped his lips. "You see what I told you? The fabrication is masterfully done. She thought of everything." He turned his eyes to a very confused Trenara and smiled. "You're going to hang for this, witch. Did you really think you could get away with it?" The guards laughed and pushed the guider hard into the wall before she could respond.

Pravius turned his attention back to Joshan and began to pace. "As I was saying, this little trinket can be quite useful if handled correctly. For example..." He suddenly took on the voice and mannerisms of the meek councilor again, his voice quiet and intellectual. It was strangely odd and twisted to watch. "Placed in certain areas of the body, this brand can cause some interesting effects."

He held the scepter under Joshan's chin, lifting his face close to his own. "It works off the receiver's own fears, you see. But here... let me demonstrate," he said quietly, the baleful eyes shining in the torchlight. The councilor grabbed a handful of hair and pulled Joshan's head back, placing the scepter in the middle of his bare chest. An agonizing scream escaped Joshan's throat as unspeakable pain consumed him. He felt as if his body were on fire, as if layers of skin were being peeled away. The burning was so intense he blacked out.

Haiden let out a cry and strained against his holders; the other guards had to relinquish their hold on the guider. Trenara saw her chance; she snatched the jar of tavelson from her pocket and uncorked it. With a surprisingly quick gesture, she threw the contents at the unsuspecting tormentors. It hit the guard standing closest to her in the face, sending him screaming blindly across the cell. At the same time, it caught Pravius across the back of the neck, causing him to drop Andelian. Splashes of the liquid fell across all the guards. Cries of pain echoed through the chamber as the Tavelson burned them, causing sudden chaos.

Once loose, Haiden was quick to disarm a guard and drive a point into another, his skill swift and deadly. It was for good reason Haiden was the lead trainer in the Keep. No one could match his talent with a blade. He rushed to the prince's side to put his weight around him, dragging him to the door. Two more guards felt the sergeant's blade and fell. Haiden held out his sword, Trenara in close pursuit.

Pravius was the first to recover. "Stop them!"

The three ran into the corridor, steps ahead of the guards. Haiden heaved on the heavy iron door and it shut with a clang, the snick of the lock echoing down the corridor. Shouts could be heard from every prison cell, when more guards appeared. He recognized them immediately as the councilor's and cut them down with a graceful quickness that caught them unaware. They fell before the cell door. One of the guards on the inside reached through the bars and fumbled to get the key into the lock. He managed to get it turned, but the bodies in front of the door wedged it into place.

A third guard charged around a bend in the passageway and stopped abruptly, his mouth open and his eyes wide as he scanned the dead guards on the stone floor and Haiden with a dripping sword in his hand. He gathered enough wits to draw his blade, but did not move. The young man could not have been more than seventeen or eighteen seasons, yet he wore the golden braids of the Elite, the emperor's personal guard. Haiden had known this boy since he was a baby, but stared at him now as if he were a stranger. The guard advanced nervously, but the glare in Haiden's eyes made him stop.

"Jona," Haiden said darkly, "you've been a good friend for a long time and I've known your da well for many seasons, but I'll cut you down where you stand, if you so much as lift a finger against the prince. I swear to the gods."

The boy looked at the young man clasped in Haiden's grip, saw for the first time the tattooed symbol on his exposed arm, and stared hard at his face. Jona's eyes widened in recognition as his blade dropped with a clang to the stones. His face contorted strangely as he turned and ran.

Trenara had scooped up a sword from one of the downed guards and was valiantly battling another guard, but had received a nasty gash to her arm during the melee. Haiden rushed to the guider's aid and quickly dispatched the assailant. The guider's wound was deep and bloody.

The corridor was clear for the moment. The remaining guards and Pravius were trapped in the cell, the dead bodies wedged tightly in front of the iron door, but it was opening slowly as shoulders were put to it. More guards could be heard advancing down the passage.

"I think we best be moving," said Haiden grimly as he lifted Joshan to his shoulder. "Can you run, guider?"

Trenara was holding her injured arm, blood soaking her sleeve and robe. "Like I have a choice. Let's go."

They set off down the passageway, but their progress was very slow. Haiden's burden made running awkward, and Trenara had been deeply cut. They rounded a corner, and Haiden caught sight of a deserted closet.

"Here," he hissed. They dashed into the darkened room and closed the door. Haiden lay the prince down gingerly and stooped next to Trenara, as a group of guards went rushing past. "We're going to be hard put getting out of this one. The guards are going to be all over this place soon." Haiden helped Trenara tear a strip from the bottom of her robe and tied it around the gash in her arm. Trenara winced in pain, but didn't make a sound. She was breathing heavily and her face was very pale.

"There must be a way," she whispered. "There's a tunnel that leads to the streets of Keepton on the other side of the hold entrance, in the west hall. Do you know it?"

"Aye, behind the fifteenth panel on the north side. I know it well. I'm a bit surprised you do." This had been used in times past when previous emperors wanted a discreet visit to the brothels in town.

"Yes, well, I'm full of surprises," she replied testily. "It hasn't been used since before the siege, so I think it might be safe. At least I'm reasonably sure Pravius doesn't know about it. If we can get through the hold entrance and then to the hall, we may be able to escape to the city."

"Aye," Haiden said doubtfully. "But that hold entrance will be the hardest to take, unless we get some help."

"Help often comes from strange places, Haiden," Trenara replied, opening the door a crack and looking down the now empty corridors. She grimaced in pain.

A groan came from Joshan and he sat with a start. "No!"

"It's all right, lad," Haiden said helping him to his feet.

"Where…"

"There's no time now. Are you hurt? Can you run?"

Joshan was dazed and shaking, but otherwise whole. "Yes."

"Well, there's nothing for it, but to do it." Haiden glanced down the cell block, wiping sweat out of his eyes. "Now."

Again, they sprinted down the corridor. They picked their way through the intricate maze of tunnels carefully. Trenara's wound was deep and she was weakening with each step, falling behind the others. When they ran around another bend, Trenara caught her foot and fell sprawling against the stones. Joshan looked back at the guider's cry and stopped.

"Haiden!" he shouted and ran toward her. At the same time, a group of northern guards came around the bend. All froze. Trenara was caught midway between them. Pravius made his way to the front of the guards and lifted the wand, sending a beam of light toward Joshan.

Haiden was quick to tackle the prince and throw him back before the beam could reach him. Instead, it hit the wall with a resounding crack that shook the hold and spread a translucent barrier before an already exhausted Trenara. She struggled to her feet and charged into the field, but it held her fast and her face twisted in agony. The energy shimmered like mirrored water, then glowed sickly as it drained the last remnants of strength from the guider. Her two companions looked on helplessly, as the guider's face turned ghostly white.

Joshan lunged at the barrier, but Haiden held him tight.

"Get him out of here, Haiden," Trenara grated as she sank to her knees, sliding to the stone floor. She did not move again.

Haiden hurled the prince in the opposite direction and stumbling, they bounded down the passageway. Tears streaked the dirt and blood that stained Joshan's face. *If only I could summon the power now*, he raged to himself. But it lay dormant in him like a sleeping storm. They heard running steps in front of them, so Haiden pushed the prince and himself into a dark corner. The pursuers passed. Again they ran, now hiding behind a rock or crevice or shadowed doorway, now fighting a bewildered guard, stopping only long enough to listen for pursuit or to conceal themselves.

Joshan noticed Haiden was very discriminating with his killing, selecting only the darker northerners for his blade and merely immobilizing the regular guards. He was having difficulty himself distinguishing between the two, but the old fighter was very precise with his violence. After what seemed like an eternity, Haiden stopped at a bend and lay next to the wall listening. He was covered with blood.

"Beyond this point is the guardhouse and the entrance gate," he whispered, wiping his face with a bloody sleeve. "It's bound to be held tight, but with a little luck and maybe a miracle or two, we'll make it. I ain't going to lie to you, son. Our chances are slim. Without the guider…"

"I'll need a sword," Joshan replied, exhaustion and grief making his voice mechanical.

"Aye, that you will." Haiden looked carefully around the bend. "We'll see what we can do." He listened and then stepped fully into the corridor. A lone Elite guard came around the corner, suspicion heavy in his eyes. "Good," Haiden breathed. "There's fighting heavy up the passage there. Pravius sent me to find help. Run, lad. I'll get others."

The guard saluted and sprang off, but as he passed, Haiden lifted his blade and expertly struck the youth on the nape of the neck. He went down and Haiden caught him before he landed on the stones, setting him down gently and grabbing the blade from his limp fingers. He tossed it to Joshan. "There, lord," he said, looking down the tunnel again. "Follow behind and keep your distance; you'll only get in my way. I'll clear a path as best I can." Haiden sprinted down the corridor.

Joshan turned the sword in his hands, feeling very inadequate. He was not a good swordsman, but he was determined to fight. He would not let his old friend fall. Not like Trenara. He gripped the hilt tightly and dashed into the tunnel.

As he ran, a strange tingling began in his hand, and the sword took on a barely perceptible glow. His mind, so dulled by exhaustion, didn't notice it. He rounded a bend, only to see Haiden engaging two swordsmen who had been caught off guard. Three lay dead or unconscious on the ground, and four others were advancing, all of them northerners. He sprang to his friend's side and began to fight with one of the guards, relieving Haiden's plight. As he fought, a new strength began to build in him. A confidence spread to his bones and he suddenly realized that the *power* had awoken again.

More guards poured into the passage. He cut down his assailant and advanced on this new group with a vengeance. His eyes glowed with the *power* and the blade gleamed like a torch in his hands. As a whole, the group stepped back. The leader, a ruddy man of heavy girth, mustered some courage and moved toward Joshan. Before he had taken more than two steps, a beam of *power* shot from the sword and hit his chest. As he crumbled, the remainder of the guards broke and ran. The light died instantly.

"You're going to have to teach me that," Haiden said, wiping his blade on the shirt of one of the downed men. For the moment, the guardhouse was empty except for the fallen.

Joshan nodded grimly. "I can't trust that to happen again. It seems the *power* comes at its own time." His eyes were steely in the gloomy dark.

Haiden shot him a look and turned to the door. "This leads to the west hall." He stuck his head carefully through and looked both ways. "If we can hold out for about thirty more spans, we'll be home."

They ran down another hallway and Haiden pushed Joshan through a door before some advancing guards could see them. The Keep's west hall was clear, but they moved very cautiously, staying close to the wall. They did not speak and walked very carefully, because the marble hall magnified every sound. The elaborate ballroom had been built many seasons before, when Joshan's great-mother reigned. In those days, it had been brightly lit, full of stunning tapestries and paintings of priceless quality. But the beauty was gone.

The austere elegance of flax veined marble was now dulled by lack of tending; dust and cobwebs covered the walls and ceilings. Dirty adornments decorated the walls, viscid mockeries of the bright and lively days. The curtains were tattered and decaying and the room gave one a feeling of deep loneliness as the boarded windows gave little light. Joshan felt the dreariness of the place and was appalled by the lack of upkeep. His heart ached to cleanse the sorrow from this place. Although he did not know its source, the grief attached to this room was ancient and disturbing.

They walked on in silence, slowly, and Haiden appeared to be counting as he looked at the north wall. He raised his hand suddenly to stop Joshan and put a finger to his lips. Looking around, he found a large drapery that had fallen from one of the immense windows. He slowly and quietly tore the remainder of the cloth, tested it for strength, and then spread it out on the floor before a large door. He then motioned Joshan to stand behind a dusty alcove.

Joshan heard them now. A group was searching the rooms one by one; voices were raised and doors carelessly slammed. Haiden pantomimed that he wanted the drape pulled when the group entered. Joshan nodded mutely. The sergeant took his station beside the door, with his back to the wall. They waited.

The handle turned, and a lone northern guard entered. Joshan readied to pull the drape, but the sergeant shook his head. When the guard was in the room, Haiden took him from behind, throwing a hand over his mouth, turning his head to the side, and neatly cutting his throat all in one fluid motion. Blood flowed from his neck making a black puddle on the stones. He dragged the body carefully out of sight and returned to the shadows. Joshan was amazed at the old soldier's skill and deadly accuracy. He would never want Haiden as an enemy.

Moments later, the remainder of the group came through the door. When they were all in the room, Haiden jumped from his hiding place and shouted, "Well, lads. You've caught me at last."

Swords were drawn, and when Haiden gave Joshan the signal, the four guards were flung helplessly into the air, coming down with an echoing crash on the hard marble floor. Haiden wasted no time. He smashed the first two Elite guards unconscious and ran through the northern one, but the fourth was on his feet with lightning speed and advanced toward him. The man parried the old guard's sword and lunged at him, nicking his leg badly. Haiden winced, but deflected another blow before it could hit its mark.

As they circled, Joshan recovered his senses and went to Haiden's aid. He recognized the assailant as the guard at Third Gate who must have turned them in the night before. Before he reached them, Haiden shouted, "No, lad. This one's mine. I have some unfinished business with this fellow." He parried a thrust and lunged, just missing his mark. "Something Trenara wanted attending to." Joshan stopped and then ran to the door to watch for other guards.

The two swordsmen circled slowly, each gauging the strength of the other; then both stepped into the duel. For every lunge, there was a parry. Haiden hit his mark only once, but it buried into the man's shoulder and not his heart as he had hoped. As skilled as Haiden was, he was dead tired, and this man was relatively fresh and quite skilled with the blade. Haiden was losing strength quickly, but he was determined to get this victory for the starguider. The man lunged again, just missing by fractions.

Haiden knew he could not hold up long and would have to call for Joshan's aid. A glimmer of a smile came to his face as he grimaced in pain and stepped back, causing the man to press harder. Haiden took another blow, but the blade deflected and left a welt on Haiden's undamaged cheek, which would blacken later. He stepped back again, holding his injured leg and hissing in pain.

The man grinned as he cornered his adversary. Haiden stumbled, and his blade clattered to the ground. The man lifted his sword slowly to strike the final blow, relishing the moment. Haiden recovered with incredible speed, as he grabbed his sword and thrust it to the hilt into the man's exposed gullet. Blood soaked his hand and wrist as he pulled the sword out with the precision of a graceful dancer. A look of surprise covered the man's face as he fell to the floor. He shuddered once and then died, as Joshan reached them.

Haiden struggled to his feet with Joshan's help, and the prince just shook his head. "You'll have to teach me that," he said.

"It was a close thing, but we've no time to waste." He gestured to the opposite wall. "Quickly, lad, before others come. Over to the panel there." Haiden's leg was bleeding badly, and he leaned on Joshan as they ran. Even now, they could hear guards coming down the corridor. Joshan stopped the old guard and grabbed a piece of cloth from the floor.

"We can't have you leaving a trail of blood." He wrapped the cloth around the wound and tied it tightly to staunch the flow.

Despite his pain and imminent danger, Haiden laughed. "I guess you were listening during your lessons."

They covered the distance to the wall at a sprint. Quickly cleaning his bloody hands on his trousers, Haiden pushed on the panel, slid it up, and then pushed the prince inside. He jumped in after him and slid the panel back into place. Just then, shouts and the sound of running feet were heard in the hall. Joshan and Haiden stood in the darkness holding their breaths.

Pravius strode into the room and reviewed the scene, completely losing the façade of the councilor. "Fools!" he shouted, scanning the bodies and kicking one hard. He glared at the northern guard who entered with him and grabbed him by the front of the shirt. "Find them! Or I'll skin you alive, I swear." He let go of the man, sending him sprawling among the bodies on the floor. "I don't care if you have to tear this Keep apart stone by stone. I want them found and brought to me!" He whirled on his heel and disappeared out the door.

Haiden and Joshan heard none of this. They were well on their way down the tunnel to safety.

CHAPTER SIX
THE BARGAIN

When Trenara woke from the nightmare, gruesome visions echoed behind her ears, pounding violently at her temples. Her head whirled and spun into consciousness, until she nearly retched. Her heavy eyes reluctantly opened, afraid of what they might see.

However, the guider no longer felt the icy grip of the field, or the power that had so thoroughly crushed her before. Instead, she lay on a soft bed, with clean wrappings surrounding her upper arm and the faint scent of boiling herbs drifting on the air. Trenara struggled to sit, the sling holding her arms firmly against her chest.

She threw the covers aside, exposing a clean heavy nightgown. The guider recognized the room as one of the servant's quarters on the lower level. It was dimly lit, being on the inside of the castle and away from the afternoon sun, but neat and plainly decorated. When she tried to rise, nausea took hold again, and she put her head in her hand until the spinning stopped.

"I am happy to see you awake."

When she turned to look behind her, Pravius sat in a chair next to a small window, the smoke of a pipe curling about his head like a gray wreath. Trenara frowned at him and stared for a moment, taking care to guard her thoughts and emotions, not knowing how extensive this man's abilities were. She stood a little too quickly and fell heavily to her unbound hand and knees. "You bastard," was all she could manage and that in a scraping rasp.

"Come, you mustn't exert yourself." He motioned to a page who came forward to lift Trenara to her feet. The guider shook off the young woman's hands and edged her way toward the councilor, holding onto the bed for support. "Yes, that's a good idea. Sit. There is much we need to discuss," he said gesturing to the chair opposite him, apparently taking on the pretense of Pravius for the aide's benefit. Trenara sat down awkwardly.

"The only thing I wish to discuss is your death, demon," she snarled weakly.

Pravius chuckled. "You are hardly in a position to threaten my death." He tapped his pipe into an ornate ashtray sitting on a small wooden table. "I would worry about my own, if I were you." He rose and crossed to a window, pushing aside the curtain and taking in a long breath. "But I have not come here to bandy threats with you, my good guider. I came to seek a truce." He turned to gaze at Trenara, who returned it narrowly.

"I hardly think that possible, *Pravius*," she said, emphasizing the name.

A small light flashed in the councilor's eyes as he raised a dismissing hand. "Leave us." The page bowed quickly and ran for the door. Pravius crossed to a table and poured himself a cup of tea. "Won't you join me? It is quite good, from the emperor's stock."

"No," Trenara replied dryly.

Pravius sat and sipped his tea, regarding the guider from above the porcelain vessel. "It is such a small matter, really," he said. "I need the young stranger, and I believe you can lead me to him."

So, Trenara thought happily, they had not caught Joshan. *Good boy!* She was certain she had Haiden to thank for that. Pravius gave her a nasty look.

"Yes, the young man is still free, but that is not a permanent situation, I assure you. We *will* find him." Although his voice was smooth, his hand clenched the chair unconsciously. "But I am forgetting myself. I came to ask your help in finding the stranger."

Trenara lifted her hand in weary protest. "Let's not play games. You know as well as I who that stranger is."

"Very well," he nodded after a solicitous pause. "Joshan, then; no one will believe it if you spread that rumor. I have seen to that."

"What do you mean?"

"Why," Pravius said sympathetically, the disguise again prevalent, "haven't you heard? Joshan's eecha came back without a rider yesterday morning. We were all quite alarmed, you see, afraid something awful must have happened to him. Soon after, the boy's body was found." He paused to sip his tea and let the knowledge sink in. "I'm afraid there was nothing much left, save a few scraps of clothing and some badly charred bones. Very sad." His scowl was almost authentic. "I left no doubt."

Trenara gripped the arms of the chair tightly. What innocent has been sacrificed and why? "You monster! What have you done?"

"Save your righteousness, Assemblage," he said. "It is of little consequence. The boy we used was a peasant. Your judgment doesn't concern me." He relaxed his anger and managed a smile. "But as I was about to say…"

"Who are you?" Trenara hissed.

Pravius cocked a brow and smiled. "You are very perceptive, my friend."

"The corruption that fouls my guider's *sense* can only be for one reason, devil." Her eyes flashed, but Pravius just laughed.

"Devil? No, you have not met the devil." His laughter stopped as he lifted his eyes to take full measure of the guider. Trenara was horrified by the fear and hate she sensed in those briefly unveiled eyes. She shrank back in terror. "But I have." Pravius's whispered confession spoke volumes. He lowered his eyes and sighed deeply, quickly covering his moment of indiscretion with a derisive snort. "Let's just say I am a messenger and leave it at that."

"From whom?"

Pravius smiled. "In good time, guider. In good time." He stood and stretched his neck. "I want to strike a bargain with you. Consider well before you answer, for I will offer it only once." He pursed his lips, and a fire began to sparkle behind his eyes. "If you tell me where the boy would go or where the sergeant would take him, then I will do this for you. I will release Jenhada from his illness and Saldorian from her imprisonment. I will disappear from all of your lives and never return."

Trenara's face became dour. "Along with the boy, I take it."

"Yes," he replied evenly. Their eyes locked for a moment and Trenara caught the burning fire beneath the surface of the councilor's outer calm.

"And if I refuse?"

"Then I will do everything in my power to destroy this Keep and everyone in it—starting with you."

Trenara nodded solemnly. "That doesn't leave me much of a choice, does it?"

Pravius's face smoothed; satisfaction showed in the lines around his eyes. "None at all. You have made a wise decision."

Trenara's eyes flashed. "Do not mistake me," she spat. "You must know I would never betray Joshan, no matter what the bargain."

Pravius stood back and his voice became sweetly bitter. "Certainly. I should have known. You've always been obstinate, Trenara," he responded viciously. "But you will help me. Your refusal means very little. One way or the other, you *will* bring Joshan here." There was a moment of silence in which Pravius lowered his head and composed his anger. "Myself," he continued smoothly, "I would prefer your voluntary cooperation. It would make matters much more pleasant for you—and him. It is your choice. I mean to have the boy in any event."

Trenara looked at the man, carefully weighing her words. "What do you want with him?"

"Unfortunately, I am not at liberty to say," he replied, picking up his pipe. "However, I assure you no harm will come to him. I want the prince alive and well as much as you."

"It didn't seem so last night."

Pravius's eyes flashed. "I will not abide insolence in anyone. The boy's manners needed checking."

Trenara rose stiffly. "If this is your idea of 'no harm,' I will have to decline your kind offer." She stumbled to the bed and sat. "I'm tired. I have no patience for games."

"Nor I," Pravius replied blackly. "You will not aid me?"

Trenara met his gaze. "Not in this lifetime."

The councilor's eyes narrowed and Trenara could feel his building wrath. "You are a fool, Assemblage," he growled as he pulled a cord that hung from the ceiling. "He said you would be stubborn. I should have listened."

Pravius crossed to where Trenara sat, grabbed her shoulders, and pulled the wounded woman from the bed. She winced in pain as his strong fingers dug into the torn flesh, but she did not cry out. "Hear me well, Assemblage. You will regret this. You have sealed the fate of the Imperium. He has ways of rewarding those who serve him—and those who do not. I will enjoy watching you die, as you should have long ago."

The chamber door flew open, admitting three stout northern guards with chains. Pravius threw the guider and sent her sprawling before them, painfully opening the gash in her arm and soaking the binding with blood. "Take the bitch," he screamed. "At dawn, hang her to the stake." They pulled Trenara from the floor and roughly bound her arms. She stared at Pravius in disbelief.

"The stake," she whispered, for the first time frightened. "Why not kill me now and have done with it?"

"Because, you old fool," Pravius intoned washing the blood from his hands with a napkin, "you can't catch fish with dead bait. Get her out of my sight."

The guards dragged Trenara away, fighting for her life.

CHAPTER SEVEN
REFUGE

For most of that night and the better part of the next day, Joshan and Haiden made their way through the maze of tunnels under the castle through Keepton, and finally just passed Second Gate. They lost their way many times and had to retrace their path to where they had begun. Crawling for hours in pitch blackness through centuries of filth, their hands and knees became bloody from the stones, their wounds gathered grime, and their strength was almost gone. Joshan thought more than once they would die in those hideous tunnels. Haiden's unwavering instincts and perseverance saved them more than a dozen times. But the guard's strength was quickly fading.

Finally, the tunnels became larger and they could stand upright, much to their relief. They were under the streets of The Village and light began to filter in from a series of grates overhead. Try as they might, they couldn't get any of the grates to open and were trapped in the tunnels for most of the day.

Without warning, they splashed into a sewer before they even knew they had found it. They almost choked on the vile sewage, but somehow forced a street cover open where they crawled out into the night and relatively fresh air. No sooner had they emerged, than two guards on swift eechas came thundering down the cobblestones, heedless of pedestrians, and almost rode them down.

The riders reined in their animals, turned them about, and galloped after the two. The companions ran for their lives, only to round a corner into the arms of a squadron of mounted men. Had it not been for the *power* that suddenly burst from Joshan's palms, they would have been taken. The fierceness of the blaze terrorized the eechas and sent them bolting off with their riders. Joshan helped a shaking Haiden up from the street, and again they ran.

Joshan's concern for his friend deepened as they went. He was limping badly from his wound and they had to stop too often for the prince's comfort. He didn't know where they were heading, but he trusted Haiden's judgment. The old guard was failing fast. If he were to collapse, Joshan would be completely lost. He had never ventured into the Village, except along the main road. The place was as foreign to him as another country.

They stopped to rest behind a garden wall and stooped quietly to catch their breaths. Haiden was panting heavily and his face was very pale. "Listen," he said, rubbing his hands in the cold. "I don't know how much longer I can keep on my feet. My leg is hurting bad." He wiped the sweat and muck from his eyes. "If I can't make it, you got to try it on your own."

"Haiden, I won't leave."

"Begging your pardon, son, but shut up and listen," he said. "There's an inn, by the name of Foresons, a few leagues north of here. We'll make for it. I know the people there and they'll help. If I don't make it, you go on alone and tell them I sent you. Then, if you can, you send someone back for me." He rubbed his leg, which was beginning to numb. "I've no intention of being left, but I got to see you safe first. It's the least I can do for Trenara. Come on." He winced as he rose and started down the road again.

At the mention of Trenara, Joshan couldn't prevent the tears that began to blind him. He stopped briefly to wipe his eyes with the back of his sleeve. When he was grabbed from behind, it took him totally by surprise. He opened his mouth to shout, but the arm locked down on his windpipe and effectively cut off his voice. Joshan was pulled into an alley and pushed roughly through a door.

Inside, the dwelling was inky and reeked of fish and stale beer. A massive hand shoved him toward a bench. He fell heavily and struck his forehead against something sharp, causing painful sparks to go off behind his eyes. Tinder was lit and Joshan could make out the features of a huge, ominous man.

The giant lit a lamp and turned it very low, giving Joshan a sinister stare. He was very dark, with a tangle of black hair and beard that meshed together to hide most of a rugged, stormy face, with one black eye visible and the other covered by a dirty patch. He towered over Joshan by a good five hands and exceded his girth by half again as much. There was a long jagged scar that ran from under the patch to the general vicinity of his chin, disappearing in a snarl of unkempt beard. Joshan regained enough composure to weakly stand, but his knees buckled under their own weight.

"Well," echoed a booming voice, "looks like I caught myself a pretty fish, doesn't it?" He pulled a long, nasty looking dagger from his boot and advanced on Joshan. "They say there's a handsome reward for the likes of you. But they want you alive, mores the pity." Joshan backed against the wall, trying desperately to summon the power, but it could not be coerced from its slumber.

In a sudden move, he jumped for the door, but the man was too quick. He lunged at him with his knife and neatly pinned his shirt to a post. "Going somewhere? Just remember, I'd just as soon throttle as look at you. And they say alive, but not how alive, if you get my drift." His breath was foul in Joshan's face. The giant removed the knife and pushed Joshan back to the bench. "Wert! Get your arse in here."

A beam of light fell into the room from a door slowly opening. A small man with a bad limp came in, looking like he lived in constant dread, the worry lines deep in his face. "Yes, Van?"

"Lookey here what I caught." He held the light to Joshan's face. "I'm thinking it might be that escape prisoner them guards were talking about earlier."

Wert nodded and looked closer. "I think you're right, Van. Leastwise, he kind of looks like what they said."

Van grabbed the little man by the shirtfront. "Kind of? Exactly, I say." Wert nodded silently and the giant let him go. "Now, here's what I'm thinking. I stay with the lad and make sure he don't get any inclination to run, and you go after them guards and tell them we got them a package."

"Yes, Van."

"Then you and me, we got us some spending money, eh? Now, get going and make it quick." He stood over the hunched man. "And get the booty first. You tell 'em we'll meet them just inside Second Gate. Got it?" He held the dagger before the timid man's face. Wert nodded once and then stumbled for the door. When he was gone, Van laughed, picked up a skin of wine, and poured the contents into his mouth, much of it running down his beard and shirt.

As Joshan stared up at the giant, a deep bitterness left him numb and uncaring. He was tired to the bone, hurt all over, and knew this was the end. He'd die before returning to Pravius, and that resolution hardened him. He settled into the bench, folded his arms, and stared darkly at the huge man.

Van turned the light higher and sat down at the table across from him, picking up a piece of half-eaten bullion-beast. "That sluggard'll take a couple of hours to get them guards," he said from around a mouth of food. "You better get comfortable." He spat out a bone. "We got a wait."

Joshan merely glared at him. Van returned the stare and a glint came into his one good eye. He picked up the lamp and held it to the boy's face again. "You look familiar to me. You ever been to sea?"

"No," Joshan replied flatly.

Van furrowed his brow. "Still… I know you from somewhere. What be your name?"

Joshan opened his mouth to give a nasty reply, thought better of it, and looked down at the table instead. "You wouldn't believe me."

In an incredibly quick movement, Van grabbed Joshan's shirt and stood up, pulling him off his feet. The prince dangled helplessly before the giant. "I asked your name," Van said dangerously, putting his dagger to the exposed throat.

"Listen, you drunken sod. Either cut my throat or break my neck, but have done with it!"

Van grinned broadly and let him go, sending him crashing to meet the bench. Joshan straightened his tunic and rubbed the back of his neck. "I like you. You've got backbone, and that's a fact." He gave the boy a long look, and Joshan began to see a masked intelligence in the giant's eye. "Here," the giant said, throwing the wine skin to Joshan who caught it clumsily, astonished he hadn't been beaten to death. "Take a swig."

"No, thank you."

"Come on, boy. It'll do you good."

Joshan shrugged and put the spout to his nose. It smelled very strong and somewhat foul, but he turned it up and most of the contents spilled into his face. He put it down sputtering.

Van threw his head back and howled with laughter, hitting his thigh with a massive hand. "Well, you're no drinker, I can see that."

Joshan wiped his face with his shirtsleeve, his eyes glistening angrily. When Van's chortles subsided, he looked long and hard at the young face. "What's your name?"

He met the look squarely. "Joshan," he replied evenly.

Van's eyes narrowed. "Joshan is dead or haven't you heard?"

"I told you, you wouldn't believe me," Joshan replied looking down at the table. The big man rose and Joshan flinched, but the giant merely crossed to the fire to tend to it.

"Now you mention it, you do look like him, but you're older than he could be now. You some sort of kin or something?"

"Something," he replied bitterly.

"He was a fine boy, that one," Van said quietly. "And had the most gracious mother I ever did meet, and the most beautiful, I'll wager."

"When did the likes of you ever meet my… the Lady Saldorian?"

"It was a long time ago, lad." Van's face softened in the glowing firelight. "I sailed the lady and her boy to the isle once, for the Festival of Midseason. The lad was no more than five or six then, but he was a smart one and as cocky as they come." Joshan had to hold his hand over his mouth to keep from shouting.

Vanderlinden! Captain of the Imperial Fleet. One of the finest sea captains in the provinces—in the world, as far as the young Joshan had been concerned. Vanderlinden had been highly praised and decorated by the emperor many times, as well as countless Assemblage honors for his bravery against Sirdar. Few people not of Assemblage could claim these honors. Joshan thought he was dead; they all thought he was dead—lost at sea, they said. He and Trenara had been very good friends and Joshan remembered how the guider had grieved when the news hit the Keep two seasons before.

He looked at the man now. Yes, it was the captain. Only one man in the world could be as big as Vanderlinden. As a boy, he respected and admired him, but he had been quite handsome then, with both eyes and not the ominous, dirty figure standing before him now. By the gods, what had happened?

"Captain?" he asked aloud.

Van whirled on him and raised his fist. "What'd you call me?" Joshan shrunk from the blow, but it did not come. Instead, Van sat down and stared at him.

The prince couldn't contain himself. "What happened to you? Trenara and I thought you were dead. That's what they told us. Look at you. Why, you used to be the bravest man in the world. You'd take on fifty ships and bring them through any storm, then laugh about how you had beaten the sea god one more time. You used to tell me tales about sea monsters and sailing and all about the ethics of the sea. You were going to take me away one day and make me a proper seaman…"

"Joshan, stop!"

They looked at one another, and a long silence hung in the room. For several seconds they stared at each other as if believing, yet not believing. Finally, Van blew out a breath and leaned across the table. "There's a scar," he said hoarsely.

"Yes, on my left arm, where the main boom hit me during that same trip."

"Let me see it."

Joshan quickly rolled up his sleeve and showed the arm to the mariner. The scar lay as it always had, long and red down the length of his forearm. Van used to tease the prince about it being his first to manhood. The giant reached over, pulling the tunic off Joshan's shoulder. There the distinctive red and black imperial tattoo stood, and Van stared at it a long time before taking in a shaky breath.

"You got a lot of explaining to do," Van said at length.

"Me?" he exclaimed. "What about you? Where…"

Just then, the door burst open and Haiden came charging in, wielding his sword straight for the sitting giant. Joshan jumped up. "Haiden, no!" Van whirled around, dove for the floor, caught Haiden by the legs, and sent him flying through the air into a fish bin.

Joshan leapt over the table and helped Haiden out. "Are you all right?"

"Well enough," Haiden replied, rubbing the back of his arm where it had been wrenched, death in his eyes toward Van. "You lay one hand on this lad and I'll cut you down where you stand."

"No, Haiden. He's a friend."

Haiden took a few hesitant steps toward the giant and retrieved his sword from the ground. "This ain't no friend. I caught me a sneak outside who says so. Or didn't you tell the lad you were going to turn him in?" he said, keeping the blade on Van.

"No, Haiden. He thought I was an escaped prisoner, that's all. He sent Wert to get the guard, not knowing who I was."

"And now he knows?" he asked, giving Joshan a sidelong look. Joshan nodded. "Well, I'm thinking he might be figuring you're worth a bit more, ain't that right?" He adjusted the hilt in his hand and narrowed his eyes at the giant, who just sat there looking amused.

"Haiden, listen. This is Vanderlinden—Captain Vanderlinden of the Imperial Fleet."

Haiden screwed up his face and looked the man up and down. "Vanderlinden, eh? Vanderlinden I remember was lost at sea, couple of seasons back, wasn't it? If you are this Vanderlinden, why haven't you made yourself known for all this time?"

"That's a long tale and we ain't got time for no tales, mate," he replied. He rose and took a cloak from a peg. "What'd you do with Wert? You didn't kill him, did you?"

"Nah. He's sleeping it off in the alley."

"Good," Van shrugged. "As good a place as any. As long as he's not getting the guards." Turning the lantern down, he spat in the dark and donned the cloak. "We need to get the lad safe. Where you be heading?"

"Hold on there, mate," Haiden replied without moving. "I'm responsible for the boy and I won't be needing any help, thanks just the same. So, how about you just stand aside and let us go peaceful-like?"

Van looked at Haiden, judging the strength of the man and instantly liking him. "Just how far you think you'll be getting with that leg," he asked, gesturing to the bleeding limb.

"A good spell yet, I'll be bound." Haiden tightened his grip on his sword.

"Not bloody likely. You'd probably bleed to death 'fore you get where you're going, leaving the boy to fend for himself."

Haiden glared at the giant and raised the weapon. "How 'bout I show you just how far I could get?"

Joshan turned toward the door. "Well, if you two gentlemen will excuse me, I have to reach the inn by sunup. When you two are finished fighting over who gets to protect me, by all means, join me." He strode out the door without another word.

Haiden and Van looked from the door to each other and Van broke out laughing. "That's my boy."

Haiden sheathed his sword. "We'd better catch the young idiot before he runs into trouble."

"Aye."

They dashed out the door, hoping to catch him before he ran right into the hands of the guards, only to see he was nonchalantly leaning against the outside fence, looking at them sagely.

"You young rascal, I ought to box your ears, running off like that!"

"Quiet," Van hissed and skulked down the alley toward the street. He disappeared around the corner. Haiden gestured to Joshan to hide behind some barrels at the back of the alley.

"Begging your pardon," Haiden said, "but I don't trust this cut-throat. It don't matter what he was before. Men change, go rotten, like anything else. 'Sides, this is a rough part of town and full of his kind—and worse."

"To be honest, Haiden, I don't know if we can trust him either, but something tells me we can. In any event, we haven't much choice. In one thing, he's right. You're not going to get very far on that leg without help, and soon," he said gently. "Trenara used to tell me sometimes you have to look for help where it is least expected. In this case, it couldn't be any less expected."

Haiden sighed. "Aye, it's good advice. There's many a time when I got help when I thought there was none. Just the same, I'm not turning my back on him, that's all."

Just then Van came around the corner at a dead run. "Get moving. They're coming this way." As they bolted for the end of the alley, a guard appeared from the street.

"You, there! Stop!" He pulled his sword. "Commander, here…" But he didn't finish the sentence. Van neatly threw and buried a dagger into his neck. Eechas could be heard clattering down the road at a fast clip.

"Trapped!" Haiden cried.

"Not by a long sight," Van said, turning around. "It'd be better this way. Come on." They ran to the back of the alley again and the giant began to wrestle with a bulky barrel almost twice his size. He moved one side forward a crack. Behind it was an opening cut into the ancient stone fence that ran to what appeared to be an alley on the other side.

"In you go," he said pushing Joshan to his knees and through.

The two men followed and the giant fought with the heavy barrel to get it back in place. He gave it a hard pull and it grated into its niche. He wiped sweat from his brow and motioned them to silence. Eechas could be heard in the alley now, and men began to shout. The sound of men rummaging through the debris strewn along the alleyway made them tense in the darkness.

Van's black eye gleamed as he looked at Haiden and nodded toward the barrel. There were two notches on the back, making firm hand holds. Haiden got a good grip while Van adjusted his own, and together they pulled. Almost immediately, they felt the pressure of men pulling from the other side. It took every ounce of their strength to hold the barrel in place, but soon the pressure diminished.

"I don't think they headed this way, sir, unless they vanished into thin air," they heard from behind the barrel. "It'd take a few good stout men to move any of these."

"Frightened men can do amazing things, corporal. Still, you're probably right. They must have ducked out before we got here. If I catch the scum that cut down my lad out there, I'll skin him alive, orders or no."

"Commander, here," they heard. "There's a man behind one of these barrels." Haiden shot a quick look at the giant and mouthed *Wert*. The giant's nostrils flared for a moment, but he just gave the old guard a curt nod.

"What's that?" The commander's voice receded.

"Yes, sir," they heard. "Appears to be dead."

"Dead drunk, more like. I don't think he saw anything, but we'll bring him in just the same. Here, you two, take him to the hold and sober him up. I'm sure the councilor will want to question him." They heard some wrestling and then an eecha gallop off.

"What's that?" the commander shouted. There was some reply, but the companions couldn't hear it. "Where? Well, let's have a look." The eechas thundered away.

Haiden relaxed his grip, which had been unconsciously strained on the handle, and sat next to Joshan. Van appeared troubled.

"That was a little too close, by my way of thinking," Haiden said quietly.

"Come on," Van replied gruffly, leading them to the end of the alley.

"Now, where're you heading?"

"Foreson's," Haiden replied. "I can trust them there."

"Aye, it's a good choice." Van studied the street before him and spat into the dust at his feet. "This road'll lead you there and cut your journey by half."

"Captain, what is it?" Joshan asked, seeing the strange look in his eye.

"Nothing, lad. There's just a thing or two I don't want them guards to find out. Wert's a good man, but ain't no good under pressure."

"What sort of things?"

"Never mind. It'd take a lot of explaining and I don't have the time. Come on." Even whispering, Van's voice was deep and penetrating. He led them through the streets and stopped them at a bend in the road that curved sharply north.

"You shouldn't have any more trouble. Guards don't normally travel down this way—too dangerous. This road's not used much these days, but it'll lead you where you want to go. Use your heads. There are a lot of strange characters about. I'll see someone keeps their eyes on you."

"You're not going with us?"

"I got some things to take care of. I'll meet you at the inn when I get my business done." He looked at Haiden's leg, nodded, and then sprinted back the way he had come without another word.

Haiden scratched his head and then shook it. "Well, I'll be damned."

*****

What Van had told them was true. They encountered nothing while on the road to the inn. By the time they arrived, they were exhausted, and Haiden was leaning on Joshan heavily. Mati Foresons had greeted them with a sickle nearly twice her size, thinking them to be robbers. Luckily, she recognized Haiden's voice or they might have had a nasty end.

It had been days since the two fugitives had eaten, so when bread, cheese, and sweet milk were placed before them, they ate ravenously. It was simple fare, but it seemed a feast.

Mati Foresons waddled into the room, carrying a large tub of hot, soapy water. She was almost as round as she was tall with deep, jolly eyes and rosy cheeks surrounding a quick smile. "Ho, there," she cried, setting down the tub. "You gentlemen are going to make yourselves sick, eating like that. Slow down now, for I won't be cleaning up no mess, I can tell you."

She placed her hands on her hips and gave them a scornful look. "A fine sight you look, Haiden Bails and smelling like the very devil. We'll have to clean you up and tend to that wound. No telling how you kept it from festering, and me with the house to clean and all. Ain't no work for one woman, I keep telling them. No, sir, ain't no work for one woman, running this inn, keeping the books, raising the young 'uns all. And then, on top of everything else, you two scalawags come sneaking up and about scare me to death!"

"Now, Mati…" Haiden pleaded.

"Don't you 'now, Mati' me, Haiden Bails. You're the worst of the lot, dragging this poor young one through—who knows what." She wiped her hands on her apron, then turned. "I've got other guests to attend. You two get yourselves cleaned up and then we'll talk. It'll take me a month to get the stench out." She turned her head and wagged a finger. "And, Haiden, I don't want you leaving no water and soap on my floor. This room had better be as clean as you found it, or I'll tan you good. I'll be back presently to dress that wound, but I want you smelling like decent folks when I return."

"Yes, ma'am," Haiden said sincerely. "And may I say you get more beautiful every time I see you."

Mati turned scarlet to the ears. "Oh, go on now," she said with a smile, "I haven't time for such frippery." She quickly waddled out of the room laughing.

Haiden chuckled to himself and went back to his food.

"I don't think she likes us," Joshan said quietly.

"Eh?" Haiden replied through a mouth of food. "Mati?" He wiped his mouth and smiled. "That's just her way. A kinder woman you'll never find. She'd give you everything she had, if there was a need." Then he chortled loudly. "Course, she'd burn your ears all the way through the giving."

"Are you sure we can trust these people, Haiden? We've almost been caught more times than I'd care to count."

"Not to worry, lad. In a way, these are my kin—well, as close to kin as an old bachelor like me is ever likely to have. It was them that took me in when I came to this province. I lived here at the inn 'til I went to the gates." He paused to swallow. "Believe me when I tell you, lad, these folks may be simple and rough around the edges, but they're the best kind, to my way of thinking."

"I'm sorry, Haiden. I'm sure you're right."

Joshan thought back on the last two days and dived into his food hungrily, feeling almost at ease for the first time in days. He thought through all that had happened and felt, by rights, he should have been dead. He owed much to Haiden, Trenara—and even to that strange ghost with the one eye, Vanderlinden. Yet, what had he returned for their courage and aid? Only pain, grief and possibly death. His mind wandered to Trenara.

When they were clean and dressed, they felt better than they had in many days. "Much better, I must say," Mati said, coming in and looking them both up and down. She was carrying a large tray of bandages and medicines for Haiden's leg. After a thorough examination, she scowled at him. "Well, it'll mend, but we'll see what we can do." With an indifferent gesture, she motioned Haiden to sit and began to clean the wound.

"Ouch," he cried when she squeezed the filth and infection from the cut, causing it to ooze down his leg.

"Oh, pipe down, you big baby, 'fore I use the brush."

Haiden's mouth turned down and he scowled at her, but he made no more outbursts, though he did wince now and again.

While she was tending the wound, he turned to the young prince. "What now, lad?" Joshan was staring at the fire, thinking. He sighed deeply.

"I wish I knew, Haiden. Should I go back to the Keep, leave the province, or just turn seaman and sail away from the whole mess?"

This made Mati sit up, and Haiden let out a yell. "Begging your pardon, sir," she said, ignoring the outburst, "but I near forgot. Sailing put my mind to it. There was a man here earlier, asking for you. An evil looking fellow, all black, with an eye patch. Said he was a friend, but I set the dogs on him just the same, thinking he was up to no good. Told him I'd never seen you. He sounded like one of them sailors, though what the likes of him would want with you there's no telling. I'd say more pirate than respectable sea."

"Vanderlinden?"

"Yes, sir, that was his name—leastwise what he said. Said he'd be back in an hour and that I was to tell you—even if you weren't here." She furrowed her brow. "You know this man?"

"Yes, Mati, and you are to let him in when he arrives."

"As you say, sir," she said doubtfully, going back to Haiden's leg. "It's your own business, and if I've done some harm, I'll be apologizing, but I wouldn't trust the likes of him." Mati finished tying the cloth around Haiden's leg much to his relief.

"I had less pain when I got the wound."

"Oh, quit your whining and get up so I can see if that dressing's going to hold." Haiden rose stiffly and moved his leg until Mati was satisfied. "It'll mend." Mati gathered her medicines onto the tray. "Now, don't get any dirt in it, Haiden Bails, or I'll take a scrub to it," she said, pushing the tray against her hip and brushing a lock of white hair from her eyes.

"Yes, Mati."

"Now, I got other things to attend. Here, give me those clothes, so I can burn them. No use smelling up the place." Joshan tossed her the bundle and she lumbered out the door.

They sat by the fire, each lost in their own thoughts as the mid afternoon sun came streaming through the window making everything smell fresh. The room was plain, but immaculate, and put Joshan in mind of happier times—in his nurse's room back in the Keep, playing with his mother in the gardens, or riding his eecha with Trenara in the woods. He must have dozed, for the next thing he knew Haiden was shaking him from a dreamless sleep.

"The captain's here, lad."

Joshan got up and saw the ominous figure standing in the doorway. He had a guarded look in his eye and his face was hard and tight. "Captain…"

"Before you say anything, I think you better hear this." He moved to the window and pushed open the shutters. Joshan and Haiden looked at each other and then joined him at the window. They could hear a crier's bell ringing down the street and looked out to see a man on an old, swayback eecha, holding a sheet of parchment.

"Hail," the crier's voice rang through the streets. "Hear this royal decree. Hail." He lifted the parchment to read.

"By issue of his Majesty, Lord Jenhada, Emperor of the Eight Provinces and Keeper of Mathisma, as executed by the Council of Justice, it is hereby ordered, adjudged, and decreed:

"For acts against the kingdom, for the murder of the First Prince, and disturbance of the peace and prosperity of the land; the traitor, Trenara of Mathisma, is found guilty of high treason.

"It is further ordered that the traitor shall lose all title and claim to her rank as starguider and further;

"Any man, woman or child who speaks her name shall hang from the neck until dead.

"For crimes against the realm, the traitor shall be punished thus: to be stripped of all belongings and bound before the sight of her people, she shall be taken to the High Cliffs at dusk and there hanged from the stake until dead. There shall she stay until time can wash clean her transgressions against the land." He lowered the parchment. "It is so ordered."

The death knoll hung in the air as the sky darkened.

CHAPTER EIGHT
SIRDAR'S CURSE

The sound of eecha hooves echoed morosely down the street as the golden day darkened when low clouds sailed across the face of the sun and a dismal rain began to fall. Van closed the shutters and leaned against the polished wood, striking tinder to his pipe. He eyed a stunned Joshan, who looked at the window with dull confusion, while Haiden sank to a stool and shook his head mutely.

"She's alive," Joshan whispered, half joy, half dread.

"Aye," Van replied, taking the stem from his mouth and wiping it on his shirt. "She's alive, right enough, but it'd be better if she was dead." There was a strange sadness in his eyes that struck Joshan.

"Why, captain? What is this stake?"

Vanderlinden went to the hearth, stirred the embers thoughtfully, and threw in a piece of wood to stay the sudden chill. "The stake's not been used in the provinces for near an age," he said, brushing his hands and looking at the gathering flame, "but there're places I've been where they use it. It's a kind of torture and execution. They take a long piece of wood, ten spans high and as wide as a man. They strip the prisoner naked, bind her hands and neck to the top, and her feet and legs at the bottom, stretching the body as tight as it'll go. They haul the lot straight up, and down it goes into a deep hole with a massive jolt. They just leave you there hanging, until you die."

He stared at the cracking fire and shivered. "It's a grisly sight, lad. When the stake hits the ground, your bones come clean out of their sockets, snap. If you're lucky, your neck will break and you'll die right away. If not, it could be more than a week hanging there, in agony the whole time. There's no worse death, they say." He stirred the fire again and grew silent.

"He can't," Haiden whispered.

"Aye, mate, he can." Van rose. "It's just like that rotten sod to do it, too."

"Then you know who's behind this?" asked Joshan.

"Aye," he said. "It's that accursed Pravius and his band of sneaks."

Joshan furrowed his brow. "You know him?"

"Know him?" Van pointed to the dirty patch over his eye. "He left me a little souvenir last time I saw him."

The bitter tone sent chills through Joshan, and he didn't question the giant further when Van stepped to the window and gazed out sullenly. "If he hurts her, I swear to the gods, I'll…" The captain's voice was so low, Joshan barely caught it.

"As much as I love the guider," said Haiden, "we got to get Joshan out of the Keep, before we do anything else."

Joshan flashed him a look. "Now, wait a minute. I won't go cringing off while my family and Trenara are in danger. I'm going back to the Keep."

"Aye, lad," Vanderlinden replied heavily. "That's just what that devil wants—wants it bad enough to set just this kind of stinking trap."

"For once, I agree with you," said Haiden. "Lad, you can't go back there. You'd be caught sure and who knows what's in that oily sod's mind—nothing good, I can tell you. You saw what he's done to your da. With your abilities, only the gods know what might happen. No good, I'll be bound."

"Haiden, I'm going back to the Keep. I ran out on Trenara once, I will not do it again."

"Begging your pardon, son, but you got no sense. You go back there now and he'll kill you for sure—or worse. Then where would we be? What about your father, now, not to mention her ladyship. You want to start a mass murder? 'Cause, sure as I'm sitting here, once that stinking Pravius has got you, there won't be no stopping him. Meaning no disrespect, but he'll bend you as sure as he bent your da! You said yourself the *power* wasn't under your control—what happens if it gets under his?"

"I don't care. That is exactly why I have to go back—to fight him—to put everything right. I can't just walk away from…"

"Pipe down!" Vanderlinden's voice boomed with such intensity, the bottles rattled. "I'm thinking," he added more quietly, effectively ending the debate.

Haiden sat sullenly and Joshan walked to the table fuming, as Van went back to the hearth, tapped his pipe on the mantel, and looked at Joshan a long time.

"Come over here and sit yourself down," Van said. "You, too, mate. I've got a lot of telling to do."

"But, Trenara is…"

"Laddy, she's got to go through Last Defense in the morning, and there ain't nothing can be done before nightfall. Sit."

Caught by the sudden gravity in his voice, Joshan and Haiden settled on wooden chairs before the giant and became silent. The room darkened, and a steady rain began to beat a dull rhythm against the slated roof as the giant slid to the hearth and folded massive arms over his chest. The firelight caught strange crags in his face when he turned to stare at the closed shutters, and a sudden clap of thunder sparked the prelude to his tale.

"Two seasons back," Van mused so softly his voice seemed to mingle with the rain. "Aye, more than two seasons, now." His mouth took on an odd curl from beneath the tangle of beard as he began.

*****

During high season, the emperor would send out the fleet to sweep the coast and patrol the lands between Badain and the Keep. This particular season had been no different from most at the onset. These patrols had started after the fall of Sirdar when his creatures still roamed the outlining areas, and criminals hid in the remote forests and mountains. In the early seasons this had been a hard, thankless job, taking Vanderlinden and his crew away from Thrain for months at a time as they tracked down the remnants, flushed them out of hiding and either destroyed or imprisoned them. After many seasons, because of the giant's vigilance, the provinces became safe once again.

Since then, these patrols were usually smooth and uneventful. The giant looked forward to them. It gave him a chance to train new sailors as well as sharpen the skills of the old ones. But the vigilance lessened as seasons passed. Fewer sailors came to the enlistment offices each season. Where Van once had a fleet of thirty of the best ships, he now captained only five, the rest gathering dust and rot in the moorings of Keep Harbor, or re-rigged to furnish smaller merchant crafts. He hadn't begrudged the merchants their vessels, but the decline of the imperial fleet unnerved him. At the time, he passed it off as vanity. After almost thirty seasons of war, peace brooded heavy on the weathered veteran.

Before leaving on this trip, the Council of Trade had passed a bill to consider salvaging the rest of the old fleet for yet more merchant vessels. Van appeared before the council arguing that the ships should be refitted, not scrapped. But he was overruled and almost thrown from the proceedings when he threatened to place the entire council on an unprotected merchant ship and attack it with one of his much larger brigs. His popularity hadn't been bolstered that day, and accusations of treason were murmured from the whispering council as they shook in their chamber chairs.

If the emperor had not intervened, cooling both the giant and the council with his usual calm words, the captain may have found himself in the hold. In Jenhada's chambers that night, Van and the emperor sat on the balcony overlooking the sea. "You mustn't let them get to you, Van," said Jenhada. "They are a long way from a unanimous vote and until then, the ships won't be touched." He looked at the giant as he sipped his mead.

"Aye, Jen," Van replied, sitting on the edge of his seat, toying with his glass. "I know. It's just those damn thread peddlers haven't a clue what they're doing. If an attack was to come, we'd be defenseless. You think they'd see that? Hell, no. They're so busy counting their money, they're blind to everything else."

The emperor had smiled. "It's our money, Van, the Imperium's. Without it, we'd crumble almost as surely as if we were attacked. The restorations alone took millions. It was worth it to see Tola reconstructed and the provinces restored. Don't begrudge them their idiosyncrasies, Van. They've earned them. They've rebuilt this nation and made it better for all of us."

"Jen, the only thing those pocket pinchers have done is implement your policies. They wouldn't know how to wipe their own arses unless you were there to tell them. If it'd been up to the council, we'd still be arguing over which road to build or where to send the workers."

Jenhada laughed and shook his head. "Maybe, but you're forgetting—without the council I can't move to implement them."

Van shrugged good-naturedly and lifted his glass. "Well, here's to the council—may it ever be deadlocked." They both laughed and downed their drinks.

"You're leaving tomorrow, then?"

"Aye, with the sun. It'll be good to get back and break in those new recruits, though there are damn few this season. They look like a likely bunch—young, tough, cock-sure, but willing. I only hope I got a fleet to send them out on next season."

"You handle your sailors and I'll handle the council."

"Aye." He looked down at this drink. "It's just… a black feeling comes on me now and again. I can't explain it, so I won't try." He regarded the emperor seriously. "Jen… just don't let them get my ships."

Jenhada regarded the captain a long time and then placed a hand on his arm. "It's been almost thirty seasons. The threats are gone, the forces scattered or appeased. Not that I would have that weigh my decision about the ships; they'll stay for other reasons than that. But your fear is baseless, unless there's something you're not telling me."

Van shook his head. "Perhaps baseless, because if you're looking for something you could touch, it wouldn't be there—maybe just the ravings of an old soldier." He stood and looked down on the docks sadly. "Sometimes, when I'm on the pier looking at the fleet—the old fleet—I get a pit in my stomach that goes right to my heart, if you understand me. It makes me want to go to the council and beat some sense into them." Van smiled down at his drink and gave the emperor a sidelong look. "Did I tell you I bought the *Evenstar*?"

"You're joking. Why?"

Van smiled and shrugged, turning his eyes to the sea. "Not sure," he chuckled. "One night I got that feeling and up and bought her—lock, stock, and keel. I asked myself the same thing next morning."

"Were you drunk?"

"Nope, sober as a judge." He looked at his drink and smiled. "Ravings, huh."

Jenhada gave him a searching look and narrowed his eyes. "I wonder." The emperor shook his head. "A young man came to me from Badain some thirty seasons back—with strange feelings. He wondered then if they weren't just ravings. He was wrong, wasn't he?"

"Aye—that I was."

"While you're patrolling this season, keep your eyes open, Van. I've always relied on your instincts, and they've never failed me," said Jenhada, rising and grabbing an old hand-carved cane.

"You can count on that. You'll get reports," Van said as he set his empty glass on the sideboard.

"And you'll get your ships, if I have to sit on that council."

The giant smiled broadly and took the emperor's outstretched hand. "That's all I can ask." He tipped his hat and bowed. "Evening, sire."

"Captain," Jen replied as Van strode out the door.

The patrol went smoothly at first, without incident, and Van did keep his eyes open. It wasn't until he reached the far south that something odd happened. They anchored *The Evenstar* outside the Bay of Cortaim, the capital city of Badain, about half way down the southern coast. The lookout shouted down to Van that they were flying the yellow flag. When Van looked through the glass, he saw the quarantine symbol and cursed. He hadn't seen that flag since the great plague thirty seasons before, and it sent chills up his spine.

"Mister Bano," he said to his first mate.

"Aye, sir?"

"Get me a longboat and two rowers."

"You're going ashore, sir?"

"Aye," the captain replied raising the glass.

"But, sir, the yellow flag…"

"Now," Van replied evenly, lowering the glass.

"Aye, sir." Bano saluted and ran to the boats with orders.

Van had seen too many such flags and the sight unsettled him. He swallowed the gall in his throat and scanned what he could see of the port town. Beyond the flags, he didn't see any outward signs of plague. The market was bustling with people, the roads alive with riders and wagons, but the docks themselves were virtually empty, the ships deserted and the yards unmanned. The other signs of plague with which he had become well acquainted, were absent. No burnings, no bodies carried through the streets, and none of the misery usually sketched in people's faces. He thought he was being overly sensitive. Quarantines were called for many diseases these days, with the advent of the health inspectors.

The first mate came to his elbow and told him the boat was ready. As he boarded, he gave final orders to Bano and had the sailors row within hailing distance of the pier.

A lone soldier in red and black livery paced the dock and turned to face them as they approached. "Come no further," he called, holding up a hand.

"Hold, mates," Van said quietly. The oars were lifted and the boat drifted to a stop some five spans from the pier.

"What's your station, soldier?" the giant asked.

"Private, First Class, Dock Patrol, sir," he answered crisply.

"What's the trouble here, son?"

"Quarantine, captain."

Van closed his eyes patiently and smiled. "I can see that, lad. What's the ailment?"

The private hesitated a moment. "Pocks, sir."

Van started. "Pocks?"

"Yes, sir."

"Boy, there hasn't been a case of pocks in the provinces for over fifty seasons."

The soldier seemed uncomfortable. "I know, sir, but that's what the healers tell us. It broke out two weeks ago."

"Why hasn't the emperor been informed of this?" Van had stopped at almost every port between the Keep and Badain and there wasn't even a whisper of pocks. Normally, runners were sent so travelers from the affected area could be isolated to keep the disease from spreading. This was an ancient law, and violation of it was considered treasonous, as whole provinces had formerly been decimated before its adaptation.

"Messages were sent, sir—at least, as far as I know."

An old soldier appeared from behind the private. He was dark, swarthy and thick boned, very unlike the native Badainians, who were generally fair. "Good morning, captain," he said, his northern accent heavy and unmasked.

Van nodded coolly. "Sergeant."

"What seems to be the trouble here?" he asked good-naturedly.

"No trouble. I was just asking your private here about the quarantine."

"Pocks. Damndest thing, too. Took the healers a month just to figure out what it was. From what I've heard, there hasn't been a case of pocks for fifty, sixty seasons."

"Aye. Have messengers been sent?"

"Yes, sir, two days ago."

"Has a guider been called?"

"Guider, sir?" the sergeant replied blankly. "There hasn't been but one guider here for seasons. That was Palarine. But he's been gone since the last full moon. Went back to the isle I heard. But the healers have things well in hand. There are fewer cases every day." His words seemed too well rehearsed to the giant's sensitive ears.

"All right, sergeant." He sat back in the boat, gesturing for the men to lower the oars. "We'll send our ship's healer ashore to lend a hand," he added, watching the man closely.

There was the slightest trace of hesitation in his response, but he covered it over with such subtle ease, Van was not sure he even caught it. "That really won't be necessary, captain. Our healers have it well under control. And they've been exposed. They're saying fifteen, maybe sixteen days, and the quarantine should be lifted—maybe sooner. No use exposing your healer if it's not necessary."

Van regarded the man for a long time. "Maybe you're right. Tell your Baron if he needs help, we'll get a message to the health inspectors for him. This is the last run of the coast until springtide, so if he's going to do it, it'll have to be now."

Van was aware that the new Baron, placed in office only months before, was young and inexperienced. The emperor had complained repeatedly about the Baron's lack of communication on important matters concerning Badain. When reminded about these breaches in protocol, the Baron always relayed his deepest apologies and pled ignorance. The old Baron had died rather suddenly, he said and left little, if any, references regarding the office in relation to the emperor. The emperor had requested the new Baron's audience in Thrain, so he could train him for the office and answer any questions. The Baron replied that the emperor could rest assured he would be there very soon.

"Also," Van added, "his majesty wishes to know when the Baron will be arriving in Thrain. He's anxious to meet him."

"If you'd care to wait, captain, I could take the message right now," he said kindly. "As luck would have it, I was just on my way to the castle for audience with the Baron."

"I'll just bet you were," Van said under this breath, instinctively disliking this man. He had a stockpile of loathing for northerners and the sergeant's satiny tongue did nothing to deplete it. "Very well, sergeant. If you don't think it'd take long."

"Not long at all, captain. I'll be back presently."

When the man left, Van lifted his eyes to stare again at the massive structures that filled the sky just beyond the docks. The Cortaim castle never ceased to amaze him, second only to the Keep itself.

There were three tiers of massive stones, cold and black, and five large towers with their pointed spires that seemed to impale the ice-blue sky. The sight sent shivers through Vanderlinden, as always. The first level, the castle wall, was tall and smooth with long, sharp spikes lining the top. The second tier had a tower on either end that soared to lofty heights without window or opening, while the third was a miniature of the second. On top of the third stood the great tower, now black and menacing, even in the light of the morning sun. It measured a hundred and fifty spans across the bottom and loomed almost as high as the peaks of rubble far behind it.

It was within this tower, the monster had ruled thirty seasons back. It was from there he and Balinar had been driven into the catacombs that wound endlessly through what used to be a mountain behind. It was nothing more than a pile of fused rock and glass now, but the castle itself remained standing, a sinister reminder of darker days.

Van noted with interest that construction was occurring, as men and wagons poured over the thick wooden draw bridge that arched above the deep black moat beneath it. Over the wall could be seen the tops of wooden cranes laboring with heavy stone blocks and massive timbers. It was odd to see laughing young women talking in front of the black gate and even children sailing toy ships along the sluggish moat, where once scores of hideous creatures had prepared for war and tortured souls begged for death. It was very disconcerting.

The sight of the castle had never been a cheerful one. The giant was strangely relieved he didn't have to go into the nightmare fortress, and he wished the sergeant would return quickly, so he could escape the memories it brought.

"Have you known the Baron long, captain?" the sergeant asked when he returned, panting to catch his breath.

Van glared at him. "I've never met the man."

"He seemed to know you," he said. He lifted a piece of parchment and read. "Tell the good captain the Baron is honored by his visit to Cortaim. He wishes he could see you again after so many seasons, but his duties prevent it at this time. He apologizes. He thanks you for your kind offer of the health inspectors, but feels the healers are doing a good job and have the disease under control. He will certainly summon help if needed. He also extends his best wishes to your emperor."

"*My* emperor?"

"Oh, I do apologize—my mistake. *The* emperor, of course…" He cleared his throat and went back to the paper. "The Baron extends his best wishes to *the* emperor and expects to make an extended visit at the end of the season. Then he says he may see you before then, but he'll send a messenger." The sergeant finished and folded the paper neatly.

"Why the devil would he want to see me?"

"As for that, captain, I wouldn't know," he replied smoothly. "I'm not in the Baron's every confidence. Perhaps regarding the patrol or passage to Thrain. He did say he would send a messenger, sir."

"Aye," Van replied flatly. "Extend my thanks to the Baron. Good day, sergeant."

"Captain," he replied with a bow.

Van ordered the men back to the ship with a nod. Something in the exchange with the sergeant made the giant uneasy, but he couldn't put his finger on it. The sergeant's words and those of the Baron sounded fair—but felt foul, somehow. He rubbed his eyes and smiled, shaking his head.

I've been around Trenara too much lately, he thought. *I'll be damned if I'm not developing guider's* sense. Van was appalled at the idea. He was no guider and the idea of being buried alive under mountains of books for the rest of his days turned his stomach. He slapped the back of an oarsman and laughed.

"Come on, lads, let's go home. I want a cold tankard of whillen beer and a warm bed."

*****

Several days out of Cortaim, after a tedious session with the Regent of Quitain over fishing lanes and taxes, Van fell into his bunk exhausted and fuming. What had started out as a routine patrol was rapidly turning into an imperial nuisance with political intrigues and diplomatic overtones the giant was not trained for, or willing to bear.

Every port, practically from the day they left Cortaim, had some kind of squabble with the empire, ranging from confusions over taxes to the outright declaration that protection had been withdrawn. When traced down, almost every incident turned out to be a misunderstanding originating from some baseless rumor, the source of which could never be found. Reports on the first few were sent by land to Jenhada, as was customary. But Van sent carrier fowl, the fastest route possible, with this last one. He stated in his report that he was bypassing the rest of the stops and coming straight back to the Keep. He suggested the emperor send out an envoy immediately to investigate. Van had no way of knowing none of the reports ever reached the emperor's hands.

That night, he started out of a fitful sleep and sat up rubbing his eyes. The cabin was pitch-black; an icy chill filled the air. His breath came out in frosty patches as he grabbed his robe and wondered at the cold. When he wrapped the robe around his shoulders, it gave little warmth, the freezing air finding its way through the fibers. The giant groped for the door, but found it locked tight. "What the devil?" he cursed and pulled again.

While he examined it, a faint light appeared from behind him. He whirled around to see the wall suddenly glowing with white radiance. Sidestepping to his bunk, he pulled his sword out of its shaft with a hiss and bent his knees in ready stance before the wall. Van was no stranger to magic.

Tiny flashes of static permeated the room, which crackled in his ears and made his hair stand on end. A black speck, growing rapidly, appeared in the center of the wall. The giant shaded his eyes against the glare, making out the shadow of a robed man. The tiny charges converged in front of him as the form began to take on dimension. With a last flash of brilliance, the figure stood tall and black against the glow.

Van sucked in his breath and took a step back, bringing his sword level with his eyes. The figure lifted the cowled head and gazed at the giant silently, his eyes barely visible as gleaming lights beneath the hood.

The captain lifted his sword above his head to strike, but there was an earsplitting crackle as a blue charge wrapped itself around the weapon and wrenched it from his hand. He let out a cry as he was thrown against the door. A sickeningly sweet aroma saturated the air and made the giant's eyes water. The concentration of *power* in such a small space was overwhelming. He slowly rose rubbing his hand where it had been scorched. The giant's knees felt weak and rubbery as he glared at the figure.

"Who are you? What do you want?"

"Forgive me, giant. I did not mean to harm you." The voice was muffled by the hood, but seemed old, smooth, and pitched to sound kindly. Van felt strangely ashamed of his anger. "I didn't want you to strike me down in haste, before you had heard me," the figure said and then reached up and pulled back his hood. The static immediately faded, leaving a bent, old man leaning laboriously on a tall, gnarled staff. His spotted hands caressed the well-worn wood as he studied the giant amiably.

"If you don't mind, I'd like to sit down. I'm getting too old for journeys of this sort. It has quite taxed me." Without waiting for a reply, he tottered over to a chair, lowered himself, and smiled. "And if I could trouble you for a glass of water, I'd be most obliged, young man."

"Certainly, father," Van found himself saying as he obediently went to the sideboard to pour a tankard of water. After he handed it to the man, he sank into the chair opposite him.

"I do apologize for the dramatic entrance." He smiled as his ancient hands tapped on his glass. "I don't normally drop in on people unannounced."

"Who are you?"

"A messenger, my boy, with grave tidings, I'm afraid."

"From whom?" Again, the hairs on the back of the giant's neck began to rise.

"From a benevolent master who cares deeply for humans and wishes them nothing but goodwill and prosperity. He hopes to aid them in their troubles." His words flowed like honey, but the giant could not fight the lump of fear rising in his chest. He had heard words like this before.

"Unless I miss my guess, old man, you're Assemblage."

The man inclined his head in acknowledgement. "For almost fifty seasons now."

Van swallowed hard. "Who's your master?"

The man's smile was beneficent. "The master has many names, giant, and not all of them known. But you perhaps know him as the king of the south: Sirdar the Wise."

"The Usurper?" Van hissed, standing away from the table.

The old man stared at him kindly. "His enemies once called him that, yes."

"He's dead!"

"Oh, no, my good captain, he's very much alive."

The guider's face began to change, the benign lines hardening as he locked eyes with the giant. Van felt himself slipping, felt his will begin to fade, his mind begin to numb. He tried to fight, but the more he struggled, the deeper he fell into those milky green eyes until the room began to spin.

"Relax." The old man's voice was firm now, strong, persuasive. Van sat mechanically, his arms hanging limply at his sides, the fear, the loathing, draining away until there was nothing left but obedience. "You need to listen carefully, giant," the old man said with a clean edge to his voice that echoed through the chamber. Van knew his head was nodding, but felt detached from it.

"I deliver a message and an honor for you. The master is gracious and more powerful than you could know. He bestows his graces rarely. Assemblage sent their most powerful starguiders, but they could not stop him and were themselves destroyed. He has been weakened, yes, but now finds new strength. He *will* take what is rightfully his." He stopped for a moment and smiled serenely.

"The master is a hero, Vanderlinden, not an enemy. He is maligned by so many," he whispered, his eyes tearing. "If you only knew what he has fought for—what he has done in his past—what sacrifices he has made, you would not judge him so severely. He is not evil. This is what Assemblage would have you believe. He only wants to bring peace to this land, growth. The master wants knowledge and riches for mankind, not to make them slaves to starguiders with their small *power*. The master knows *all* humans have power within them, if it were only acknowledged and released. But the guiders, this Assemblage, would not see their control undermined. They seek the weak-minded, the easily controlled, to train. They hoard the *power* and keep it from mankind. Sirdar has the ability to give this gift to *everyone*. Don't be blinded as I was. Assemblage has swayed the common man with their lies to weaken him, because they fear what he can do, they know he has found the way—and they nearly succeeded.

"He is a forgiving lord, captain, and doesn't blame the misguided people who fought against him. He wants only an alliance and their help in destroying the true evil in this world—Assemblage. That is why we need your strength, to take back what is rightfully yours, the rule of the empire. This is your destiny, Vanderlinden. By helping the master in his war against this evil, your reward will be handsome. You will rule as you are destined; *you* have the will, the wisdom, the experience to help your kind take back its freedom."

Such was the authority of his voice, flowing sweetly in the giant's ears, that Van began to see visions of grand armies, strong and invincible at his command, the glory of war ringing in his ears with the voice of thousands of free people speaking as one. Fleets of ships, majestic and shining, with masts of gold and silver, their numbers so great they faded into the horizon. People praised and bowed before his kindness and just rule; Vanderlinden, King of the Imperium. His rein would be benevolent and bring mankind into a new age of enlightenment. The world would lie at his feet.

"You see it now, don't you, the glory that could be yours, the gifts from the master. All this will be yours, if you join him now."

In the stillness that followed, Van saw in his mind a powerful master: kind, generous, and long-suffering at the hands of ignorance; a kind benefactor who forgave those who would destroy him, bestowing honors even on his enemies. The spell wound so tightly around Van's mind, that without knowing how, he found himself on one knee before the stranger, his hands folded, anxious to promise his life to the master.

Van was not a religious man; in fact, he thought the gods and all their accompanying foolery were ridiculous. He and Trenara had debated the issue countless times. But now, here in the dark of his cabin, on his knees before this strange messenger, a soft caress seemed to touch his soul. It was as if someone had reached into his heart, had shielded his mind, taken his will, and bolstered it with compassion. He couldn't put a name to the feeling, but it was as close as he had ever come to believing in the gods. Van pulled in a startled breath as it seized him and forced open his mind, forcing harsh memories to open before him like a bloody gash.

Many seasons before Van had been attacked and almost killed by a flying tarsian lizard. He still carried those scars. Now, the healed wounds, painless though they had been for countless seasons, began to throb and ache, as if the lizard's talons were freshly buried in his shoulders, as if the messenger's words rekindled the agony of that night. Old recollections formed out of the pain. Van saw the lovely face of a slip of a girl he had saved from that same lizard, the siege of the Keep, and the annihilation of his troops at Placent Crossings.

He remembered clearly the firing of the great woods of Tola and the score upon score of valiant soldiers who fought and died because of the treachery of Sirdar. Their dying screams echoed through him as the new visions pushed the glory from his mind, filling it with old sorrows he had succeeded in burying so long ago. With each old memory, the spell, which was woven so expertly through his mind, slipped away, bit by bit, until his vision cleared into stark reality. He suddenly saw Sirdar for what he was—a menace, a liar, a black disaster.

Van was free from the spell. He thought for a split second and realized he could not pass up this opportunity. His face did not betray him. "What does the master wish done, my lord?" he asked, his face still alight with servitude.

There was a glint of self-assurance in the old man's eyes as he looked at the giant. "Good," he said smoothly. "The master will be very pleased.

"First, you must return to the Keep and go before Jenhada. You are his closest counselor and he will listen to you. Convince him of his peril, for even now the guiders conspire to take his throne from him. He needs to turn against them. There will be men sent to help you from the south and the north. They will lay out plans for you, Lord Vanderlinden. Keep your counsel secret, for there are many Assemblage spies. They will do anything to protect their plots. They think the vigilance of the empire asleep, and the master dead. You must watch especially Trenara of Mathisma, for she is deep in the schemes of Assemblage, their greatest weapon. Do not trust her!" The man's voice betrayed his fear and hatred of the guider as he spat her name with venom.

At the mention of Trenara, Van stood and stared down at the old man as he tightened his fists. "Take this message back to your master. I will never bow before him or his deluded slaves. Nor will I betray those I love for glory. Say this to him: I remember the past, the memory of that pain is clear in my mind, and still aches in my heart. I remember all the good people he destroyed, the purity he corrupted, the love he stole from me! Fair words and pretty lies can never bury that. Tell him there is power yet in these hands, and they will work all the days left in them to destroy what he has made."

Such was the strength of his conviction, the old man seemed to cringe and bend before him. "Fool," he hissed like a cornered animal, pushing himself away from the table and throwing the cowl over his head. The old man changed before the giant, shifting and shimmering, like hot haze on the distance. He became darker by degrees, with gleaming eyes and a hideous melting face, aglow with red fire. The blackness became larger and larger, until it filled the room. Van knew the shadow of Sirdar stood before him, and the giant's anger melted into terror. He quaked in the master's shade, but could not move.

"On your knees before me, mortal!" The words echoed through the giant as if he were nothing more than wind. Darts of terrible red fire engulfed him, and an unrelenting pressure forced Van to his knees. He screamed in pain trying to resist it, but it was useless. Van's head began to whirl, making him nauseous as he threw his palms over his ears to stop the misery the voice inflicted.

"Hear me, Vanderlinden, for your deeds against me, your theft of something I once loved, and now these words have earned you this curse. Those things you have built with your own hands will perish, and you will live that others may die before you. Nothing you can do will stop it. Your life will become base and degraded, until others call you thief and blackheart. You will betray that which you love most, delivering it into the hands of your enemies. Your hands, you say, have power still to defy *me*? Those hands will earn you nothing but anguish. In the end, they will take your own lifeblood."

There was a hideous, blinding red flash and then suddenly the figure was gone. Van vomited violently and blacked out.

CHAPTER NINE
THE FIRST ALLIANCE

The rain continued to pour and the sun slipped behind the hills to wink for a brief moment from under the canopy of clouds before it disappeared for the night. The fire had burned down until there was nothing left but fragile coals and gray ash in the hearth. Van's head was bowed as Joshan and Haiden stared at him in silent horror, numbed by the story and the news—the news of a monster that would not die.

Tears sparkled in Joshan's eyes as he regarded the giant in pity. Vanderlinden lifted his head and looked at them quietly, his face very old and very tired. "There's more," he said softly. "This was just the beginning.

"When I woke, I was in my berth, soaked to the skin. The room was light with a gray dawn. The experience tasted vile in my mouth, like a bad dream—and that's rightly what I thought it was. When I rinsed my face and head in the basin and looked in the glass, I knew it was no dream. Behind me, lodged in the wall just above my chest, was my blade where it had landed after being ripped from my hand. When I went over to pull it out, the alarm bells started clattering.

"When I got to the bridge, the crew was aft, staring at the biggest, blackest storm front I've ever seen in all my days at sea. It was clipping toward us at sixty, maybe seventy knots, straight from the south, like a giant black hand. I ordered the crew to turn her hard aport and to unfurl the sails. I figured the winds would hit us and that we might be able to skirt her and make for land to the west." He looked up at them and his eyes were very dark. "But there was no wind," he whispered. "Just that damn bank of clouds sailing at us faster than some devil. There was no way we were going to outrun her, so I had the crew secure, when a shout came from the bow. Another bank was now heading straight at her from the west, meeting the first and pacing it. I ordered her hard starboard. No sooner than we get her due north again, another bank of clouds and then another, come from east and west. We were completely boxed in.

"The sea started churning, slow at first, but picking up speed. I had the crew secure and waited for the damn thing to hit. We battened down best we could, but I figured, from the size of the clouds and the pitch of the waves, best we could hope for was she'd hold together and ride it through. There wasn't anything else we could do.

"All of a sudden, just before the clouds reach us, they stop; waves, wind, clouds, everything. There was a damn bloody quiet, death looming over our heads and all around us. Then, the clouds started to move. Round and round they blew, pulling the sea with them, and my ship starts to spin. The crew got flung around like straw as the whirlpool picked up speed."

Van's voice cracked and his eyes began to glisten. "I watched her die," he continued slowly. "Pulled to bits, piece by piece and man by man, like she was made of paper, the sea rising above her, sucking her down to her death." He sank his head to his chest and wiped the tears from his face.

"I watched them, one by one, either smashed against the railings or sucked into the water to drown. My body was frozen to the deck where I stood, not able to move or lend a hand—not even to fling myself into the sea when the last man went down. A hundred and eighty sailors," he whispered. "I prayed to the gods 'til I had no voice left, but they didn't answer—so I cursed the bastard over and over before the nightmare was through. When it was done, darkness came.

"I don't remember much of the following days. Only nightmares of the screams of my crew and the thunder of the breaking timbers of my beautiful ship, the ship I had built with my own two hands and the crew I had trained and known for seasons. Many of those people had served me from the northern war and others were no more than lads or lasses, even younger than you.

"That voice…" The memory widened the giant's eyes until they were dark crystals glistening in the firelight. "The curse kept ringing in my ears. I thought I had gone mad, and screamed until I wanted to die—to ease my mind and escape that voice in my head.

"When I came to myself, I don't know how long after, I was on a raft and riding the swells, weak from want of food and water." Van bowed his head again and sighed.

"By luck or fate, I don't know which, in a couple of days I saw land. Thrain, just below the Keep, which was strange enough, but I was too relieved to care. I stumbled onto shore and saw the guards, thinking they were there to greet me." He chuckled dryly. "They greeted me right enough. I was slapped into irons and hauled to the hold before I knew what hit me. One thing's certain—whoever sent those bastards must have thought me dangerous. There must have been twenty, thirty guards to take in one weak and starving man. I was thrown into a cell and chained. It must have been days I spent in that stinking hole, not seeing the light of day and nothing more nourishing that a crust of bread. When they finally arrived, I was near death. The first light I saw came from the guard's torch when the emperor and Pravius came into my cell. I could hardly move and couldn't rise from the floor…"

*****

"So, this is where you've been keeping him?" asked Jenhada, stooping down to look at Van.

"For your own protection, my lord," replied Pravius. "We felt it best under the circumstances. He's dangerous."

Even though Jenhada had known Vanderlinden for almost forty seasons, he looked down at him as if he were a stranger. "He doesn't look dangerous, councilor," he said. "He's near death." Jen leaned down, turned the giant's face to him, and then shook his head. "The confession was given freely, you say, not tortured out of him?"

"As you can see, sire," the councilor answered, "the torturer's hand has not touched this man. The confession was freely given when he was arrested."

Somehow, by some miracle, Van found his voice but it was weak and barely a whisper. "I haven't confessed to anything. I haven't done anything."

"I thought you said he couldn't speak, councilor," the emperor said.

"Above senseless ravings—no, my lord. The physicians say he is quite mad, hears voices, and has fits. It was for this reason I cautioned you against coming here tonight."

"I had to see for myself. To desert a ship at sea leaving all hands to die is a grave charge, Pravius. Vanderlinden has served me well in the past and has earned at least this."

"But you read the confession, my lord."

The emperor looked back at the giant gravely. "How could you do this?"

But Van couldn't speak and looked every bit the madman, his eyes bulging and his mouth waging without sound. The effort sent his head spinning and he blacked out again.

Van remembered little of the days that followed. He was fed better and he started getting his strength back, bit by bit. By the time he saw Pravius again, the guards had left him chained him to the wall.

"You are fortunate, captain," the councilor said when they were alone, "the emperor has been lenient. He could have you executed for what you've done. Because of your earlier service, he banishes you instead. You are to be taken from Thrain to the Northern Waste, where you will remain in exile for the rest of your life, which hopefully, will be very short."

"You've done your job well—for your master," Van snarled at him.

"Better than expected. The emperor has grown weak and is quite open to my suggestions. He will be more susceptible with time. The master is very pleased, you know. I warned him you couldn't be bent, but he had to try. He doesn't realize how much stronger you are than Jenhada. In your folly of refusing him, you have brought upon yourself more anguish than you yet know. His curse will follow you to the end of your days. Sirdar is more powerful than anything you could possibly imagine."

Van strained at his chains and cursed him. "I'll kill you."

Then Pravius laughed. "You will try, giant, but even if you succeed, you are much too late. The Imperium is ours. It's only a matter of time." He reached into his robes and pulled out an ornament like nothing Van had ever seen. It was red and glowing sickly, the crystal tainted and ugly as it rested in an ebony cradle in his hand. Pravius brought it to the giant's face and smiled. "Of course, you won't have to worry about any of that. Goodbye, Vanderlinden. I'm certain the north will welcome back her wayward son. You should have died there before, and now perhaps you will." With that, he put the crystal over the giant's eye…

*****

"I have never felt a greater pain," Van continued in the gloom, "not even the torture of the tarsian's talons, than the agony that crystal shot through my body. By mercy, I blacked out.

"When I woke, I was tied up, face down in the back of a wagon heading to the Northern Wastes. The drivers were paying more attention to the bottle they were passing, than to me. Inch by inch, I wormed my way to the back of the wagon. I finally slid over the edge and landed in a ditch.

"How Wert found me, bound, bleeding, and half dead, I never knew. He said something made him leave his house that night. I thank the gods he did. He nursed me back to health until I was strong enough to be on my own again—strong enough to plan.

"Wert did something else for me, too. He introduced me to the worst sort of cutthroats and outcasts that exist. By clawing my way up, I became one of them and finally became their leader. Blackheart, he said, and blackheart I became—the leader of blackhearts and cutthroats.

"Because of this, I've been able to keep myself hid. I got Pravius worried. He knows I'm not dead; he knows I never got to the north. Even though he's been hunting me these two seasons now, I disappear like smoke thanks to my band of thieves. He's mysteriously lost many of his best men. But each blow we deliver is nothing more than an inconvenience."

Now Vanderlinden rose and pounded his fist into an open hand. "The time for inconveniences is over. We're ready to strike. I have an army—mostly pirates and bandits, but good people and loyal to Thrain and the emperor. I've told them my tale and they're willing to follow me to Pravius's downfall—and beyond, if I ask. My life in the bowels of this city hasn't been pretty, and there're things I've done for which I'm not proud, but I've been preparing for this for two seasons, and we're ready. Ten score men and women with arms, personally trained by me."

Van fell to his knees before Joshan, his eye blazing with conviction. "I give them all to you, sire," he said, putting a hand on the prince's arm. "Let's smash this bastard, once and for all."

Deeply stirred by the giant's words, Haiden leapt from his chair and knelt alongside the giant. "Lad, come what may, I'm with you, too. If the giant has these people, I say go with it. We may all get killed and others with us, but no one will say we didn't try."

Joshan looked at the two men. Van's words and his tales had added seasons to the youth. He knew what was required of him, as if it had been painted in blood on the brows of these two men. He sighed. "Two hundred warriors against ten times that many?" Joshan's voice was very tired. "A one-eyed sea captain, a lame gate-keeper, and a changeling prince with the body of a man but the skill of a boy to lead them?" Joshan lowered his head and ran a shaky hand through his hair. He closed his eyes, the room chilled and dark, the companions breathless for an answer.

"We'll go to the Keep," he said quietly. He then looked up at them, his face twisted with hate. "Sirdar will never rule, not while I have breath in my body."

His eyes blazed with a *power* that made both of the older men bow their heads in reverence.

CHAPTER TEN
THE BROKEN WAND

Trenara paced her cell, furious at being so helpless and allowing herself to be put in such a state. She knew the outcome very well, as Joshan's tenacious nature and impulsiveness always seemed to rule him. She only hoped Haiden was with him and would save the prince from idiocy. *Damn it,* she thought. *Surely, Joshan will realize giving into this snare can only make the situation worse.* Even as she thought it, she knew better.

She whirled around when she heard the jingle of keys in the cell lock. It couldn't be time yet; hours remained before dawn. Two Elite guards stepped in and parted, admitting Pravius. With a hand gesture, he dismissed them and placed a torch in its rack. Trenara stood looking at him with her hands in her sleeves, but refused to give him the satisfaction of knowing the depth of her concern. With her Assemblage training, she made her features as impassive as possible. Pravius stood gazing at her, but said nothing.

"Well," Trenara said at length, "if it's time, let's get on with it."

"You seem quick to greet death, magician."

"Death doesn't frighten me," said Trenara looking him squarely in the eye.

"Perhaps," he responded and sat on the bunk, "but it isn't time yet."

Trenara narrowed her eyes. "If you've come to torment me, you might as well save your breath. I really don't care."

"Torment you? No, I come only to bring you solace in your time of need."

"What do you want?"

"Only to relieve your conscience. It seems your young companion has decided to return to the castle, much to my relief. Despite what you may think, I do care what happens to the prince."

"Like hell you do," Trenara mumbled.

"I can see you don't trust me. But let me assure you, my information is quite reliable. Apparently, your young man is very resourceful. It seems he's enlisted the aid of an old friend of yours—Captain Vanderlinden."

"Van?" Trenara exclaimed, her façade fading. "But…"

"You thought he was dead." His face was such a mask of smug confidence, Trenara wanted nothing more than to beat it off him. But the news of the giant brought her new hope. Vanderlinden was the one man she would trust with her soul. If anyone could help Joshan, he could.

Pravius just smiled. "I shouldn't get my hopes too high, my dear. I controlled the giant once and I can do it again. Or do you think it chance that brought them together?" He laughed. "You would be more of a fool than I thought if you didn't think I would plan for every contingency."

"What have you done?" Trenara shrieked, trembling in rage.

"Calm yourself. I have only done what is necessary." He began to rise. "It's a pity you won't be around long enough to see our plan take fruition."

Trenara lunged at Pravius, but the back of his hand sent her sprawling into the stones, opening the wound and sending blood gushing from her nose and mouth. His strength was unexpected and Trenara stared up at him in shock. With an effort, she stood brushing herself off and glaring at the councilor. Using the sleeve of her robe, she stanched the flow of blood from her nose.

"If I'm to die—so be it. I have lived a long and full life. But this I swear to you: I will haunt you until you scream for redemption, as Ethos is my witness." Her voice was low and venomous.

The councilor chuckled. "Do you think your feeble curse warrants reply, Assemblage? It is not the first—and, I think, hardly the last. Many will curse me before it is over, but in the end, I will be the one standing." He turned to leave, but when he was at the door, he looked back.

"Oh, I almost forgot." He pulled a leather pouch out of his sleeve and tossed it on the cot. "A little memento of your visit." He slammed the door with an echoing snick of the lock.

It was sometime before Trenara could calm the tremors that shook her. When she finally crossed to the cot, she opened the pouch, suspicious of its contents. She sucked in a startled breath as she poured the contents onto her open palm. Shattered into five pieces and all the fire gone, was her precious *via,* Andelian.

Trenara threw the pieces against the wall in rage and buried her face in the cot. Soul wrenching sobs shook her, and tears flowed unabated, until at last they washed away the deep seated grief that suffused her soul, cleansing her spirit as only tears can, leaving her finally with a resolute calm and a grim determination.

She silently moved to the discarded bits, gingerly placed them back in the pouch, and tied it to her sash.

Trenara was not defeated—not yet.

CHAPTER ELEVEN
THE SCOUNDRELS

Night hung like a shroud in the street. A cold fog had rolled up from the sea that lay damp and quiet on the still air as the companions stood in the shadows, beating the chill from their arms. Van had brought them through a maze of back alleys, broken cobbled roads, and muddy lanes until they stood under towering buildings. This section of town was extremely old, and the smell of garbage drifted up from the roadside. Feral curs and rodents ran everywhere. The buildings, which once must have been majestic, now lay in ruins about them.

"What place it this?" Joshan's words were deadened by the misty air.

The giant grinned broadly and made a formal sweep with his arm. "This, m'lord, is my home. You've just entered the sacred place of all cut-throats, derelicts, and pirates. Welcome, sir, to the Village of Scoundrels." He placed a hand on his chest and bowed deeply. "I am its master."

Haiden curled his lip and gave the street a dubious look. "Nice place you got here."

"Ah, now," Van replied, lifting a finger. "What you see on the surface of a thing isn't always the best view. It may not be pretty, but it's saved my backside more than once. It's what's inside that counts."

Van peered around the corner and then gave a nod. "All right, gents, I've got to go alone for a bit, but I'll be back presently. Stay in the shadows and keep your voices down. There're a lot of bad sorts around." He stopped himself and laughed. "None quite as noble as me." He sprinted off, disappearing in the gloom.

Joshan and Haiden leaned against the stone wall and folded their arms against the cold. Joshan surveyed the lofty buildings and speculated on the ornate carvings, which were magnificent even in their decline. "This must have been a beautiful place once."

"Aye, I think this was the old Keep. I never been down this way, but the buildings are right enough. From what I've heard, it was grand in its day, back when they built it. These buildings were the first ones that went up and the first home of the emperors." He rubbed his hands together and hunkered down into the collar of his cloak. "But that was close to a millennium ago. Decent folk don't travel this way anymore. I guess the beggars and riff-raff are living here now." He wrinkled his nose at the stench. "Though how they do it, I couldn't guess."

Haiden stared quietly into the gloom for a long time. A shudder ran through him. "Lord," he said tentatively, "this tale of the giant's—what does it mean? Are we never going to be shed of this evil?"

Joshan didn't answer immediately, but stared at the patches of fog beginning to dissipate and the rutted cobblestone at his feet. "It means—things will change, Haiden." Joshan's eyes were fixed on the night. "It explains much, though the answers are not entirely clear or comforting. We are on the threshold of grim events, I'm afraid. Much will depend on what happens tomorrow. If we do not win against Pravius, then…" His voice trailed off and he said no more.

Haiden looked at him and let out a quivering breath. "Do you think…" his voice was almost a whisper. "Do you think this Pravius is really…" He couldn't bring himself to say the name, so nodded instead to the south.

Joshan glanced up at him. "No, I don't think Sirdar is in the Keep—a servant, perhaps, or, as Vanderlinden guessed, the same messenger that came to his ship. That doesn't make him any less deadly. I wish I knew more of such things, and I do so wish Trenara were here."

After a long silence, Van reappeared across the road and signaled them to cross, then led them down a long, gloomy back road. He stopped outside a very dimly lit doorway, with a deteriorating hanging sign that read simply *Paps*. Van opened a door—ornate by design, but beaten by age—and led them into a hallway containing a bench along one wall and rows and rows of pegs on the other. Several cloaks were already hung there, weather beaten and aged for the most part, or dirty and in great need of repair, and the companions hung theirs beside them. Van then led them down a long flight of grimy veined steps that wound endlessly through the massive stone structure. They passed several landings that contained arched and darkened entrances that lead to other parts of the building, or closed doors leading to silent rooms.

When they reached the bottom of the stairs, a large wooden door blocked their way. Van knocked on it softly. An eye appeared at a hole in the center, and a bolt grated against the iron hinges that held it. When the door opened, thick smoke and the smell of stale beer rose up around them to sting their eyes. Van strode in with familiarity, Joshan and Haiden in close pursuit.

The room was very large with chipped marble stairs that led to a dingy, littered floor. The ceiling was high and vaulted with richly carved wooden beams. The walls bore long mosaic murals, obviously designed by gifted craftsmen, but they were now stained and cracked, many of the original figures missing. Along the back wall was an immense fireplace, apparently engineered by a skilled mason, for even after hundreds of seasons and ten thousand fires, the intricate brickwork still remained whole and solid. Along the left wall were rows of thick wooden benches and heavy tables, both scarred by seasons of use and pocked with chips and gouges. Along the right was a narrow wooden bar with stools lining one side and stacks of casks behind it. The room was dimly lit by smoking lamps and a huge crackling fire lay on the ancient grate, making the room hot and close.

Around the fire was a group of men and women, who were the most sinister figures Joshan had ever seen. A few glanced up to scowl at them, but went back to their conversations without looking again. The giant motioned the companions to a table near the fire, while he went off to talk to a man and a woman at the bar.

Haiden looked around with doubt in his eyes. "This is the seediest bunch of people," he whispered. "They look as if they'd just as soon cut your throat as look at you." Joshan didn't reply, but looked around at the men and women. Many of them were beggars; some maimed, crippled, or missing limbs. Others were menacing and dangerous looking, usually scarred, many missing teeth, and all of them dirty. Three or four were better dressed, but held long notched blades at their sides, and the women were hard and seamed by the weather with seasons of arduous experience shining from their keen eyes.

There were also one or two serving wenches with matted hair and soot covered faces that were neither young nor lovely anymore. The man behind the bar was a round, jolly fellow with a bright eye and a kind face, though the black bludgeon strapped to the side of his greasy apron showed he, too, could mean business.

The two people speaking with Vanderlinden were as menacing as the captain, though of less stature. The man had long stringy black hair and wore a short sword on one side, a dagger on the other, and an axe strapped to his back. The woman was tall, well-muscled, and relatively neat, but had a long scar that ran down the length of her chin and thick bushy eyebrows that rose and fell as she spoke.

Van nodded to them, and they left to join other groups at opposite ends of the pub. He exchanged a brief whisper with the pub keeper and then joined another group at the fire. The barman drew a flagon of ale, grabbed three cups, and came around the room to join the companions at their table.

"Evening, gents." He flourished a wide, good-natured grin and set the mugs on the table. "Van asked me to come and sit with you a spell. I'm Pap." He wiped his hands on the apron, gave one to Joshan, then to Haiden, and sat down. "Not my real name, of course, but it kind of came with the pub and I figured it'd be easier than changing the sign." He laughed loudly and then poured.

"There'll be a council soon, and he wanted me to answer your questions should there be any, and to fill your glasses, if not." He winked at them and then nodded to a man near the door. The man, who had been leaning back in a chair, got up and threw the bolt over the door.

Other people began to appear from some hidden recess at the back of the pub and the room began to get very crowded. A bench was pulled from the wall and Van mounted it. "Get your arses over here and listen up. We got a lot of talking to do and not a lot of time. You all know why we're here, and I'm not going to repeat it. But what you don't know is we can't wait another five days to strike. We strike at dawn tomorrow."

A loud cheer went up from the crowd as tankards were lifted. But he looked at them grimly and the noise soon died down.

"This isn't a strike fast and get out proposition anymore." He stopped and searched several faces. "This is war." Murmurs ran through the group. "Some of you know what that means. Those of you who don't, soon will. I'm not going to paint a pretty picture for you. Chances of winning this are maybe a hundred to one. But if we don't win now, I think we'll have ourselves a new master—from the south."

This sent frightened, angry noises through the crowd and several people made the sign against evil. "You all know what that means. You got six hours to get ready. Get with your lieutenants and go over the plan one more time. Kiss your children goodbye and weapon up. We'll give that bastard a fight he'll never forget." Again, they cheered and raised their tankards, but as the noise subsided, there was a sudden clamor at the front of the pub.

The man who had been sitting by the door was now standing before a very large group of people, trying unsuccessfully to stop them. The leader just pushed him aside and brought his group in slowly, watchful. Many hands went to the hilts of their swords, but none were drawn. As they moved into the room, the crowd parted to let them through. Their leader detached himself from the others, and he stood looking up at the giant.

He was a dark, handsome man who wore a self-assured arrogance on his face and had an intense, penetrating stare. He was dressed in a long black weather-stained cape, high muddy boots that reached his thighs, and a bright red gem on his left ear.

"Who is that?" Joshan whispered to Pap.

"That be Sark, sire. A meaner character you wouldn't find."

"Dangerous?" asked Haiden.

"Aye, very dangerous—to his enemies, but a dedicated and brave man to his friends. I don't think he's a threat to you now, sire. He's faithful to the emperor in his own way. You see, it was him that was master of the village two seasons back. Van bested him for title of it, but he took those that would follow and went to the eastern side. He's master there now. Rivals they are, but not enemies." He eyed the two with an amused glint in his eye. "This ought to be very interesting."

"Vanderlinden." Sark rested his foot on a bench and leaned toward the giant with an arrogant smile. "Good evening to you, sir." His voice was so smooth and cultured, it made the giant's seem harsh and common in comparison. Sark had a heavy western accent, but his mastery of the language was excellent.

"Sark," Van replied dryly, stepping down from the bench. "What do you want here?"

"I heard, good captain, you and your lieutenants were planning a little—revelry at dawn. Not being one to hold a grudge, I thought perhaps we could come with you."

Van snorted and folded his arms. "Since when does the likes of you come offering me aid? You've never been what I'd call a joiner."

Sark's face turned very hard. "Since that bastard attacked the east village and took some of our women and children hostage."

A murmur went through the crowd and many people pressed closer. Van motioned to his lieutenants, who were at his side instantly. All pretense of mirth disappeared.

"When?"

"About six hours back. We chased them down, but we were exceedingly outnumbered. I lost some good people."

Van put a hand on his arm. "I'm sorry, Sark, I didn't know. You'd be welcome to join us—in fact, more than welcome. You were a good lieutenant once."

Sark raised an incredulous brow and smiled. "I was a good master once—captain."

"Aye, that you were." Van grabbed the arm of one of his own lieutenants. "How many soldiers do you have and where are they?"

"Sixty, maybe, but some are wounded. They're at Diamonds, except these here."

"That's good news. We'll need them." He turned to his man. "Boric, take two others and round them up. You'll split them between you and Shawn. Bring them back here. Use the underground."

Sark turned to a tall rugged woman at his back. "Tige, go with him. Tell Donnally to meet me here when the fighters are mustered. And, Tige, you watch your temper. We're joining forces—for the time being." He glanced at Van. "I want no fighting amongst the rank. Understood?"

"Same goes for you, Boric," Van added. Tige and Boric eyed each other doubtfully, but nodded and left together by the back entrance.

"The rest of you get to it. There ain't much time," Van called. They broke up into their respective groups and disappeared into the shadows with their leaders.

A man came up to Van and handed him a rolled parchment before going to his group, and the giant led Sark to the companions' table. "Pap," Van said, "you better get those stores divvied up and get drinks passed around." Pap got up, but Van took his arm before he could leave. "Tea and coffee, nothing stronger."

Pap winked and gave him a cheerful smirk. "Aye, captain. Evening, gents." He bowed and then lumbered off to the pantries.

"Sark," Van said, turning to his companions. "This is Haiden Bails, Sergeant of the Gates." Sark smiled amiably and shook Haiden's hand. "And this," Van added proudly, "is Joshan Jenhada Thoringale, First Prince and heir to the throne."

Joshan stood and held out his hand, but Sark gave him a wary look before taking it. Joshan caught the doubt in his eyes, but said nothing as he sat. Van unrolled the parchment until it hung over the edges of the table. It was an immense map of the Keep. Joshan ran his fingers over it softly, and whistled. "Where did you get this?"

Van just looked up and winked. "Let's just say I borrowed it." He folded it in two and pointed to one corner.

"This is the sewer that runs under the city and through the castle," he said to Sark. "Unit one will be headed by Haiden here, who will enter through the west hall. Now, problem is, that area's bound to be full of guards. But it's the only way to get a group in all at once. The other one," he slid a thick finger down the map, "is a series of tunnels. The prince says you have to go in single file. One advantage is we can get people into many areas, but only one at a time, so that west hall is going to be important."

Sark nodded, looking at the map intently. "So, you are going to need a diversion to pull those guards out of that area, is that it?"

"On the mark. It's got to be something that would take all of them out without alerting the whole bloody castle—something big. That's been the only weak part of the plan. I didn't have enough fighters to cover all three areas. Bar knocking at the front door, those are the only ways in. Any suggestions?"

Sark stared at the map and ran a long finger down his chin. A slow grin covered his face. "You'll get your diversion, captain."

"What do you have in mind?"

"Trade secret, my dear master."

"You devil! All right, have it your own way. You've never let me down before, but it better be good."

Sark smiled knowingly. "Oh, it will be very good."

"Units two, three, and four will go up the tunnels. Timing is going to be critical. Too soon and we'll lose it."

"And too late…" Sark folded his arms. "Well, why clutter things with conjecture, hey? After we're in, we engage the guard, right?"

"Right. But it's got to be done quietly. Then, the lad and I go and find the councilor."

"Yes," Joshan said. "He has to be at Trenara's Last Defense before her sentence is carried. Pravius is a clever man. He won't run the risk of exposing himself by violating the law. I must go against him alone. I don't know if my *power* is strong enough, but it's worth the risk. If we can remove Pravius, I think the rest will be easy. Not all the guards at the Keep are under his sway and most are just obeying orders—which brings me to another point. Your people are to be ordered not to kill unnecessarily. Many of those guards are still faithful and either don't know what's happening, or are just so overwhelmed by the whole thing they don't know what to do, this side of writing the matter up and waiting for justice through proper channels."

"All right, then." Van rolled up the parchment. "That's about it, unless you have any questions."

"Just one," Sark answered, staring at Joshan intently. "How do we know this boy is really the prince?" All three men stared back at him astonished.

Van blinked back at Sark and frowned. "What—besides my telling you he is? What's that supposed to mean?"

"Just what I said. How do we know this is Joshan? Seems to me if that snake wanted to catch you, he'd be clever with his trap, yes?" Haiden's eyes began to fire up as his hand went to the hilt of his sword.

"Now, wait a minute." Van said, rising from the bench. "I've known this lad since he was a boy. Besides, he's got the imperial mark on his shoulder and a scar on his arm from seasons ago."

"Aye, but marks and scars can be forged and so can features, if you have magic enough. I might point out—he's no longer a boy, though he should be. Don't you find that rather strange?"

"He changed when he went through *first trial*."

"So he says. But how do you know?"

Haiden jumped up from the table and leaned into Sark. "You got no need to doubt the prince. I've been with him since he came back to the Keep with Trenara, and I tell you this is him. I've seen him cure a woman with just his hands and lots of other things besides. I've raised this one from a pup and I know him better than anyone." He began to draw his sword and Sark stood away from the table, putting his hand on the hilt of his own. The other people heard the outburst and started to gather around the table. Several drew blades on both sides and eyed each other.

"All I'm saying," Sark pierced through Haiden's anger with steely eyes, "is what proof do we have, beyond your word and his? We've been vexed before by this bastard, and I can't think of a better ruse to gain our trust."

"Why you…" Haiden would have leapt over the table, had not Joshan jumped up and caught his arm, impelling him backwards. The room became suddenly very tense.

"No!" Joshan's voice stung at the guard like a slap in the face.

"But, lad, this insult…"

"No, Haiden. He's right. What guarantee do you have?" He turned to Sark and regarded him a long time. He could see strength in those eyes and a fierce concealed pride that he had seen in very few men. Joshan knew that he would want this man on his side at any cost. He saw something else in those eyes. The *sight* sent a wave of foreknowledge through him that panged of future strength and reliability; this man would be very important to his future—and the future of his nation.

"All right, Sark," he said evenly. "I concede your reasoning, but what would you have of me? I could show you the scar and the mark, but you're right, they can be fabricated. I can't change myself back to the boy. So, what would you have me do?"

Sark put the sword back in its shaft and walked to the hearth. The people relaxed instantly. "I heard once that the prince was a starguider—or, at least, training to be one."

Joshan stiffened, but smiled dryly. "So, it is magic you want to see. What trick shall I perform for you?" His voice was edged with such distain Sark involuntarily flinched.

Assemblage was a very high order and well above reproach as far as their *power* went. They were very proud of this fact and Joshan was no different. To ask for proof of the *power* by requesting some showing of its ability was considered no better than a request of a fool to perform some acrobatics. It was the highest insult you could pay a starguider and therefore extremely dangerous. Sark knew this and apparently so did the others, since audible breaths filled the room. Haiden's rage was building to the point of complete abandon, but Van stopped his outburst with a cold, grim shake of his head.

"If you *are* Joshan and therefore a guider, I will make my apologies then. If you're not…" But Sark stopped and Joshan found himself admiring his courage. Not many would insult a starguider, and few lived to repeat the error. "If I'm wrong, captain, make sure my heirs get what's due them, will you?"

Van just regarded him coldly. "Sark, you always was a suspicious bastard. Joshan, you don't have to do this. I know who you are and you got nothing to prove to me."

"No, captain," Joshan said slowly. "I admire his caution and it's warranted. I do appreciate your faith, however." He crossed to the center of the room. The crowd moved to the sides and watched curiously.

Joshan motioned to Haiden to help him move a bench. Haiden looked at him grimly as they lifted it. "Lad," Haiden whispered, "will the *power* come to you?"

Joshan gave him a sidelong look and a half smile. "I certainly hope so." Haiden moved to stand next to the giant, who planted his arms firmly over his chest.

"I must warn you," Joshan rolled up his sleeves, "I am just recently from *first trial* and the *power* may be… unpredictable." Sark gave him a mute nod and Joshan turned to the pub keeper. "Pap, put out those lamps, will you?" The barman nodded and smothered the flames.

The only light in the room came from the embers burning softly in the massive fireplace. The air was still, and though Joshan appeared assured, his heart labored in his chest and his mouth went dry. He raised his hands toward the fire and looked at it intently. The crystals, which were now spread across his palms, caught a flame and sparkled with fire, throwing reflected lights to dance against the walls. His brow became moist and his voice a quiet chant on the air, lulling those about him with its purity. Gasps were drawn at the sound of that first clear note.

The music bounced off the marble like a peel of thunder and sent people closer to the walls. Nothing happened. Nervous murmurs ran through the ranks. Sark rose from the bench, slowly, watchful. Joshan took a deep breath and focused again on the fire, while his eyes sparkled like black opals in the gloom. His face became cold with sweat, and water poured down his back and sides.

He sang again. More gasps followed, and one or two covered their faces; but again, nothing happened. Sark regarded him with a disappointed sigh and then turned to the giant.

"Van," he said slowly, "this boy may not be who he claims."

The giant shook his head and furrowed his brow, tightening the sinews in his neck. It would be a sorry loss if Sark and his people withdrew, but he would not desert Joshan now. "Lad," he said to Joshan stoutly, "you don't have…"

The room exploded violently.

A sudden earsplitting thunder shook the building to its foundation, toppling people, casks, and benches, sucking away Van's words. A brilliant flash of white mist poured from the ceiling like a giant fireball to engulf Joshan. Men and women froze in wonder or crouched on the ground in fear, covering their ears as the sound grated at clenched teeth and frozen necks. The giant's face was a stonework of astonishment, while Haiden's shifted from humility to wonder to pride, not knowing where to stop.

Sark was lifted from his feet by the blast and thrown back so hard he tumbled over the bench. He sprawled in a huge pile of ash at the side of the hearth. He sat up coughing, sputtering, and looking very much like a large floured dumpling.

In the silence that followed, Joshan began to laugh. But it wasn't the laughter of ridicule, derision, or spurn; rather, it was the clear unblemished peal of absolute joy as the *power* overflowed his heart and wrapped his soul in ecstasy. It danced around him and flowed through his veins like a glorious fire, burning away both wound and sorrow. His peals of laughter, amplified by the ceiling and enhanced by the *power*, flowed through the room like a storm until it touched everyone it could reach.

It started with Vanderlinden, his deep throaty chortles mixing with the delight of Joshan. Then Haiden's guffaws joined the chorus, and one by one, the others joined in. The laughter spread through the ranks rapidly, and had they known it, down the alley and through the streets until all those awake for many leagues in all directions joined them, many wondering at its source, but grateful for its bliss.

The Village had not felt such mirth in many, many seasons and they laughed until they felt the weariness of seasons fade away to exhilaration. This was the long awaited miracle. It allowed them, for a fleeting moment, to forget their destitution and pain— and see an unexpected flash of hope.

Finally, in the midst of all, even Sark began to laugh. Looking down at himself and then dancing a merry jig before the fire, he laughed until he could no longer stand. Haiden and Vanderlinden leaned on one another for support, the giant wiping a tear from his eye and the guard holding his belly and sides. After all were spent, content and revived, the laughter subsided and Joshan looked at Sark warmly, as the *power* flowed around him like a flurry of sparkling snow.

"Now, good Sark," he said, his voice echoing into the rafters, magnified by the *power* and edged with a clear serenity. "What trick would you have me do?"

Sark wiped his face on a towel and looked at Joshan with a shining light in his eyes. He strode toward the glowing prince with unabashed dignity and stopped before him, his face reflecting the bright light. Taking his sword slowly from its scabbard, he raised it in salute.

"No trick, sire. Except perhaps, to forgive a foolish man his doubts and take his sword instead." He sank to one knee and laid the sword at Joshan's feet. "It is yours, along with what little honor it may possess and the arm of Sark the Mercenary, should you desire it. I name you Ganafira, which, in my tongue, is Master of Men. I pledge myself and my fighters, though we're little better than rogues and thieves, but what strength we have is yours."

He lowered his eyes and bowed his head and the others looked on in wonder. Sark the Mercenary had *never* bowed to any man. A cheer went up from the party until the timbers shook with the sound. To the man or woman, all went to their knee before the boy.

CHAPTER TWELVE
THE ELITE

"I don't care what's been said. I saw what I saw." The young man stood sullen at the guard station, his lieutenant scowling at him. The older man glanced out the door and then closed it without a sound.

"All right, Jona, I want you to tell me everything you saw."

"Gods," Jona grumbled, but then shot a wretched look at his senior. "I'm sorry, Lieutenant Thiels, but I've been over this a hundred times."

"And you'll make it a hundred and one. I want you to tell me what you *didn't* tell those miscreants working for Councilor Pravius." Thiels sat down and rested his elbows on his knees, his wise blue eyes and rugged handsome face calming the younger man as they always did. "Start from the beginning."

"Yes, sir." Jona sighed and rubbed his eyes halfheartedly. "I was coming down the corridor, because I thought I heard a commotion. All I knew was there were prisoners being questioned in number eleven. When I heard the shouts, I started running. As I turned the corner, Haiden—*Haiden Bails,* mind you—was standing right in front of me. He was holding a man in his arm and behind him, her ladyship Trenara was crossing blades with one of the council guards. Then, I noticed the dead men in front of the cell door. I guess I drew my blade, because Haiden looked like he was about to run me through." He swallowed. "He said if I did anything to harm the Prince, he'd kill me where I stood, friendship or no. Then I saw the man he was holding and took a good look at him." Jona's eyes became urgent. "He had the imperial mark on his arm and I'd know that face anywhere. I've been Prince Joshan's training partner since he could lift a sword, sir. I'd swear to the gods, it *was* him—just... older."

The lieutenant looked at the young man and frowned. "Did you tell the council guards what Haiden said?"

"Not me... no, sir. Lately, people who have seen a bit more than they should, seem to be... dying suddenly. I didn't say a word."

"Isn't that the truth?" The older man said pensively.

"But I swear, Lieutenant Thiels, that man I saw *was* Prince Joshan." He shook his head and looked down. "I just don't understand what's been going on. All this strangeness—the decree and then all of those *extra* council guards showing up from nowhere—and northerners, too," he added with a derisive whisper. "It's just not... right."

"I don't understand it all myself, son." Thiels stood and rubbed the bristles on his chin thoughtfully. "If what you say is true, then there's something terribly wrong." He raised his hands in exasperation. "But what? That's the question." He looked at the young man and his expression changed as if he had come to some decision. "I'll have my own investigation launched; something a little... independent from the councilor's. I'll get to the bottom of this, one way or the other. In the meantime, we've just got to keep our ears and eyes open and see what happens."

Jona took a deep breath and stared at the lieutenant. "So, what do we do now, sir?"

"We do our duty and follow orders, until someone tells us not to. We're the Elite Corps, private, remember that—the emperor's own guards. We do his bidding, even when that's hard to do. If we know something's wrong, we write it up."

Jona curled his lip. "Fat lot of good that does anymore."

Thiels turned on the boy and pointed a finger. "Son, the man who sees the crime is just as guilty as he who commits it, if he doesn't write it up. You remember that."

"Aye, sir," he said, knowing the code well.

"Of course, we're emperor's guards. That doesn't mean we can't poke around and maybe find out a thing or two. Like, for example, if some of the orders coming down weren't exactly from the emperor, but from a certain councilor, well, then…"

Jona brightened. "Then no one could blame us is we didn't…"

"Exactly." The lieutenant smiled.

He took the keys down from their peg. "Come on, private. It's time to take her ladyship before the judgment. It's near dawn."

Jona grabbed the lieutenant's arm. "But, if what I saw was true…"

"Then the woman is innocent. That order was signed by the emperor." Then a slow smile came over his face. "But we'll see what happens. The guider's not dead yet."

Jona looked at the glint in the man's eyes and wondered at it. "Yes, sir." He opened the door with a brisk salute.

When they entered the corridor, they were met by a group of Pravius's men. They were dark and unkempt with dirty uniforms and black eyes. Thiels scowled searching out the lead man. "You there! This isn't the honor guard. Where the hell are the rest of my guards? You're not even part of the Elite."

"Begging your pardon, lieutenant," the man answered unpleasantly, slurring the title as if it were a jest, "but we're part of the Elite now. I just got my orders." He smugly took out some papers and shoved them at the officer.

Thiels examined them carefully and saw they were in order, disgusted the emperor could name these ruffians to the Elite. "All right," he said stiffly, handing the papers back. "Fall in!" The man began to take his place at the front of the line, as the other ragtag stumbled into place behind him. The lieutenant took the man's arm and stared down into his sneering face. "Behind us," he said. "You've got no rank in this guard as yet."

The man merely shrugged and shot an amused looked to his comrades. "As you wish, mate, makes no difference to me." He turned back to his men. "Come on, you slugs, get in line. You heard the man." When the men managed to get in place, the leader bowed to the lieutenant with a flourish, indicating the front of the line. "Sir."

Thiels bristled noticeably, but did nothing. If there had been time, he would have shown this weasly little man there was more to being part of the Elite than a piece of paper. As it was, they were late already. He resolved he was going to teach this reprobate a much needed lesson in the art of humility—or break him trying. He motioned to Jona, and they took their places at the head of the line, ignoring the snickering at their backs.

The law stated that a noble, as Trenara certainly was, had the right to an honor escort to Last Defense, regardless of the crime or punishment. The escort, also by law, was made up of the emperor's personal guard. Their function was to protect the royal family and the court, and to see to the security of the Keep. Only the finest men and women were appointed to the Elite, and only by the hand of the emperor.

At present, Thiels felt very much a token in this strange game and didn't care for it much. He led them to Trenara's cell.

CHAPTER THIRTEEN
CHANGE OF PLANS

"Wert!" Van bellowed when they entered the house. "Wert, we're back." He hung his cloak on a peg and lit the lamp above the door. "Make yourselves comfortable," he said to Joshan and Haiden, while pouring tea.

Wert lived in a rundown house situated near the northern border of Keepton. Van had moved much of his operation there, since his street in the Village, and many around it, were being closely watched. Although Wert's place was inconvenient and farther away, it was safer and less likely to be observed.

"Wert! Come on, man. There isn't much time."

The little man appeared from the back of the house looking much the same as before, although there was a bruise on his forehead where Haiden had clipped him *and* he seemed, if it were possible, more nervous. He wrung his hands and looked at the floor.

Van was rummaging through a locker, taking out several small arms. "Wert…" he started to call again. "Ah, there you are. How's the head?"

Wert touched the wound softly and winced a bit. "It's all right."

"I'm really sorry, if I would have known, I'd have gone a lot easier on you," Haiden said with genuine regret.

Wert glanced at him. "It's all right," he repeated.

"Haiden and Joshan will need weapons. Get them some and then you better get ready yourself. We're leaving within the hour."

"Yes," Wert said meekly and turned to the closet.

"Here, sire." Van tossed a dagger and case to Joshan. "That'll be better for close-in fighting than that long blade you've got." He slammed the locker lid, and Wert jumped with a cry. Van scowled at him. "What's wrong with you, man? You're as jumpy as a cat."

"Nothing—it's just—well the fighting and all."

"Ha!" Van gave him a wink. "You're still nervous about those guards that almost got you last night. I got your scrawny arse out of that mess, now didn't I? You were out cold, so no harm done. Hell, they didn't even get you to the gate."

"I know," he said, still looking at his hands.

"All right, then, quit your fretting. What you need is a good fight." But Van noticed a strange look in Wert's eyes. A hot flush of fear rose in his face as he stood up slowly and regarded the hunched man suspiciously. "There's something else, isn't there?" He suddenly felt like the world was about to cave in.

Haiden and Joshan turned, suddenly caught by the wariness in Van's voice. Wert seemed to melt under the giant's keen stare.

"Van… I… that is, you…" His brow began to glisten with sweat.

"Spit it out, Wert."

"Van…" He looked up at the giant with tears in his eyes. "I'm sorry," he whispered.

The giant placed his hands on his hips and scowled. "What's wrong with you?"

Joshan was grabbed from behind, and Haiden was knocked unconscious by the hilt of a sword. Joshan had his hands wrenched violently behind his back and his mouth savagely bound before he could sing to call the *power*. It happened so quickly, by the time the giant whirled around, pulling his sword from its scabbard, it was done. There were ten of Pravius's northerners behind him, with Haiden in a heap on the floor and Joshan held tight, a sword at his heart.

"Put it down, giant." Pravius emerged from the shadows.

"Bastard!" Van brought his blade up sharply, heedless of his peril.

"I wouldn't, good captain," the councilor replied, motioning to Joshan. The prince's eyes widened in pain as the blade at his chest broke the skin, and blood stained the fabric of his shirt. He let out a muffled cry.

Van screamed and hurled the blade with such force it shattered against the farthest wall. He turned on Wert and clenched his fists. "I'll kill you for this!" Van screamed, but Wert just covered his face and sobbed. "Why would you do this?" Wert could only cringe.

"Shall I tell him?" Pravius asked, turning to the giant. "You've been a fool, Vanderlinden. Do you think Wert here found you by chance two seasons back? I knew you would escape. Why else would I convince Jenhada to exile you? Everything has gone according to plan. I have Jenhada and Saldorian. I have Trenara and Joshan— and now I have you."

He motioned the guards to bind the giant's hands and Van gave no resistance; the sword at Joshan's heart afforded him none. Pravius ordered them to put a yoke around Joshan's neck.

"You mustn't blame Wert," Pravius whispered into the giant's ear. "He is an honorable man, but he has a weakness."

Wert brought his hands down and looked up at the giant desperately. "He's got Katin. He says he'll…" He broke into sobbing and bowed his head.

"Your daughter?"

Wert nodded wretchedly. Van looked at him a long time, pity moving him. His eye misted as he threw his head back and screamed in frustration.

"Every man has a weakness," said Pravius. "Hurry now, there isn't much time. Bring the giant and the boy." Wert screamed and sank to his knees.

The guards pummeled Van toward the door, but he broke from their hands to look at Wert a last time. "I'll find you."

"I don't think so," Pravius said as Wert looked up. "He'll be dead within the hour, along with the sergeant." The guards pushed Van though the door.

"But, you said…" Wert looked up at the councilor from his knees.

"What?" Pravius voice was now silky. "That I would reunite you and your daughter? And so I will." He removed a pouch from beneath his robe and threw it at Wert's knees. The little man opened it with trembling fingers, and his face became a mask of pain. The bag was filled with fine ash. Wert screamed.

Pravius turned to the door and took his guard's arm. "Kill them both when we've gone. Clean up when you're through; I don't want any of that village scum to know what's happened here."

Outside, they forced Joshan into a waiting carriage as Pravius stopped before the giant and looked up at him. "The first thing you are going to tell me is where the scoundrels are, or where Sark will lead them.

"Go to hell," Van hissed.

The councilor pulled his gloves on tightly. "It doesn't matter; there isn't much he can do anyway, now that I have all of you. Killing Sark and his followers will be easy. Of course, you could change that. Tell me where they will strike, and we'll spare them."

Van shook his head evenly. "I've got nothing to say to you."

A smile dusted the councilor's lips. "You'll have plenty to say before the day is over." He removed the red crystal from his robes. "It's time to pay your debt, captain." Pravius began to sing.

Van looked at the crystal and tried to take a step back, but it was too late. A ruby fire sparked in his eye, and his face became as still as stone, as the red glow settled into a cloud around him. When the mist touched him, Vanderlinden became immediately obedient.

A slow smile covered Pravius's face as he moved to be close to the giant's ear. He removed his gloves. "Now, my dear captain, this is what you are going to do…"

The sky began to gray as the sun shot its first beam of light against the fading night.

CHAPTER FOURTEEN
MARCH TO JUDGMENT

The sea was calm as hundreds of scalards peppered the shore and floated on the air above it. The only sounds were their lonely cries and the soft, faint hiss of the tide hitting the sand to wash away the old death and carry in the new. As the first beam of light sparkled on the horizon, a single bell chimed from somewhere in the castle, and the rippled clouds that lined the skies like barren hills caught the morning light and dulled it to the gray ghost of dawn.

Trenara stared across the Ethosian Sea from her cell at the bottom of the cold Keep. Her eyes were grim, but clear in the morning light. Her face was drawn with fatigue. She had no thoughts—only a dull pain that bit into her heart. The jingle of the keys echoing through the chamber, and the creak of the door opening and closing, touched the guider's senses, but she did not stir.

"Ma'am?" said a small voice behind her.

When she turned, she regarded Ena with pity. Her young aide's face was red and swollen with grief and tears sparkled in her eyes. Her yellow hair was mussed and her clothes wrinkled from sleepless nights and long painful hours. The young woman stood alone, clinging to the guider's formal robe, mantel, and sparkling sash, as if they contained some semblance of consolation. Ena looked down at the garments and ran her fingers over them lightly.

"They said I could bring you fresh robes, lady." Her voice was tight with suppressed tears and her bottom lip quivered, despite her attempts to stop it.

Trenara crossed to her slowly to brush a tear from her cheek and then took the clothes. "Tears?"

"I… I've tried to be brave, lady," the girl said, her voice hoarse. "When they told me…" The aide's eyes filled with pain and she couldn't say anymore. She lowered her head and wept.

Trenara lifted the young face and looked gently into her eyes. "Ena, don't waste tears on me. You are so young and have many seasons left for sorrow. Death, should it come to that, will only mean a new beginning for me; but for you…" Her voice faltered when she thought of the legacy she would leave. She sucked air into her lungs to ease her heart. "But for you, there are many battles to fight, many deeds to perform and many tears yet to shed before it is through. Save them for that. Now you will need to be strong. Do you understand?"

Ena threw her arms around the guider and buried her face in her robes. Trenara brushed the young woman's hair gently and threw her head back to fight the tears as they welled in her eyes. She embraced her and finally took in a quivering breath.

"Come," she said at length, holding Ena out by the shoulders. "Help me dress. I shouldn't go before the judges looking like this, should I?" She smiled at the girl, but Ena simply nodded.

When Trenara had pulled the mantel over her robes, Ena held out her gold and blue sash and the guider took it formally. The blue denoted her rank as a starguider and the thirty-four gold bands that ran through it represented her seasons of Imperium service. Trenara wrapped it around her waist and tied it in Assemblage fashion at the front, but couldn't stop the morose feeling that it would be the last time. Her guider's *sense* lay as dead in her as if it had never been alive. She pushed back the trepidation, tried to get her hands to stop shaking, and managed a smile at Ena.

After running a brush through the long gray hair and braiding it at the back, the girl stepped back and gazed at her proudly, then fell to one knee. "You look beautiful, lady," she whispered.

"Thank you, lass," Trenara helped Ena to her feet. "You had better go now. The guards will be here soon."

Ena bowed low and went to the door. "Lady?" She turned to look at Trenara.

"What is it, child?"

"I promise I'll be brave."

Trenara's heart quietly broke, but her face did not betray her. "I know you will."

Ena knocked on the door to be let out, imparting one final look at the guider before she left.

*****

Thiels stopped the line of guards formally at the cell door. As one, they turned smartly on their heels and stood at rigid attention. Jona took a step forward, unbolted the door, and opened it ceremoniously. He stood to one side and saluted.

The woman who emerged was not the huddled old woman they expected to see, but rather a tall, stern, noble figure, as regal as a queen and grim as a seasoned warrior. The torchlight caught the gold and blue at her waist and sent it glimmering around her, so she appeared to be girded in golden flame and cobalt mist. Her eyes shone like polished blue gems in the dim corridor, ageless and clear. The guider's gaze moved from guard to guard, one by one and held each pair of eyes until she knew the heart of each. None could bear that gaze for long, and to the man, they bowed their heads before her knowing eyes. When finally her eyes fell on Thiels, guilt filled him and he deplored the task at hand.

The lieutenant nodded to Jona stiffly, and they took their places on either side of the silent guider. When Jona raised his hand to take the guider's arm, Trenara turned to regard him and Jona knew at once that this woman would not be held. He swallowed hard against the knot of apprehension climbing up his throat and awkwardly lowered his hand. At a word from the lieutenant, they marched solemnly through the hold.

In the castle they passed several groups of guards and spectators on their way to the hall, but such was Trenara's bearing, that all sneers died on somber lips and all cruel gibes were forgotten. Even the northerners were struck by the majesty of the starguider and instantly silenced themselves. Awe replaced derision and people bowed their heads in silent homage as she passed.

When they arrived at the huge wooden doors that led to the Hall of Justice, the group stopped as a whole. With a face of iron, Trenara watched the doors silently open. A long expanse of marble stairs lay before her, leading down to an immense chamber with high vaulted ceilings and somber stone walls.

A throng had gathered to witness the Last Defense, lining the stairs and filling every bench on either side of the arena. All Trenara could see in those faces was the rank carrion coldness that scavenger fowl carried while waiting for their dinner to die. The faces changed to wonder, the murmur hushed when she entered, and the doors closed with a dull thud at her back. The escort descended the stairs to take up their respective stations.

Trenara stood alone, gazing at the three tiers of marble benches before her, the twelve judges who occupied them, and the huge podium that stood at their center. At the highest tier, now level with her eyes, Pravius sat with his hands folded and his face as grave as death. Around him sat the other eleven council judges, all silent and watchful, their red robes bright against the dull marble. The man to his right, the Chancellor of Judgment, sat solemnly staring at the guider. Jenhada sat to one side, his eyes closed, his head weighted down by grief.

Pravius regarded the guider with cold eyes from behind the tall podium, but then faltered under the guider's penetrating stare. He cleared his throat and looked instead at the parchments that lay before him. Trenara silently descended the stairs and stood alone at the center of the arena, gazing up at the judges as if to challenge them merely with her staunch forbearance.

CHAPTER FIFTEEN
THE DIVERSION

"It's too bloody quiet, if you ask me," the northerner hissed in the gloom of the west hall. "Something should have happened by now."

The other man, dark and scarred, just looked at him and smiled. "Ah, quit your jawing, Anno. It's dawn. The guider's before the judges and the giant and the boy are caught, so what can happen? No one would be fool enough to attack when there are so many hostages. When this is all over we can have our pick and take of whatever we want. There's one or two of them uppity ladies I kind of take a fancy to. Wouldn't that be a handsome gift for a cold night, hey?" He smiled, winked at the other men gathered around, and they all laughed.

"All right, you slugs, get back to your stations. There's work to be done, and we got to at least look like we know what it is we're doing," he added with half a smile. The men rose and lazily spread through the west hall, most leaning casually against the marble walls, or sitting on the floor.

"Hey, Kit," Anno said after the other men had gone. "You know what I'd like?"

"Gold?" Kit snorted.

"Gold, sure—and jewels. Those royal jewels are worth a pretty penny on the market, but you'd have to cut them up. Ain't no one has that kind of money—not to buy them whole, I mean. But it weren't gold nor jewels, I was thinking of." He sank to the floor and rested his back under a boarded window.

"What then?" Kit asked, joining him on the floor.

Anno scowled and spat. "There's a certain lieutenant I want, from that stinking Elite with all their airs." A wicked grin spread over his face. "I think slow torture— maybe over coals. Aye, cook him, I will."

Kit laughed. "You mean Thiels? You'd have to get in line for that one."

"It'd be worth it just to see him crawl. He's gotten more of our boys in hot water—him and those accursed Elite. Why didn't the councilor lock him up with the rest of that scum?"

"Ha! Lock up Thiels? Listen, Anno, that Pravius is a smart one. Thiels is too popular with the rest of them. He would just have to lock up the whole frigging lot, and then he wouldn't have enough men to run the Keep."

Anno spat. "I can't see where it'd hurt none. Them damn pretty boys with their uppity ways and all their gold braids. And women! Women guards to boot. There's only one good use for a woman and it ain't that. Too good for the likes of us, they are. I'd like to show them just how much better they are."

"You'll get your chance, mate—and soon, from what I heard. Some of our boys got into the Elite last night. I heard it from Barra himself, 'cause he was one of 'em.

Six, as a matter of fact." He shook his head and laughed. "That's the councilor's doing, I'll be bound; though how he got that old buzzard to sign the papers, I couldn't guess. More of his magic, I guess."

"Shhh…" Anno looked around quickly. "No one's supposed to know that."

"Ain't much of a secret. 'Sides, by the time the party's over—couple of days maybe—I'm thinking everybody's going to know it—and where he's from," Kit added in a low whisper. "No use kidding ourselves, mate. He ain't exactly lord good, you know."

Anno looked at the floor and furrowed his brow. "Aye, I wonder about that sometimes," he said, a glint of shame in his voice.

"Ho, now! You're not going honest on me, are you? Let me remind you—honor never lined nobody's pockets and goodness never paid enough to buy a good wench or a mug of beer. Nah, you stick to the power, mate—that's where the money is."

"Right you are." He shuddered. "But ain't Pravius the one, now? I've heard stories that'd set your hair on end. Every time he comes in, I get the willies all up and down my spine. I'd hate to be on his bad side."

"Aye, he's a blood freezer, that one. If you're talking bad sides, I can't see where he's got anything but."

A man who had been sitting near the double doors whirled around to Kit. "There's someone out there!"

Kit was instantly on his feet and whistling to his men. "All right. Look alive. This may be it." The men jumped to their feet and started to advance to the door, pulling out their swords. When they were within reach, Kit put out his arm to keep them from moving any closer. "Stay put. We'll make them come to us." The door handle turned slowly, and the men raised their weapons.

When the door opened, they all gaped in wonder. There stood twenty of the most beautiful women any of them had ever seen—blondes, brunettes, redheads, all shapes and all sizes, dressed in bright colors and lewd loveliness. The lead woman, a brassy blonde with large, half-exposed breasts, bright red lips and lusty eyes, smiled at Kit languidly and took a slow step through the door.

"Put down your sword, darling," she said, her voice deep and sultry. "Molly doesn't bite. Least wise, not unless she's asked."

Kit lowered his sword and swallowed hard. "Who… who are you?"

"Why, I'm Miss Molly and these are my girls," she said cocking her head to the side. "Come on in, ladies. How about introducing yourselves to these fine gentlemen."

The women, all well figured, fragrant and equally alluring, came through the door and picked a man from the faction, wrapping their arms around their necks, helping them put their weapons down with soft words and stealing off with them into dark corners.

"We're gifts from the councilor, love. Kind of a surprise package, you might say."

Kit looked at his men wildly as they disappeared into the shadows one by one.

"But… but we're on duty." He swallowed nervously as Miss Molly wrapped her arms around his neck and caressed his leg. "You can't…"

"Shhh. You wouldn't want to spoil the councilor's surprise, now would you? We've come all the way from the Village, just to entertain you boys." She brought his face close to hers and planted an intoxicating kiss on his lips. His sword fell with a clatter as he wrapped his arms around her and closed his eyes to take full measure of Molly's experience.

Thirty seconds later, he and all his men were sprawled on the floor, every one of them knocked senseless by a sudden rap to the back of the neck inflicted by either Sark or one of his people. Sark stood over the fallen Kit and put his sword back in its shaft. Molly brushed her hands and gave the mercenary a sidelong look, to which he smiled. "Molly, you are a wonder."

She snorted and curled her lip. "I'd have to be to be to kiss that thing."

"All right," Sark called to his fighters. "Let's get this bunch packed up and stored. Move it." The group began to gather up the unconscious men, bound their hands, legs and mouths, and dragged them into the darkness.

"Come on, ladies," said Molly to the milling group of women. "You're not broken. Lend a hand."

Sark surveyed his people and checked the door quickly. "Listen, Molly, Tige will take you back to the Village, but you're not to return to the House—at least not until this is over. It won't be safe."

"Oh, you were always the gallant one. Molly can take care of herself and her girls. But we'll do what you say. I never could refuse that handsome smile of yours." She regarded him seriously, as he put his arms around her waist.

"You are a good woman, Molly."

"Not for a long time, love. Now you take care of your hide and that shark bait, Vanderlinden, too. Don't go getting those pretty faces all scratched. I don't know what I would have done without you two the last couple of seasons, but if you go and get yourselves hurt, I'll never forgive you."

Sark gave her an arrogant look. "Madame, think to whom you are speaking. Now, get your ladies together. I want you out of here before the fighting starts."

"They're all secured, Sark," called Donnelly. "But shouldn't Van have been here by now?"

Sark scowled and scanned the rows of panels. "Donnelly, get them to their stations and…" Just then, a panel at the back slid up, and forty of Sark's fighters poured out of the wall. Sark searched briefly, but there was no sign of the giant, Joshan, or Haiden.

"Sark," Boric said breathlessly as he reached him.

Where are they?"

"We don't know. They didn't show at Pap's, so I sent a couple of my lads to Wert's." He gave Sark a frightened look and shook his head as Molly came up to join them. "Place was empty, Sark, and tore up bad. We found the giant's sword busted, and one of the northern guards dead, but not a living soul in the place. There was a trail of blood leading out, but it ended on the road. No one saw anything, but there were carriage tracks leading toward the Keep—made fresh." He looked down as Molly let out a cry. Sark's face was strained with repressed fury.

"Sark," Molly's voice was trembling, "do you think that bastard's got him?"

"Aye! He's got him." He pounded his fist against the wall. "Damn!"

He lowered his head and took a deep breath to calm himself, knowing the need for haste. "Boric, get your crew to their stations. Donnelly, you get to the east wing. And Tige, get the ladies back to the Village." They all just stared at him. "Nothing has changed. Now get going." His words got them moving quickly. Boric called out orders, and the hall was soon empty except for Molly's women, Tige, and Sark. Tige stood at the tunnel and helped the women in.

Molly turned to Sark and squeezed his hand gently.

"Thank you, Molly."

"Ah, I'd do it again." She then gave him a troubled look as a tear went down her cheek. "You find him. His carcass ain't worth much, but you and him are all I got."

Sark picked up her hand and kissed it softly. Molly touched his cheek, bit her lip to hold back the tears and then let Tige help her up to the tunnel. "Tige will take you back and make sure you're safe."

"It'll be interesting to have Tige protect us. It's usually us protecting her, when the authorities come around."

The tall warrior woman gave her a grin. "They only come round 'cause I'm following Sark's orders."

Sark shook his head. "Go… both of you!"

Tige imparted one final look at him before stepping up into the opening. "I'll take care of them, captain."

"I'm counting on that, Tige. If I don't see you again, it's been a great twenty seasons."

Tige's face melted into a frown, and Molly mirrored her expression. "Don't even tease about that." They disappeared into the darkness of the tunnel as Sark closed the panel.

CHAPTER SIXTEEN
LAST DEFENSE

"Trenara of Assemblage," said Pravius, his face assuming the placid façade for the benefit of the crowd, "you have come before the Council of Justice for Last Defense." He glanced at the slumped figure of Jenhada and then scanned the room. "The emperor has requested I rule over these proceedings. If anyone opposes this, let them voice it now." He waited for a challenge, but the hall was silent. "So be it. You have heard the charges against you. What is your defense?"

"My defense is this: Joshan lives." Trenara's voice was smooth, firm, the intonations persuasive. Murmurs rose from the crowd.

"Silence!" the Chancellor of the Council shouted. Trenara knew the man well. He had been in Imperium service almost as long as Trenara and was known for his unbiased rulings. The dusky blue eyes gleamed out from beneath jutting milk-white brows, giving him a comical, almost child-book quality, which camouflaged his serious nature. Trenara was hoping the chancellor was still free from the influence Pravius seemed to be exerting over Jenhada; it was all she had left.

Pravius put his elbows on the podium and folded his hands. "You say the prince lives," he said reasonably. "Do you have proof of this?"

Trenara looked at the remaining judges. "There is a deception among us that sounds so much like the truth, even I and others like me did not see it until it was too late. It is undermining our laws, destroying our freedoms and will make slaves of us. The personification of that lie stands in this room." Her eyes scanned the dais and fell on Pravius. "He has at his command a terrible power that has corrupted the hearts of many good people and swayed our leaders' judgments."

Pravius smiled down at her as if the words meant nothing at all. "Please, guider, present your evidence," he said gently.

Trenara ignored him and looked instead to the other councilors. "Judges, if you will permit me, I would like to bring forth someone who has seen the prince in the last two days."

Pravius looked at Trenara suspiciously and then turned to the chancellor. "The guider is within her rights, of course, but I must warn you, she is Assemblage, quite capable of any sort of mischief with her magic. I vote we do not open ourselves to these tricks. With her talents, we could fall prey to the same enchantment that lost us our heir."

The councilors began to talk among themselves, but Trenara raised her hand. "Please. It is my right to present my case." She closed her eyes for a moment to calm her anger. "However, Pravius has challenged it by implying I possess powers which would sway your judgment. That power no longer exists. It was stolen from me." She reached into her robes, removed the pieces of the Andelian, and with an effort, cast them before the councilors where they scattered before the marble podium, chiming against the stone. "That is what is left of my power." The blue eyes flashed in the early morning light as the crowd murmured around her. "It was taken from me the night I was arrested." Her words came out raw and brittle as if the pain were still too new to speak. The councilors bent their heads together and came to a decision.

"It is your right to present your case," the Chancellor said, "whether or not you held the *via*. We will listen to all defenses, as prescribed by law. You may present your witnesses."

Trenara's face was bleak as she bowed her head in acknowledgement. Turning to the crowd behind her, she motioned to Jona. The young man cast furtive looks at the ground as he made his way to Trenara.

"Ma'am, I…" he whispered. "How did you know?"

"There's no time now. A witness can't be prosecuted for giving testimony—or so it was. You have no obligation to me, young man. Decline, if you need to."

Jona touched her arm and smiled sadly. "No, lady, I don't have the stomach to decline. If they wish to prosecute—let them." He turned on his heel and spoke to the benches. "Yes, I saw him the night before last in the hold."

A deafening noise went through the crowd and Pravius brought his fist down on the podium. "Silence!" His voice reached out with a hiss that burned the room of sound. But his eyes were not on the crowd; they bore through Jona as if they could boil his blood. The guard lost his moment of confidence, stepped back, and fell against Trenara's hands as Pravius came around the podium and softened the lines of his face. His eyes became limpid as he crossed.

"It is quite all right, son." His voice was smooth and comforting. "You have nothing to fear. Speak freely." He placed his fingertips together and paced before the guard. "Under what circumstances did you behold this—sighting?"

Jona looked down at his trembling hands and clasped them together to keep them from shaking. "I was in the hold and saw Haiden Bails with a young man in his arms. I would have known him anywhere. Joshan and I have been training together daily since he could lift a sword—at least five seasons. I swear to you, that man *was* the First Prince." The young guard quickly relayed what had taken place in the hold, reporting every detail as he had been trained by Thiels. When he was through, the councilors talked briefly among themselves and Jona wiped his brow.

Pravius simply nodded. "You say he had changed—how so?"

"He… he was older and larger, like he had grown up." The councilor's eyes still unnerved him.

"He had… grown?" Pravius whirled on the young man. Jona couldn't breathe and a flash of panic made him shudder. "Yet you testify this… man was the same boy of ten seasons."

Jona almost denied it all in a fit of terror, but Trenara grasped his arm tightly, sending a wave of relief through him. He straightened his shoulders, stood up tall and his eyes sparkled with conviction. "I swear by all the gods," he said through his teeth, "the man I saw was Joshan Jenhada Thoringale. No one can tell me otherwise."

Pravius held his gaze for a moment and then bowed his head in assent. He turned to the other judges and shook it solemnly. "Undoubtedly another feint of the guider's to deceive us. My heart sorrows for the lad, for Trenara has obviously bewitched him. I'm certain he knows nothing of this terrible crime and believes wholeheartedly in what he thought he saw."

"And I reiterate," Trenara cried, before that controlling tone could take hold completely. "My *power* was removed from me *before* I was placed in the hold." She sent Jona back to his place.

The Chancellor looked from Trenara to Pravius and regarded them a long moment while he contemplated, then looked into the crowd. "Is there anyone here who can either confirm or refute the claim made by the guider?"

"Yes, sir," called a voice from the back of the room. Muted whispers rose from the crowd.

The Chancellor squinted to make out where the voice came from. "Step forward and make yourself known."

A man made his way to the front of the crowd and Pravius let out a hiss that only Trenara heard. For the first time, Trenara saw fear in his eyes.

"Lieutenant Connan Thiels, is it?" the Chancellor was saying. "From the Elite?"

"Yes, sir," Thiels responded smartly. "For thirty-five seasons now."

"Yes, Thiels, your record is well known to this court. What do you know of the guider's claim?"

Thiels pointed to Pravius and the councilor flinched as if the finger were a weapon. Thiels ignored him completely. "I observed Councilor Pravius with the guider's wand when she was first arrested. It's all in the reports, sir, the ones lying in front of you and the other judges." He glanced at Pravius. "Sorry, councilor, but when it came to making copies, I'm afraid I was one short, so you didn't get one. Purely an oversight."

He gave Pravius an innocent look edged with calm defiance and the councilor's nostrils began to flare. Thiels simply smiled at the man and returned his attention to the judges. "You'll note from the report, sir, I also observed the starguider's wand, or *via*, which I believe to be the proper name, in the possession of Councilor Pravius exactly seven times over the last two days. Most recently, four hours ago." The judges read the reports while the crowd waited breathlessly. Pravius did not move, but his face became livid with fury.

Finally, the Chancellor looked up and regarded him sternly. "Is this true?"

Pravius tightened his lips into a hard line; he was having difficulty maintaining his composure. "Yes," he hissed through his teeth, knowing Thiels' word would not be contested.

"Excuse me," said Thiels to the council, "but I'd like to make a statement and have it entered into the record." The Elite lieutenant had testified in countless trials over the seasons and his reputation was undisputed. He was one of the finest investigators in the Imperium. Often his word was held above even hard evidence.

"Very well, lieutenant," replied the Chancellor. Pravius turned around and regarded the man in shock.

"I understand this witness's background, but I must protest this obvious…"

"Councilor Pravius," the Chancellor replied crisply, "you know the law. This testimony will be heard. Proceed, lieutenant." Pravius went back to the podium. He said nothing while Thiels spoke, but it took a great deal of effort to smooth the disapproval that lined his face.

"Thank you, sir," Thiels said. "First, the reports before the council are true and accurate. Second, Trenara of Mathisma, a second trial starguider of Assemblage, has an unblemished record. Based on the facts of this record and the many honors bestowed on her by the Imperium, there can be no provocation to insinuate her in the murder of Joshan Jenhada Thoringale, if indeed the prince is actually dead. Since an eyewitness has testified to seeing him after the fact, then there is, of course, some doubt about this accusation.

"Third, the starguider's *via*, Andelian Trucrystal, is her rightly awarded crystal scepter presented to her by the Provost during her ordination thirty-six seasons ago. The *via* is her source of *power*, not the guider herself. Without her *via*, which by testimony and written statement was not in her possession within the last two days, Trenara of Mathisma could not use her *power* on anyone," he nodded toward Jona, "including, sir, the previous witness." Thiels turned to regard Pravius with a fine twinkle in his eye. "With the judicial council's agreement, I would suggest we bring the Elite Corps into the investigation. If you will allow us to substantiate… or disprove these accusations, I believe this would serve both the council and the accused. I would deem it a personal honor to render my services to this noble body."

"Sir," Pravius's voice broke for a moment, but with an effort, he smoothed it. "As much as I respect the good lieutenant's status, I do not see where this has any bearing on the case at hand," he stated plainly, his voice edged with silky persuasion.

"Yes, councilor," the chancellor replied thoughtfully. "I agree. These observations do not appear to have any bearing on this case."

Pravius gave a smile of assured relief as the council spoke together quietly for a moment. The chancellor regarded all of them this time. "However," he said, "because of this testimony and that of the young man earlier, there does seem to be some doubt as to whether the prince is indeed dead. We will accept the Elite's offer to clear up that doubt before proceeding with the guider's sentence. We have no choice, therefore, but to…"

"If you please, Chancellor," Pravius compelled, "perhaps this matter can be clarified by the evidence our own investigators have uncovered." Trenara and Thiels exchanged puzzled glances as the Chancellor looked down at Pravius curiously. "I would be more than happy to present it when this witness is excused."

The Chancellor thought for a moment. "Very well, councilor, but if the evidence presented does not clarify that doubt, we will proceed as suggested by the Elite."

When Thiels returned to his place, a man came up behind him and put a hidden knife to his back. Thiels froze. "Say one word in the next five minutes," the man murmured in his ear, "and I'll cut out your liver and have my mate over there cut out the boy's at the same time." Thiels looked across the arena and saw Jona, stiff with fear, a northern guard close to his back. "Believe me, Thiels, I'd enjoy doing it and wouldn't hesitate a second. Understood?" Thiels nodded once.

"All right, councilor," the Chancellor was saying, "present your evidence."

"Thank you, sir," he said turning back to the chamber and smoothing the pile of parchment on the podium seductively. "I have here the complete report of the evidence against Trenara of Mathisma. May I read it to the council?" Pravius asked, looking at Trenara.

"Are you prosecuting, Councilor Pravius?" the chancellor asked formally.

"I am."

"Objections?"

No one replied and Pravius began his oration, barely glancing at the parchments in front of him. "Much of what you are about to hear will be disturbing. It is the culmination of months of investigation, the information painstakingly acquired. I'm afraid this crime is more comprehensive than originally thought, so I ask the council's indulgence as I lay out the extent of this woman's actions over the last two seasons." He looked back at the chancellor who nodded.

"Several months ago, we received information of suspicious activities, potentially detrimental to the empire. Because of this, we sent two agents to Mathisma to investigate. After careful observations and an informant interview, it was discovered that a seditious group of starguiders had banded together to undermine the empire. We believe now that the accused was not only a member of this group, but one of its leaders. I will not go into detail regarding the group at this time, as the investigation is continuing and this matter can be taken up later. I will only brush upon this group's activities as it relates to the crimes now before the council.

"These dissidents believe the Imperium should be run not as a cooperative effort between the emperor, councils, and Assemblage, but should be a religious state with the councils of trade and justice under Assemblage rule. They believe the imperial model is obsolete. Since they have been unable to convince either the councils or Assemblage to accept the dismissal of the emperor and his line, they have taken it upon themselves to overthrow him, using Trenara's position of importance to implement the plan." There was uproar, as this knowledge sank into the council and the observers. Trenara just looked at the man dumbfounded. The chancellor called for silence.

"These are grave charges, councilor. Do you have proof?" the Chancellor asked.

"Yes, I do," he replied quietly and handed the chancellor a stack of parchments.

"Those are letters found in the starguider's chambers after she was arrested. As you can see, they clearly lay out the group's overall plans. However, I only introduce this evidence to establish the motive of the accused. As I said, we will need to pursue this other matter later, when we have put this one to rest. Agreed?"

The chancellor looked up and nodded. "Thank you, sir," said Pravius. "The plan was to poison the emperor so it would appear he died of natural causes, neutralize the heir, and then supplant him with someone else. We believe once the preparations were outlined, Trenara recruited the emperor's consort to aid her, knowing Saldorian was an ex-starguider—and a dissatisfied spouse. Each night Saldorian gave the emperor poison, which Trenara prepared for her. Here," he said pulling out a bag and handing it to the chancellor, "are the remains of several vials we found in the consort's chambers, and with it, a mortar and pestle we discovered in Trenara's quarters. Both contain the same ingredients, a combination of poisonous chemicals that make it appear the victim is dying of a long-term disease.

"We do not know what motive the guider could have given Saldorian to betray her husband and child, but after extensive interviews with the consort, we know what occurred. Here is her signed confession." He handed the parchment to the chancellor.

"According to the confession, Trenara convinced Saldorian that Jenhada was planning on disassociating his union with her for a princess from the south. The guider told Saldorian this woman was younger and more beautiful. She was shattered by the news and susceptible to the guider's... influence. I would point out that the emperor had no such plans. It was then that the accused committed what was probably the most atrocious part of her plan. She lied to the consort about Joshan. Trenara told her since Joshan would not be of age for many seasons, Saldorian would then become regent in his place. It appears the consort was reluctant at first, but eventually agreed. It is likely Trenara threatened her with Joshan's death if she did not cooperate. Saldorian has been devastated by this loss. Her confession is at times... vague. Regardless of the motive, the consort began the slow murder of her husband.

"It was then Trenara recruited a sailor to impersonate the young prince and began his training to take Joshan's place. We have testimony of an artist in the Village who tells us the guider arranged for the young man to be tattooed and scarred exactly as the prince was. We will come back to that later. Here is that testimony," he said, handing another parchment to the council.

"This is absurd," Trenara whispered, hardly able to believe what she was hearing. She was so stunned by the complexity of this lie, her mind reeled with the implications. Every bit of the deception began to fit exactly into the facts. She couldn't disprove any of it. She realized with a sickening rush of fear that, whoever this was, he had been planning this from the beginning. Every nuance, every fact, every detail painstakingly accounted for; even Joshan's change was sewn into the fabric of the deception, probably at the last moment, but brilliantly. This was the product of an unqualified genius.

Thirty seasons ago, she had seen evidence of the same warped intellect at work. It belonged to only one soul—Sirdar. Her heart labored in her chest, when she realized everything she had done over the last two seasons must have been watched, reported, and twisted beyond recognition or denial. With a shock, she remembered seeing the same dark men frequently, in the Keep, on the roads, in the forests. Trenara was astonished she hadn't realized it then—it seemed so obvious. It only proved that this man was incredibly skilled at manipulation. Her life had ceased to be her own. The guider felt defiled by the knowledge. Pravius just ignored the outburst and stared at her.

"We believe she planned the final coup for many months," Pravius continued persuasively. "By taking Joshan up to the High Cliffs several times, it appeared to the Elite that she was no threat to the heir, coming back with him each time. When Jenhada became increasingly ill, she finally put her plan in motion.

"We believe the starguider took the prince one more time to the cliffs when no one was around. We think she must have convinced the child that he was attaining *first trial*, probably by use of her own magic. Unfortunately, when the prince allowed the *power* to touch him at her encouragement, he was not ready and the child was burned to death, leaving little trace of his small, young body." There were growls of exclamation from the crowd, but the chancellor again called for silence.

"Fortunately for our investigation," Pravius continued, "she missed some of the remnants—most likely in a hurry to complete her scheme.

"We assume after Trenara disposed of the boy, she met up with the young sailor and rode into the Keep. There she attempted to pass the stranger off as the prince, concocting a story of how he had been changed by the *power* into a young man, since this would make the imposter, conveniently, old enough to rule the empire.

"We think, based on the amount of fresh poison in Trenara's room, she must have been planning to have Saldorian give the final dose to Jenhada that night. Fortunately, her plan fell apart. This was due to her lack of foresight and the vigilance of our agents.

"While Trenara and Joshan were gone, the prince's eecha returned to the Keep without a rider. This sparked considerable suspicion, and the animal was examined thoroughly. The eecha's saddle was covered in blood, and pieces of burned fabric were in her mane. Obviously, the animal ran away before the guider could destroy it.

"Men were sent to investigate immediately. They found pieces of burned bone and flesh scattered in a clearing on the High Cliffs. Miraculously, one piece of skin contained a fragment of the prince's tattoo." He sighed compellingly and pulled from the podium a small glass bottle filled with liquid and a suspended piece of flesh. "Forgive me. This is unfortunate, but necessary. This is the object we found at the sight," he said, handing the glass to the chancellor. Cries went out from the crowd and many sobbed.

"When we discovered this," Pravius's voice was pitched with an edge of repulsion,

"I went to the consort and shared this evidence with her, hoping to garner a confession about her part in this crime. Saldorian realized she had been betrayed, and her son had been murdered by Trenara. The consort finally revealed the entire plot and signed her confession. I went to the emperor with all of this evidence. In his wisdom, Jenhada had Saldorian confined to her chambers and issued a warrant for Trenara's arrest. He accused no one at that point, but wanted those involved held until we could sort this out.

"When Trenara and the stranger appeared at the Keep, she was aided by her long time friend, Haiden Bails, to avoid the arrest. Two agents saw Bails helping the guider and reported to this council. They reported there was a stranger with Trenara who looked much like the prince. Unfortunately, this confirmed our worst suspicions. The pieces began to fall into place.

"We sent out all the council guards to hunt down the guider, Bails, and the young man. A gate guard reported that Bails tried to enter Third Gate, and with quick thinking, had him followed to an Inn where they were later arrested. Unfortunately, Bails and the young man escaped the hold." Pravius looked up from the report and stared at Trenara briefly. For a quick moment, she could see a glint of satisfaction in the languid eyes, but he quickly covered his lapse and continued.

"Sadly, when we arrived at the home where the young man and Bails were hiding, Sergeant Bails resisted arrest and was killed by the council guards." A note of remorse made the words stick in his throat. "It is disappointing to lose a man like Haiden Bails, a brave and noble fighter, because of the deceit of this woman." His eyes actually misted for a moment and he sighed deeply. "With the council's permission, I would like to now introduce a witness."

The chancellor spoke to the other council members and then nodded to Pravius.

"Thank you, sir." Pravius nodded to one of his guards stationed at the top of the stairs. The guard saluted and opened the doors.

Through them, in chains and badly beaten, came Joshan. Vanderlinden was holding his arm roughly and looked as if he had been drugged, his eye glazed, his face stony. Joshan's appearance had been altered, his hair lighter and his bone structure changed. For a moment, Trenara didn't recognize him. She had to fight the spell that touched against her guider's sense leaving her perception foggy. With an effort, she saw him clearly and took in a startled breath.

Trenara felt the world dissolve beneath her. Her fingers itched for her *via*, but it lay broken. There was nothing more she could do. Her *power* was gone.

CHAPTER SEVENTEEN
RAISING THE VEIL

The Chancellor rose to his feet. "Who is this man?"

"This, sir, is the man the guider claims is the young prince. As you can see, he is not."

The chancellor looked at Trenara, his eyes full of doubt. "Guider, is this true?"

Trenara was numb and she barely heard the question, giving Pravius a precious chance to close the trap. "If further proof is needed, sir," he continued smoothly, "then I would ask his keeper." He motioned to Vanderlinden who didn't look up. "He can cast some light on these proceedings."

"Speak then," the chancellor demanded of Van.

"If you will allow me, sir, the giant has been through a terrible ordeal. I will discuss this later with the council. For the present, I would ask you allow me to question the witness, as I have a certain—rapport with him," he said, shooting a look at Trenara.

The Chancellor frowned. "This is very unusual, Pravius."

"Yes, sir, and I do apologize. If you will allow me, I believe this will expedite the truth, so we can end this matter."

The chancellor thought for a moment. "Very well, Pravius," he said at length sitting, "question the witness."

"Thank you, sir." He turned to Vanderlinden and made a slight gesture, which only Trenara caught. Van's face contorted painfully as Pravius began.

"Now, sailor, you came to me with information regarding one of the men you have had occasion to work with. Is this correct?"

Beads of sweat began to form on Van's brow as he resisted the enchantment. With a great effort, he withstood the onslaught and did not answer. Pravius made another gesture that twisted the captain's face with agony. Trenara looked around frantically and was amazed that the council would not stop this. But they were not seeing what she was seeing, their sight clouded by the blackest magic. She felt helpless and clenched her fists.

"Come now, man, you are among friends. Is it true you came to speak to me a few hours ago?"

"Yes," Van rasped through his teeth.

"Good," Pravius replied smoothly. "You told me this sailor—and correct me if I'm wrong—came to you with some wild story. Is that right?"

"Yes." Van was losing control.

"Then you told me this man had been hired by a starguider to impersonate the First Prince. Is that correct?"

Sweat began to soak the giant's tunic and his eye went wide. His brain burned, his ears pounded and rang. The councilor again assailed him with another wave of pain, and he nearly stumbled.

"Yes," he finally whispered.

"Stop it!" screamed Trenara. "You're killing him."

Pravius ignored her and smiled. "And isn't that the man standing there beside you now?"

Tears fell from the giant's eye as he closed it in defeat. "Yes," he said in anguish.

The councilor smiled. "Thank you, giant, you have been most helpful." He turned to the judges. "This is the case against Trenara. I believe, unless the accused has any further witnesses, we should get on with the sentence as the law prescribes. Last Defense is well ended."

Joshan had seemed dazed before, but Trenara thought she saw a light in the young eyes. She wasn't certain. The betrayal of Vanderlinden was a heavy blow and it clouded her vision as she turned back to the council.

"Trenara?" the chancellor said to her, but she was completely at a loss for words.

The guider wanted to scream up at them that it was all a lie, a trick. Couldn't they see that? But she knew of no way of saying it without sounding completely insane. Trenara had no proof, no evidence of the falsity of the reports, nothing she could say to discredit the immensity of the lie—the trap was simply too intricate to undo with words. It would take months to prove any of it false, if then, and she had no time.

Pravius and his master had planned this from the beginning. His master... the thought sent terror through her veins like a poison, and she became sick to her stomach. Sirdar was alive. Trenara realized only he could have orchestrated this deceit. Only he could have released this kind of power. Her world collapsed with the realization. In the end, all she could do was look up at the judges and numbly shake her head.

"It's not true... it's all a lie. That man *is* the prince, I swear to you. You've been deceived. This man is not Pravius." But her words fell on deaf ears and the council seemed not to have heard her at all.

The judges talked among themselves for a long time. The chancellor at length motioned Pravius to join them. They spoke together for some moments, and then Pravius took the podium once more. He looked down at her and could barely keep the mirth from his face.

"Trenara of Mathisma, your sentence is carried," he said sadly, as a murmur rippled through the crowd. "By the vote of the Council of Justice, by and through Jenhada Thoringale Kanaine, Emperor of the Eight Provinces and Keeper of Mathisma, your title and name are hereby expunged from the hearts of our citizens."

In her sorrow, as each word hammered against her disbelief, shattering her faith, a solitary comfort surrounded Trenara's mind, the voice of the goddess—*take heart.*

"Your rank is hereby forfeited."

Fear nothing and you will endure.

"You are to be stripped of all worldly possessions and taken to the High Cliffs, where you will be suspended from the stake until dead, the gods' own time to claim you back."

Have hope—trust—know your fate.

Pravius motioned to his guards who formally stepped from the ranks and stood on either side of the stunned guider. He took his seat with a swish of his robes and a barely covered look of exulted joy.

The Chancellor's face was lined with grief as he looked down at the starguider. "Take her robes." The council guards saluted him and placed their hands on Trenara.

A single note infused the air with sound—so incredibly high and piercingly elegant that all ears began to ache with its richness. A second note followed, higher and more compelling, sending people to their knees with disbelieving gasps. The music rang out with a fierce beauty. It held such compulsion that the only movements were Trenara spinning around to confront the source and Pravius bolting from his chair.

Joshan shone at the top of the stairs, encircled by a blinding white light; the yoke shattered at his feet and the chains melted away from his outstretched arms like so much wax. He appeared to be engulfed in a silver cloud that pulsated with brilliance. Propelled by a torrent of wind, his long black hair became fluid and danced as if suspended in water, as his eyes turned white with *power*. Those who had been close to him lay singed and groaning at his feet. Vanderlinden lay in a heap on the cold marble, some feet away, unconscious.

Joshan lifted his arms above his head and broke the remaining chains. Then, slowly, he looked at Pravius in fury. "I know you," Joshan's voice boomed through the hall while people crouched down and covered their ears. "What have you done?" Joshan's face became frightening, making everyone look away. But Pravius could not move. He stood before Joshan like a pillar of stone.

"Go to your knees, misguided fool—cur to the southern devil. Go to your knees and beg these people for forgiveness, before you lose your soul." Joshan's voice rumbled against the high ceilings as a beam of light escaped his hand and struck Pravius full in the chest. The councilor screamed and fell to his knees. "These people have a right to know who you are. Open your eyes," Joshan cried to the crowd. "You have put your trust in a lie. The man before you is not Pravius. Before you stands Balinar, Sirdar's captain." A cry went up from the crowd.

At the sound of his true name, the councilor began to change. His hair faded to white, strand by strand, until it was as pale as snow, rumpled and thick. Around his forehead, the familiar flesh began to peel away, followed by his eyes, nose, and mouth, melting into folds of ancient skin that ebbed under the unruly white mane. The eyes darkened to holes above his wrinkled cheeks, and he looked down at his changing hands in horror and then touched his chin. Balinar stood before them an ugly, stunted man, bent and twisted from seasons of wicked deeds and degradation.

Trenara was shocked. It had been over thirty seasons since she had seen Balinar; he looked nothing like the robust young starguider she used to know. Instead, he was old beyond his seasons, as frail as ash—a sick perversion of a man.

He stood slowly and gazed up at Joshan when the transformation was complete. He reached into his robe and pulled out the red crystal as Elite guards advanced on him. With a sweep of his hand, they crumbled where they stood, a red glow illuminating their last screaming agony as a deformed red fire slowly consumed them. They melted into the stone floor and the other guards retreated in terror.

Balinar looked at Joshan and turned the crystal toward him, but the prince's *shield* held, and the meeting of the two powers spit sparks in all directions. People scattered, stumbling before the flames.

The man who had been holding Thiels, jumped up at the first volley and the Elite lieutenant lost no time in disarming and killing the man with his own blade. Thiels whistled for his troops. They rushed to his side dodging running people, guards, and sparks. Jona, a bloody gash on his side, joined his commander, the body of his assailant sprawled on the marble slab where he had left him.

Thiels got the Elite organized and armed as quickly as he could, and they began to work together to get to the prince or his father. But the deadly *power* spilling fire everywhere, made it impossible to reach them. Helpless, they stood where they were, watching in horror as the battle raged.

Joshan lifted his hand against the deceiver's attack, and the fire fell back. Trenara gazed at Joshan in wonder. She had never seen the *power* wielded so masterfully.

"So, you have unmasked me," Balinar sneered. "Fool. Do you think you have defeated me? You have freed me, you contemptuous whelp." Slowly, the red power began to move the white back. Doubt began to creep into Joshan's mind, as Balinar's voice made its way into his certainty. Concentrating, he willed the *power* to stay, but it began to weaken. "You haven't the strength, son of a whore," Balinar said. "You are failing even now. You can't fight—not against me—not against him. It is useless. Give it up."

Trenara knew instantly what was happening. "Joshan! Don't listen. Shut him out. Remember your training!" With a sweep of his free hand, Balinar sent a bolt that would have killed Trenara, but she dived out of the way. She couldn't stop herself before hitting the heavy podium and crumpling to the floor beside it.

The diversion gave the prince a chance to push back the red power. Balinar whirled around and increased the pressure as a ghastly light came into his eyes. "Shall I tell you about your mother?" His voice was slow and soft. "Shall I tell you how she gave herself to me? How she came into my arms willingly, like the whore she is?"

Images invaded Joshan's young mind—visions of his mother and this monster. They were vivid, stomach retching, powerful, making the rage raise in him like a tidal wave, threatening his control. Pravius pushed his memories into the young mind, each one worse than the one before, each one crystal clear. Joshan couldn't shut them out. The mental portraits of what Balinar had done to Saldorian were overwhelming, and the white ray fell back. Joshan was beginning to weaken.

He had to do something. He needed Trenara, but the guider was helpless without Andelian. Joshan lifted his free hand to the broken pieces scattered before the benches and began a different kind of music: low, gentle, almost soothing, shaping the *power* into a fine thin series of waves that surrounded the shattered crystal. A gleaming light radiated from the crystal fragments as they moved with a tinkling roll toward one another. In a sudden burst of brilliant green fire, they merged. Andelian was whole again and lay with new fire in her.

But the exertion had cost him. The red flame leapt at him nearly unabated, and he caught it within inches of his face. A blinding headache crushed his skull and the room began to spin, as his sight got hazy. Joshan threw his head back in anguish. "Trenara!"

She shook off the daze and struggled to her hands and knees. Balinar lifted his hand to stop her, but with the agility of a youngster, Trenara rolled and the bolt missed her. She landed behind the podium. Then she saw Andelian sparkling on the marble in front of her. Joy washed through her as she stretched her arm out from behind the barrier and grabbed the crystal scepter before Balinar could attack again. She threw Andelian up and caught the sunlight coming through the window. The crystal scepter shone like a star in her hand. Her voice rose richly from her throat, and her music combined with Joshan's, the harmony perfectly blended, as she stepped out to confront Balinar.

A deep rumble shook the Keep and a shaft of light engulfed the guider, filling her with rapture. She threw back her head, drinking in the *power* until she was filled, and then she laughed just to hear the sound. Trenara lowered her gaze to Balinar, and the traitor's mirth melted away as he saw the raging storm to his side, her hair blowing everywhere, her gown a torrent of blue and her eyes piercing through the light. Joshan gained on the red power, moving it back several feet.

Trenara smiled in exultation, staring at the terrorized man. She changed the note, and the wave of resonance that came from the blue tempest merged with the green from Joshan. The lights swirled around one another, a brilliant ballet flowing like a twisting waterfall. When they finally fused completely, a sudden surge of radiance struck Balinar's *via* and fractured it into thousands of splinters. A scream echoed through the Keep, and Balinar was thrown back violently, hitting the marble and crumbling into a limp pile on the floor, unmoving.

The *power* faded at once as Joshan bowed his head and fell to his knees. Trenara took the stairs two at a time and rushed to his side, taking him into her arms as he fell. "Are you all right, child? Speak to me."

He touched her hand. "I'm all right, Trenara."

She helped him to his feet. With the aid of two of the Elite, she brought him down the stairs and set him on one of the councilor's benches. Trenara called for imaka, sending a guard to her room. She smiled at the prince. "You did it, lad."

"We did it, Trenara." Joshan looked down at Balinar who lay beaten at his feet. "That was close," he whispered, fighting back the exhaustion. "Too close." He looked at her and frowned. "We tried to get here sooner, but Balinar has some kind of power over Van. He didn't mean to do it, guider. I think Balinar..." But he couldn't continue as fatigue began to take him.

"Don't worry," Trenara said taking his hand. "We'll sort this out. I'm just glad you're all right."

"What... what's going on?" said a voice from behind them. They turned to see Jenhada lifting his head slowly, his face dazed.

"Father!" Joshan ran to him and took his hands. Jenhada was still pale, but his eyes had lost their vacant darkness.

"Joshan?" He touched the boy's face and looked puzzled. "What's happened to you? Have I been gone so long?" He rubbed his eyes. "I must have been dreaming."

"I'll explain it all later, father," Joshan assured him. "For now, I'm just grateful to see you well again."

"Have I been ill?" Jenhada asked as Trenara joined them.

"Yes, sire, dreadfully ill," she said.

"Trenara, old friend, it has been too long."

"Yes, your majesty. You must rest now."

Just then, a deep rolling thunder shook the Keep, and all three of them stood as Balinar stirred. He lifted himself to his knees and reached to the ceiling in one fluid motion as if pulled there by an invisible string. Before Trenara could take hold of Andelian or Joshan could call the *power*, Balinar threw back his head. "Sirdar, deliver me!" His body began to shimmer so brightly they covered their eyes against the radiance and he began to fade, his words echoing through the hall.

They held their ears as a booming drone answered, toppling benches, people, and drapes. In a wisp of crimson smoke that rose to the ceiling, Balinar was gone. In the stillness that followed, a heart-stopping laugh vibrated through the hall. "I will conquer in the end. I alone."

Trenara was stopped cold by the sound of that voice, a voice she had heard before, a voice that reached deep into her soul as it always had—a voice she loathed.

"You are a great healer—Starsight," The words swelled around them until they were everywhere at once. "Heal this."

A crackling blast flared from the smoke and pierced the emperor's heart like a knife. Jenhada screamed and fell, as a fountain of blood splashed on the cold marble floor. In a sudden burst of red, the smoke was gone, taking the echo of that horrible voice with it.

Jenhada lay in Joshan's arms, his life pouring out of his chest with each heartbeat. No matter what he did, Joshan could not call back the *power*. He screamed in frustration, trying with his bare hands, to staunch the flow of blood spilling life from his father.

"Father," Joshan sobbed. "I don't have the strength to help you. Please!"

The light in Jenhada's eyes began to fade. The lingering light of afternoon poured into the hall from the massive eastern windows and fell on the emperor for the last time.

"Be good to them, Joshan," Jenhada whispered, grasping his son's arm. "Don't forsake them…" and then he died.

"No!" Joshan shrieked and clung to the dead monarch as if his arms alone could give Jenhada back his life. Trenara sank to her knees and wept, as Joshan screamed over and over again.

CHAPTER EIGHTEEN
REQUIEM

Thiels and his crew were charging down a long echoing corridor after a group of Balinar's guards. The northerners, in their escape from the furious fire fight, had killed several people in the hall, cutting down innocent men and women in their panic. The Elite immediately took after the group, but not before Thiels put Jona in charge and ordered half of them to stay with the emperor. "Protect the emperor and the prince," he shouted as he ran from the hall after his guards.

After a long chase, the northerners hit a dead end as they rounded a corner. They turned to meet the furious Elite behind them, but the conflict was brief and final. To the man, the northerners lay dead on the floor.

Thiels turned around to see another group of ruffians running down the opposite way toward the hall. He called to his Elite and ran after them. The other group ducked out a veranda door into a garden courtyard surrounded by stone benches. There was only one way in or out of that courtyard and they were trapped in the middle, as the Elite poured through the doors after them. The group went back to back and lifted their blades.

"All right," Thiels called to them, gesturing his guards to hold back, "put your weapons down and your hands on your heads. This doesn't have to end this way. We really don't want to kill you."

"Well, that's good," called their leader, "because we really don't want to die." He was a dark handsome man who skillfully spun his sword and smiled at the lieutenant charmingly. "So, I have another idea. Why don't you put *your* weapons down? That would work better for us."

Furious, one of the Elite took a step toward the man, but Thiels stopped her with a look. "I've had about all I'm going to take. Surrender your weapons and we'll go easy on you."

The man shrugged. "Likewise." They both lifted their swords, and the two groups began to advance.

"What the hell are you doing?" The cry echoed from the veranda door. Both groups turned around to see Haiden standing with his hands on his hips, staring at them in disbelief. He was bloody and dirty, but otherwise whole. "You're both on the same side! Thiels, meet Sark DeMontaire from the Village, recruited by Joshan to fight the northerners. Sark, meet Connan Thiels of the Elite. Now come on, all of you. There's plenty of real fighting inside."

They eyed each other dubiously, but followed the sergeant into the Keep. It was an icy truce, but everyone behaved themselves.

*****

When Van regained consciousness, he groaned and looked up to squint at the sun that dazzled his eye from low eastern windows. He struggled to sit, feeling the sting in his arms and side. They were scorched, but his leather jerkin and tough hide had kept the flames from doing much damage. Many of the guards who had been hit by the blast didn't fare as well. Most were being taken off in litters.

"Good morning, captain," Trenara said from behind him, her joy at seeing Vanderlinden alive muted by her grief.

"Trenara!" He sprang up and took her in his arms, but seeing the sadness in the guider's eyes, his smile disappeared. "What's wrong?"

Trenara looked up at him and sighed deeply before turning around to gaze toward the prince and the figure in his arms. Joshan had not moved from the spot for over an hour. He sat on the stone floor holding his father, rocking softly and silently, as tears flowed down his cheeks. They were surrounded by a ragged line of Elite guards, standing stiffly at attention, many wounded, but refusing to leave.

Van's lip began to quiver as his legs buckled beneath him, and he fell to his knees. "No," he whispered as tears began to well in his eye. "No. No!" Memory and pain washed over his face as the demon's curse echoed behind his ears: *You will betray that which you love most, delivering it into the hands of your enemies.* "What have I done?"

Trenara put a gentle hand on his shoulder. "This was not your doing. You couldn't have stopped it. That you resisted at all is an amazing feat. I doubt any Assemblage could have withstood as well."

When Trenara told him what happened, Van bowed his head and shook it, weeping deeply. Trenara wrapped her arms around the massive shoulders as far as they would go.

Finally, when the tears stopped, he ran a hand through his matted hair. "Balinar," he growled. "It must have been him on the ship."

"Ship?"

Van looked up at the guider. "I'm afraid there's going to be much to explain on both sides, before the whole tale is known." He then turned a sad look to Joshan. "I should have seen this."

"There's no way you could have, Van. We can't predict the future; we can only feebly try to shape it. I have told you so before." She turned towards the figures. "My greatest concern is for Joshan. Sirdar will not destroy him as well. Not while I have breath." Her voice was not spiteful, only dour, and the conviction seemed to age her noticeably. "But there are other matters to attend to at present."

"Yes." Van pushed back the paralyzing grief as he had done too many times before. His face turned hard with the strain. "I need to find out about my troops and Sark. They'll need to be gathered to flush out the rest of the northerners. What happened to the council guard?"

Trenara's smile was tired. "When Balinar disappeared, they bolted out of here like a pack of rodents, but the Elite went after them. None will escape." She shook her head. "You should have seen the look in Thiels' eyes. I almost pity the poor bastards when he catches them."

Van nodded curtly. "This is going to be a long day, but if we don't move now, some of them will escape. What do you want done, Trenara? I'm at your disposal, along with my soldiers."

Trenara looked at the massive man and gave a wan smile.

"First, I would suggest you find what you've lost."

"What is that supposed to mean?"

"Your voice, man. You are beginning to sound almost civilized."

Van gaped at her a moment and then chuckled. "Aye, guider, you be right again. It's easy to do, when I'm with them I trust, eh?"

"Your secret has always been safe with me."

"Now, what do you want done?"

"Yes… done." Trenara sat at the top of the stairs and stared at Joshan. She wanted nothing more than to escape the responsibilities that faced her. How had this even happened? Sirdar alive and Balinar loose—tremors she couldn't still shot through her. She gritted her teeth against the sorrow. Decisions had to be made and quickly. "Balinar is gone; I wouldn't think he'll be back soon. But there are still many of his men about. You say you have soldiers?"

"Aye that I have, guider."

"Can they be relied upon to help us?"

"Help us? Guider, unless I miss my guess, they're probably in the Keep doing just that right now."

Trenara raised her brow. "Well, I guess there *are* some tales that need to be exchanged. I don't know how extensive the damage is to the guards, but I fear the worst. Any help will be welcome. I wonder how long this has been going on."

"Two seasons, roughly," Van replied slowly.

Trenara frowned. "Two—my gods!" she lowered her head. "Ethos, forgive me, but where the hell have I been? If you knew, why didn't you try to get word to us?"

"Try? For almost a season I tried to get to you. Jen first, but he was too far gone by then; they had him completely boxed in. Then Saldorian, but she was a prisoner long before the edict. In case you didn't know it, you were followed and watched every step of the way. There was always someone right on your tail. I couldn't get to you no matter how hard I tried and believe me, I did. Joshan, too, but he was being watched even closer. I knew if I got too near you'd both be in danger, so eventually I kept my distance, least wise until I could get up enough strength for a real attack."

"We will need to root out the rest of his men," said Trenara, "and either send them back to where they came, or for those who are not corrupted, incorporate them back into the guard. I'll wager that's few."

"I got just the crew. That is, if I can find them. If they followed orders, then the job may be more than half done already."

"I will leave it in your hands. In the meantime, you should find Thiels. He can tell you who are true and who not." A thought struck her. "Haiden," she said in sudden panic. "Balinar said he was dead. Did they…"

Van touched her hand to comfort her. "He was alive when we left, so don't worry. The man he was with I know pretty well, although Pravius didn't, seemingly. Wert may seem weak, but he's a skilled man in a fight. If anyone could protect Haiden, he could. That guard weren't no match for him. I'm certain Wert didn't go down without a fight. But I'll find him, guider, and see what's happening with the scoundrels."

"I don't think you'll need to worry about the northerners. They'll have no heart for battle once they hear of their change in fortunes."

The giant gave her a crooked smile. "Uh—those weren't exactly the scoundrels I was talking about." Trenara shot him a puzzled look. "Never mind. Right now I've got to find Haiden." Trenara took the captain's hands to help her stand.

Van turned to leave, but then looked back at Joshan. "Do what you can, guider."

As Van left, fatigue blurred Trenara's vision for a moment. She massaged her eyes and gripped Andelian for strength. She felt once more an old woman—bent, tired, and full of grief—and the day was just beginning. There would be much to do and many hours before she could rest. She wondered if she would ever truly rest again. Wrapping her robes around her to stay the chill of the early evening, she slowly descended the steps to Joshan, her more pressing problem.

The cold marble of the lower bench shot through her as she tentatively sat. Joshan continued to hold his dead father, his eyes vacant as he swayed. The blood that covered them both was dark and matted now, making them look like an open wound. The guider wanted nothing more than to take away the hurt.

Trenara caught sight of a group of Elite, headed by Jona, coming with a stretcher. She raised her hand and shook her head. They saluted and stood where they were. She carefully leaned toward the prince and lightly touched his arm. "Joshan, you need rest. There's nothing more you can do here."

With a sudden movement, Joshan stood, lifted his father in his arms, squeezed him gently to his chest once, and then advanced toward the guards. They saluted as he laid the emperor on the litter and kissed him on the forehead.

"Walk gently with him, Elite," he said, looking into his father's face and folding Jenhada's arms across his chest. "Prepare him now for his final voyage. It is fitting you do so."

Tears flowing, they lifted their burden. Joshan watched after them as they solemnly marched Jenhada from the Hall. "Sleep well, father," he whispered. He bowed his head and Trenara caught him before he could fall. The guider managed to get him to the floor and motioned more guards over, as the prince lay unconscious in her arms.

"Take him to his chambers and let him rest now," she said, looking down at Joshan.

"Aye, guider."

Trenara shot a look at the guard. "Haiden!"

"Shhh—you won't want to wake him."

"I'm delighted to see you, but a little surprised. Van had all but given you up for dead. Where the devil did you come from?"

Haiden lifted Joshan easily into his arms. "Vanderlinden told me where you were, and those that were here earlier told me what happened. I'm sorry I missed it, but it couldn't be helped. When I woke up at Wert's I wandered out, staggering like a drunken man from the blow to the back of my head. Good thing I got a tough skull. It was well after dawn when I finally reached the gate, and the fighting was pretty heavy then, so I joined in." He looked at Joshan. "Very sorry I wasn't here," he said slowly, an odd glint in his eyes. "It's a mighty thing, this *power*."

"Yes," Trenara replied simply.

"Well, I best be getting the lad to bed."

"He's no longer a lad, Haiden, despite how we may feel. He is emperor now."

Haiden gave her a half-crooked smile and nodded. "That he is." He left with his burden, followed by several of the Elite guard.

*****

The next three days were a nightmare. The crowds that had gathered for the launch of the emperor's barge clogged the harbor, the streets and the castle, creating additional problems the Elite and Trenara didn't need. But they couldn't deny the people their rights and left the funeral open to the public.

The ceremony had been long, formal, and difficult for Trenara. Despite the emperor's recent illness, the guider still loved him deeply and grief took her wholly when his funeral barge was finally lighted, his body consumed to the pyre and the ornate boat driven out to sea. But there was no time for her grief.

Skirmishes broke out in the Keep, when the last of Balinar's men were cornered. Vanderlinden, Thiels, Sark, and their crews fought bravely as the remainder of the rabble were routed, much to the guider's relief.

The prisoners were taken in droves to the mines in Tola. Trenara's guess hadn't been wrong; few were worth salvaging, being for the most part bandits and criminals from the north. There were more of Balinar's men than anyone expected, and they had infiltrated almost every echelon of the Imperium. All told, over four hundred northern men were counted. This number amazed Trenara, Van, and Sark, as they watched the caravan leave for the mines.

"How can there be so many?" Van asked, watching the last of the wagons disappear through the tunnel of First Gate.

"Balinar was a powerful guider once," Trenara answered. "Be grateful there were not more—there could have been, or worse." She scowled deeply.

"Well, if you ask me," Sark said, "I'm glad we're getting rid of the lot. It's scum like that gives us honest scoundrels a bad name."

"Your scoundrels are welcome any time. I wish you would reconsider my offer. Are you certain you won't stay?"

Sark looked after the wagons and pulled up a glove. "No, guider. I do appreciate the offer. My place is in the Village. We're always there should you need us. You have but to give the word."

Trenara took his hand and shook it warmly. "Then, I'll accept this for Joshan and all of us. Should you need us the reverse is true, if you won't take a position here."

"Maybe one day, but for now, since our good giant is staying with the prince, someone has to run the Village. I, personally, can't think of a better choice."

"You always were modest, Sark," Van said with a laugh. "You take care of that hide of yours. I'll be down from time to time to check up on you. Tell Molly if there's anything she needs, all she's got to do is ask."

"I'll do that, Van." Sark mounted his eecha, a gift from the guider, and wrapped his hands around the reins.

"And, Sark," Van added, "if you get any word on Wert, let me know. I want to let him know…" but his voice trailed off.

"I will," Sark replied, but his face was not hopeful. Wert had disappeared that day without a trace, although many had been sent to find him. Both Sark and the giant feared the worst, but neither of them would abandon the search. Sark tipped his hat to Trenara and bowed low. "Good day, my lady." He cried to his eecha and they went thundering down the road.

*****

That night, Trenara woke with a start as a commotion from the corridor echoed against her leaden eyes and pounding head. Her face was a mask of fatigue as she yawned. She had been up for three days and had finally fallen into bed in the small hours of the morning.

Shouts were muted through the wooden door as Trenara groggily sat up. An Elite guard burst through, with Ena following behind him frantically.

"I'm sorry, ma'am," Ena said. "I tried to stop him."

The guard ignored her and bowed his head to Trenara. "Begging your pardon, lady, but there's trouble. Lieutenant Thiels said to come and bring you."

"Will there be no end to this day?" Trenara grumbled as she threw a robe around her shoulders. Ena skirted the guard to help her with her slippers. "More fighting, swordsman?"

"No, ma'am, it's the prince, at his mother's chambers. That's all I know."

"Come on." Trenara strode quickly from the room with the guard stumbling after her.

Joshan had not said more than ten words in the last three days and stayed in his rooms. During the requiem, the only time the guider had seen him since the trial; he had been cold, silent, and severe. Trenara was anxious about his condition, but had done everything she could. The grief of Jenhada's death touched them all deeply, but it left Joshan hard. This frightened the guider who knew *detachment* could come at any time. With Joshan's abilities, it was difficult to gauge what might happen if it did.

As they approached the chambers, they could hear the argument, Joshan's voice and a woman's. Trenara and the guard rounded the corner and saw a small woman with her hands wringing the weave out of a kerchief, her face red with sorrow, looking pleadingly up at Joshan. She was Dottie, the consort's lady and up until recently, Joshan's nursery maid.

Trenara knew this confrontation was imminent and dreaded it. She just learned what Balinar had done to Saldorian, but thought the news would not have to be added to the prince's grief until later, when Trenara could think of what she would say. Joshan knew so little of such things, only having the experience of a child and not of a man. Still and all, Trenara thought dismally as she prepared herself to confront Joshan, he had to know.

"If you don't unlock that door, Dottie, I will break it down. Do you understand?" Joshan towered over the small maid, and his voice echoed down the corridor. Doors on both sides were cracked open, but closed quickly when Trenara shot a glance down the hall.

"I know, sire," Dottie replied in a whispered rasp, "and you'd be right doing it, too. But, my lady, she said she didn't want to see you. Forgive me." She buried her face in her hands. "I can't go against her orders, and I ought not to go against yours. What do I do?"

Trenara came over and put her arm around the nurse. "Do as your mistress asks."

Dottie lifted her head and looked at the guider gratefully. "Thank you, ma'am."

Joshan set his jaw and glared at his mentor. "Have you lost your senses?"

Trenara spun on him, lack of sleep making her quick to anger. "Don't speak to me of senses. I am not the one who has lost them. Don't you know what has happened here? Haven't you the decency to respect your mother's wishes in her grief?" Joshan looked at her as if she had slapped him. Trenara sat wearily on the couch outside the chambers. "I'm sorry, Joshan. I wanted to tell you, but not like this. The light of day would be better."

"I don't understand. I only wanted to see my mother." He looked at the guider with the same guileless eyes the guider had always associated with Joshan, the youth. It sent a pang of remorse through her at the prince's lost childhood. Could it have been merely days ago?

"I don't doubt it, and I will do my best to explain." She motioned Joshan to sit, feeling awkward. He took the seat across from the guider, watching her intently. Dottie appeared to be about to leave, but Trenara motioned to her. "Stay, Dottie, please. I may need you."

"As you wish, lady."

"Son," Trenara began slowly, "your mother has been badly—abused. She almost died. Do you understand what all that means?"

"I know *exactly* what that means." There was a bitter edge to his voice.

"You know?"

"Balinar's thoughts were extremely vivid."

Trenara looked at Joshan a long time, trying to fathom how deeply Balinar had affected him, for the first time realizing how horrible it must have been for that innocent mind to be forced to see those images. She forcibly unknotted her hands. "Lesser women, after such an ordeal, would have found it difficult to look at any man. Your mother is strong. I think she would have taken this in her stride and recovered quickly. There is something else you may not know."

"What?" Joshan asked when Trenara hesitated.

She turned to Dottie. "Tell him."

Tears filled the servant's eyes and her lip began to tremble. "Oh, Mistress Trenara, please. I couldn't tell him… I just can't."

"Please, Dottie. You were there. You need to tell him."

She nodded silently and wiped her eyes. "I was there, sire." She said it like a confession. "He had locked me in my room and I heard it all." She started to weep, but controlled the tears by biting her lip.

"I wanted to go to her and help her, but I couldn't. I pounded and pounded on that door, until my hands were black with bruises." Dottie absently lifted her hands to look at them, as if they had betrayed her. "I screamed at him to take me—to spare my lady. He only laughed at me. I could hear his voice and the hideous things he said to her—I've never heard such foul language or such loathsome words. She didn't let out a sound, not even when he hit her. She wouldn't give him the satisfaction. Her silence seemed to enrage him, so that he hit her again and again. How she stood it, I don't know. I only know it was the bravest thing I've ever known. And then he took her and…" She stopped and looked at the guider, her hand over her mouth. "Forgive me, ma'am, I can't tell him that part."

"It's all right, Dottie. What happened after?"

"After…" She faltered, the memory painful. "It was quiet for a time and I was afraid he may have killed her, but then he said something I couldn't hear." Dottie looked up at Joshan as if accusing him. "It was about you, sire. I heard him say your name twice, clear as day. Then she screamed—after all his abuse it was the words that made her scream, like he had taken the heart right out of her. I'll never forget that sound." She began to sob.

"Go back to bed, Dottie," the guider said, helping her to stand. "I am so sorry—I wish I could have spared you this." Dottie nodded and lumbered off to her chamber.

Joshan rose and went to the open window at the end of the corridor. The prince's face was difficult to read—very stern, very still, very quiet. It unsettled the guider as nothing else had in the last three days. She joined him at the window and wondered what was going on inside this unfortunate child. She had expected pain, grief, even confusion. But Joshan simply stared at the black pre-dawn sky, his feelings and thoughts his own. Trenara watched in horror as every drop of youth drained from Joshan's face, leaving it pale and bleak. She quietly mourned the child.

"When Dottie was finally allowed to go to the consort," Trenara continued, feeling that if she didn't, she would break down, "the lady was unconscious and barely breathing. The maid sent immediately for the healers. They did what they could to mend her broken body, but could do nothing more. The spirit in her had snapped, Joshan. She breathes, her heart beats and blood runs through her veins, but there is no light in her eyes. She lies there, as if reality is too harsh to bear.

"Dottie came to me earlier tonight and asked me to go to the consort. She let Saldorian know that you were safe, thinking Balinar must have told her you were dead, but her reaction was… well, unexpected. The consort said that she didn't want to see you. It is the last thing she has said since that night.

"When I went to her, your mother lay in her bed, white and small, like a young child. I spoke with her at length and gave her herbs, but nothing could get through that blank stare. Even the news of your father's death didn't change that blank expression. The *power* was useless and she was oblivious to everything I did to help her." The guider felt she was rambling, for Joshan showed no sign he heard her.

Trenara didn't tell him the rest—she didn't tell him of the images that came flooding into her mind the moment she had taken Saldorian's hand, didn't tell him of the awful lies that Sirdar had used to poison the consort's mind. She thought Balinar had put them there for the guider's benefit. Something about being lost in the forests… something that had happened ten long seasons ago. Trenara had no idea what the visions meant, but wasn't going to add them to Joshan's grief. She would wait until his mind was stronger—until she had the courage to speak.

"I gave her a draught of imaka and it seemed to alleviate some of her pain. She slept, at any rate." Trenara stared into the night, feeling quite hollow. "I don't know what further evil Balinar has woven, but I swear he will pay for this degradation."

"That will be in another's hands," Joshan responded so quietly Trenara hardly caught the words. He turned and held the guider's eyes a long time, as though reading her thoughts. His eyes became hard for a moment and then confused, but soon his face softened. "Go back to bed, guider. You are exhausted. You need rest."

"I think it best if I stay with you tonight," she replied feebly.

"That won't be necessary." Joshan looked back at the stars. "There's so much I want to think about. I need to be alone for a while."

"But, lad, you are…"

"I assure you, I'm all right. If it will ease your mind, I will have Haiden stay with me. I've already sent for him."

Trenara's concern deepened, but she knew the boy was right; she did need rest. Even now, her eyes were heavy with fatigue and keeping them open took some effort. "Very well. I will look in on you later, if you are certain."

"Don't be troubled, Trenara. You see," Joshan said without taking his eyes away from the night sky, "everything you've told me, I've seen before. The *visions* are forcing me toward—something."

"You've seen these things?"

"Yes." He glanced at her. "Even the parts you withheld."

"I have withheld nothing from you."

"You said my mother didn't want to see me. In fact, what she actually said was, she wished I was dead and never wanted to see me again."

Trenara gaped at him. "You saw this?" Joshan nodded silently. "Perhaps you're right. It seems your *vision* is getting stronger." She wrapped the robes around her shoulders. "Good night, then. Call me at need."

Before she could step away, Joshan suddenly took Trenara into his arms and laid her head against his chest. To her surprise, the soothing warmth of his embrace melted away her fear, her anger, and her doubt. As she listened to the distant beat of his heart and closed her eyes, an overwhelming wave of sorrow surged through her. With a sigh of relief, Trenara finally succumbed to the sobs that had been teetering on the edge of her emotions for days. Joshan rested his head against the soft gray hair and let her cry.

The light from Ethos pouring through the window threw their shadows against the night.

CHAPTER NINETEEN
THE REGENT

"What is this?" Trenara had just finished a late breakfast and was reading a book on Imperium law, when Ena entered her bed chamber and handed her a parchment.

"I'm sorry, lady, but the prince's guard said to deliver that personally, early this morning. I would have given it to you sooner, but my instructions were not to wake you." She bowed her head so she didn't have to look at the angry face of her mistress.

The now crumpled parchment had been clear. With seals affixed and signatures of all twenty-three members of the Councils of Trade and Justice, Joshan had officially appointed Trenara to the post of Emperor's Regent. She had been empowered with all the authority and duties of the emperor for an indefinite period.

"But what of the councilors?" she raged to herself, but Ena misunderstood.

"That's another thing, lady. They are waiting for you."

"What? Where?"

"Uh—in the corridor, ma'am."

"All twenty-three of them?"

"Yes, ma'am—and they said it was most urgent."

"Do they expect to meet in my bed chamber?"

"I don't know, ma'am. Shall I ask them?"

"Is that all?"

"Uh, well, no… no, ma'am. Captain Vanderlinden wishes an audience, and some others are waiting with business as well. Forgive me, lady."

"Oh, hell." Trenara picked up her cup and calmed her anger. "Send them all away. We'll see about this regent business." She sipped her tea as the girl bowed to leave. "On second thought, send Vanderlinden in and tell the rest I'll meet them in the east hall after the noon meal."

"Yes, lady." Ena gave her a brief curtsy and bolted from the room.

"Damn nuisance," the guider growled, slamming her book shut.

Vanderlinden didn't improve her mood any. He took off his hat, bowed low with a flourish, and then got to one knee before her, laughing hysterically. The giant looked much better than the night before. He was washed, his beard and hair were trimmed, and, except for the new black eye patch and multiple bruises, he looked like his old self again. Trenara had almost forgotten what a handsome man he was.

"Good morning, your Excellency," he said with a flamboyant sweep of his arm.

"Spare me!"

Vanderlinden sat down and helped himself to tea as Ena put a plate of toasted knoshkin in front of him and then left them alone.

"I wish I could have seen your face, but that girl of yours wouldn't let me in." He chuckled. "Emperor's Regent. It's got a nice ring to it, don't you think?"

Trenara narrowed her eyes. "Don't add salt. How would you like to find yourself vice-regent?"

"Now, don't get nasty. I'm only having some fun. No harm intended." He lit his pipe.

"How long have you known?"

"For hours now. There're notices all over the province. They went up just after dawn."

"I'm going to skin that boy alive," Trenara said folding her arms. "Regent, indeed."

"You shouldn't take on so, guider. It was the only thing he could do under the circumstances."

"What's that supposed to mean?"

"Well, think about it. The lad's mother isn't in any condition to run the provinces. The lad himself hasn't any training for it, being in actual fact only ten seasons, remember. You're the ideal choice, all things considered. You know more about running the Keep than anyone else I know, and the Councilors are a bunch of bumbling clowns when it comes to making a quick decision. It'd take them days just to decide who's going to stand watch, if it weren't for the Elite." He puffed his pipe. "Pretty smart appointing you, I'd say. The boy knows his business."

Trenara didn't reply immediately, trying to find fault in his logic. "Well, perhaps you're right. At any rate, it's done now. I don't suppose there's much I can do about it. But, if you think me jesting when I say you'll be vice-regent, careful you don't laugh too quickly."

"Can't be done," Van said, pulling his pipe from his mouth.

"You seem to forget, I have been empowered to do just that."

Van shrugged. "Still and all—Your Most Highness—can't be done. That's one of the reasons I'm here." He pulled a parchment from his jerkin. "Here, look at this."

She scanned the page and lifted a white eyebrow. "The boy *has* been busy," she said at length, handing the paper back.

"Aye, but I think I'm a bit more appreciative of my appointment."

Trenara looked at the man proudly. "Grand Admiral Vanderlinden. Now, *that* has a nice ring."

"Aye, that it does."

"So this must account for your almost presentability."

"If you're talking about my being cleaned up, that wasn't my idea. He says if I'm to be in charge of *his* fleet, that I should look the part."

"I quite agree, my dear admiral. Perhaps some of my training has rubbed off on the lad after all. I can only hope it continues, if the results are so delightful. You look absolutely charming."

"All right, you can stow the humor," Van replied dryly.

The guider couldn't suppress a smile. "I can hardly wait to see you in the dress uniform."

"There's no way I'm going to wear that poor excuse for an upside down chandelier."

"But, my good friend, you have to. That's the custom."

"Custom or no, there's no way. And that's just what I told his highness myself."

Sobering, Trenara offered Van more tea, which he accepted with a nod. "You've seen him, then?"

"Aye, early this morning."

"How was he?"

"Well enough, I suppose," he replied, pulling the pipe from his mouth and toying with it. "But there wasn't any humor there. He was gloomy and withdrawn. I guess them that goes through hardship to come of age, aren't likely to be cheery after."

"I suppose you're right. I'll look in on him later."

Ena came in to restock their tea and toast as Van repacked his pipe. While waiting for Ena to finish, Trenara found herself unconsciously studying the jagged scar that ran from Van's eye patch to his beard and the deep engraved creases along his cheeks. It was the haunted look in his one good eye that betrayed the depth of his grief.

It painted his face with a buried sorrow that only the guider could see; in thirty seasons of familiarity, she had explored that face more than her own. Something had aged Van more than the two seasons of his exile. She knew the loss of Jenhada had been hard on him, harder than he could express to anyone else; but this was something different—a ghost she couldn't see—and it bothered her. The guider wondered if her own face held the same shadows.

When Ena left, she looked down at her tea cup and wrapped her hands around it. "Something is on your mind."

Van looked back at her and raised a bushy brow. "Aye. I need to tell you a few things before you meet with the councils this afternoon."

"Go on."

"It's the fleet mostly." He sucked several times on the pipe until a billowing haze of smoke circled his head like thunder clouds. "I went down there this morning to see what kind of shape it was in. I'd expected it to be bad—it was heading that way two seasons back, but I wasn't prepared for the fact of it. Seems some of Balinar's men got off with a couple of our ships the other night. My guess is they took those that were least damaged. The rest of the ships aren't seaworthy. Some of them we're just going to have to scrap. That bastard planned it well. There's not a ship at harbor that doesn't need some repair, and not one of them would I trust for a long voyage." He stood and crossed to the balcony, the gray smoke trailing behind him as he puffed angrily. "I'd hate to tell you what could happen if we were attacked by sea right now. We'd be holed up here like rodents."

Trenara joined him at the railing. "What needs to be done to get them ready for a battle?"

"You expecting one?"

"I don't know. But your news brings to mind past history. Remember what happened just before the siege?"

"Aye, I'm thinking along those same lines. It seems treachery always foretells doom."

"Not doom—the provinces have always landed feet down."

"Aye, it's always survived *his* attacks, but at what cost?" He stoked his pipe a few moments in silence.

"There's something brewing," the giant continued. "I only wonder what devilry he's hatched up now."

"I wouldn't even begin to second guess Sirdar. He came close to defeating us before. I don't think his plans include being beaten a second time. He'll learn from his mistakes, unfortunately." She couldn't keep the contempt out of her voice as she watched the sparkling ocean. "Joshan seems to be the key to this new madness and that's what concerns me. Sirdar obviously wants him, but why? And why wait until now to spring his trap through Balinar? Joshan could have been his months ago, when we were unaware of his presence. He took Jenhada easily enough. Why not the boy?"

"My guess is Sirdar was waiting for him to come to *power*. Maybe that sneaking bastard knows something we don't. It wouldn't be the first time."

"All these riddles," Trenara said irritably. "We won't answer them by guessing. I think we need a meeting to compare notes of all the people who had contact with Balinar. I'll set up something later today." She turned to Van. "But I'm getting off track. You were talking about the ships."

"You see that brigantine?" He pointed to the far end of the bay. "She's the closest to being ready, but she'll take a couple of weeks just to re-rig. She's well built and sound, as far as it goes. Her name's *Morning Star*. Should be as good as new in a fortnight, if I can get enough builders."

"Take whatever you need. I will sign all the necessary papers, but it is imperative you get her on her legs," the guider said solemnly. "How long for the others?"

Van shrugged. "Half a season for the ones that can be salvaged. That's if we work around the dial. I got to have builders, sail makers, and sailors."

"We will get you as many people as you need. I'll see that messengers are sent out today. The rest I leave to you." After looking at the sundial on the balcony, she went back into her chambers.

"It's nearing noontide. I need to get ready to meet with the councils and I'd like to check on Joshan before that." She put on her formal mantel.

"Yeah," Van snorted. "Good luck with that."

"Meaning?" Trenara asked, tying her Assemblage sash in place.

"You'll see." Van smiled. "I got things to do. G'Day, Madame Regent." He bowed fluidly and left the room.

"Humph."

Trenara finished getting dressed, tenderly put Andelian in her sash, and called for her aide. The girl came in quickly and curtsied.

"Find the council leads and tell them we will meet within the hour."

"Yes, lady."

"And Ena, you can have the afternoon off. I shouldn't need you."

"Yes, ma'am," she answer brightly. "Thank you, ma'am." She bowed quickly and left the room.

Trenara smiled to herself. In all likelihood, she would need Ena that afternoon. *Maybe I'm getting soft-hearted,* the guider thought. After all, the girl needed rest. She had been up with the guider most of the night and probably rose at dawn, as well. Trenara put her robes in order and went to check on Joshan.

The guider was waylaid several times by servants, guards and various other Keep officials with questions, problems, and comments for the new regent. She dispatched them quickly, but politely, saying she would see them in the east hall. She had learned a great deal during that walk, however.

There had been even more treachery during Balinar's reign. Pravius—the real Pravius—had been found dead along with his wife and three children in their rooms at the Keep, butchered brutally by Balinar's men. More good people had either been killed or disappeared, and the weak and dimwitted had been sent in to replace them.

Trenara was beginning to feel rather dimwitted herself. She should have kept her eyes more on the Keep and less on Joshan and her books. Thinking the evil in Badain destroyed, she hadn't looked for more disaster and had gotten lax in her duty to Assemblage as their ears and eyes in the Keep. However, the damage was done, and all she could see was a long and harsh road to repair it.

When she finally arrived at Joshan's chambers, her mood was brooding and touchy, so seeing four stout Elite guards barricading the door didn't do much to improve it. When she advanced to enter, the guards saluted respectfully, but did not budge from the door.

"Gentlemen," she said gruffly, "I have business with the emperor. If you would be so kind."

One of the guards stepped forward and motioned to the bench nervously. "Pardon me, madam regent, but if you will take a seat, I will inquire within."

"Guardsman," Trenara started nastily, but put a damper on her anger and merely snorted. "Be quick about it. I haven't all day to idle here."

"Yes, ma'am." The guard disappeared through the door. He returned after a moment and took his station back at the entrance. "Marshall Bails will be with you shortly, ma'am."

Trenara gave a curt nod and sat on the bench. Marshall Bails? Well, it was no great surprise. Haiden certainly deserved it. But the guider's mood was worsening. She was unused to cooling her heels in waiting, even for the emperor.

Haiden came out presently and greeted the guider with a warm smile. The multi-colored braids at his shoulder and the deep blue uniform lent him an air of nobility. She was quite impressed. "Good morning, guider. I'm truly sorry for the delay, but I was in the midst of something and couldn't come at once."

"Never mind that. I had hoped to see Joshan before I went to speak with the councils." She sounded a bit harsher than she intended, but she was irked Haiden was greeting her in the corridor like some common servant. "Besides, I'd like to give that young pup a piece of my mind about this regent business," she added lightly.

Haiden smiled. "Aye, he said you'd say that. But the lad—I mean his highness, is indisposed at the moment. He says he doesn't want to see anyone. I'm sorry, guider."

Trenara sighed deeply, surrendering to the fact that Joshan's privacy was now his own. She had to accept the fact that the "boy" was no longer a boy, but a man and the emperor. It was going to be a long time before the guider would get used to that. There was so much she wanted to ask Joshan. Trenara desperately needed answers. She wished they were well on their way to Mathisma, so more knowledgeable minds than hers could ponder the questions.

"What is he doing in there?"

Haiden shrugged. "My guess is he's reading."

Trenara blinked. "Reading?"

"Aye. He ordered up near the entire library a few hours ago."

"Don't you know?"

"Not for a certainty. I've only seen him three times this morning. Once at dawn, when he gave me my instructions, once when Vanderlinden came in, and then when we brought up the books and scrolls."

"This seems an odd time to read."

"Aye, I agree. But when I asked him why, he just said, to learn. That was the lot of it. I haven't heard another word out of him."

"I imagine I have a hall full of people waiting for me and I'm late as it is. Tell him it's urgent I speak with him. Plans have to be made, and we need to start preparing for a trip to Mathisma. Tell him that."

"Aye, that I will. Oh and there's one more thing, I near forgot. He says to tell you that he'd call at need—said you'd understand."

Trenara curled her lip. "Well enough." She placed her hands in her sleeves and stalked away scowling.

The guider hadn't been wrong about the amount of people in the east hall. It took her the rest of that day and a good part of the next two weeks just to sort out what problems existed and how to solve them. She was well versed on the running of the provinces, having been closeted with Jenhada countless times over the seasons to discuss the running of the empire. However, she was not good with individuals, being stern and impatient with people's shortcomings. It was difficult at first, and she spent most of her time in those first weeks just smoothing over hurt feelings and raging disagreements. However, after the initial shock was over, she began to enjoy her new role as emperor's regent.

The Elite were badly affected by Balinar's meddling. It was the most powerful group, closest to the emperor and therefore vulnerable to the *emperor's* orders, which were Balinar's at the time. The young and inexperienced were put at the top and easily controlled. The older, more experienced of the Elite were demoted, discharged, or imprisoned. A score of Elite, who had no family ties, had either disappeared or died mysteriously. Thiels hadn't known it at the time, but his own death was planned for the afternoon of Last Defense.

Trenara passed on the lesser duties to subordinates she could trust and took on the job of revamping the Elite. Their first order was to start recruiting and training an imperial army. This was a difficult order for Trenara to give. She did not want to admit they would need one, but knew it was necessary. The thought of yet another war was bitter to her.

She appointed Thiels Commander of the Elite, much to the lieutenant's delight, although he staunchly denied he could handle it. "Excuse me, lady," he said to Trenara the morning of his appointment, "but I think there's been a mistake. This paper says I'm to be Commander of the Elite."

"So?" Trenara had said sharply, looking at and signing a mountain of parchments.

"Well, ma'am, I was just thinking there are those who would be much better for the job."

"Really?" Trenara commented impatiently, having a lot to do yet that morning. "Name one."

"Well, ma'am, there's—no, he's dead. But Hoskins, now—no, his wife's about to have her baby…" He paused, fumbling for others, but the guider had interrupted.

"You see?" she said, going back to her papers. "But if you don't want the job, then I'll just find someone who does."

"Now, I didn't say I didn't want the job… it's just…"

"I know, Thiels, but I haven't time for your modesty this morning. I need someone I can trust and I know I can trust you. It's as simple as that. From the reports I've received, not to mention your contribution to my Last Defense, you were one of the few who stayed true during Balinar's control and kept your head—you and your people. You have no idea how helpful the reports were to the investigation. But give me your answer now. I haven't all day to sit here and argue with you!"

Thiels accepted the role and attacked it wholeheartedly. From the first day, a new esprit de Corps began to spread through the Elite and rapidly to the rest of the Keep. The moral and physical darkness of the place began to dissipate, and Trenara was delighted with her choice.

But many anxieties were growing in the guider's mind as the days passed. She had discovered almost at once that Balinar had effectively undermined the communication systems to the other provinces. Little news had come out of the other countries in the last two months. What little news that made it through was greatly embellished, or for the most part false. The regent had sent a score of messengers to find out what was taking place in the provinces. When the reports started coming in, they were not encouraging.

The main mine shaft in Tola had mysteriously collapsed one day, killing hundreds of workers. Since mining was Tola's main source of income, it was a shattering blow. There had been a massive infestation of insects in the agricultural province of Palimar; a civil uprising had broken out along the coast of Gorka, when a decree came down from Thrain (authored by Balinar, it was later found) ordering three-quarters of the profits from their fish trade to be sent to the Keep as taxes. There had been much blood spilled.

Trenara had sent envoy after envoy out to the troubled areas to bring some order to the chaos. Some succeeded; some did not. Reports from all the provinces had come in, except one. There was no word from Badain. Every messenger the guider sent south did not return. At the insistence of the Council of Trade, she finally sent a company of soldiers. When they also did not return and no word was forthcoming, she sent no more. Instead, she ordered the Elite to increase their recruitment efforts and to fortify the other provinces.

The regent was not the only one who sent envoys. Two weeks after Trenara's appointment, Vanderlinden was loading a wagon with lumber for the rebuilding. Sark rode up and dismounted.

"Sark, you old devil," the giant exclaimed, taking his hand. "How you been?"

"Well, admiral. I almost didn't recognize you. You look wonderful."

"How's the Village?"

"The same as ever." Sark grabbed the end of a piece of timber and helped Van load it into a wagon. "Molly says to tell you that if you don't come down to see her soon she'll pine away into nothing."

Van laughed. "I somehow doubt that. What brings you all the way up here?"

"I was summoned," Sark replied arrogantly.

"Summoned? What would Trenara want with the likes of you, now?"

"Not by the good guider, Van. I was summoned by his majesty, the emperor."

Van raised a brow. "Joshan? I haven't even seen the lad in two weeks. Do you know what about?"

Sark adjusted the straps on his eecha. "Not entirely. All the dispatch said was he wanted to discuss a trip north with me and needed a group of tough, seasoned recruits."

"North? I wonder what he wants up there?"

"I wouldn't know, my friend." Sark threw his leg over his eecha and wrapped his hands around the reins. "And I won't find out if I don't get to it. I'm late as it is."

"Goodbye, Sark. If I don't see you before you leave, good luck."

Sark shook his hand and sprinted off to the Keep.

The days passed quickly and Trenara was constantly embroiled in the problems of the Keep and the provinces. Things were going quite well, but still her anxiety grew—not for the empire but for Joshan.

The guider had received little communication from the boy, since she became regent. She had stopped by to check on him, but was always politely told to go away. Late at night, the guider would often find herself wandering by Joshan's quarters to see if she could pick up any news. When Trenara thought no one was looking, she would stand on her balcony and stretch to see if she could catch a glimpse of him on his. The guider would haunt the stables where Whirl was kept, or the training yard where Joshan used to spend so much of his time. All these places were distinctly void of his presence. Trenara missed him terribly. She had only Haiden's assurances that the emperor was well, but this assurance did not cure the gnawing concern she lay awake with at night.

The guider had received a brief note one night requesting she send him all the scrolls she had on the *power*, Assemblage, the history of the empire, along with any information or dispatches she might have regarding the stationing of each of the active guiders. This particular request was unusual, but she complied. The last line in the note had bothered her for some reason. *No matter how trivial or mundane you think the materials, it is imperative I have it all.* She had grudgingly given the guard who came for the materials all the references she could find in her library and all the dispatches she had received from Mathisma, with the strictest oath they would be returned as soon as the emperor had finished with them.

The second communication came when Haiden entered her study one day with a bolt of cloth over his shoulder.

"What have you there, Haiden?" Trenara asked as the marshall set the cloth on a large table.

"His majesty said you might like to see this." He untied the leather thongs as Trenara joined him at the table. Lifting the bolt to the ground he started to unfurl it. "Here, grab an end and we'll see together what the lad's been up to. I haven't seen it myself."

They unrolled the banner and laid it on the table. On a field of brilliant blue, lay a golden snake with red jeweled eyes. The serpent glittered in the dappled sunlight from the balcony, its gilded scales dazzling with regal beauty. It was coiled, but not to strike, with its head held high—the royal banner of Joshan Jenhada Thoringale.

Haiden whistled as Trenara ran her fingers over the serpent gingerly. "It's beautiful," she whispered.

"That's a fact, guider," Haiden replied, shaking his head.

"Why a serpent, I wonder?"

"Now, that I do know. He said the snake was the—now, how did he put it—ah, the survivor, that's it. He says the serpent was here before us and would be here when we're gone, and that as long as the serpent was here, the world would be safe." He looked at his hands ruefully. "'Course, his words were a lot prettier than mine. In fact, he's said lots of pretty things lately—well, not pretty exactly, but the kind of words that go to your heart, if you take my meaning."

Trenara looked down at the banner thoughtfully. "I'm afraid I wouldn't know."

Haiden blushed and cleared his throat. "Well, as for that, I'm truly sorry the lad won't see you." He shook his head as he started to roll up the banner. "I just plain can't figure him out sometimes. Meaning no disrespect, mind you," he added quickly.

Trenara smiled. "No one could ever accuse you of that, Haiden. I know you serve him well, whatever else. I'm glad you're with him."

Haiden lifted the bolt to his shoulder. "Well, I don't know about that, guider. If the truth were known, I'd just as soon you were with him." The old guard adjusted the load and looked at his feet. "He's strange, sometimes, and I don't know how to take it. His face gets harsh and hard and cold—always sets my knees to quaking, I can tell you—and he'll get this look in his eyes, like he's far, far away and no one can reach him. I mean, what do you do?" He looked up at Trenara and the guider smiled.

"You watch, you wait—and you love him."

"Aye, I guess so." He headed for the door. "Well, I best be getting this banner topside. The emperor said he'd have my head if it weren't flying by noon. 'Day, guider."

The only other communication of any kind was a Royal Order postponing the coronation of the emperor indefinitely. This haunted Trenara as well.

One night, well into high season and close to two months after Joshan's self-imposed exile, Vanderlinden came to visit the guider in her study. Trenara had just received several reports that the envoys were doing quite well and the empire, though still chaotic in parts and silent in the south, was slowly coming back to itself again. This relieved some of the guider's burdens and she was feeling somewhat elated that night, so when Vanderlinden came in with a tray of whillen liquor, she was delighted.

"Well met, my large friend."

"Especially those that bring gifts, eh?" Van laughed and poured them each a stout portion of the spirits.

"Any news, admiral?" Trenara asked, after she had fully savored the warming liquid.

"Did you hear Sark was back?"

Trenara looked at him sharply. "No. When?"

"Few hours ago, though I didn't see him when he came to the castle. He went straight to the emperor and was with him a long time. I caught him when he was coming down."

"And?"

Van shrugged. "And nothing. Sark was as closed mouthed as I ever seen anyone. Not a clue as to what he was looking for north or what he found. But I didn't press him. He looked as if he'd been on the road for weeks and was exhausted. He did say he lost a man to the cold, but that was about it. It must have been a bitter journey."

"All journeys north are bitter," Trenara responded gravely.

Van looked up at her sharply and his eyes flashed with a sudden hatred. "Who knows that better than I?" But his eye dulled and he sank his head.

Trenara regarded him sadly and touched his arm. "I'm sorry, Van. I had almost forgotten."

The giant drew a deep breath. "But I haven't; those scars run deep and make me quick to anger at a friend who deserves better. Forgive me, Trenara. Those words weren't meant for you."

"I know." The guider shook her head thoughtfully. "I only wonder why Joshan would risk an envoy to such a place."

"I wish I knew."

The sea sparkled with white fire through the balustrade as they looked. "Well," Trenara said at length, tipping the glass to the giant. "No use spoiling this fine whillen with gloom and mystery." She warmed the glass between her hands and stared out at the night. "How goes the rebuilding?"

"Better than expected. *Morning Star's* back to her old self again and we got three others that'll be shipshape in a couple of days. There's also one of the clippers ready for the sea. So, all told, we're doing half again as good as I thought we would."

"That's great news. You really are a marvel, Van."

"Not half the marvel you are. I heard about the success the envoys are having. You did a good thing there, that's for certain."

"I'm pleased with the results, but I'm afraid I can't take the credit. All I did was clean out the deadwood at the top and replace them with those that were there before, or should have been."

"Still and all, for a woman who doesn't like dealing with individuals, you sure know how to pick them."

"Perhaps," Trenara replied, warmed by the compliment.

They sat in silence for a time, enjoying the drink and each other's company, the cool evening breeze coming in off the sea. They finally made a silent toast and drained their glasses.

"You up for a ride, guider?" Van asked, stretching as he rose.

"Tonight?"

"Aye," Van answered simply.

"I'd love to, but I still have so much to do before I turn in. To be honest, I shouldn't have even stopped for this drink."

"I understand, but I have something to show you." He threw a cloak around his massive shoulders.

"Well now you've piqued my interest. What is it?"

"You'll see," Van said without elaborating.

Trenara opened her mouth to excuse herself, but something in the giant's eyes changed her mind. "All right," she said taking a heavy cloak Vanderlinden offered her. "Actually, I think a ride would do me good. I haven't seen Gliding in weeks. I'll bet he's fit to be tied."

"He's waiting outside."

Trenara raised an eyebrow and gave him a sidelong look. "You were so certain I'd come with you?"

Van smiled smugly and nodded. "Aye."

Gliding was so overjoyed to see his mistress he reared happily and knocked over the poor stable boy holding him. Trenara patted his neck tenderly, whispered in Mathismian, and easily mounted him.

Van was already on the back of a huge red-brown eecha by the name of Spietus, which meant in Tolan, the spirit of the devil. It was a fitting name for the beast. He had injured all who tried to ride him, except Vanderlinden. The admiral was the only man the stallion would bear, and at that, it was often grudgingly. Even now, the eecha was struggling.

"Down, you black hearted son of a bitch." Van swore viciously at the beast, pulling at the reins expertly. "Settle down or I'll see you to the butcher."

"Perhaps another eecha would be better, Van," the guider shouted across to him.

"He'll settle down shortly. He's just irked 'cause I haven't ridden him today, that's all," he said through his teeth as he forced the eecha to obey the reins. "'Sides, there ain't but one eecha big enough for me." Spietus, or Spit, as Van called him, calmed at last and Van rode him to the guider's side.

"Where to, my friend?" Trenara asked, looking up at the stars. She hadn't been beyond the Keep since that last ride with Joshan, which seemed an eternity now.

"We're heading for the lower north cliffs, to the clearing at the top. I expect we'll be able to see best there." He leaned over to talk into Spit's ear. "You listen to me, you mealy buck jumper, if you toss me, I'll cut your ears off and feed them to you." The eecha haughtily tossed his head and then bolted off down the road into the darkness.

Trenara's Gliding did the same and soon they were sprinting after the mountain of man and beast. *Yes*, the guider thought, *Van certainly has a way with animals,* and then chuckled. If only Vanderlinden knew how much like the beast he was, the guider supposed he'd be gentler with the creature. On second thought, probably not. Each man controls in his own way. This was Van's way. The admiral liked to control, but not break. In all the seasons Trenara had known the giant, she had never seen him strike man or beast, except his enemies.

Once out of the Keep, they rode on at a quick pace down the main road, until Van suddenly turned into a seldom used path. The guider was certain she would have missed it had she not seen the giant turn. She carefully steered Gliding onto it. It was rocky and rutted, but wide enough for a normal eecha, although rather narrow for Spit and his rider. The guider caught up with them after taking a dangerous bend in the path.

"What is it you're going to show me?" the guider called to him, not taking her eyes from the path.

"You'll see soon enough." He squinted to see through the heavily laced trees around him.

The path could be treacherous in the daylight, but was ominous at night, as a rider or walker couldn't see more than a few paces before him. Spit had good eecha sense, and soon they were standing on a high cliff, the sea to their left and the immense castle to their right. At this height, the eastern edge of the castle's outer wall towered above them majestically. They were at the same level as the family chambers and great halls. Each balcony and terrace could be seen quite clearly, protruding from the old stone wall like pouting lips.

They dismounted and let the two eechas graze, as they stood on an outcrop of rock and drank in the grand beauty of the natural and the man-made. The night glistened around them, the sea calm and peaceful reflecting Redwyn's fire and Whilema's brilliance like mirrored glass. Ethos shone like a torch in the blackened night, dominating all of her sister stars, muting their light.

Andelian tingled at Trenara's side when she beheld the brilliant star. It filled her with contentment and exhilaration. "This is beautiful," Trenara said at length. "I appreciate your sharing this with me. I've never been this way before."

"You're quite welcome, but I didn't bring you here for the view. Look there," he said, pointing to the massive wall of the Keep.

Midway down the wall was a darkened balcony. Trenara could barely see a lone figure standing there, arms outstretched to the sky. At first, she thought the figure merely stretching, but the arms remained stationary. Then the silhouette appeared to place his hands together above his head. The beam from Ethos shot down so quickly the guider inadvertently took a step back. It illuminated the balcony with an intense white glow; from past experience, the guider could almost hear the deafening crackle and smell the bittersweet aroma of the *power*.

"What in heaven's name is he doing? I've told him the dangers involved in direct contact with the star after *first trial*. Is he mad?"

"I wouldn't know. But whatever the dangers, this isn't the first time he's done it." Trenara shot him a hot look. "Aye, this is the third time to my knowledge. I got a report of strange lights at the Keep's east wall and came up here night before last to check it out. Seen just what you're seeing now. Then, I came again last night. Same thing."

"Why the devil didn't you tell me this sooner?"

"I'm not versed in star lore," Van snapped. "I didn't think anything of it until last night. I've seen a good piece of the *power*, especially during the war, but nothing like what I saw then. I came to you straight away, but you were asleep and your girl wouldn't wake you. I didn't press it, 'cause Haiden said the boy was well. But you were in council today, and I couldn't get to you until nightfall. I didn't know it was dangerous until you just said it."

"Quite dangerous—possibly lethal, if we don't stop it at once. This has gone too far." She turned to find her eecha.

"Trenara, look!" Vanderlinden shouted as the guider was about to dash to the clearing.

When the guider turned, the white *power* began to take on an unusual hue. It became quite blue by degrees, until the whole face of the wall was bathed in cobalt light.

"By the star!"

The color changed again as they watched. It turned a bright green almost instantly and then to brilliant amber, a golden fire hanging fluidly in the air. It flowed from the balcony like a stone thrown into calm water, the ripples widening as they streamed from the figure. The two stared dumbfounded in the radiance of the light as it lit up even the sea far below it.

Trenara was the first to recover and jumped from the rock to the ground below, whistling for Gliding as she reached the clearing. Before Van turned to join her, the light suddenly vanished. He thought he saw the figure stumble to his knees and another figure rush to his side to lift him.

Van reached Trenara just as she was mounting Gliding. "You better let me lead. You'll get lost for sure. Spit, you lunkhead, get your arse over here." The eecha came galloping up. Van jumped to his back and sprinted off into the woods, the guider close behind.

When they reached the Keep, Trenara leapt off Gliding and took the steps two at a time, with Van a close second. The guider flew past baffled guards and servants as she ran, nearly knocking down several more. They reached the chambers quickly.

"Let me in there now!" she demanded, fingering Andelian dangerously. The guards parted at once. She and Van broke into the front chamber. Haiden was just closing a door and rushed to them.

"Where is he?"

"He's resting," Haiden answered quietly. "It won't do no good to rouse him now."

"I shall rouse him for this, by god. Open that door immediately or I will break it down." She imparted such viciousness that Haiden took a step back and then shakily crossed to the side table to pour himself a drink. Trenara suddenly saw how tired the old guard looked, but was beyond caring.

"I'd like to, guider, but I just can't. You see…"

"I don't care about your damned orders, Haiden. I want answers and I want them now. Open that door."

"That won't be necessary, Haiden," echoed a powerful voice from behind them. Trenara turned sharply and drew in a startled breath.

Joshan stood in the doorway, so different, she barely recognized him. He was seasons older now, perhaps thirty, his hair as black as night, flowing to the small of his back with a touch of white at the temples, and salted sparsely through the crown. He had grown by two hands and was almost as tall as the giant. But what struck the guider almost at once, were the eyes. They were deep and black as pitch, old and incredibly wise, as though the experience of countless lifetimes lay in them. Even exhausted, the beauty of his face was breathtaking. Trenara's lips trembled.

"Joshan… sire, I… that is, we…"

"I know, guider, a million questions and much to be said. Your questions will have to wait until we're on the ship."

"Ship?" was Trenara's dazed reply.

"We sail for Mathisma tomorrow," he said quietly. "The waiting is over, Trenara. I can't linger here any longer. We have to begin."

"Begin?"

Joshan looked deeply into the guider's eyes and a small smile dusted his lips. "Tomorrow, guider." With that, he turned, walked into his bed chamber, and closed the door behind him.

Never in her life had Trenara known such fear. She quaked at the knowledge that from this moment forward her fate, the fate of Imperium, rested in the hands of an innocent. The dream that had haunted her from the very beginning, loomed in her mind—a foreshadow of providence.

A feeble shaft of light opened the blackness for a fleeting instant and showed her once again the only promise against destruction: a frightened child—and a broken wand.
The starguider screamed.

STARSIGHT – VOLUME I
BOOK II – THE EMPEROR

CHAPTER TWENTY
ALTERNATE FUTURES

Ena carefully packed the last of Trenara's books, strapped the bag down tightly, and dragged it to the front parlor. Just as she sat down, Trenara and Vanderlinden came bustling in. The guider was obviously irritated, the giant amused.

"Ena!"

"Yes, ma'am?" Ena answered quietly, jumping up from the chair.

Trenara started and whirled. "Quit sneaking up on me like that." Van gave the girl a smile and a wink. Ena blushed to the ears and looked awkwardly at her hands.

"Sorry, ma'am."

"Now," Trenara unbuttoned her collar, "take the bags down to the docks and mind you don't break anything. Then see what you can do on board to help. I'll be down presently. You'll be berthing with the other aides. Take along something warm for yourself. The seas can be quite cold, even during high season."

Ena's eyes widened with a sudden sparkle in the morning light. "I'm going with you?"

"Don't be a dunce. Of course, you're going with me. You'll need to pack quickly now. If those bags are not boarded and stowed by the time I get down there, you will spend the trip scrubbing the decks."

"Yes, ma'am." Ena hefted the bags and ran out the door, a loud cheer going down the hall with her.

"Well," Van said as he took a chair, "you've made one person happy today anyway."

"Humph." Trenara took off her formal sash, kissed it, and placed it in its velvet box. "Damn nuisance, if you ask me," she grumbled over her shoulder as she walked into the dressing room.

They had just left Joshan's coronation, which had been small and rushed. Trenara had to preside over it, being the only member of Assemblage present in the Keep. This was extremely irregular and, the guider thought dismally, probably illegal. The emperor had always been starblessed by the Provost. But the lad had insisted, even though Trenara assured him the coronation could be done on Mathisma when they arrived. Joshan was adamant and would not elaborate on the urgency for it. This annoyed the guider, but she conceded and performed the ceremonial blessings. They were awkward, at best, as the guider had only that morning gone over the chants.

It was made more difficult by the fact that the ceremony had been written in old Mathismian and many of the symbols were unfamiliar to her. Not being much interested in ancient language, she had studied only what was necessary, seasons ago as a young woman. Joshan had filled in all the symbols Trenara did not understand, as they went through a brief rehearsal. The guider was amazed at how much he had learned over the short few weeks.

One consolation, Trenara thought as she changed, *at least I saw Vanderlinden in his dress uniform.* She and Haiden had laughed until their sides ached, causing Van to turn around and head for his chambers to change. Joshan waylaid the giant and convinced him to proceed to the coronation as he was. Trenara would not easily forget the withering look Joshan gave them when they passed into the Holy Chambers. She decided she would never want the emperor's enmity and resolved to watch herself more carefully in the future. Haiden was miserable.

She walked out of the dressing room to see Van sipping a glass of wine with another across from him. "It's a little early in the day for libations, isn't it?" Trenara started to put miscellaneous items into her satchel, things Ena had forgotten.

"Not at all," Van replied, holding up his glass. "It's customary to honor a new lord with a toast. Since we didn't have time to do it proper before, I figured now's as good a time as any."

Trenara smiled. "You're right." She reached for her glass and held it aloft. "Here's to Joshan Jenhada Thoringale, Emperor of the Eight Provinces and Keeper of Mathisma, may his reign be long and peaceful." But her smile dissolved and they both became somber, knowing that peace may never come for the young emperor.

"Aye." Van said and they drained their glasses.

"Well, I got to be off." Van stretched and headed for the door. "We sail at noon. Don't forget your spectacles," he said over his shoulder as he left.

Trenara groused, but looked in her satchel, and sure enough, she had forgotten. She snatched them from the bookcase along with a few books, stuffed them into the bag, looked around to ensure she hadn't forgotten anything else, and then headed to the docks.

*****

Van walked down the massive castle stairs and jumped on Spit's back. He rode the eecha over to the last few wagons heading for the ship and spotted Saldorian's canopied litter in the garden with Dottie sitting next to it. Around them, several Elite guards were stationed, with Thiels giving quiet orders in the shadow of the trees and scowling up occasionally around the garden. Since the death of Jenhada, the royal family was closely watched, and Thiels protested loudly when he found out the new emperor was traveling without his royal escort. Haiden had to assign six additional Elite guards to ship duty before Thiels was grudgingly appeased.

The morning was superb, promising bright skies and warm weather, but the canopied divan where Saldorian lay looked out of place in the dappled sunlight. It was shrouded in black and nothing could be seen of the consort, as the veils were staunchly opaque and tightly drawn. The admiral spurred Spit over.

"Oh, good morning, sir." Dottie jumped to her feet and curtsied politely.

"Morning, lass. How's her ladyship?" Van kept his voice low as he glanced at the curtains dubiously.

"Well enough, sir. She's asleep right now. The guider—that is the regent, gave her a drink of something to help her rest. She hasn't said a word, though." Dottie caught sight of someone and became somewhat agitated when he motioned her to join him.

"A friend of yours, lass?" Van smiled roguishly.

Dottie blushed and looked very pretty with the color. "In a way, sir."

"Why not go over and say hello to the lad?"

"I'd like to, sir, but I have to stay with her ladyship. The guider said for me not to leave her." She wrung her hands and shot surreptitious glances at her young man, who had turned around awkwardly when he saw who Dottie was talking to. He occupied himself by pretending to admire the flowers.

"Now, I'm sure the guider wouldn't begrudge you saying hello to a friend. You just get yourself over there and I'll watch the lady."

Her eyes sparkled. "Oh, could you, sir? I mean, I shouldn't even ask, seeing how busy you are and all—but just for moment. I swear I'll be right back."

"Go on."

"Bless you, sir. I won't be but a moment—less than that."

She ran to the arms of the young man and Van smiled to himself, reminded of happier days. He spurred Spit over to the litter and frowned at the dark silk, thinking the lady should never be surrounded by black, but by bright, lovely colors. A small sound came from inside and he looked around, feeling a bit self-conscious. He leaned over to the curtain and pushed it aside.

Saldorian lay with her eyes closed, the long, dark lashes brushing her face and the delicately etched features white against the bed of black. Her long ebony hair fell over wide shoulders and across long fingers as they rested over her slim form. She looked young lying there. The consort was a tall woman, as tall as Jenhada had been. She reminded Van of a stately tree, a lofty birch that sways with the winds, but remains ever noble. The heavy velvet gown she wore made her look thin and pale in the morning sunshine and the months of silence and pain showed in the lines at the corners of her mouth. But for all that, she was still the same striking beauty that had touched Vanderlinden's heart those many, many seasons before on Mathisma, when they had all been young.

Even now, her splendor took his breath away. He had never begrudged Jenhada his bride, for he knew he could offer Saldorian no better. Van had loved her in youth too much to watch her wither of loneliness, while he whored around with his mistress, the sea. After many seasons that love had turned to a rich friendship and he looked upon her now as a sister, relishing that relationship more. His heart had long ago been stolen by another and Saldorian, his confidant, was the only one who knew it. He had shared secrets with her he had never shared with anyone else, not even Jenhada or Trenara.

He picked up a small white hand and pressed it gently to his lips. "If only I could take your nightmare away, Sal," he whispered.

A soft moan escaped her lips, and she turned her head away from him. On the side of her neck was a black bruise that swelled the skin, even after two months. Rage flashed in his eyes when he realized that everything he held sacred, the monster had somehow spoiled. *By the gods! That bastard will pay for this!*

He gently replaced the curtain and turned Spit away from the memories, as Dottie came up panting.

"Thank you, sir."

"Aye," he grumbled and dug his heels into Spit's sides to rush down the road to his mistress.

*****

When everything was secure, the servants and guards were brought on board and settled, the sails were set to fly, most of the moorings untied and the ship made ready to sail. The admiral, the marshall, and the regent stood side by side at the railing, watching for any sign of the emperor.

"Where the devil is he?" Vanderlinden pulled hard on a rope and glanced unconsciously up at the riggings. "Noontide's well underway and if we don't get it now, we'll miss it for sure."

"He said he'd be here. I've no doubt he will," Haiden responded. "Said he wanted to see a bit of the place before he left. That it'd be a good piece before he'd see it again."

"What does he mean by that I wonder?" Trenara leaned on the railing and scanned the harbor. Off in the distance, she saw a speck charging down the road. "Here he comes."

"'Bout bloody time," Van muttered and then turned to his crew with orders. "All right, mates. Hoist anchor. You there, secure that sail. Get them moorings up. Come on, ladies and gentlemen, we're not here for a party. Let's get this bucket to sea!"

Joshan reined in, jumped off Whirl, grabbed a pack from her back, and threw it to Haiden. He noted quickly that Van left the deck and joined his sailors, obviously piqued. As the ship lurched forward, Trenara and Haiden each took an arm and pulled him aboard.

"I'm so sorry," he said, brushing the dust from his boots and tunic. "I had fully intended to be here sooner, but completely lost track of time."

"That's fine with me, my boy," Trenara said, "but I wouldn't get too near the admiral at present." She bowed. "May I make the first official act and invite you to mid-meal?"

"By all means," Joshan replied. "Will you join us, Haiden?"

"I don't think so, sire." Haiden rubbed his hands together and scanned the decks. "I best be checking on my guards. 'Sides, I expect you two have some high things to discuss, and I'd just as soon get back to plain talk, if you take my meaning. I need to start acting the part you gave me, sire. What kind of Marshall of the Guard am I when I don't even know what my people are up to?" He tipped his chin and strode to the deck.

"If you don't mind, Trenara, I'd like to go to my cabin and put some comfortable clothes on. These boots are killing me." Joshan retrieved his pack from the deck and followed after the guider.

Trenara felt curiously awkward with Joshan, as though the boy had somehow— outgrown her. She could get used to the graying hair, the mature face, and the tall, muscular body, but the eyes unsettled her; they were almost too deep, too knowing.

As they walked down the companionway, Trenara caught Joshan staring at her, and she stopped to glare back at him. "What are you gaping at?"

Joshan smiled. "You." He searched her face a moment. "You're uncomfortable."

"Maybe a little. I'm sorry. I had just gotten used to you the way you were."

The emperor shook his head. "You haven't outlived your usefulness—quite the contrary."

Trenara curled her lip. "If you can read my mind, then I *am* in trouble." The guider shook her head and smiled.

Joshan laughed. It was good to hear that sound. "It wasn't your mind I was reading. It was your face. But come. You promised me lunch and I'm starving."

They entered an elaborate cabin at the end of a long passageway and found two valets unpacking. Joshan dismissed them, saying they could finish later. Trenara left to find lunch.

When she returned carrying a tray laden with food and fresh mead, Joshan was coming out of his wardrobe, tying a golden sash around an ornate green robe.

"Good heavens, sire, you are starting to look like a proper starguider."

"Disgusting, isn't it?" Joshan made a feeble attempt to adjust the hemline. "They only brought me robes. I'll have to talk to the valet about this. I feel absolutely ancient."

Trenara raised an incredulous brow. "I'll try not to take that personally."

"Sorry," he chuckled, sitting down to lunch.

After they had eaten, they retired to Joshan's study with their mead. During the meal, Trenara didn't push him for news, although she was very eager to hear it. At the same time, the guider was oddly relieved. When they were settled, she poured them each a glass of wine and sat back.

"You have kept our plans as quiet as possible, yes?" Joshan asked at length.

"As requested. I still don't understand the need for secrecy."

Joshan smiled at her. "There is a method to my madness, guider."

Trenara just looked at him. "Which brings us to the point, doesn't it?"

Joshan looked at his hands and thought through all he needed to share. It was difficult to decide how much he could say to Trenara, difficult to gauge just how she would react. His mind reeled again with the thousands of alternative *visions* that had begun to assail him the night he was at his mother's room. It had taken him weeks to control the continuous barrage of thoughts that circled around his mind, and every ounce of his strength to keep them from destroying it. Joshan had buried himself in books to help silence the screaming voice of the *visions* as they hurtled through his psyche. When he reached *fourth trial,* the voices stopped and he could finally control them, but he had to work to keep them in check.

"Sire?" Trenara said quietly.

Joshan looked up at her and smiled. "I'm sorry. I must be drifting." He took a deep breath and sat back in his chair. "How did Thiels take to being in charge of the Keep in our absence?"

Trenara smiled at the memory. "He'll do fine. And, what's more, he knows it. The Elite have been running the Keep for seasons."

"I was delighted with your choice. He should be able to handle it very well." Joshan's voice was distant as he went to the port to stare at the sea and sip his wine.

"Handle what?" Trenara asked tentatively, knowing he didn't mean the Keep.

Joshan regarded the fading coastline as it disappeared into haze to the north. "Trenara, what do you think of our going to Mathisma now?"

Trenara looked down at her drink and furrowed her brow. "I will support you in whatever orders you give. You know that."

Joshan shot the guider a glance over his shoulder. "That doesn't answer my question."

"Well," she replied looking up at him, "I think leaving the Keep right now is ill-advised."

"Why?"

"The silence in the south can't be ignored. We know... he's there; we know he's gathering strength." She took a sip of her drink. "I think Sirdar has retaken Badain and may be ready to strike us any day."

The emperor nodded solemnly. "I agree."

Trenara frowned at his back. "I have done what I can to muster the forces, but it could take months to get them ready without guidance. Going off to Mathisma now could be fatal to the empire." She stopped at the force of her own conviction and relaxed the muscles in her shoulders with a feeble shrug. "You asked my opinion."

"You have no idea how right you are."

"So, why the hell are we going to Mathisma?"

"Because if we don't," Joshan replied turning around to look at her, "then that will *certainly* be fatal for the empire. Sirdar would conquer us within a matter of weeks." He grew silent and Trenara sank into her chair. Joshan's words took on a significance she could see in the deep black eyes staring back at her.

"But how?" she breathed.

Joshan toyed with his glass then looked up at the guider. "That's going to take some explaining, but first, I have questions, starting with *fourth trial.*"

Trenara looked up at him. "Not many know about *fourth trial*. Quite frankly, when I saw you on the balcony last night, I thought you'd be dead when we arrived at your chambers."

Joshan looked at his drink and sighed. "I know, guider, and I apologize—for many things—but mostly for shutting you out the last few months. I didn't mean to hurt you. It was necessary. I think you'll soon understand why."

"Lad, you don't need to apologize to me. I'm not your teacher anymore. I'm afraid you've outgrown me."

Joshan looked at her sharply. "No, you're wrong. I need you very much. You have no idea," he said intently, his eyes blazing for a moment. He got his emotions under control with an effort and smiled at her apologetically. "I'm sorry, Trenara. Please go on about *fourth trial*."

Trenara was strangely thankful for the change of subject. "I'm certain you've read about this, so if I become redundant, I apologize. I can tell you what I've learned. You should talk to Grandor when we reach Mathisma. He's the Assemblage historian, or rather Keeper of the Books, officially. He has authored most of the books I have on the subject, and he's the best.

"*Fourth trial*—the *master of power*. The amber light denotes a combination of all the lower *powers*. The accepted philosophy is that the amber increases the discipline that comes with the white, enhances the *sight* that comes with the blue, and gives more control over nature that comes with the green. To my knowledge there hasn't been a guider of that level in many seasons. At least, not until now…"

Joshan did not take his eyes from the fire. "Don't you think that rather curious?"

Trenara shrugged. "Not particularly, since there have been few as far as we know. Others might have existed at one time or another. There are guiders all over the world, Joshan. It would be difficult to keep close tabs on them all."

"Yes," Joshan replied heavily. "You told me sometime back that the original *via*s were made from the crystal itself. When did that stop?"

"Some ten or twelve seasons after the first Assemblage was created. The order grew so rapidly they realized they would soon run out of crystal. A pocket of similar stone was found in Tola and mined. When Cessas discovered *via*s could be made from this substance, he started immediate production. Actually, that was why Assemblage expanded so rapidly and one of the reasons they moved to Mathisma. The same stone was found there as well."

"Do you have any idea how many *via*s were made from the crystal and what became of them? Who has them now?"

"There were fifteen, one for Cessas, and one each for his fourteen disciples. When Sirdar rose thirty seasons ago, before Balinar had been corrupted, the original *via*s, stored on Sanctum, were converged back into the crystal to give it more *power*. The ironic part is, when the crystal was stolen, that's why we were so powerless. If we had kept even one of the original *via*s…" her face faltered a moment, "the guiders that went to Badain may not have been lost." She grew silent then and looked down. Shame had flared for a moment in her eyes, but she suppressed it. Joshan regarded her sharply, but said nothing.

"There was a rumor going around that only thirteen of the original *vias* were merged with the crystal. It was said Cessas' *via* and one of the others were not among them. I don't know how much truth there is to it. I do know they feared Balinar had taken them before he stole the Crystal.

"Most of this is in my books and I'm certain you've read them. This last about the original *vias* would not be in any of the books I have. Many of the scrolls relating to that are back at Mathisma in the Sanctum Library and most are confidential. Only third trial guiders are allowed to see those and only through the discretion of the Provost."

"Really?" Joshan replied, shaking his head. "That's unfortunate—knowledge should be shared."

"I agree." Trenara pulled her chair closer to the fire as if the glowing embers could sear the burning memories that had nearly risen, for a moment unguarded, from the recesses of her mind. Her voice sounded evasive. "However, the Prelacy is ruled by the Provost and rarely goes against his doctrines."

"Still, it's a shame, but does explain some things," Joshan said, looking at the golden liquid in his glass. "Do you think it was one of those two *vias* Balinar used at the Keep?"

Trenara shook her head. "No. The red crystal Balinar used is something I've never seen before," she lied. "I don't know where he got it. Rumor has it both the missing *vias* are scepters."

"Hmm. Balinar, yes." Joshan gave the fire a thoughtful nod. "Trenara, did anything strike you as odd about this most recent attack on the Keep?"

"All of it was odd, sire. What are you saying?"

His brow looked slightly pained. "His fall was entirely too swift and easily done."

Trenara just looked at him.

"And other things…" Joshan continued. "Did you examine any of the northerners before they left?"

Trenara frowned. "By that time, I hadn't the stomach."

"Well, I did. The northern race is notorious for being clever and capable of survival where other people would soon flounder; yet, to the man, that lot was as dim witted as a stone. Almost all of them were criminals and none of them literate. Something else—when I was battling Balinar, when I forged Andelian back for you, there was a split second when his face changed—just for a moment. It is only recently I even thought about it. Balinar's expression was almost—joyful." He sank his head in frustration. "But I don't know why after two seasons, a clever man like that, certainly trained in every art his master has, would leave himself open to me, my hands bound in front and my mouth ungagged. He certainly was cautious enough at Wert's. Why not the Keep where it was more important? This man conquered five provinces during the first reign of Sirdar, without lifting so much as a weapon. He is *third trial* and wields a crystal that is incredibly powerful. It's as if…" But his voice stopped.

He seemed to forget that Trenara sat there clinging to every word as though each were more precious than the last. So starved was the guider for answers, her voice sounded suddenly harsh. "As if what, sire?" she whispered.

Joshan looked at her a moment. "As if he had been sent to do exactly what he did." He shook his head. "It doesn't make any sense, does it?"

Trenara sat back in her chair. "Perhaps Balinar was over confident."

"Perhaps," Joshan replied thoughtfully. "Or perhaps he was sent to test us…" His voice went low, "…me."

The guider's eyes sharpened. "But why?"

Joshan shook his head. "I wish I knew."

"To gain time."

"What?"

"To gain time… to distract us while they built their forces in the south. That would fit perfectly. If he could embroil us long enough it would give them time to…"

"To build an army? Trenara, you seem to forget, Balinar could have completely crushed us without lifting a weapon." Trenara's face fell. "I'm sorry, but we have to be honest with ourselves. We were *allowed* to win that battle."

"Are you so certain?" Trenara's voice was pleading.

"Reasonably."

Trenara couldn't restrain her anger anymore. "Then why the hell are we going to Mathisma?"

Joshan leaned forward and poured himself a golden splash of mead. "How long since you've been to the isle?"

"About ten seasons… why?"

"I'm afraid you might find it changed from what you remember."

Trenara furrowed her brow. "Changed how?"

"Let me back up a bit. I want to tell you what's happened to me. It might explain a lot." Trenara's nod was stiff.

"The last night I saw you outside my mother's chambers, something happened to me. Something snapped in my—*sight*, I would say. A thousand visions appeared in my mind all at once. They were strange and distorted, like a scattered dream or a complex child's puzzle with thousands of pieces. When you told me what happened to my mother, that piece fell into place. I still don't know what Balinar told her, but I do know that it fits into one of the alternate futures."

"Alternate futures?" Trenara looked at Joshan intently.

"My word for it. One of the things I've concluded about those visions that night. I suppose my analogy of a child's puzzle is not entirely correct. I guess I should say the pieces fit several puzzles or several alternate futures. These futures will depend on what we do over the next few days."

"You mean there is more than one solution to this whole thing with Sirdar?" Trenara asked hopefully, but Joshan's eyes were tired suddenly.

"No, Trenara. What I'm saying is there is only one solution to Sirdar. My task is to find out which one that is. All the other futures lead to oblivion." He grew silent and Trenara sat with her heart pounding.

"Lad…" she breathed, but Joshan put a hand on her arm.

"If it's any consolation, at least I know several routes I can't take. That narrows down the choices." He got up and gazed at the fire, warming his hands, but it couldn't take away the chilling implications in his heart. "That's why I've been spending the last two months in study.

"There was little I knew, Trenara—so little you or father, or anyone else had told me. There was so little anyone really knew. I had to fit together many pieces to find answers.

"I think I first suspected trouble on Mathisma when Vanderlinden spoke about his lost ship. Has he told you?"

Trenara looked up at him. "Yes, but only sketchily. I know about the curse and his exile."

"Fortunately, Van chose to tell me that story in detail. Otherwise, we would have fallen immediately into Sirdar's hands. I read something else there. But again, I didn't know what it was I was seeing. Not until I started to do some investigating.

"Van had told me that during his exchange with the guard on the dock in Cortaim, the man said there had only been one guider in Cortaim for many seasons."

Trenara looked at him in alarm. "There shouldn't have been any guiders in Cortaim. That was the agreement."

"Exactly. Fortunately, I remember you telling me that or it might have been missed."

"But Van didn't even mention that to me." Trenara rubbed her hands together and looked up at Joshan.

The emperor looked back at the fire. "He probably didn't think it was important."

"Who was this guider in Cortaim?"

Joshan turned his back to the fire. "A man named Palarine."

Trenara furrowed her brow in concentration. "Palarine—Palarine," she mused softly. "Where have I… wait. Palarine of Quitain." She glanced up at the emperor. "He went north with several others right after the first war. They were there to establish a school for the northerners."

Joshan nodded. "That's what I found out as well. Dispatches you had received from Mathisma bore this out and that he had been there for many, many seasons. That's when I began to wonder how this sergeant in Cortaim could say that Palarine had been there. It was then I sent Sark to the north."

Trenara smiled. "So that's why."

"Yes. I needed to know if Palarine had actually been in the wastelands. When Sark returned, I found out otherwise. Apparently, Palarine had left the north twenty-five seasons ago, leaving instructions with his assistant. He was ordered to continue the reports to Mathisma under Palarine's signature. That explains why Assemblage didn't know."

The implication made Trenara's mouth dry. "If I remember correctly, Palarine was held above reproach, one of the finest guiders we had. Do you think he was corrupt then?"

"I don't think so. To tell you the truth, I think when he went south he suspected something. Some rumor about Sirdar he took upon himself to verify. That would fit his character precisely. He wouldn't want to risk anyone else on such a bold venture. I think he was then corrupted by Sirdar. I believe it was planned just that way to ensnare the good guider. Sirdar used the voice of a giant bird to bend starguiders to his will. Do you know of it?"

Trenara's face became pale. "Yes," she hissed.

Joshan scowled at the guider. "Trenara, what is it?"

The guider cleared her throat and managed a nervous smile. "Any guider who has seen a Mourna remembers nothing pleasant about the encounter." She rubbed her face to get the image out of her mind. "Do you think Palarine was ensnared by this creature?"

Joshan felt the guider's pain but did not broach the question. "Yes." There was a whetted edge to his voice. "Ensnared and devoured. It must have been devastating."

Devastating echoed through Trenara's mind.

"After Palarine was taken by Sirdar, I think the plan was to overthrow my father and take me back to the south. Why, I don't know, yet. I believe the visitor Van had in his cabin that night was Palarine."

"That clears up some mystery. But I still don't see what this has to do with going to Mathisma."

Joshan would not look at the guider. "It has everything to do with it. Trenara," Joshan said slowly, "Palarine has been on Mathisma for almost two seasons now."

Trenara blinked at him in disbelief.

"I checked and it's true," Joshan said. "He has a following and he's becoming more influential every day. Something else Sark brought back to me from the north. At least six northern ships filled with soldiers have left to travel to Mathisma over the last six months."

Trenara was having a hard time grappling with the volley of information she was receiving. "Lad, do you realize what you're saying?"

"I know exactly what I'm saying, guider." He looked down at Trenara. "We might very well find the isle held against us."

"Saminee would never allow such a thing to happen. Northerners are no match for a group of starguiders!"

"Trenara, you haven't been listening," Joshan replied quietly. "Palarine has already garnered the trust of over half of the guiders on Mathisma."

"Half?" Trenara spat. "Saminee would never allow…"

"Saminee is dead."

The words left Trenara silent. Joshan rubbed his knuckles and stared at the fire to ease the sight of her grief. "He fell ill two seasons ago, soon after Palarine arrived on the island. I'm certain that's no coincidence. He died in his sleep four nights ago. I received word of it only yesterday. I'm sorry, Trenara, I know you were fond of him."

Trenara allowed her frayed nerves to sink into the chair and she closed her eyes against the pain. "By the gods." But then the truth struck her. "They will elect another Provost within fifteen days."

"Precisely. They will elect Palarine—unless they are stopped. After he is elected he will have access to the Crystal and everything else on the island, including the other guiders. Do you understand now?"

Understand? Trenara wished she didn't. The provinces on the edge of war, Assemblage being taken over by Sirdar's servant, Vanderlinden cursed by a power she didn't understand, Jenhada dead, the boy changed and strange. All of it, on and on, a progressive nightmare with nothing to wake to but more nightmares. *Like before…*

"Yes," she whispered, not knowing what else to say. "What do we do?"

Joshan shrugged. "That will depend on what we find when we arrive. We could find it totally held against us. In that case I will have no alternative but to fight Assemblage to save the Crystal. If it is not and if we can get there before the appointment, then there will be… another solution. This is one of those alternate futures I was speaking about."

"It seems a bitter choice in either case." Trenara's words contained no comfort. "Even if the isle is not held against us and we can win it back before Palarine is named, we still leave the Keep and the provinces virtually unprotected."

"Well, not unprotected." Joshan's wry smile was contradictory to the weight of his words. "I haven't been idle, guider. There is a legion of soldiers from almost every province from Selas to Thrain encircling Sirdar's borders at this moment. Also, a handpicked team of highly skilled fighters has been sent to penetrate the High Ingress. Scouts will be sent in to see what's happened on the inside."

Trenara's face shifted to wonder. "How did you do all of this?"

"Thiels and Haiden put most of the people into action," he replied. "It is Thiels's handpicked team going to the borders to penetrate the Ingress. Haiden took the troops that you had ordered and saw to it they were prepared. It wasn't difficult since most of them were seasoned veterans anyway. Sark took the commission and is leading them south."

Trenara's face seemed to shift like sand under the storm of conflicting emotions and stopped at indignation. "Why the hell didn't you tell me?"

Joshan searched her face a long time before answering. "I couldn't, Trenara, not until after we left the Keep."

The guider looked down and cleared her throat. "You don't—trust me, then?"

"It isn't you I don't trust. It is your relationship with someone that could make an innocent slip of the tongue destroy everything I've planned."

"Who?"

Joshan sucked air through his teeth. "Vanderlinden."

"Are you mad? Why, Vanderlinden is…" But she stopped herself before she could go on, her face horrified at what she almost said.

"Is what, guider?" Joshan's eyes were suddenly intent.

Trenara stared down at her knotted hands. "I… I can't tell you, Joshan. I've sworn an oath that I won't break."

Joshan opened his mouth to insist, but stopped when he saw her face. "And I won't make you," he said, patting her arm. "I've known before now that Van is more than he appears."

"You must believe me, sire," Trenara pleaded, "Van *is* above reproach. What happened in the Keep was an enchantment, nothing more. He is as faithful to you as I am."

Joshan looked at the guider wearily and shook his head. "I wish it were that simple. I know Van is faithful to me and always has been. But he was touched by something other than enchantment. Don't you ever wonder why he was blinded?"

Trenara shrugged. "Cruelty?"

"A blacker cruelty than I could have imagined until a few days ago," Joshan said. "Balinar implanted something in the giant's eye to make him bend to the will of Sirdar."

Trenara scowled. "What could make him do that? I know of nothing that would…"

"It exists, Trenara." Joshan closed his eyes over the admission. "Sadly, I now know it exists."

"What exists?" Trenara's voice was shaking.

Joshan stared at the fire and seemed to be having an internal debate. "Before I tell you," his voice came low and thick, "there is something I need you to tell me first." He was struggling with his words.

Trenara's internal *sight* flared hotly for a moment, making her swallow hard against the knot climbing up her throat and the flash of fear sending needles up her chest and arms. "What?" she forced herself to say.

Joshan turned slowly to pick up Trenara's eyes. "I need to know what happened to you thirty seasons ago. I need you to tell about your trip—to Badain."

Trenara gasped and her mouth hung open in numb apprehension. *No,* she screamed soundlessly—or was it aloud? Suddenly the dread turned to anger. "No one knows about that! You don't understand." But her voice broke and she couldn't continue.

Her fists were clenched so tightly that Joshan flinched from the pain that was surely piercing the guider's palms.

He felt only pity. He knew this was Trenara's most closely guarded secret and regretted deeply having to ask for it, but knew of no other way. "I know, Trenara," he said, "and no one will ever know, if that is your wish. But I *must*. Believe me, I would not ask otherwise."

The flame in Trenara's eyes was quickly extinguished by tears. "I have spent thirty seasons trying to forget that journey—and its end." She wiped her eyes with her sleeve. "How did you know?"

"I knew it the night you told me about my mother. It was another of those pieces of the puzzle. I didn't know what it was I was seeing and didn't get any clear idea until I read my father's diaries. He makes mention of your leaving and your return, when Van brought you back—close to death. He said you and Van had been to Badain and brought back invaluable information, but said nothing about how you had been hurt. You were in recovery many months and wouldn't tell anyone what happened, nor would the giant. It seems just as you have made an oath to him, he has made one to you. Am I wrong?"

Trenara shook her head.

Joshan got on his knees and took her hands in his. "Trenara, you are the only person living who has personal knowledge of the evil in the south. I have read too often in your eyes the pain of that moment. Believe me, I do not ask lightly." He kissed her hand and held it to his face. "I would not see you hurt for anything, but this memory has festered inside you for too long."

She touched his hair, looking strangely peaceful. "I will tell you—because I love you," she finally said with a sad smile. "It's strange. You see, after that, I swore I'd never love again." She closed her eyes as a tear went down her cheek and lowered her head, the long mane of gray hair shimmering for a moment in the firelight. Joshan squeezed her hand, closed his eyes, and used what power he could to help her remember.

CHAPTER TWENTY-ONE
BADAIN

The young Trenara, lively and lovely with long braided tresses of deep red and brilliant blue eyes with specks of brown, was new from *second trial* and just shy of twenty-five seasons. The world was peaceful in those days; the war with the north was over and the roads open to all. The guider had six months to idle in the provinces before her next charge was ready for training, so she headed out to visit the land she had heard so much about, having been no further than Mathisma and Thrain before then. Trenara was bold in those days, self-assured and arrogant in her youth and ability, without the experience to cause her hesitation or prudence.

The tenacious guider left the Keep in disguise, traveling with a bright wagon of wares and trinkets, the role of merchant somehow pleasing her. She headed first west to Tola and decided early in the journey to remain in her pretended profession. Even in those days, Assemblage guiders were often sought out and begged for favors. Trenara knew she would use her *power* at need, but enjoyed being part of the masses. The guider could embrace the common folk, feel what they felt, hear what they heard, and be warmed by a welcome inn at the end of the day or a chance meeting with good earthy people, to laugh or cry as the mood set them.

The guider enjoyed seeing the land that had been only tales before. It was nothing like what her imagination had painted. She was awed by the north ridge, tall and resplendent white-capped, jagged peaks, which could indeed be the borders of the world, as in the old mystical legends. They gave way to rolling foothills that were carpeted with shining grass and delicate flowers, so fragrant they could make the unsuspecting traveler forget her journey.

She soon came to the Great Forest, so named as it spread from Thrain, well through Tola, into the cold northern lands, and dwindled finally into the Plains of Palimar, to the south. The magnificent conifers were tall and straight, fading into distance to the north and south. It was here the Meridian Gorge began, beautiful with its milliard of trees blanketed by the bright and colorful autumn season, the leaves beginning to turn bright red. Farther and farther she traveled, each site capturing her heart.

It was when the guider arrived in Tola that she first began to hear rumors of the south. Trenara sat at an inn in the mining city of Silverland and listened to the talk about her.

"I tell you, Cam, you're wrong. There're mighty strange things happening down there, if the stories are true," remarked a cheery-faced young man to his rather portly companion.

"What stories have you heard?" the round man asked.

"I heard tell that springtide's passed over them and the sun's as hot as the devil already—not even past low season. I also heard there's not a river or stream running and the fields are dried up."

"And I heard," said another man sitting with them, "that the desert's moving right up to the borders like it's growing."

"I think you're all full of hooey. You been listening to those southerners and fell for those tall tales," the fat man said, laughing uproariously. "They're no doubt laughing in their beers right now, thinking you fell right nice for that line of prattle—growing desert indeed." He buried his face in his hands and howled. The others began to laugh as well, making fun of their own gullibility.

Trenara did not find it amusing. This was like numerous conversations she had heard since coming to Tola. She knew rumors began as facts and were then twisted with misuse. She paid for the ale and was retrieving her cloak, when the innkeeper came up and motioned her aside.

"Ma'am, excuse me for bothering you, but there's a gentleman over there says he'd like a word with you." He pointed to a darkened corner, showing a large pair of boots sticking out from a shadowed booth.

Trenara was tired as it had been a weary day of travel, and felt rather put out a stranger should ask the innkeeper to fetch her like a round of drinks. But those days were younger and Trenara was feeling rather adventurous, so she decided to see what the stranger wanted. The guider gave the Keeper a curt nod and made her way to the back corner.

Trenara was greeted by a giant of a man in his late twenties. He had curly black hair and piercing dark eyes in a face that was swarthy and weathered, handsome in a rugged way. The guider was a bit startled at first, both from the man's size, but more from the strength radiating from those eyes.

"The innkeeper said you wanted to speak with me," Trenara said.

"Sit down, guider. There's much we need to discuss."

Trenara was stunned silent for a moment at the use of her proper title and by the fact that he towered well over her head. He sat down to load his pipe and she narrowed her eyes at him. "You seem to know a deal more than you should, stranger."

"Aye, I know a thing or two."

"Since you seem to know me, may I ask who you are?" Trenara spoke with as much indifference as possible to cover up her annoyance that his man could know what she was. She thought herself rather careful of her identity.

"I'm known by lots of names, but you can call me Vanderlinden. Most everyone else does."

Trenara regarded the giant for a long moment. "All right—Vanderlinden—what business have you with me?"

"I'm going south and thought it might be good to have someone like you along. I'm no guider and I'm thinking from the tales I've heard, we'll need some *power* before the journey's through." Van looked at her through the smoke that rose from his pipe.

Trenara instantly liked this fellow—and his proposition. "Do you think there is truth in these rumors?" She couldn't keep the enthusiasm out of her voice as she sat down.

"Truth enough, though the stories have been blown up a bit. The changes are subtle, but growing rapidly. And the desert *is* moving."

"You've been there, then?"

"Aye, back in Ethosian, toward the end of Meridian. It was hard to get in and out, too. Those mountains are murderous toward low season."

Trenara frowned at him. "Why not take the road? Surely that would have been easier." Trenara had seen many maps and remembered that Badain was enclosed within two mountain ranges, the Foles Range to the west and the Arms Range to the east. Where they met along the northern border of Badain was a large gap called the High Ingress, where the North-South Road wound to the desert and the southern shore of the province.

"That way's closed, guider. I can't say more about it. Only those that try to enter or leave don't return or go forward. They simply vanish. What evil befalls them, I can't say."

"Word must be sent to the emperor. I'm amazed it hasn't reached him before this."

"It may have already. I sent messages to Thrain some time back and hope they were received." He began to relight the huge briar pipe.

Trenara eyed him suspiciously. "Sounds like you have the emperor's ear, giant. Do you know him?"

"Well, guider," Van replied while lighting his pipe. "Very well."

"This seems too risky. I will return at once to make certain." Trenara began to rise, but was held by a massive hand.

"Begging your pardon, guider, but I've been on your trail for two months and I'm not likely to lose you now."

Trenara looked at the man and touched her *via*. "Let go of my arm." Van released the guider. "What right have you to follow me?"

Vanderlinden shrugged. "In case you haven't noticed, there ain't but one guider from here to Gorka. And that's you. The rest have been pulled back to the isle, three months ago."

"What?" Trenara's exclamation was so loud, many curious heads turned in their direction.

"Keep your voice down, guider," Van replied quietly. "This isn't public knowledge, and we'd sure enough have a panic if it was widely known."

Trenara sank onto the bench. *All pulled back? Why?* The other guests returned to their own conversations.

"How is it you know so much?"

"I've been keeping my eyes open. I went to Gorka to find a guider I know, and he said he was called back to Mathisma and had to leave right quick. I didn't tell him my purpose; the less said the better. He told me to go to Thrain and find you, but I wasn't to be surprised if you weren't there, 'cause as far as he knew, all the starguiders were called back. He didn't tell me why."

He took the pipe and packed it down. "I got wind you had left the Keep and was heading to Tola. I cut across country and finally picked up your trail at the Gorge."

"This is insanity. What could have possessed the Provost to pull back Assemblage?" Trenara looked at the table and toyed with her glass. She looked up at Van. "Unless he knows something of the trouble in Badain and is forming a council. But why Mathisma? Surely the Keep would have been a better choice."

Van eyed the patrons scattered around the Inn and got up to pick up his cloak. "Let's take a walk."

They walked through the streets of Silverland for hours and talked well into the night, planning their journey to the south and deciding to take the quickest route along the North-South Road to the High Ingress. There they would gather what information they could and get word back to the Keep and Assemblage. Trenara returned to the inn, sent word to the Keep outlining their plans, and spent a restless night worrying about their journey.

The guider sold her wagon and goods the next day and bought needed provisions for the trip, including two very nice eechas that the merchant guaranteed were swift and hardy. They left by the main road out of Silverland, an odd pair—the massive dark-haired giant and the tall redheaded beauty, galloping out of town at breakneck speed.

The riders came into trouble barely an hour into their journey, when a band of strange looking men in masks surprised them by jumping out of the trees lining the road. Had it not been for Andelian's fire and the giant's strength, they would have met an untimely end.

When the robbers realized they were outmatched, they took to the forest and disappeared among the tangled foliage and dense trees, with the exception of one who lay dead in the road, the giant's dagger protruding from his chest and his black blood staining the gravel beneath him. When Van pulled off the mask, they both stepped back in disgust. The creature's face had no nose to speak of and only a slit for a mouth lined by a set of sharp yellow teeth. His skin was hairless and leathery with strange markings standing out boldly on his forehead and cheek.

"By the star." Trenara swallowed. "What is that?"

Vanderlinden frowned and covered the man's face. "I think the word in Mathismian is laminia, though I've never seen one in the flesh."

Trenara regarded the thing with horror and covered her nose. The stench was terrible. Laminia were monsters from myths, creatures that could not eat as normal men, feasting instead on the blood of the weak and helpless. They were merciless in their quest to satisfy their blood-lust and often preyed on young children and the old.

"I've never heard of them being this far south." Vanderlinden knelt down and closely examined the tattoos on the creature's face. "Slave marks." He rose and wiped his hands. "I'd wager my life on it. But I can't tell whose. Only slaves left would be in the north. This isn't good, guider. We need to go." Before the guider could collect herself, she was thrown onto the back of her mount by a pair of massive hands and set off racing down the road.

They traveled like the wind now, the darkling forest blurred by their passing and the road alight with sparks from hoof meeting stone. Trenara began to experience real fear. This swiftly ceased to be just an adventure, and turned alarmingly into a flight for their lives. For the first time, Trenara confronted her mortality, and it seemed suddenly fragile. She left the first part of her innocent youth behind on the graveled roadway. The rest would soon follow.

After many leagues, the forest thinned until they burst through the trees into the bright daylight. The companions halted on the borders of the Great Forest and saw row after row of mounds covered in tangled turf that led to the golden Plains of Palimar. It was said that civilizations were entombed beneath the Border Mounds, civilizations older than even Kerillian. Seeing them now, the companions could believe it. They were awed by the hundreds of dark green hills rolling to the spacious plains beyond. The honey colored grasses blew in waves beneath a late afternoon sun. Van and Trenara dismounted and surveyed the shadowed mounds.

"It'll be dangerous traveling those hills in the light. We don't know if there are more of those creatures, but I'm not willing to risk it." Van tightened the eecha's girth strap and scanned the terrain.

"I agree. I think we should stay off the road." Trenara joined the giant and shaded her eyes. "I'm feeling strange, like we're being watched."

"Aye, I felt it, too, though I didn't see anything. Come on, guider," he replied, mounting his eecha. "There's a patch of woods to the east where we can stay until dark." He yelled to his beast and they galloped toward the east, leaving the road behind them.

As they rode, Trenara watched as long shadows leapt from knoll to knoll, cast from the setting sun. A deep uneasiness began to creep up into the base of her neck sending shivers down her spine. The feeling of watchfulness grew stronger as they galloped east, and despite her best efforts, she couldn't shake it.

They reached the woods without incident and alternated watches so they could rest before attempting the ride to the plains. Van took the first watch, but Trenara did not sleep well and had terrible nightmares. When the giant finally woke her, she was trembling.

"You all right, guider?"

"Yes," Trenara replied, sitting stiffly. The small forest had a strange feeling. Trenara got to her feet quickly.

"Aye, I've been feeling it for about an hour now," Van said.

"Why didn't you wake me?"

"Wouldn't have done any good… I've been all through these hills looking for whatever it is. It's got itself hid pretty good."

Trenara wrapped her cloak around her shoulders. "You better get some sleep, Van. I'd like to leave this place as soon as we can."

"We'd best leave now, then." Vanderlinden went to his eecha and threw the saddle on her. Trenara's eecha was already saddled.

"You're going to need sleep before the night is over," Trenara said, but she was actually relieved the giant was willing to go on.

"I can go a good piece yet tonight. 'Sides, the place where I'm taking us isn't far and should be safe enough for tomorrow. I'll rest then."

Mounting, they sped into the night, their silent predator stalking their tracks. The eecha reared in terror from time to time, but their riders were firm on their backs and kept them on the trail through the hills. They headed southeast, and the mounds began to diminish. It was treacherous going, as the darkness at the base of the hills was absolute, making it hard to find any path. They didn't dare risk a light, so Andelian lay unused in Trenara's robes. The giant guided them swiftly, using the stars and his wits as a guide.

They finally arrived at the last of the Border Mounds and gazed south to the Palimar Plains and the Minan River to their left, a distant ribbon of glistening black in the moonlight. The night deepened around them as Redwyn disappeared behind the horizon.

Van regarded the midnight black plains. "The place we're heading is about ten leagues down the Minan on the other side. It's called the Grotto by the Palimarians."

"I've heard of it. Aren't there tales of it being enchanted?"

"Aye, enchanted it is, but not like the *power*. It's the feel of the place mostly; makes a body feel welcome and content. It's been like that for ages, by all accounts. Enchanted or no, I just want to get to it before whatever is stalking us gets there. We'll head straight down the Minan and cross the bridge, but we're going to have to fly, guider." With that, they goaded their eechas into a swift race across the plains.

They flew through tall grass that beat at their legs brutally and found its way through thick leggings and boots. The companions only looked forward to the river, which glistened faintly in the sparse light as they drew nearer. They paused when they reached the noisy white crested rapids. The river was relatively narrow here and broadened as the water flowed south.

Vanderlinden stood up in his stirrups to survey the surrounding land. The trees that bordered the Minan were sparse and twisted by decades of windy low season weather and offered little hope of concealment against searching eyes, but the thin forest was better than the open plains, where they stood exposed on all sides like naked prey. When Van seemed satisfied, he jerked his head to the right, and Trenara followed him in silence. Whilema slid behind the horizon and the night became dark, only the stars shining to light their way now.

A quarter league from the grove, Vanderlinden's eecha suddenly reared, throwing the giant heavily to the grassy turf. He sprang up and just caught the eecha's reins as she went bolting past. She reared again, but Van had a good hold on her and calmed her down enough to mount. He shot a frightened look at Trenara, who returned it. The presence was at their heels as they spurred their eecha onward at a frantic pace.

They could see the Grotto ahead of them now, across the water. It was only a dark line of trees this close to dawn, but reassuring nonetheless. As they sped for it, the night became for a moment darker, as if clouds had sailed across the sky above them. When Trenara looked up, she couldn't see the stars for a moment. Fear chilled her bones. The eechas fretted beneath the riders, and they had trouble keeping them under control until the shadow passed. Trenara took Andelian from her robe and held her tightly to her breast for strength, knowing she would need the *via* soon.

They saw the bridge now, towering high above the broadening river. It was almost fifty spans before them. They stopped their eechas as one, and Van carefully considered the landscape. Dawn was almost on them and they stood in the open, a pre-dawn breeze circling around their trembling beasts.

"It's on the bridge," Trenara said grimly.

"Aye. We can't cross the river here, it's too deep toward the middle, and the eechas are too tired to swim. Besides, the only way into the Grotto is that bridge. There're thickets full of bristle berries and stinging gorse, running all along the outside of the place, so that way's out." He paused for a moment as if trying to make out the bridge in the darkness. "What do you suppose it is, guider?"

Trenara shook her head. "I don't know. Something… bad," she replied, scowling at the darkness.

"Well, it knows its business. We can't go forward, nor across, and we can't likely go back either. If we cut across for the road, my guess is we wouldn't make it, if there be any more of them stinking laminia. Aye," he spat, "it knows its business."

A deep calm settled over the guider as she confronted the choices before her. They could no longer go by road; they would be dead within minutes of reaching it. There was only one choice and it hardened her resolve. She had to confront this monstrosity. Trenara furrowed her brow in concentration and held Andelian tightly.

"Come on," she said hoarsely and kicked her eecha forward. The scepter began to tingle in her hand and brightened with each step she took. She stopped the animal at the foot of the towering bridge and dismounted slowly. Vanderlinden's eecha reared again, but the giant managed to dismount and throw a cloak over the beast's head. He grabbed the reins of both eechas and followed in silent apprehension.

The guider moved cautiously, the dread increasing with each faltering step. She came to the first plank and stopped. On either side of the bridge were intricately carved railings and down the center was a line of worn white stones. Its width could easily admit ten full grown men, shoulder to shoulder and the curve of the span was such that one could not see the other side without mounting to the apex. Trenara felt extremely small on the massive bridge, as she unconsciously stood on her toes, trying to see the other side.

A pre-dawn gust came from the east, carrying a vile smell that made their eyes water and their nostrils burn. It was the smell of fire and burned flesh, sickly sweet and putrid. The stench was unmistakable.

Trenara slowly advanced up the bridge, but before she reached the summit, she paused and held her scepter toward the sky, singing so softly the notes were a whisper on the air. The *power* glided down as a graceful white torrent that swallowed her. In seconds, the light swirled into a blazing blue, undulating around the figure at its center like the heart of a flame.

Vanderlinden had never heard anything more beautiful than the lyric music of that voice, and his heart danced to the sound. He saw Trenara as if for the first time. Her hair was an auburn fire in the wind of *power*, her figure, slim and strong, her face more lovely than anything he had ever seen and her eyes, those beautiful eyes that had conquered him the first moment he saw them, now blazed gloriously. The giant knew instantly that he loved Trenara and the intensity of the emotion left him breathless. He suddenly wanted nothing more than to take her in his arms. Vanderlinden realized his foolishness at once and looked away from his own weakness.

There was a loud, rumbling hiss from the other side of the bridge, making the wood tremble beneath their feet. Andelian flared with sudden fury in response and filled the guider with calm assurance. She took the last few steps to the top.

Beyond the summit, standing three spans in height and filling the width of the bridge, was a giant lizard. It had scales running down its back to an enormous tail that fell over the side railing and dangled in the river below. A pair of powerful hind legs, each as thick as tree trunks, supported a massive scaled belly, and in its taloned hands was what appeared to be a blackened human leg. Around it laid gnawed bones with pieces of uneaten flesh still clinging to them. Its bloody face seemed to smile back at them, the immense jaws lined by three rows of needle sharp teeth. The huge mouth curved to large pointed ears, making a permanent sardonic grin. Behind it, between two of the many humps that ran the length of its body, were enormous bony wings that fell over either side of the bridge.

Trenara lifted her eyes slowly to take in the abomination. There was no doubt as to what she saw. A flying tarsian lizard, extinct for thousands of seasons; here stood the terror of the ancient lands. The lizards were singularly vicious, killing for the mere pleasure of it. It was said they possessed high intelligence and could speak in the common tongue.

As the blue flames surrounding Trenara flared at the sight, the lizard hissed again and shrank back from the light, dropping the half eaten leg to cover large, cat-yellow eyes with a bloody hand. Disgust sent a sick rush through the guider as she looked up at this creature. She took a deep breath and repeated to herself the axiom of strength: *evil cannot exist without fear—it has no power over those who are not afraid.*

"Ssso, Asssssemblage." The tarsian hissed so quietly, it was difficult to hear. "You have come at lassst."

"Step aside, lizard, we wish to pass." Trenara's voice sounded feeble in the gloom as she held Andelian before her, her knuckles white with strain.

A sound escaped the lizard that could have been a laugh. "Of courssse, Asssssemblage, it would be our pleasssure. But asss you can ssssee," it said, opening its arms to the bones laying before it, "we have jussst now finsssshed our meal. It isss difficult to fly away with a full belly, hmm?" A black forked tongue came out and licked blood from its massive jaws.

"Move aside, lizard!" Andelian flared and the dragon took a step back.

"Nasssty, nasssty," it hissed viciously. "We are king of lizzzardsssss, Asssemblage. You will call usss majesssssty." It took a menacing step forward and Vanderlinden drew a long blade from his side with a metallic whisper.

"You *were* king, lizard, but you rule no more in this land," Trenara called up to it. "You have been asleep long, tarsian. What has brought you out of your slumber?"

The creature regarded her with slanted eyes. "We sssee no reasssson for Asssemblage to know what wakesss usss, but we will tell her, asss we think ssssshe won't be able to tell anyone." He took another step forward, the bridge shaking under his weight. "Wasss the massster in the sssouth that breathed life back into usss from our place among the sssstonesss."

"Who is your master?" Trenara demanded, Andelian punctuating the command with fire.

The lizard swiftly leapt into the air, spreading its wings and letting out a piercing screech. The eechas screamed and broke from Vanderlinden's grip as he covered his ears and put his head down. They bolted off the bridge, disappearing into the midnight plains.

Trenara kept her footing as Andelian protected her from the earsplitting shriek. Sparks began to fly away from her where the vibrations hit her *shield*. The tarsian ceased its cry and hovered over the two on the bridge. Vanderlinden fell to his knees when the scream stopped, trying to shake the sound from his head.

"Asssemblage would like to know, would ssssshe?" the lizard said. "But we have no time to tell her. Massster gave usssss an errand to do and sssaid there would be a tasssty morsssel in it for usss, though we imagine Asssemblage meat to be ssstringy and giant meat to be tough."

The beast unhinged his jaws until his mouth became a cavernous black opening above them. In a blinding flash, a column of white-hot fire erupted from the black, surrounding the two victims on the bridge. As it hit, Andelian shot out a circle of brilliant light that settled into a blue dome around them, absorbing the heat and flame. The bridge, however, did not fare as well and caught fire in many places. The tarsian shrieked in rage.

Van's ears had been ringing violently after the initial trumpet call of the lizard, and the pain in his head was so intense he thought he was going mad. When the dome encircled them, he saw the lizard rise, send fire raining down on them again, and then rise further with another screech. All Van could hear now was the numbing hiss of silence.

Trenara's arm rose and two bright beams of blue light came from Andelian with a crackling blast, one right after the other. The first missed its mark and exploded in a shower of sparks in the sky. The other caught the lizard's wing and scorched it badly, causing the monster to double its efforts against the *shield* around them. Just as the *shield* kept the blaze out, it also kept the protected in and the bridge was soon a blazing firestorm around them. Vanderlinden knew it was only a matter of seconds before they would plunge into the rushing rapids or crash against the jagged rocks below.

More *power* shot from the guider's wand and again the tarsian deftly dodged the bolts. It began to fly higher and farther away. For a moment, the giant thought the wing was damaged badly enough, the creature would give up the battle. However, the tarsian stopped and hovered over the two. Vanderlinden guessed the monster's game: it would wait until the bridge gave up and they fell to the rocks below. If there was anything left, the beast could swoop down and pick up the pieces. Van knew it was swift enough to pick them both up before they hit the water. It infuriated him to be completely helpless in the dark, caught between fire, water, and a lizard's whim.

The timbers beneath them began to crack and moan as Vanderlinden lost his footing and fell, and the bridge began to teeter as the side sagged toward the rapids. More bolts flew from Trenara's scepter, and one hit the beast on the right side. The animal screamed in pain. Stopping the fire abruptly, the creature began to dive. The great distance allowed it to pick up speed as it threw the giant wings flat against its body and readied its talons to strike.

Completely spent and all her magic gone, Trenara fell and the *shield* disappeared. Van dived at the guider, wrapping his body around her frail form to protect her from the tarsian's vicious claws and the fire. As if on command, the bridge gave up and Van went down without letting go of Trenara. Wind rushed up to flail against them as they fell toward the river helplessly. With a rush of foul air, the lizard swooped down and neatly caught Van's shoulders in its talons. It began to rise, the leathery wings beating the air with rhythmic precision, and the eyes blazing with yellow fire. The giant screamed in pain, the weight of the unconscious guider making the talons bury themselves several inches into his soft flesh and muscles, but he wouldn't let go. From the tarsian's throat came an exulted cry that mingled with Van's screams and echoed repeatedly across the plains.

The echo of that triumph would be the monster's last. The tarsian didn't realize it was flying backwards into the arms of the waiting Grotto… and that is exactly what Vanderlinden thought he saw, although in latter days he was never quite certain. Shadowed now by a rising dawn, were two huge, fir-clad arms, stretching out to three times the width of the tarsian's wings. It was as though the trees had suddenly come to life and were waiting to take the screaming beast into their embrace. The limbs engulfed the creature with such alacrity, they cut off the cry in its midst. All that could be heard in the silence that followed was the grating crack of bone and sinew. The lizard dropped his victims, and the last thing Vanderlinden remembered was the first sound he had heard since the loss of his hearing, a heart rending shriek of agony and defeat. The sun broke over the horizon as the beast fell and Van lost consciousness.

*****

When Trenara woke, it was late morning. The bedding of subtle grasses where she lay was warm as sunlight streamed down, and a soft whispered breeze went through golden-green leaves above her head. She sat up at once and felt refreshed. There was no one around, but she didn't feel lonely, as though the trees and grasses were company enough. The guider began to wonder if the battle on the bridge had been nothing more than a dream; indeed, she began to wonder if it all wasn't some kind of dream. In this place, nothing of evil, hurt, or weariness could be very real. Only the grass, the trees, and the birds that chattered on every bough possessed this place and left it in peace.

The guider knew the tarsian had been all too real, as well as her mission. There were other things she knew as well, but didn't know why. The lizard was dead, although she didn't remember it, and she had spent several days asleep while all her hurts were healed.

The guider got up to the sound of rustling and turned to see a small man with a bright eye advancing on her as if his feet never touched the ground. The little man, perhaps half her height, was clad all in green from his leather stockings to his bright leather hat. He wore a smile that would have melted grief from the gravest situation.

The guider was instantly delighted. A Clurichaune, a rare find these days. They were a delightful people, reclusive, living chiefly in forests and on one or two small islands in the far west. Few females were born to the tiny people, which was the reason for their scarcity. Trenara had known one as a girl. She had met him on a night long ago, when she had crept from her father's house and often wondered why she had never been punished for these small breeches of familial law. She found out much later that her father, too, had done the same as a boy.

Clurichaunes were not magical in the sense of power, but rather in their charm. Their voices were high and lyrical. When you first talked to one, you got the impression they were scattered and garrulous. However, if you listened long enough, you would realize they made perfect sense. Indeed, they seemed to have more sense than the truly wise among *regular* people. The guider's pleasure was two-fold, for Vanderlinden came lumbering behind the little man, making him seem even tinier.

"*Questasta cordican, Clurichaune haditant,*" Trenara said, bowing with lavish formality.

The Clurichaune clapped his hands and did a somersault in mid air, touching the ground in the exact spot. He began to laugh and wiped a tear from his eye. "Well met, indeed, oh, thou wondrous master of tongues—would that I could hear those words more oft these days. From thy way of speaking the Great Tongue, my guess would be thou art either from the grand isle to the east, or a brother has taught thee thy notes, to sing so sweetly." He cocked an eyebrow, did a small dance in the middle of the grove, and took the guider's arm.

"Both, my dear friend, for I am from Mathisma and a brother did indeed teach me pieces of your language. I have forgotten more than I learned." Trenara allowed herself to be led from the glen down a small path.

"No matter then," the tiny man replied, "for I shall continue thy lessons and be glad of the teaching. I have been here too long without kith or kin and would greatly be obliged to do thee such service. Thou may call me Tak, short for my name, but long enough for thee. If it was Mathisma from whence thou fares, then it must have been the self-same Etaletalon who has taught thee. No doubt, he's filled thy head with tales and rumors of our kin and kind. He always was a liar and I shall have to set thee straight afore the night is gone." Tak skipped on ahead as if his exuberance could not keep him still in the glorious morning. His running tread was so light it left no mark on the delicate grass.

Vanderlinden caught up with Trenara as the Clurichaune disappeared around a bend in the path. "He be strange, that one," he said, walking beside her. "But he sure makes a body feel good."

Trenara smiled as if it were easier than any other expression in this forest. "Consider yourself fortunate, Van. Few people see a Clurichaune in a lifetime. To have known two is a rare treat. I wish there were more of his kind."

Van looked her over carefully as they walked. "You all right, guider?"

"I'm good, Van," she said. "But it seems you took the brunt of the attack."

Van shrugged. "Not bad, really."

She stopped and peered up at him. "Let me see your shoulders."

He let out an exasperated breath and grudgingly opened his shirt so she could inspect the wounds. When she reached to expose his left shoulder, he pushed her hand away. "It's just in the front and back," he said quickly.

Trenara gave him a sidelong glance, and then inspected the damage. On each shoulder was a large circular scar where the lizard's talons had held him. The wounds were white and completely healed, as if it had happened seasons ago.

"Amazing," Trenara whispered as Van shrugged back into his shirt, uncomfortable with her touch.

"Aye," he said simply and began to walk again.

Ahead of them, the path grew broader. It was bordered on either side by neatly trimmed hedges intertwined with lavender flowers. At the end of the lane was an enormous cathedral made from living trees and moss. Situated inside the grove were moss-covered stone benches and tables, so worn it looked as though they had grown there over many ages.

They both stopped and looked at the living sanctuary in wonder. Neither of them had felt such power of life. The trees, mostly evergreens, were tall and straight, yet many were aged with gnarled bark, and thick about the trunk. Some were so broad at the base it would have taken a half dozen men fingertip to fingertip to embrace them fully. Their branches intertwined high above the companions' heads until they appeared to belong to just one immense tree. It blocked the light of day almost entirely, making the cathedral dark and misty green. Only here and there did a single sunbeam escape the dense branches, shooting a gleaming shaft of yellow-green sunlight that sparkled with millions of bits of dust caught in the stuffy forest.

The Clurichaune jumped down from one of the benches and gestured to them. "Come along, come along, come along. Thou canst stay here," he whispered and then gave them a wink. "The trees, you know. There are things to do before ye set off again and long talk to have." The Clurichaune turned on his heel and strode merrily through the center of the grove.

They came at last to a thick, narrow archway made of living holly settled at the end of the cathedral. Vanderlinden had to get to his hands and knees to crawl through, but they emerged from the thorny opening and saw a carpet of green well-trimmed grass before them. The path ended here, but beyond was a lovely little cottage made of mud and fir boughs.

The little man was busily setting a short table with baskets, bowls, bottles and berries; figin fruit, fireweed and fratellas; sweet baked breads and savory sautéed salminian. He worked so quickly the larger people could only gape in wonder, as the table seemed to be made ready on its own.

Trenara broke from the spell and was about to venture a helping hand when, before she could so much as open her mouth, the Clurichaune bowed to them nobly, now dressed in silver and green, and invited them to sup. And sup they did, on a feast that rivaled the greatest boasts of tables from province to province.

They talked long into the afternoon and far into the evening, when Ethos climbed into the sky to look down at the weary travelers and the amazing little man. The Clurichaune talked on and on, as though his voice were inexhaustible. He spoke much of the grotto and its ways, about its beauty and joy. He spoke of the hard labors he had to expend to tend it. No one asked him why he did it; it would have been like asking a tree why it grew.

Few creatures visited, he said—only the birds who brought him news from the outside, amongst many a chattering frivolity about their nestlings and the lack of food. Birds were like that, he supposed, but they had brought him enough news to keep him fairly well informed. Bears would come upon occasion in search of salminian fish along the Minan. He liked bears, but they were quite insular and minded their own business, paying little heed to the doings of humans. Many people traveled the road or the river, but few stopped anymore. Tak blamed the silly rumors that the forest was dangerous.

"Dangerous indeed." He shook his head until the feather bounced. "It is only dangerous to those with evil intent. However, we approach dark days and who's to say? Perhaps one day my Grotto will again be filled with visitors." Tak laughed suddenly.

"There are only two things I miss: company and playing my little jokes. The trees do not have much of a sense of humor, I'm afraid." He threw his head back and laughed again. Clurichaunes were notorious for their practical jokes.

The travelers didn't need to mention much of their journey or their purpose. Tak already knew what they had been through and hinted at what lay ahead, though never enough of a hint to give them any kind of clear picture. The guider and the giant found it easy and even compelling to speak their hearts to this little man. Each told him exactly what they had done, good or bad, and their hearts were lightened by the sharing. Van was especially comforted, as he had kept deep secrets locked away for many seasons. The Clurichaune listened quietly and merely nodded. Trenara also remained silent, but not so much in respect, as in marvel at Vanderlinden's past; a past the guider swore she would never reveal.

The night dwindled as the moons slipped behind the line of trees each in their turn. Vanderlinden was beginning to drift into sleep as the guider and Tak talked on.

"Thou wilt be needing to leave soon, I imagine," the Clurichaune said. "Though mores the pity. I haven't had such long talk in seasons and a body does get lonely." He sighed deeply. "These eyes get sore from lack of naught to see but trees and sky. It's a wondrous thing to look at thee, if I may be bold. It does an old heart too much good." He then bowed low. "You shine like a star in many eyes, guider, if truth be known. Thou dost not know how brightly."

Trenara blushed, much to her surprise. "Thank you. What a lovely thing to say."

"It pales against thee, my lady." The little man stopped and looked at her, his eyes clouded with a sudden pain. "Do not let love go blindly by thee, lady; see it when it passes." Trenara looked at him puzzled, but he just smiled broadly, did another somersault on the spot, and clapped his hands. "Too much. Too much!" he cried and laughed again. Without missing a beat, he continued. "I shall teach thee yet the Clurichaune tongue, and thou wilt be glad. There is magic yet in the world that is not known to mortals, or so it is said—some older than the gods and twice as mighty. Thou wilt need to know the tongue for thine own protection."

Trenara became alert. "What magic?"

"Now, don't get thyself in an uproar. The magic I speak of isn't like thy *power*— no, no, no indeed. It is old, like the tall mountains and subtle like the wind in the leaves. I'm thinking thou hast seen a piece of it here and there." Trenara looked on uncertainly. "Come now, guider. Like the man who has just a little more 'luck' than he ought; or the mother who knows there's something wrong with her child when all else says there isn't? This kind of magic has always been around. Long before the Crystal of Healing came to thee. It'll be here long after, too. Of course," he mused, "that is the *white* magic, as it's called. There's also the black, though not much, thank the Mother. It's against this, the tongue will protect thee. It has protected us for a long time now."

"Tak, what of these black…"

"Shhh, shhh, shhh." Tak's finger danced before his mouth in a graceful gesture. "Enough said for tonight. Now is the time for sleep. Thy good companion has fairly won that race," he said, nodding to the slumbering Vanderlinden. "It's best we all do the same." He rose from the table and began to extinguish the lamps.

"Please, Tak, one more question. How will you teach me the language if we can't stay long?"

The little man blew out the last lantern, leaving the stars to light the clearing. "I have my ways, guider. I have my ways. Good night." He vanished into the little house and slammed the door.

Trenara would have pursued him, but a sudden deep weariness overcame her. She woke Van, and the two went off into the trees to find their beds for the night.

When she and Van woke the next morning, their bags were neatly stacked at their feet, much to their surprise. Neither of them knew how they came to be there, but they were so delighted to see most of their provisions still intact, they didn't care. Trenara hugged her *via* as a tear fell down her cheek. She thought it was lost in the woods the night of the attack.

They decided to leave immediately, agreeing they had wasted valuable time. A sudden urgency was on them that neither could explain.

"We'll need eechas or some kind of transport," Van said as he checked his satchel.

"I believe going down the Minan would be best and by raft, if we can build one quickly. How long do you think it will take?"

Van shrugged. "A day would be my guess, but it's going to be dangerous going down that river in a raft. At the Calpern fork, the rapids get rough. No raft is going to get through those. We'll have to leave the river before then and cross the Plains."

"Whatever you think. You know this country better than I do. We best tell Tak we're leaving."

But the little man was nowhere to be found. They searched for almost an hour, when Trenara happened on a note tied to a tree.

"Van, this note's from Tak. It says he had an errand to attend and that he left us boats and supplies down by the river."

"Boats! Bless the little scoundrel. If he was here I'd kiss him."

"He also says he won't be back before we leave. He wishes us good fortune." She handed the note to Van.

"How can you read this gibberish?" he asked, turning the sheet upside down and over in his hands.

"Gibberish?"

"Look at it," he said giving it back to her. "That's not common speech, nor Mathismian."

Trenara looked again. "By the gods, it's Clurichaune! I guess the little fellow does have his ways. Come on. Let's get to those boats."

They found beautifully carved wooden shells tied to the bank of the river that would hold one apiece plus their gear.

"I'd like to know how these were built and rigged," Van said as he settled into the boat. "This balance is about as perfect as I've ever seen."

"When we have time, I'll tell you how it's done." Trenara began to paddle to the center of the river. Van gave her an incredulous look and she just shook her head. "Don't ask."

They drifted down the river, leaving the Grotto and the little man far behind.

*****

The Minan was wide for many miles and didn't narrow again until it came close to the Calpern River, which forked and flowed raggedly to the Selas Straights in the southwest. Van said it would take about fifteen days to reach the fork by river and was concerned they would need to stop for provisions before then.

"I know a town off the river by the name of Clover. Haven't been there in seasons, but we can get what stores we need for the last part of our journey. It should take about a week to reach from here."

They traveled down the river by night and slept in the woods on either side of the water by day. The closer they drew to the country to the south, the greater their haste became.

As the days passed, Van and Trenara became fast friends. They would talk for hours, sometimes right through the day and have to take naps in the boats to make up the time. Other times, they would heatedly debate both empirical and Assemblage rule until they were both hoarse from the efforts. Then, they would look at each other and break down laughing until they were spent.

But the further south they went, the more strained the relationship became and Trenara started to see hesitation in the giant's eyes. He would be laughing hysterically one moment and still and sullen the next. As each day passed, his mood worsened. He would snap at the guider for no apparent reason and then apologize, saying he didn't know why, which seemed to make him more agitated.

To make matters worse, every day they felt as if they were under attack. The assailant was unknown but began to eat at their emotions. Trenara tried to explain to Van that if he feared the feelings, his anxiety would become worse, to which he'd merely grunt something about needing quiet. The weather was also becoming unseasonably hot and Vanderlinden would complain repeatedly that he couldn't sleep. More and more he would take to the woods and not return until dusk, each day looking increasingly careworn and haggard.

Trenara's concern was twofold; somehow, they had spent well over a week on the river without seeing any sign of a town and nothing to break the sight of endless plains, except an occasional thicket of weather beaten trees. Their provisions were running dangerously low.

One evening, the guider sat up suddenly from a fitful sleep, well past the time Van should have woken her. She searched the clearing quickly, but Vanderlinden had not returned. The sky was overcast and the moons had waned to slivers that hung as misty crescents under a blanket of ruddy gray. From the west, a sudden shout echoed through the plains. Trenara could see nothing as she scanned the grass and sprinted off toward the sound. When she cleared the woods, she could see smoke rising in the distance. Drawing Andelian from her robe and hoping the blue light would somehow shield her, she gazed at the distant smoke and heard the cry again. The guider crouched low and raced toward the fire.

When she got as near as she dared, Trenara stooped behind the tall grass to catch her breath and study the situation. There were several figures standing around a huge bonfire and two men tied to a large circular stone. The figures were singing and chanting, the music sour and wretched. So engrossed were they in their ritual, they did not notice when the guider moved forward cautiously. As Trenara drew near, she could smell the unmistakable stench of laminia. Peering through the grass, she saw close to twenty of them contorting wildly in a strange dance before the flames. With them was another figure the guider could not identify, as it was robed and hooded. There was an unnatural chill in the air that bit at her cheeks, as if a northern wind had escaped from the mountains. Trenara's *sense* could feel nothing from that creature—like a deep emptiness, completely devoid of life. It made her gut ache with apprehension.

When the creature raised its arms, the blaze jumped with a sudden yellow flame and the victims began to scream. Trenara recognized Vanderlinden instantly. His face was bloody and he seemed nearly unconscious. The other man was smaller, his long, black hair tumbling over his face as he thrashed about, strained against his bonds, and shot smoldering looks at his captors. Finally, he screamed and fainted.

The guider lifted her scepter above her head and began to sing. For a moment, all that could be heard was the hideous drone of laminia voices as they rose and fell on the still air. There was a sudden hiss and crackle as the *power* unleashed its light to engulf the guider with white mist. The drone of the voices died and the hooded figure whirled around at the sudden clash of fire at its back.

The laminia cringed near the ground with a babble of fear and confusion as the figure shrank back from the brilliant light embracing the guider at its midst. There was a sound like an angry growl and the laminia became at once silent. They began to stand, taking long, crooked knives from their belts that flashed blood-red in the firelight. At a sign from their leader, they began to advance slowly on the guider, spreading out in a rough semi-circle around her.

Trenara waved her hands casually, and the group crumbled to the ground as one. She then turned her attention to the hooded figure and caught the gleam of two fiery eyes smoldering beneath the cowl as it reached among the burning branches and picked up a blazing brand. The sleeve caught fire, but the figure did not move until the robe burned away completely. All Trenara could see was a deep shadow, completely devoid of light, which sent tendrils out on all sides. One held the burning torch as others curled back and forth with a strange kind of grace; the rest was a fluctuating mass of black. The figure shook the branch once and in a whistling flash of red, it changed into a gleaming staff. Trenara's eyes widened in horror, and she lifted Andelian.

When she sang, the white turned at once to blue and trickled down around her to form a pulsating cobalt *shield* shot with tiny charges. The figure seemed to float toward her with the brand held ready to strike. When the staff came down, it hit the *shield* and sent sparks cascading into the grass to hiss.

Trenara turned her scepter once and held a bright staff that glistened like white jewels in the sun. She swung it with all her strength to cut the figure across the middle. The staff whistled in the air, but the shadow jumped back and the weapon missed. The mass whirled around quickly and lunged at the guider, bringing the burning staff straight down. Trenara's ears pounded with pressure as it hit the field at full force. The figure shook violently from the impact and staggered back a few steps. Trenara shot sizzling bolts of light at the shape over and over again, but as each hit the shadow it disappeared in the darkness without impact. Trenara was staggered by the attack and sank to her knees breathlessly.

The shadow loomed above her cocoon of *power* and a gravelly chuckle grated on the air. Although the voice was no more than a whisper, each word was painfully clear.

"You do not know your peril, Assemblage. You fight the unconquered, the champion of Sirdar. Your *shield* will not hold me back for long."

Trenara struggled to her feet, but did not answer and leaned on her staff. Again, the quiet laughter rasped against her nerves and the figure brought his staff up sharply, the eyes a fiery gleam in the shadow where a head should have been. "Fight, mortal," it whispered.

Trenara stared wearily up at it. "I will not fight you, demon. Break the *shield* if you can."

The monster moved several feet back and charged toward the guider like a hellish hurricane, its staff glowing with red fire. When the demon was almost on her, Trenara went to her knees and thrust her staff deeply into the ground, until it rested at an angle level with the shadow's middle. Her song filled the air and echoed over the plains as the *shield* fell suddenly away from her.

At the same instant, the gleaming white staff shimmered faintly and became a long, sharp barb. Such was the figure's speed that he was pinioned on the spear before he could stop, and his brand disappeared in a flash. The fiery eyes went wide and the shadow fell back, leaving the spear to smoke with what Trenara could only assume was the demon's black blood. In a sudden hiss of curling smoke, the figure disappeared.

The earth shook brutally and Trenara had to cling to the shaft for support, driving it deeper into the ground. A void opened up where the form had stood, as if an immense puncture had been ripped into the night air. A powerful wind began to suck everything that was not fastened down into the hole. Rocks, earth, grass, and luckless laminia were sucked into the pit like bits of debris, as Trenara hugged her *via* for life. She felt it beginning to give under the pressure and fought desperately to keep it lodged in the soft dirt.

As quickly as it opened, the dark hole closed, and the plains were once again silent. Andelian sparked in her hands and turned at once into a scepter. The guider fell backwards onto the soft grass and simply closed her eyes for a moment to gather her wits. She sat up stiffly, kissed her via before putting it back in its niche and then slowly got up to see about Van and the other man.

The fire had been sucked into the blackness leaving only a trail of small blazes where coals had fallen. The laminia were gone, and whether they had all been sucked into the pit or some escaped into the plains, she didn't know. There was no trace of them now. Trenara lifted the giant's head and examined his face. Van had a cut on his forehead, but it seemed superficial. He would come to his senses soon, so the guider untied him and let him lie on the stone.

The other man was another matter. He had been deeply wounded, with a gaping gash on his arm that bled profusely. He was near death as his breath came in ragged gasps and his heart beat faintly. The guider feared he would not last the night. She took out her still warm *via* and with a quick musical note, Andelian flared in her hand. As she ran the white flame over the open flesh to seal it, the man struggled and Trenara had to sit on him to hold him still, but the flesh closed and the bleeding stopped. The guider cut his bonds and then tore strips from her robe to wind around the wound, then wiped the dirt from his face to check his color. She was shocked at how pale he was.

Even dirty and pale, the face was stunning. Long hair, the golden color of the Palimar fields, framed a face with perfect features reminiscent of the ancient god statues on Mathisma. He looked to be about her age, although the healed scars all over his body showed a man of much more experience, and the week or two of reddish beard growth showed a weathered traveler. He was dressed in well worn mountain clothes, a little out of place here in the middle of the plains at the end of low season. She took out the imaka, poured a small drop between his parched lips, and made certain the dressings were secure.

The guider knew there was nothing more she could do for the time being, so she returned to Van. When the imaka hit the giant's tongue, he groaned and opened his eyes. He grabbed the guider's shoulders and pulled her toward him. "Trenara!" he screamed, but then realized she was in his arms. He let her go and sat up. "Guider," he rasped, "the demon…" He looked around wildly.

"Gone," Trenara responded, helping Van to his feet. "What happened?"

Van shook his head and wiped blood from his face. Trenara made him sit down while she tended to the gash above his eye. "Don't know," he said. "I heard a man screaming and followed it. When I came out of the woods, something was thrown over my head and I was beaten down. When I came to, I was tied to that stone and them laminia were all over me… and that black devil, whatever it was. That's all I know. Are you all right?"

"Yes. Can you walk?"

"Sure," he said, stretching his legs stiffly. "I'm not hurt bad—just my pride. Except my head feels like it could fall off right enough."

"Good. Let's get back to camp. I don't like the feel of this place and there's bound to be more laminia about. We'll need to get the man to shelter in any event," she said, nodding to the spot next to him on the stone. "He's badly hurt."

Trenara gave the man another drop of the imaka. His color was better and his breathing easier. They carried him back to the camp and lit a fire to stay any unwanted visitors. If there were any more laminia, they did not appear, so Vanderlinden slept, leaving Trenara to tend her patient.

She cleaned him with water from the stream and changed him into some of the giant's spare clothes. When she examined the scars, she realized they must be from sword fights; he must have experience with the blade. Worrying about infection, she spread some of the imaka on a rag and applied it to the now *power* sealed flesh. It seemed to help; he slept easier and his heartbeat was much improved. She let him rest.

Trenara settled on the bank to think and watch. As the night waned, with nothing to break the silence but the insect calls, the soft rustle of the wind in the grasses, and the sluggish splash of the slow currents of the Minan, she began to nod. A voice startled her awake; a rich baritone that was so lyrical, she was amazed it wasn't Assemblage.

"No," the stranger cried in his sleep, rolling dangerously against his damaged arm. Trenara rushed to his side to stop him before he tore the wound open again. Just as she leaned over, he had her in his arms, his eyes flashing open, and rolled her onto her back. In a split instant, she had both her arms over her head held by a stilled hand with a dagger at her throat and the wind being pushed out of her lungs as he sat on her chest.

"Who are you?" He winced in pain when the wound on his arm opened, dripping blood onto her neck, but he did not let up his grip. He was very strong.

Trenara looked up at him, her eyes blazing. "Your doctor, you idiot. If you don't let me up, I'll let you bleed to death—fair enough?"

The man looked at her puzzled and then shook his head. He did not release her. "Where did you come from?" he demanded.

"I'm…" she began, the knife making her stutter, "I'm from Mathisma and this," she said looking behind him, "is Vanderlinden. I'm not sure where he's from." The man was yanked into the air as if he were a child and thrown several feet, coming close to landing in the fire. Fortunately, he missed it and landed instead on his good arm with a thud.

Van helped the guider to her feet and smiled. "You do want looking after. You could've screamed."

"Sorry. I didn't have time." She glanced over at the man who was trying to stand up without much success. "Now, look what you've done. I just fixed that."

She walked over and reached for his arm, which he pulled away. Trenara closed her eyes and counted. "Look," she said, intoning her voice skillfully to calm him. "I'm not going to hurt you. Let me see your arm."

"I'm sorry," he said relaxing, "I thought…" He stopped and flashed a handsome smiled. "You'll have to forgive me, lady. It has been a terrible night." There was a lyrical quality to his voice that hit Trenara like a cool breeze. He let her examine the arm and repair the dressing. The wound hadn't opened too far, so she didn't use the *via* again, but rewrapped it tightly. When she was through, she explained to him what had happened on the plains and how they had found him.

"What are you doing out here?" Van asked, helping him to sit on a log.

"I was running from them," he said jerking his head to the plains. "I thought I had lost them in Clover, but they picked up my trail and caught me in the middle of the plains. They killed my eecha, the bastards."

"Who are you?" Trenara asked, still caught by his voice and the intelligence in those eyes.

He smiled and bowed as low as he could. "Forgive me, beautiful lady, but I am Leogan, Swordsman of Foles… and your humble servant. I am grateful you came along—both of you. They would have made short work of me. Sometimes I suffer from an abundance of confidence, which often serves me poorly. I should not have come alone on this journey."

She looked at him searchingly, caught by something in his face. "Are you—Assemblage?"

Leogan's eyes widened and his laugh was glorious. "Me? Assemblage? No, sadly, I am not. What skills I have rest in my hands, my head, and my heart." He picked up Trenara's hand and kissed it. "Which belongs to you, lovely lady."

Van bristled visibly.

"I have a heart of my own, thank you," Trenara replied, taking her hand back. "When I need another I'll let you know." She stood up and folded her arms. "But now I think you need to elaborate for us. What are you doing out here?"

He nodded quietly, the firelight shining in his eyes. "I'll tell you, but you might not believe me. I hardly believe it myself." He cradled the wounded arm and stared into the fire.

"I'm a soldier, lady, or was—on the wall of Foles. My liege was his honor Baron Trenapha who keeps a villa to protect Badain from attack at the High Ingress. We were a great army, lady," he said with passion. "A great army that had held back the northern strikes for countless seasons with grand success. For the first time in so long even our old people could not recall, we had peace and were finally building a new home for our children." His voice stopped as he stared at the fire. "We did not look for attack at our backs, but that is where it came.

"Without warning, Cortaim swept over us like a raging fire, burning villages, destroying crops, killing everything in their path. The few who survived were taken to the black castle to serve under Sirdar."

"Sirdar?" Trenara asked quietly. "That creature said something about Sirdar."

He looked at her. "Lord Sirdar, lady. His soldiers worship him, calling him god and master—I have seen it with my own eyes. I can't even begin to tell you the power this man holds over others. It's like an obsession. Not just men, but other creatures we thought dead and buried for centuries. They fall behind him in huge numbers and bow at his feet." A shudder took him, as he grew quiet for a moment.

"They attacked the Ingress and took it easily. We were so unprepared. By luck or fate, five of us escaped into the mountains. From our hiding, we watched as Sirdar's strength grew. A month ago, I left to seek aid." He sank his head and breathed deeply. With a visible effort, he smoothed his face and looked into Trenara's eyes.

"And here you find me," he smiled sadly, "on my way to Thrain to beg the emperor for help. I'm afraid it is probably too late."

"We are on our way to the borders to see for ourselves," Trenara told him, "as emissaries from the emperor."

"But where are your armies?" Leogan asked. "Your intentions, though noble, are foolhardy. Sirdar has many allies and his hand has spread beyond Badain. The daligon is vile, but there are many other creatures that follow him."

"The daligon?" she asked.

He laughed. "You destroy a creature and don't know its name? The shadow you bested with your magic. This path is perilous and I'm afraid it could end up being deadly. I beg you to reconsider. Return to Thrain and implore an army from the emperor."

"I understand your concern," Trenara replied, turning to warm her hands against the fire. "However, this is our mission and we won't abandon it."

He nodded solemnly and took a deep breath. "So be it. I want only to warn you of the dangers. With my help, perhaps your chances will increase."

Trenara scowled at him. "What?"

"I'm going with you, fair lady."

Vanderlinden stood up. "Not bloody likely," he said with perhaps more force than he intended. Something sparked in the giant's eyes as he stared at the man, and Leogan looked back angrily.

"You have little choice," he said. "I am the only one who knows a safe way into the country and through the High Ingress. Without my help, you won't even get as far as the border."

"I think I could get a good spell farther than you think—and without your kind of help, mate. Me and the guider were doing just fine without you."

"Fine," Leogan replied hotly. "Go without me. I'd just as soon not return to that place." He looked at Trenara. "But I'm not going to let you take her in there and get her killed—or worse. Not while I have blood in me."

"I think we can take care of that!" Van's eyes blazed dangerously, and Trenara had to jump in front of him to keep him from tearing the man apart.

"Van," she said to him gently. The fire in his eyes faded to confusion as he stared down at her. Without a word, he turned around and walked off into the forest. Trenara watched him go, puzzled by his ever increasing tempers.

"Lady," Leogan said from behind her. "I'm sorry."

Trenara turned around to stare into a pair of compelling eyes. He was so close to her, she could feel his breath on her lips. She took a step back nervously and turned away from him.

"It's all right, Leogan," she said softly, overcome by a rush of conflicting emotions. "It's late and you need rest." She turned and smiled softly. "I have a lot to think about. Please, we'll discuss it in the morning. I think we all need a break for a while."

Leogan picked up her hand again, turned it over, and kissed the wrist gently. "As you wish, my beautiful lady. Good night." He kissed the wrist again and then laid it on her breast, causing an unwelcome flush that ran through Trenara's body. Leogan bowed low and then turned to walk slowly out of the firelight. He lay down with his back to her.

The guider walked back to the river, sat down against a tree and threw pebbles into the rushing water. There was something about Leogan… something that awoke things inside Trenara that had been dormant a long time. It was disquieting. She knew he would be joining them in the morning. She also knew he was going to be a great deal of trouble.

The next morning, Van and Leogan made a temporary, if shaky truce, when Trenara announced she needed both of them and convinced the giant they could use all the help they could get. He reluctantly agreed. They hastily threw together a small raft and tied it between the two light boats. It held together quite well under the circumstances. They traveled by day and night now, feeling a compelling urgency as they moved farther south. By luck, they reached Clover the next day, but the village was silent and fearful. Without looking for reasons, they quickly purchased what supplies they needed and continued on their journey.

It was another week before they reached the headwaters of the Calpern, and they had to carry their boats and supplies over land to avoid the rapids. Beyond the stone splitting water, the current was strong and swift, carrying them at a speed none of them thought possible. The marvelous little boats plowed through the river without taking on a drop. They were not bothered during this part of the mission, which made the guider and giant skittish. They continually looked for attacks around bends and corners in the river. When they didn't come, the companions suspected worse calamity.

"I know they're out there, guider. I can feel it. Why don't they strike?" Vanderlinden ventured one day as he scowled at the shoreline.

"I've felt it too. I wish I knew. Here, watch that log."

As the days passed, Trenara felt oddly drawn to Leogan. He awoke long suppressed feelings, and his constant attention was quickly breaking down her barriers. Too often, she found herself in his arms, wondering exactly how she got there and would have to break away from him gently, not wanting to hurt him.

Over the next few weeks, the feelings became almost overwhelming, as if it were an addiction. Trenara was trying hard to keep their relationship formal, but she constantly found herself craving his voice, his touch, and his warmth against her body. It frightened her, but it also secretly pleased her. Her defenses were dangerously low as they neared the end of their journey. To make matters worse, Van had become almost a ghost. The only time she saw him was on the river; he had become strangely detached.

By the end of Eventide, they reached the first barrier to Badain, a well guarded dam. Fortunately, Leogan was with them or they would have run headlong into the trap without warning. It was strategically located. As it was, the only thing Sirdar's guards found, some days later, were two small boats and a raft. The alarm was spread, but the travelers were well into the mountains by then.

At last, they stood on the eastern peak of the High Ingress, looking down into a valley that stretched beyond eyesight in either direction. It was here they decided to separate. Leogan would go to find his companions and see what they could do to help. It was an impossible task, but he insisted.

"We may not be able to do much, but perhaps if we can rescue even a few people, we can start some hope," he said as he, Trenara and Van looked at the open vista of valley at their feet. "You shouldn't have much trouble from here. Just stay to the road I've shown you and avoid the desert as much as possible. The heat is deadly by day. The forest along the Arms would be safest." Leogan picked up Trenara's hand and kissed it gently as she smiled softly back at him.

"Aye," Van replied, "we'll keep to the trail." He scratched his head and looked out into the forest uncomfortably. "I'm going to have a look around before you go." With that, he lumbered into the woods.

Leogan wrapped his arms around Trenara, and this time she did not stop him. She knew the feelings could no longer be ignored; she was falling in love. The realization had hit her hard when she found she wasn't able to fight his advances any more. Trenara laid her head on Leogan's chest, letting herself be lulled by the throb of his heart and the strong arms around her. "I couldn't possibly repay you for all you have done, but I'm truly grateful. I swear," she said looking up into his eyes, "when this is over..."

"No promises, my lady. You have more than repaid me." He looked deeply into her eyes. "Besides, there was no debt to begin with." Leogan lifted her chin and pressed his lips to hers sending a spark of passion that flowed like lightning down her back and into her belly. He pulled her into the kiss and increased the pressure when he felt her response.

But for some reason, something in Trenara's *sense* kindled. She broke away and looked at him strangely.

"What's wrong?" he said. His smile was so beautiful Trenara doubted her own hesitation. Leogan wrapped his hands around her shoulders and pulled her against his chest. She surrendered to the embrace without struggling, as a wave of euphoria left her weak in his arms, and he leaned down to kiss her again.

At that moment, they heard a shout from the forest, breaking the mood and the embrace. Trenara stepped back and shook the ardor from her senses, throwing a puzzled look at Leogan. Another shout echoed through the stillness. "It's Van!" she cried and sprinted into the forest.

Taking Andelian from her robes, she broke into a clearing. Vanderlinden was fighting several men with one hand planted firming on his side, and his teeth clenched in pain as he swung his sword. Trenara wasted no time in using Andelian to sweep most of the men into oblivion. Van cut the last man down and then sheathed his sword.

"You do want watching," said Trenara as she slipped Andelian into her robe.

"Sorry, guider." Van winced in pain. "I'll be more careful next time fifteen men jumped me from the trees." He laughed and winced, but then another cry echoed from the clearing where Trenara had left Leogan. They made their way back through the woods, but when they arrived, the packs were still there but Leogan was gone.

"Leogan!" the guider called. There was no reply. The forest was strangely silent as they searched the clearing thoroughly, but there was no sign of a struggle.

"He couldn't have left without a sign, guider." The giant brushed his hands. "This snow's as dry as bone, unless he flew out of here."

"That may not be too far from the mark. Who knows how many tarsians that monster has?"

"Look at the trees." Van pointed to branches that hung thickly above them. "Nothing that big could get through without breaking some branches." When he lifted his arm, a shot of pain contorted his face.

"Here, let me see that side."

"It's just a scratch," the giant responded testily, but lifted his tunic for Trenara's inspection. The cut was deep and ran from under his right arm to nearly his hip.

"Just a scratch? A lesser man would have died from this scratch."

Trenara made a dressing out of one of her robes, soaking it first with water and what was left of the imaka. Without the giant seeing, she ran her scepter quietly over the dressing with a few soft notes. She wrapped it tightly around Van's chest and then made him sit under well concealed bushes some distance from the clearing. When she was done, she stepped off to stare at the sky.

"You stay here," she said, adjusting her pack. "You should sleep until morning and it will be safe here. I'm going after him."

"What?" the giant roared and tried to get up. He fell heavily. "What have you done?" Van caught Trenara's arm and pulled her to him. "I'll be damned if I'm going to let you…" But his eyes closed and his grip slackened. She threw the cloak over his massive form and tucked in the edges against the cold.

"Sleep, my sweet friend," she said to the slumbering giant, leaning down to kiss him gently on the cheek. The guider looked again at the sky and then headed out of the clearing. As she walked, Trenara activated her *via* and sang the searching notes. The scepter guided her eyes straight up a sheer cliff towering well over her head. She sighed and tucked the scepter back into her robe. "Great," she grumbled and started to climb.

The journey to the top of the cliff was perilous. Trenara slipped several times, once or twice almost falling to the ground far below. The rocks passed slowly as she advanced foot by foot, sometimes finding tiny crags and other times solid rocks that were secure enough to hold her. She had to rest often to catch her breath in the thinning air. Once at the summit, she was wet with sweat and scratched from the falls.

Trenara rested to gather strength before pulling herself over the top. Some instinct told her to lay flat against the rock face. Three laminia walked by just above her head. She held completely still for one breathless moment while they passed, then lifted herself over the edge and stumbled to the side of a broad path that stretched to an immense cave at the top of the peak.

Fortunately, the bushes and trees were very dense along the path, and the guider had little trouble following the laminia. From behind a boulder, she saw an eerie light coming from the cave as several figures milled around its mouth. Leogan's shouting voice drifted from the entrance, sounding weak and far away. Trenara sat with her back to the rock and pulled Andelian from her place.

She knew the only way to get into that cave was by getting the guards out of the way. They were too widely spread for Andelian to take all at once, so Trenara lit the scepter with a wave of her hand and a single low note. She sang soft words in the night, praying to Ethos that the *power* would not be too little or too much. She pointed the crystal at an outcrop of rock that hung at the far side of the cavern. A thin almost imperceptible beam of light hit the rocks, causing first a fine trickle and then an abundant stream of dirt and rubble to flow down the mountain side. The roar was deafening and the creatures ran to investigate. A silent figure slid in behind them as they raced from the entrance.

Trenara hid behind a large crag in the rock until the corridor emptied. When it was clear, she ran down the corridor to the back of the cave. She could see the source of light up ahead and again heard Leogan scream. The cave was sweltering, and a sick red glow illuminated the walls with twisted shadows. At the end of the tunnel was a large arched entrance that seemed to lead to the source of light. She moved quickly and stopped just outside the chamber. When she looked in, she found Leogan.

He was balanced precariously on a round slab of stone, which seemed to float in the midst of burning rock by no more than his weight. He was bound standing by chains around his wrists, his terrorized face frozen, and his body stiff. The slightest move in any direction would tip the stone, causing the man to tumble into the fire.

Trenara had seen molten lava on Mathisma, but it was nothing like this. The stone seemed to glow with its own source of fire and gave off a strange pulsating light. It did not flow like magma, but rather—changed. At first, the stone appeared liquid in form, churning and bubbling thickly in its own heat. But then it turned solid, frozen into blood-red granite like warped bare mountains and pitted hills. As she watched, the stone transformed into a thick ruddy vapor that curled around Leogan's feet and licked the lip of the basin greedily. Over and over again it changed, as though it was constantly reconstructing itself and then tearing itself apart.

An overwhelming apprehension saturated the chamber, the air thick with it. Something inside her guider's *sense* was urgently compelling her to turn and run. Trenara could hear alarms jangling in her head, begging her to leave at once. But when she looked up at Leogan, common sense faded and she ignored the pleas. She forced down the dread and gripped Andelian until her knuckles went white. When she stepped over the threshold, the fear grew and made her feet leaden. She stopped and could go no further.

Leogan looked up from his perch, his face streaked with sweat and smoke. Tears of joy flared in his eyes when he saw the guider. "Trenara, help me." His voice was almost gone. His eyes pleaded with her. But whether it was the strange reddish glow or her own imagination, Leogan's face seemed at once cavernous and frightening, like a carrion animal that hunts in cribs at night. Her heart hammered in her chest.

The guider tried to speak, but fear clenched her throat like a vise. She looked at the firestones and shuddered. The wrongness of this place was overwhelming as she drew a shaky breath and stepped slowly to the basin, not knowing exactly what she was going to do. The slightest movement and Leogan would be lost to the stones. He was too far from the sides of the basin to reach, and she looked at him helplessly.

"The *via*," he hissed. "Use the *power*. It will neutralize the stones. Hurry, my love. I can't hold on much longer." Even now, the slab was tilting dangerously. Again, she lit Andelian, the white light seeming now small and dull against the red as the guider advanced a shaky step. Trenara raised her eyes to Leogan's, and she fell too deeply into their magic. The eyes of the beast were strong and the seduction was now complete. "Sing to me, beloved."

The notes poured from her throat as if someone else were singing. High, flawless, and devastating, her voice rose on the red air, amplified by the cave walls. Another voice joined hers, the baritone low and deep, winding around her phrases, subduing her tones, binding her music to his magic. Like a frail doll, Trenara lifted Andelian high above her head. The now blue fire radiated like rippled water from the *via* as the guider drove the point deep into the pulsating stones.

A roaring thunder shook the cavern as the two *powers* met, knocking the guider sprawling several feet back and overturning the stone on which Leogan stood. She screamed, but it couldn't be heard over the din of *power*. The guider held her ears and rose to her knees.

As the thunder subsided, a dark figure emerged from the firestones. It extended its arms to the ceiling and shuddered violently as red power cascaded like a waterfall around its arms, head, and torso. Its flesh undulated in the fire, crawling as if alive and reforming itself into something else. There was a high-pitched wail that reverberated through the room, making the ground tremble. The sound melted into a human voice that laughed joyously.

Smoke rose from the cauldron spiraling up its body, the slow caress almost erotic. There was a loud gasp of pleasure. When the smoke began to clear, it left behind it a flowing ruby robe, long fingered gloves, and a deep hood that shadowed the creature's face. The fog lingered around the shoulders like rosy sunlit clouds with sparkles of red and white shimmering inside. The mist rested on the shoulders until it became a roiling crimson mantel. When the figure turned its head to Trenara, all she could see through the strange darkened cowl were smoldering red eyes—human eyes. She shrank back in terror and screamed.

"You have freed me," he whispered, his voice so soft she could barely hear it.

"Who are you?"

"Beloved," he said slowly, his voice gaining strength, as he stepped out of the basin. Trenara shrank back and tried to crawl away. "My beautiful lady." The voice was now perfectly clear and chilling—Leogan's voice.

"No," she whispered, the raw truth now ripped open before her. "It can't be."

He came so close she leaned back against the cave wall to escape. "Was the deception so complete?" he said laughing. Trenara could only shake her head as tears flowed down her cheeks and she looked up at him. "Assemblage thought they could protect their guiders by removing them to the island. Fools! They thought none could be ensnared."

The figure shimmered before her as it began to change into the figure of Leogan, his eyes remaining red. With an overwhelming strength, he reached down to grab her wrists and pulled her violently to her feet. Leogan gently touched her cheek as he'd done so often before. But this time, it felt like acid on her flesh, and Trenara struggled to get away. He looked down at her with sad triumph.

"How else could I have tricked you into coming to Badain, bringing your precious Andelian with you? You have freed a new *power*—more potent than your feeble Crystal and more encompassing than the power of the gods. With it, I will bring order. You see, my lady, I am Sirdar, and you will be my lovely consort."

"No, no, no," she said unable to escape his touch.

"I sent the daligon to test you; you bested him. Be proud of what you have accomplished. You are brave, beautiful, a fitting companion for me. Together, we will rule the universe," he said softly as he touched her lips with his own. A wave of irresistible pleasure ran through her body, making her gasp at his touch and she felt herself responding to him. It terrified her.

"No!" she screamed. From some numb recess of her mind, Trenara resisted the spell, pushed him away, and turned to run blindly from the cavern, his laughter ringing in her ears.

Before she reached the entrance, another sound, more compelling than even the foul voice of Sirdar, froze her blood and turned her body to stone. The guider stopped where she was. It was not a cry exactly, but rather a high pitched whine that fell on her ears and made her heart pound. Numbness gripped her, making her breath come in short, rasping blasts; her lungs burned and her eyes became a blazing fire as the sound consumed her will. She lifted her head slowly and saw a gigantic bird, with black feathers and sad, almost human eyes. Its bright yellow beak was wide open and its purple forked tongue vibrated with the sound.

"It is the song of the Mourna you hear," said Sirdar behind her. "You can't escape her lovely voice, can you? She will sing for you day and night, my love—she will sing at our wedding. The Mourna will make Assemblage dance for my pleasure—as you will dance, my lady." There was a cruel laugh. The bird lowered its head and the sound stopped, releasing the guider from its hold.

"What devil are you?" she screamed as she whirled on him.

"Not a devil, my beauty. Something you would not understand."

There was all at once sadness in those glowing eyes. Trenara found her heart defenseless against them as they drew her in. "I regret having tricked you like this, Trenara." His voice was full of skillful remorse, playing with her emotions, touching again that deeply buried passion. The guider had never heard such brilliance in the way he manipulated the words, the tones, and the timbre.

They stroked her mind so subtly it made her crave the sound like an addiction. "The stones can only have their full *power* released by the touch of the Crystal." Sirdar approached her and took her shoulders in his hands again. She cringed from the touch. "You have served me well, guider," a ghastly light shone suddenly in his eyes, "as you will continue to serve me."

Tears welled in Trenara's eyes, but she set her jaw and glared at him. "I will not serve you! I will destroy you," she hissed at him, finding some deep rage inside, fueled by shame and profound regret.

He looked softly into her eyes and smiled. "How can you destroy what you have created?" She screamed and tried to push away from him, but he held her tightly, hurting her.

His voice became suddenly soft and compelling, the sound of the man who had touched her in the wilderness, who had reached deeply into her soul. "Don't fight me.

Join me instead. How powerful you will be with your wondrous voice and stunning eyes. You will become a goddess; men will bow down and worship you. At my side, my queen, you will find eternal joy and I will show you the universe. Be with me, my beautiful lady, please me, and you will have everything. I will teach you the folly of Assemblage. I will show you the might of humans and their own inward powers."

He forced her to look at the burning red stones in the basin as their fire jumped greedily into the air, and he whispered seductively in her ear. "Let the fire engulf you, Trenara. Don't fear it; it will make you strong, willing. The ache will be brief, and like *first trial,* painfully exquisite when it touches you. Surrender to us, beloved and we will show you ecstasy. Fight me," his voice was suddenly quiet and horrifying, "and you will feel my wrath." He spun her around violently, and his eyes filled with a lustful gleam.

Trenara went mad with fear and shame as a part of her began to succumb to that sweet, wondrous voice. She could feel herself slipping into his magic, and her resolve began to fade when another wave of ecstasy flowed through her, spreading a blazing fire through her flesh. She gasped, staggered by its intensity. Trenara had never felt such climatic pleasure. All at once, she knew he could have her in an instant.

The goddess came briefly to her in the darkness, leaving behind an inkling that became a beacon in the night—an unspeakable inspiration. There was only one escape that remained to her, and the guider hardened her heart to find the courage to bear it. Trenara suddenly went limp in Sirdar's arms, taking him by surprise at first. But then a slow smile covered his face as he gathered her in and held her tightly for a moment, breathing in her scent.

"Sleep now, beloved," he whispered as he kissed her forehead. "We have a long journey ahead of us tonight." He gently laid her on the floor of the chamber and then crossed to the Mourna to saddle the bird for their flight to his castle in Cortaim.

When his arms were full, Trenara suddenly leapt from her spot, grabbed Andelian from the ground, and in the same instant, the guider turned her *via* on the Mourna. She cut the bird down with one fatal sweep, and it crumbled into a pile of ash. Sirdar cried out and raised his hands, but Trenara dashed out of the entrance and blindly down the corridor. She ran with the speed and strength of ten men, Andelian sealing her in a cocoon of *power* and making her strong. Those who tried to stop her melted to screaming flames at her touch.

Trenara burst through the cave entrance and headed straight for the precipice. Without looking back or slowing down, she hurled herself over the edge. The last thing she saw as she twisted in the air was Sirdar's astonished face as he watched her fall into oblivion.

*****

The cabin was dark now except for the soft light from the embers on the hearth. Joshan looked at Trenara quietly, his chin resting on folded hands. The guider sat with her head bowed, her eyes closed, and her forehead wrinkled in a scowl. She remained still for several minutes, the only sound disturbing the quiet, the waves lapping the ship. Supper, which had been laid long before, sat cold and untouched on the parlor table. The room rocked gently with the sway of the ship.

At length, when Trenara spoke again, her voice was hoarse with self-abuse. "Vanderlinden found me two days later, broken almost beyond repair. He escaped the mountains by guile alone and carried me back to Thrain, where I eventually healed. Andelian had saved me from death, but not from shame." She stirred gently in her seat and stared once again at the dying embers. "It would have been better to let me die, I think."

"No, guider," the emperor said quietly.

Trenara shot a glance at Joshan as if begging to keep her disgrace. "You don't understand. I was the one who released this evil. Me," she whispered with tears in her eyes.

"I understand all too well, and I grieve for you." His eyes were dark with remorse. "This burden has taken its toll—it has stolen your life—unnecessarily." Trenara looked into those shining eyes. "It was not you who released that power. You gave Sirdar temporary use of it, but that is all you did. He soon found it was not enough. Why else would he corrupt Balinar? He needed the Crystal of Healing to prolong the power. Only in that way could he maintain it." He looked down at her.

"He could not corrupt you, Trenara," he said with passion. "Don't you understand that? You have shown courage that should be sung among the ballads of the mighty. It's amazing you don't know it. You are quite wrong." Joshan sat down again and took Trenara's hands. "The shame here is not in what you did in the chamber, for that was brave beyond words. It is what you did after."

"After?"

He seemed almost angry. "You let love pass you by, when you *knew* it was right in front of you. Because love betrayed you, you thought you didn't deserve it and pushed it away with both hands. You swore it would never betray you again, didn't you?"

"Yes," she whispered, "I swore."

Joshan lifted her chin. "There's the shame of this story. Not that love betrayed you—but that you turned your back on love when it would have filled your life."

She looked up at him with sudden realization. "Vanderlinden."

Joshan nodded. "But it's all right, since he *never* gave up on his love for you. It is stronger now in our good giant that it has ever been."

She shook her head slowly. "I'm so confused."

"It will pass."

"I've been wrong about so many things, Joshan," she said to the fire. "I remember everything now so clearly. I was certain I had released this upon the world."

"No, guider," Joshan said squeezing her hand and turning. "You flatter yourself to think your small *power* can awaken life in the *Catalyst*." His eyes narrowed with a bitterness that made the flames leap.

Trenara looked at the emperor fearfully, seeing something foreign in his face as his eyes glowed softly in the light. "What is it? I've never heard of it."

"That doesn't surprise me. But you have *seen* it. It was the stone in the basin. So little is known of it now. Your account of its appearance is far more than are stored in any books or notes. *Catalyst* can corrupt the heart and twist the mind. It is a grave danger to much more than simply the empire. A sliver of this stone is lodged in Vanderlinden's eye, bending him easily to Sirdar's will. I must eradicate it, before it destroys—everything."

"You're scaring me, Joshan… I don't understand," Trenara replied weakly.

"I'm sorry, guider. I will try to make it clearer. Here is what I know…"

The ship sailed on into the night.

CHAPTER TWENTY-TWO
A SEA OF RAGE

Van leaned back in his chair and gave the ship's log a thoughtful tap. The cabin was dim in the sparse light from the portholes. It was so like his quarters aboard the *Evenstar*, a pang of remorse ran through him as he gave it a cursory look. He could almost hear the foul voice of Sirdar, the faint cries, and swirling black waters of the nightmare long ago.

The giant shook off the reflection and went back to the log. He poured over the limited contents carefully, noting with a disappointed sigh that it was not the guide its predecessor had been. He knew, however, that they shouldn't run into trouble between the Keep and Mathisma. The seas were quiescent this time of season, and the weather would hold to warm breezes and gentle nights. It was nearly two seasons to the day his last ship had died in that storm. They would lose a day or two, but he was going to set course as far away from the accursed place as possible.

He took the horn down from its peg and whistled for his first mate.

"Aye, sir?" Tam's voice came thin and hollow through the tube.

"Everything secure, Tam?"

"Aye, sir. Secure and well away."

"Good." The giant rubbed his eyes wearily. "Bring her about fifty points and keep her at hundred and sixty degrees south by southeast. Don't take her from that course."

"Aye, sir."

"I'm going to get some shuteye, Tam. Wake me at eighteen bells."

"Aye, aye, admiral."

Van closed the horn and gave his bed a dispassionate look. He had decided to hold the night watch this trip out and hadn't rested much in the past two days, so thought he should take what sleep he could. He lay down with a yawn, but it was a long time before he could close his eyes. As always, his thoughts drifted to Trenara, and that gave him peace enough to drift off.

Shortly after dusk, the giant was startled awake by a hand on his arm shaking him. He shaded his eyes against the glaring flame of an unshuttered lantern and squinted up at his first mate.

"Sorry, sir, but I think you better see this." Tam's voice was urgent and tense.

Van became instantly alert as he threw the covers aside and reached for his boots. "Trouble?"

Tam shook his head. "I don't know, sir. It's land, about forty degrees east by northeast." Van stopped and looked up at him sharply.

"Land? Are you daft, man? There's no land in these waters."

Tam took in a nervous breath. "I know, sir. That's why I came to tell you." Fear edged his voice with uncertainty.

Van looked up at him darkly as he pulled his boots on. "It's probably nothing more than a swell. Get my charts and follow me to the bridge."

"Aye, sir," Tam called as Van disappeared through the hatch.

When Van reached the bridge, he saw a thick bank of clouds had sailed in from the north. Fitful stars broke occasionally through a breach in the darkness. The moons were pale, misty orbs of pink and gray, and the night began darkly. The lanterns along the railing, perched on the mizzen mast and scattered over the bridge, gave the deck a yellow-brown softness.

Van leaned on the railing and scowled at the black rounded bulk off their starboard bow. The crew was anxious, quiet as Tam handed him a chart, and the giant held it under the bridge light to scan it carefully. He hadn't been wrong. There was no land charted in this part of the sea, and an eerie premonition began to crawl up his spine to chill his neck.

"Here, Tam," Van said warily, narrowing his eye at the island, "let me see that glass."

Van squinted into the telescope and then brought it down sharply. "By the star! Hard a port! Now!"

The men scrambled at the wheel, but before any of them could get it turned, an earsplitting sound racked the ship, sending tremors into her bowels and throwing everyone to the deck. Vanderlinden leapt over the railing, rounded the helm, and grabbed the wheel. The cords at his neck tightened as he put his weight into the spokes and spun it hard. The ship swung violently to port, throwing everything unfastened into chaos. The first mate recovered his footing and joined the giant on the bridge.

"What is it?" he shouted above the din.

"That's no island!" Van bellowed, as a large wave crashed against the ship. "Shoalfish, maybe, though bigger than any I've ever seen. But it's moving right for us, whatever it is. You get those gunners to their stations, now!" Tam jumped from the bridge and began to shout orders to the crew.

The enormous black mass was charging directly for the ship at unbelievable speed. Its form was indiscernible in the gloom, but its intent was not. From the size of the wake and speed at which it was charging, the ship would be reduced to a pile of debris on the first pass without the hulk missing so much as a heartbeat. Two men took the wheel from the admiral as he ran down the deck toward the gunners.

"You there! Get that catapult mounted!"

Another wave crashed against the ship, and the sound increased with mounting fury. People ran blindly, holding their ears, silently screaming. The mountain of blackness moved with ever increasing speed eating away at the sky as it came. Van ran to the gunners, but they were paralyzed with terror. He slapped one man soundly, bringing him abruptly out of his shock.

"Get the guider!"

The man stumbled off to the cabins. Another wave hit the ship knocking her off her keel, while sailors began to jump into the sea to escape the earsplitting agony. Van looked at the bridge and saw the wheel unmanned. His ears were ringing and his head pounding like the devil, but he ran like a madman toward the wheel to bring her about. Before he reached it, a boom came out of the darkness from behind and knocked him senseless to the deck. The mountain was almost on them.

At that moment, Haiden and his guards charged from the hold and began to man the guns and put cotton in the sailors' ears to shut out the noise. Two guards leapt onto the bridge and forced the ship around, almost drowning her in their efforts. The mountain missed them by inches and sailed past. The ship tilted on her keel until the yardarm brushed the water, but the Morning Star bobbed like a cork and corrected her balance throwing people from starboard to port. Only the skills of expert imperial shipbuilders and Clurichaune engineering had saved her from capsizing.

Haiden knelt down to the giant and helped him to his feet.

"I owe you one, mate," Van said groggily.

"That you may, admiral, but I'll probably be collecting before the night's through." He pointed to the stern. "It's coming about."

Van looked at the mountain as it made a wide sweep off their stern and began to move toward them once again. The gunners wasted no time in aiming the harpoons and catapults at the mountain as it charged through the water. The archers pulled their bows and waited in anticipation.

Van took the wheel from the guards and swung her starboard, almost broadside to the mountain, to allow them the best chance of hitting it. Just as the creature neared bow range, it suddenly stopped. The wave it created spilled the ship again, but it held on.

"Thank the stars for Clurichaunes," Vanderlinden said, helping Haiden to his feet.

Haiden leaned on the railings to watch the bulk. "What's it doing?"

"I don't know, but we're not staying here to find out."

He swung the ship once again to port until the sails filled, and the ship sped toward the east. He motioned to Tam to take the wheel. "Keep her in this wind. Get her out of here!"

"Aye, sir."

Van grabbed the glass from the bridge deck and surveyed the creature carefully, but all he could make out was a greenish-black bulk. They began to make way from it.

"I don't like this," he said at length, putting the glass down slowly.

"It ain't natural," Haiden replied hoarsely.

"Aye, it's natural enough. That devil's up to something. I just hope we can get away before it makes up its mind." Van turned to set a new course, but Haiden grabbed his arm.

"Admiral, look!"

The giant turned around just in time to see the creature disappear. "It's gone under," he hissed. "That can only mean one thing." He turned to his crew and cupped his mouth. "Get them guns ready and point them down. Down! It's coming underneath." The sailors scrambled to their stations as a wake began to advance toward the ship. "At my command…" The deck was deathly still as Van jumped to an unmanned gun and sat down behind it. When the wake was within range, the admiral gave the command to fire. Every gun, bow, and catapult was launched, making the sea boil. It slowed, but did not stop.

"Reload!" The command echoed dully against the open waters. With lightning speed, the weapons were filled again and fired. Three more rounds went off, each time slowing the wake, but never stopping it entirely. Van was about to give another firing command, when the wake paused within fifty spans of the ship.

The giant rose slowly from his chair and leaned over the railing, when all at once the creature shot out of the ocean before him. The suction it created pulled the ship toward its waiting arms. It took three men to hold the wheel and keep her position.

The creature stood twice as high as the mainmast and was as broad as the ship was long. It had two long arms with amphibious hands and sharp claws, as thick as a man is round. Its head, though hard to see at that height, was long and flat with two lifeless black eyes. It let out a formidable cry that shook the ship and drove people screaming into the sea.

Vanderlinden ignored the turmoil around him and methodically spun the crank of his harpoon launcher back until the barbed spear hit the rear of the machine, twice as far as any other man could have pulled it. "I may be going to meet my maker, you stinking bastard, but not alone." Blood rose to his face and throbbed in his neck as he sighted for the monster's heart, or where he thought it should be. The tension on the bow hummed as he slowly squeezed the trigger.

When the shaft was released, it knocked the giant back into the railing on the port side and struck the monster with an audible thud. The spear went through its side and landed somewhere in the sea beyond, leaving a hole the size of a man's head.

The creature screamed. Blood turned the sea black and the brute's eyes blazed with fury. It raised massive arms above its head to smash the life from this vehicle of pain. All the crew could see was the gleam of those massive talons as they fell toward the Morning Star. All at once, a devastating flash of light blinded every pair of eyes. The monster staggered and missed its mark, bringing a cascade of sea water down on the prostrate sailors and guards on the deck.

Everything froze. The creature, the people, the ship, and even the sea held still for a breathless moment. In the silence that followed, an astonishing baritone voice sang out, the sound flowing in all directions like a warm caress. Two beats later, a graceful contralto floated beneath it, the music sweet, heart wrenching, and distinctive. The notes merged until the duet became a single voice on the air, an exultant ecstasy. It lulled the people where they lay, stood, or sat. Many gasped and all eyes rose to the mainmast where it reverberated, calming everything it touched. The sea turned to glass.

Van came out of this stupor in time to look up and see Joshan ablaze with light in the crow's nest, standing on a lake of amber fire. His arms were outstretched to the monster, and his long dark hair flew behind him in a golden wind, his brilliant palms ablaze with light. Joshan was so bright, the giant had to turn away.

As he turned, Van caught sight of Trenara and his mouth fell open. She stood at the base of the mast, misted in blue brilliance, her scepter held high, looking as she had those thirty seasons before. The magnificent pandemonium of flowing white hair whipped behind her, and the brilliant eyes and voice were a soft caress on his soul. She turned her head to look at him. Trenara's smile was a revelation. Van sank to his knees knowing what he finally saw in those willing eyes, what he had waited thirty seasons to see.

Joshan sent a blaze leaping from his hands. The light swirled and engulfed the beast until it glowed. The massive giant struggled, trying to escape. A cry escaped the creature's throat that sent tremor through the wooden planks, but it ended in a choking rasp as the web of *power* squeezed the sound away. There came a dull rumble, and the sea began to roil around the monster's waist with an icy green flame. An eerie steam, thick and churning, rose from the water and climbed the creature's body, until it was shrouded in emerald smoke.

A wind began in the east. It whistled through the sails and among the crew, its frozen fingers sending people to huddle in chilled groups to escape its piercing touch. It mingled with the mist around the creature, dancing delicately through the green smoke until the fog faded and then disappeared. When the mist was gone, the small white quarter moon came from behind a cloud to pour her light on the monster's misfortune. Standing in the moonlight was an impressive pillar of sand and brine, carved with the creature's terror still etched on its stony face.

Joshan lowered his arms, and the light died. He seemed to teeter, but recovered his balance and made his slow way down the lines. Haiden reached him as Joshan's strength gave out, and he nearly fell. When Haiden got him down, Joshan sat to catch his breath.

"You all right, lord?" Haiden asked, his voice awed.

"Yes. I need to talk to Vanderlinden."

Haiden glanced up, and a slow smile creased the lines of his face until his eyes shone in the darkness. Joshan looked up at him and scowled. Haiden just nodded toward the other side of the mast, and as Joshan stood up, he also smiled. Trenara had been swept up by Van and lifted high above his head, as the giant laughed and spun her around in a graceful waltz along the deck.

The tears on his cheeks caught the reflection of the moonlight, and his uncovered eye was gleaming as Trenara looked down at him, a sad, sweet smile dusting her lips.

She touched the course black beard with her slender fingers, and the giant's smile lit up the night. Van lowered her down until their faces met, and he gently kissed her as she threw her arms around his neck. An earsplitting cheer went up from the crew, Haiden and Joshan's voices the loudest among them.

When they heard it, the couple stopped and stared incredulously at the crowd. "Put me down," Trenara whispered to the giant.

"Oh," he said and lowered her to the deck. They were both embarrassed, but smiled just the same. Van took her hand and kissed it.

Without success, he tried to get his face under control as he bellowed at his crew. "All right, mates. Show's over. Now get back to your posts." The sailors and Haiden's guards shook their heads, stretched their muscles, and went back to what was left of their ship. Tam was already shouting orders to trim the sail and lower lifelines for the people overboard.

Without warning, Joshan lost the strength in his legs and went down. "Sire!" Haiden managed to get him sitting again. "You need rest, lad," he whispered.

Joshan raised his head. "Admiral," he said as Trenara and Van joined them. "It's imperative we reach Mathisma immediately."

Van was still stunned by all that had happened and perhaps a little slow in responding. "Sire?"

"Immediately."

The giant rubbed his eyes to clear them. "Aye, sire. I'll put up full sail tonight. With luck, we can shave off two, maybe three days from the journey."

Joshan shook his head and put a hand on Van's arm. "We have to reach Mathisma within fourteen days."

"Fourteen days?" Vanderlinden exclaimed, recovering fully. "Even at full sail with perfect wind, it'd take at least a score to get there."

"I'll give you knowledge that will speed the ship. It is vital we reach Mathisma in fourteen days or we will be too late."

"Too late for what, sire?" Van asked tentatively.

Joshan began to speak, but a voice stopped him.

"No, not at night." Trenara's earlier joy faded from her face as she took Vanderlinden's arm. She was suddenly as pale as a wraith with deep circles around her eyes and lines about her mouth. Van took her back into his arms, where she went gratefully.

Joshan looked up at them and nodded wearily. "You're right, Trenara. We should wait until tomorrow. We will have council then. But now," he said as he began to rise with Haiden's help, "I must get some rest."

"Aye," Van said, "and I got to get this ship back to normal." He surveyed the debris strewn about the deck, the tangled lines and riggings, the broken boom and water-drenched deck. "What a mess." He kissed Trenara and left with Tam to join his sailors. The three remaining companions headed for the cabins, but Joshan stopped at the railing and looked up at the mountainous statue in the sea.

"For good or ill, there it will rest until the sea takes it back." He sighed deeply. "Would that all things could be handled so easily." He turned to his friends and smiled weakly. "Come, I think a good, stiff drink and a comfortable bed are in order. Tomorrow will be a busy day." Trenara and Haiden nodded, but remained silent for their own reasons and followed the emperor below.

Trenara paused to look back at the man who had always been her friend and now would be her love. She wished her heart could be lighter, but her fear muted her joy. The guider went below to find what rest she could.

CHAPTER TWENTY-THREE
THE OATH

By daybreak, the ship was cleared of debris and mended. Despite the size of the waves, the damage was relatively minimal, much to Vanderlinden's relief. Two men suffered minor injuries and Van had a throbbing knot on the back of his head the size of an egg, but these were the only casualties.

At dawn, the sail maker, a fellow by the name of Sal Carriman, was summoned to the emperor, along with Trenara and Ena, but Van and Haiden were told there would be a council later in the day. The emperor and Carriman were closeted in Joshan's cabin for hours.

Vanderlinden was getting anxious. He paced the decks fitfully, noting the wind speed and direction, the flow of the tide, and the smell of the air. It was going to be a torrid day with little wind and sluggish currents. If the emperor intended to speed the ship, Van had no idea how he was going to do it, this side of giving her wings. After the display of *power* the previous night, the giant wouldn't put it passed him.

At length, when the admiral was at wit's end, Sal finally came up from below completely absorbed in incomprehensible figures on a piece of parchment. He was muttering quietly to himself, oblivious to everything. He would look at the riggings, shake his head, make another notation on the paper, and lick his stylus thoughtfully.

Sail makers, by profession, were known to be an eccentric lot and were considered almost a class of their own (second only to ship builders in Imperium society). They kept to themselves, showing little concern for the world beyond the masts and sails, wholly wrapped up in the geometrical perfection of their craft. Sal Carriman was the best and worst of the lot, having achieved his status only after forty seasons of imperial service.

Van caught up to the old sail maker as Sal squinted one eye and rubbed the graying bristle on his chin thoughtfully. The giant didn't want to seem over-anxious so bade the man good morning. Sal continued to look up at the mizzen, carefully chewed his bottom lip, and then walked right passed the giant without a word. Van was not easily daunted, so followed beside the sail maker as the old man muttered softly.

"Could be done. But I'll need more canvas certainly, and rope. Much more canvas." He made another notation on the paper. "We'll have to work 'round the dial." He scribbled again and then crossed it out with a huff. "No, no. He said eighteen degrees starboard and nine port." He corrected his error and smiled. "There. That's the ticket."

"Sal," the giant bellowed, as the little man continued to ignore him. "What did his majesty say?"

"Oh, good morning, admiral. Beautiful day, don't you think?" He went back to his scribbling.

Van took in an aggravated breath and counted mentally. "Sal," he said smoothly, "what did the man say?"

"The emperor? Yes, brilliant man—simply brilliant. I would have never thought of it." He paused long enough to glare at the sails. "Perhaps I would have eventually. It's that simple." Then he realized a question had been asked. "He said we could re-rig the sails to get more speed." He shoved the parchment toward the giant. "See for yourself."

Van motioned the paper away. "Sal, you know I don't know what all those figures mean."

Sal pulled back the paper, knitted his brow, and pursed his lips. "Ah, yes. Quite right. You build them, I make them sail." Then he moved on. Van held back his annoyance and walked after the old man, knowing he wouldn't get anything worth knowing out of the sail maker by pestering him. Sal was quite pester-proof.

"Re-rig, you say?" he called after him.

"Yes, yes," Sal replied with a wave of his hand. "Ingenious, really," he muttered. "An angle here, a twist there, and you've got it. Sails as swift and efficient as you could wish and lines that move like silk with little effort. Ingenious." He continued down the deck, not even aware he had stopped.

Vanderlinden decided not to pursue him further, learning all he was going to from Sal for one morning. He smiled as the man came close to walking into the sea at an open railing. He was saved by a hair's breadth when a sailor grabbed his shoulders gently and stirred him in another direction. Sal never missed a step. Van shook his head and turned for the emperor's cabin.

*****

"I am not *third trial*. I can't do it!" Trenara paced the parlor floor furiously.

Joshan sat back and eyed the guider quietly. He knew he had pushed Trenara to her limits and regretted having to push her further. "Sit down," he said, motioning to the chair across from him.

She frowned, but sank into the chair heavily and put her elbows on her knees. "What you ask is impossible."

"It may be more than what you think you can give, but I know differently. I am well aware you have not reached *third trial*, but only you can create the winds we need. Do I need to remind you of the urgency?"

"You needn't remind me," Trenara replied testily. "I have tried so many times. Thirty seasons of trying."

"Who was it that said to me once, 'if you try to do something, that's what you will do the rest of your life—try. You've got to take hold and do it'? A wise woman as I recall."

Trenara gaped at him, her own words rising against her. She pursed her lips. "You win. I guess there's nothing for it, but to do it, as Haiden would say."

"That's the spirit."

"Damned strange you guiding me."

Ena came in and bowed. "Admiral Vanderlinden would like to see you, sire."

Joshan looked at Trenara. "Are you ready?"

"No, but let's get on with it. I'm not looking forward to this."

"Show him in, Ena, and ask Marshall Bails to join us."

"Yes, sire." Ena bowed and left.

Vanderlinden came in, tilted his head to Joshan, then went over and lifted Trenara off her feet so he could kiss her soundly. "Good morning," he said, setting her down. They sat next to each other on the couch as Haiden came through the hatch, gave Joshan an examining look, and then took a seat across from them. When the four companions were seated, Joshan had Ena bring in two decanters of mead and then dismissed her.

"What are these for?" ventured Haiden, motioning to the drink.

"I think by the time we are finished, you will know." Joshan's face turned grave and the old guard stirred uncomfortably in his chair.

For the next two hours, Joshan spoke quietly, with an urgent rhythm to his voice, repeating what he and Trenara had discussed the night before, including the guider's trek to Badain and the shrewd guesses she had made regarding Sirdar. During it, the companions sat as if spell-bound, absorbing each syllable with intense interest.

As his words flowed, the companions became increasingly pale. Joshan mentioned nothing of his suspicions about Vanderlinden, but near the end, the giant bowed his head as if the weight of knowledge was too much for him. Trenara stroked his head gently and held his arm. There was a long silence that followed Joshan's last words, as the companions each assimilated the news.

Haiden made the first move by reaching for the decanter of mead and pouring himself a stout portion, spilling much of it on the polished table.

"Here," said Trenara gently, taking the wine from his trembling fingers. "I have had time to recover. I'll pour."

Van lifted his head to meet Joshan's eyes. "Will Sark hold the borders?" His voice was so hoarse with trepidation it was no more than a whisper.

"I wish I could tell you he will, but I can't. The best we can hope for is he will hold them until we return."

"How long?"

Joshan's frown was grim. "Thirty days, maybe, if he's fortunate." Van pushed his chair back violently and stood to stare out the port. "Van, if I had any other choice, I would not have sent Sark, you must know that."

The giant whirled around. "All I know is it seems bloody strange you kept all this secret until we left the Keep."

Joshan looked down at the table. "I had my reasons."

"Aye, like maybe you didn't trust any of us." Even as he said it, he looked down and shook his head. "I'm sorry, I didn't mean that."

Joshan smiled. "It's all right, Van. It's forgotten. I think we're all on edge. Here, sit down and have some wine."

Van slid into his chair and downed a glass of mead.

"Sire?" said Haiden at length. "Who is this Sirdar anyway? That is to say, is he some kind of guider, like you and Trenara here?"

Joshan looked suddenly tired. "I wish I knew, Haiden. What little I do know is mostly guess work. I would like to say he is just a man, who has digressed to evil. But I can't. In the beginning, I thought so, but found that he is not—normal. The only guess I can make goes back to ancient times.

There are people—beings in myths—much like Sirdar and wielding a similar power." He banged his hand against the table in frustration. "So much knowledge has been lost over the centuries. Little is left and most of that is worthless." Joshan sank his head and became lost in thought.

In the stillness that followed, a lonely voice began to chant softly.

Deep beneath the ancient earth,
Below the sands and stones and cold,
There lies the bane of life and birth,
The Catalyst of young and old.

Woe to thee, oh delvers deep,
Who search the dirt for precious stones,
For you may find just what you seek,
Amid the ancient cries and bones.

It cannot stop. The die is cast,
For one shall rise who cannot fall
To take the stones up from their past
And bring them forth for good and all.

Into the world will shine their might.
For good or ill cannot be said.
If ill doth come, then call the Sight
To cast them back into their bed.

Sing no praises, people free,
Of their fire or of their light
For the Catalyst shall only be
Broken by the gods' Starsight.

The room became dark as the words flowed with an icy chill through the air. The companions stared in amazement at Haiden as he finished, but he merely looked at the table thoughtfully. No one spoke until the darkness had passed.

"Where did you learn that?" Joshan leaned toward the silent guard.

"That was a just a piece of ballad. Just came to me then. I haven't thought of it in seasons, not since I was no bigger than this. We used to sing it to scare each other. It did the trick, right enough. Your talking about ancient times put my mind to it, though I don't know who wrote it, or where it comes from. My mum used to tell me it was near as old as the mountains. I didn't doubt it."

"Indeed, it could very well be as old as the mountains," said Joshan. "It is an expanded version of a ballad in one of Trenara's books on Kerillian, but I thought the entire verse lost. You seem to be full of surprises, Haiden. I'm grateful that such ballads are still taught. Write it down for me, will you? Do you know any others?"

Haiden blushed to the ears and smiled. "Well, none that would be fitting here, sire. I'm sorry. But I'll think on it."

"Good. Even a child's rhyme may be of help against Sirdar. Whoever he is, the power he wields may well be the exact stones described in this verse. There are frightening implications in this. Although I'm certain the *Catalyst* could be quite capable of good, in the wrong hands it is a formidable weapon." Joshan stretched as he rose and crossed to the porthole.

"Are you the Starsight the ballad speaks of?" Van asked Joshan. "Isn't that what Balinar called you at the Keep?"

"Yes, he did call me that, but why I don't know. Starsight, as the ballad implies, is a kind of deliverer. I'm afraid I have difficulty placing myself in that role. But who's to say?" He stared out at the sea and sighed deeply. "For whatever reason, I have been given so much *power* it scares the hell out of me. It isn't without limitations, however. Every since I attained *fourth trial,* something's changed in my control—not that I had much to begin with. It only comes at night now and dwindles with the rise of the sun. It doesn't always come when I call, either. Sometimes it comes when I don't call it. It's frustrating! Last night it took everything I had to destroy that creature. The *power* is discriminate—it seems to run by itself. My control is very confused."

"I think that will change," Trenara said. "Although you're not exactly a common pre-guider, there are some similarities between your limited use and *first trial* students. It is not uncommon for young pre-guiders to have what we refer to as *dispersion* during their pre-guider days. In time your control of the *power* will improve."

"I hope you're right, guider. Because without it, I can't hope to win against Sirdar." The companions sobered under the pronouncement. "It will be during the day I will lean heavily on the three of you. In the months to come I will demand the limits of your knowledge, experience, strength, and courage. I must know that those things will be there when I need them." He looked at the three for a long time and tried to piece together what he read in each. "Van?"

The giant's face was pale, but a steady light burned in his eye. "Lad, what I done to you at the Keep don't deserve that kind of trust, but this I will swear to you… I'll never betray you again. I'll follow where you lead and do everything I can to keep you from harm."

Joshan frowned. "From harm, giant? Even if I *must* be harmed so that all else can live?"

"What?"

"Could you watch me die if it were necessary?"

Van did not answer and bowed his head instead.

"You see? This is the oath that you must take—all of you. Not to protect *me*, but to protect those things Sirdar would destroy, no matter what the cost. Even if you or someone you love must die to save everything else. Can you take that oath?"

There was an awkward silence before Van finally spoke up. "Aye," he breathed. "I'll take it; to stop Sirdar, no matter what. You don't mind if I try to save your hide at the same time, do you?"

Joshan laughed. "Certainly not. Believe me, I'm going to do everything I can to survive this. If it comes to it, I must know the three of you will carry on."

"That I'll guarantee you—come what may."

"Good. Haiden?"

"I've come this far, son. I ain't likely to turn back now," Haiden replied with his usual half-smile.

"Trenara?"

The guider looked at Van and smiled, then back to Joshan. "For good or ill, my purpose is clear; to guide you through the best and worst of it. So, if you don't mind a cranky old woman, you're stuck with me for the duration."

Joshan regarded the three and contentment smoothed the lines in his face. "No man is luckier than I to have such friends."

"What now?" asked Trenara.

"We must stop Palarine first, before he gets to the Crystal. How, I don't know yet, but we'll know by the time we reach Mathisma. Then the real battle will begin. Sirdar. My greatest weapon will be knowledge, something I gravely lack at the moment. I must learn how to destroy him. So, I will seek the answers in the Books of Kerillian and in anything else I can find. Even, perhaps, through the Crystal itself. Then I will find out what I can about these."

He slowly removed the leather gloves and placed his hands palm up on the table, revealing the now expansive crystalline structure that covered nearly three quarters of his palms. Even in the darkened room, they glowed brightly and sparkled with exquisite color. They seemed to shine with different hues each time light hit them, pulsating from white to blue to green to amber, and then back to white. Van whistled softly as he leaned over to look at them and Haiden gazed down in silent wonder.

Trenara touched them gently. "It's twice the size it was yesterday."

"Beautiful, isn't it? I must know if this has happened before. Trenara says it hasn't." He closed his hands and then leaned back in his chair.

"And after all this?" Trenara asked.

Joshan closed his eyes and drew a deep breath. "We'll have to see."

Trenara was not appeased. "You know already, don't you?"

Joshan opened his eyes and looked at her. "Does it matter?"

Trenara opened her mouth, snapped it shut and smiled. "No, I suppose not. I'm just curious."

Joshan leaned over and kissed the guider gently on the forehead. "You must trust me, guider, in this, as in all things." Trenara bowed her head in acquiescence.

"Speaking of curiosities," interjected Haiden, "why bring all of us along, sire? That is to say, seems to me it would have been better to leave the giant and me back at the Keep. I can't think where we'd be any good fighting guiders and such."

"My reasons are simple, Haiden. Van's duties are specific regarding the transport of the emperor. Plus, I'd like to see what we can do about getting that eye of his fixed."

Van gave him an incredulous look. "Can you do that?"

Joshan shrugged. "It's worth a try."

Haiden was not satisfied. "But what about me, sire? Meaning no disrespect, but I'm beginning to feel like a piece of unwanted baggage."

"To be quite frank," Joshan said after giving him a long look, "I honestly don't know where you fit into all this. But in every alternative future, you've been there. Good or bad, there is Haiden standing at my side. I don't know what part you have to play, Haiden, but I could do nothing else but bring you along—baggage or not."

Haiden screwed up his face in a comic expression of pride, humility, and confusion until the companions laughed at his attempt to decide on one. "I don't know whether to thank you or leave insulted."

"When it is all over," Joshan laughed, "you decide. Right now, we've got to prepare this ship to get to the island."

"Lad, even with the sails fixed until they're as perfect as they can be," Van said, "that doesn't change the fact that we have to have wind to fill them."

"I know," Joshan said. "The guider will provide the wind during the day, and I will do it at night. That should give us a steady source."

"If I can," Trenara said.

Van looked at each of them in turn and raised a bushy brow. "How's that? I mean, I love my beautiful lady here and have nothing but respect for her abilities, but I thought only *third trial* guiders could summon the wind."

"That's correct, Van. Therefore, Trenara needs to reach *third trial*."

Van turned to the guider. "Can you do that?"

The guider curled her lip and rose. "We'll see," she said pensively. "But I better get to it. It's late already and there isn't much time. Is there anything more, sire?"

"No, Trenara. Good luck."

The guider snorted. "It's going to take a bit more than luck, I'm afraid. Come on, big boy," she said to Van taking his hand, "I'm going to need some help."

"Sure. We'll see you later, then," he called to Joshan and Haiden as he and the guider left for Trenara's chambers.

Haiden looked at the table and shook his head as Joshan rang for a servant. "Out of the kettle, into the flame," he muttered.

Joshan gave him a sidelong look. "Exactly."

CHAPTER TWENTY-FOUR
THIRD TRIAL

For hours, Trenara knelt in the cabin, gazing into Andelian while the furniture glowed with blue fire, and shadows danced on the walls like phantoms against a dream. At first, the song had been soft and minor, a questing euphony to test her strength. Then, as hours passed, the melody melted to somber notes of tedium, the blue light unwavering. At last, as the guider's strength ebbed and her body ached for rest, the music became a shrill demand. Trenara's head throbbed, her throat ached. She drove herself, but her mind played tricks on her will to continue.

You are old, it whispered to her. *Too old for such games. All you have to do is stop and go to bed. Rest now. Tomorrow you will be stronger.*

The thoughts lulled her, her eyes began to close, and the guider almost gave in. From deep within came a strength that brought her out of her daze with a start. "No!" Trenara doubled her efforts.

She grew weak maintaining the blue at such intensity. She would faint soon without relief, and often, in a delirium, the guider thought the color changed, only to look again at a steady blue. When she couldn't take it any longer, she clenched her teeth and squeezed Andelian until her hands went white. "Change, you bastard!"

The color flared, fighting to stay, but Trenara concentrated until she shook with effort. In a sudden blinding flash that threw her against the opposite wall, the light became a shower of glistening green that shimmered down around her and touched her with triumph.

"Yes!"

She laughed, she cried, she reeled like a drunkard with the wine of joy coursing through her veins. Her world became a wonder of new experiences as though a veil had been lifted from her eyes. Exhaustion melted away into exhilaration. Nothing was the same.

A rumpled robe cast unwanted on the floor, became an intricate marvel of thread and design. A polished panel turned from dull wood to an amazing work of nature as she saw the seasons of slow growth that went into its creation, and the hands of a man who had bent those seasons to his will. The bronze and copper ornaments were dirt, then ore, then hammered chunks of shining stone, hot gases and molten metal. All at once, she knew the secret of *third trial* and laughed at its simplicity.

Trenara realized she had a new power in her hands. Bringing those hands before her face, the realization hit her; she could bend it further than she had ever dreamed. That responsibility sobered her as she stood to look at the sea through the porthole. It teemed with life and she tingled with fascination.

The guider didn't know whether it was the same day or the next. The westerly sun now sparkled on the water like a field of jewels and it was so blue, she wondered if she had ever seen color before. The sky began to dim as though clouds had sailed in to mar it—but there were no clouds. A shade of panic touched her. She had heard of guiders who had been blinded at *third trial*, especially those who were older. It wasn't blindness she sensed, but something much more frightening.

A pang of scintillation began in her neck and spread through the rest of her body like liquid fire, making every function sharply apparent in the guider's mind. Her heart beat loudly and the blood in her veins rushed through their channels with an audible hiss. Her joints creaked and moaned with weight, as vital juices thundered their music against her ears.

Trenara knew the feeling, though it had been a long time. The body, sometimes more aware than the mind, was preparing itself for the *visions* that would come. The guider braced herself. As if a curtain had been drawn, she lost sight of the sea and saw instead a deep black that spread before her inner sight. On the mental canvas appeared a tiny mote of color that grew as it approached.

She saw first a mane of fair hair, tousled and matted, then a young chin, mouth and nose. Ena. She couldn't see the eyes, as they were misted with smoke or fog. Trenara wondered what she was seeing, but when she tried to focus, it vanished. Another *vision* flooded the darkness in a brilliant flash, and where the other had been vague, this was patently clear.

Joshan stood on a platform of glass, a shrouded world of white in all directions around him. In his hand, he held a shining black sword with red fire smoldering along its edges. His face was stunning, powerful—terrifying. Mad joy danced in his eyes. At Joshan's side, towering well above his head loomed a sleek figure with outstretched wings and almost human eyes. Mourna. Joshan lifted the blade and looked at Trenara. She trembled. A horrible betrayal coursed through her awareness and sickened her heart. Before the guider could see more, the image faded.

Trenara eyes misted. Was this an alternative future or the real one? Tears streaked her cheeks as the images shifted again. A woman's face appeared, surrounded by a soft train of billowing hair, the color of autumnal grasses streaked with strands of silver. The hair bordered eyes that were young, yet old at the same time, the color of dark violets in the sun and half again as large as normal eyes. Her mouth and nose were small and delicately proportioned.

When the woman smiled, Trenara felt the weariness of seasons fall away, and her heart was overwhelmed. The guider knelt before the vision and bowed her head, content for the first time in her life. When she lifted her eyes to gaze at the sight again, it was gone, and all Trenara saw was the gleam of polished wood and bronze. She touched the wall where the vision had been and felt only sadness at her passing. The green fire had gone, and she was mortal once again.

Trenara smiled. "It is so simple. Why, any child could reach *third trial.*" Then she laughed just to hear the sound. "What a fool I've been." She stood and scanned the disheveled room. "Oh, my," she said, scanning the mess. A sparkle of mischief brightened her eyes and she had a superb idea. "I wonder if I could…"

*****

Vanderlinden and Haiden had been speaking quietly by the bridge, watching the sail maker and Joshan direct the workers, when an explosion shook the ship, knocking several people off their feet. It is difficult to say who arrived first, but what greeted the two men as they rounded the corner at a dead run were swelling clouds of smoke rising from the guider's cabin.

"Trenara!" Van shouted in horror, and then screamed for water to quench the blaze as Haiden grabbed a blanket to wrap around his head and shoulders to rescue the almost certainly devastated guider. Before either of them could enter, Trenara emerged coughing and fanning smoke away. She was black from head to toe, but otherwise whole. Van took her into his arms and swung her away, but when Trenara saw Haiden shrouded in a worn blanket like a little old woman going to market, she roared with laughter. Van put her down and exchanged a muddled look with Haiden, as they led the hysterical guider away from the carnage.

Trenara sat on a barrel and wiped her eyes against her sleeve, as a sailor ran up to tell them there was no fire, but the cabin was destroyed. The giant waved the man away, and Trenara continued to laugh.

"I'd like to know just what's so funny. You gave me one hell of a fright."

Trenara put her arms around the giant and squeezed him tightly while she regained her senses. "I'm sorry, Van. It was unintentional. I was simply trying to clean my cabin." She started laughing again.

"Clean your cabin? You got a funny way of doing it. You made one hell of a mess of my ship." He calmed down when Trenara kissed him, wiping the black smoke from his face she had smeared there.

"A small price to pay," Joshan replied walking up to the group. He knelt beside the guider and handed her a towel. "Are you all right?"

"Oh, lad," she smiled. "I haven't felt this grand in seasons. Though, for a moment there, I didn't think I was going to make it."

Joshan's eyes sparkled with pride. "Tell me."

Trenara's smile took seasons from her face. "It was—everything. It was as if I had never seen before. Then *visions* came—some terrible and confusing, but others beautiful beyond words.

"I saw Ena first, but only for a moment, and I couldn't see her eyes clearly. And then you, standing high on what looked like a sheet of glass… with a sword in your hand." But for some reason, Joshan paled and shuddered. "Lad, what is it?"

Joshan shook his head as the darkness passed. "It's nothing, Trenara. Please go on."

"Then I saw a face—but what a face it was. Golden hair and eyes that could cure a broken heart."

Joshan's face lit up. "Dark violet eyes, with flecks of gold," he said quietly and Trenara stared.

"Yes. Then you have seen her, too."

"Often."

"Who is she?"

"I don't know, guider. She is at the end of a long road. If we win, we will see her there. Was there more?"

"Isn't that enough? No more. It was perfect as it was."

"If you have seen this woman in *vision* as I have, perhaps she will be there. I thought her to be an alternative future. Maybe I'm wrong." His face turned somber and his voice was almost cross. "What color was the sword I held?"

Trenara did not answer immediately, caught by the conflict in Joshan's eyes. "Is it important?" she replied hesitantly.

"Very important."

Trenara licked her lips and looked down at her hands. "Black, shot with red."

Joshan bowed his head and closed his eyes.

"The *vision* was brief. Who's to say what it is I saw or what it means? I can't, and I honestly don't think you can either. It isn't good to add more to *sight* than is actually there. We've talked about this before. *Visions* are clues only, not destinies. Be careful, my boy, that's a slippery slope."

He looked up and smiled. "You're right."

"Now, wait a minute," Van said, scratching his head. "You two aren't making a lot of sense. You mean to say, she made it? She reached *third trial?*"

"Yes, my friend," Joshan replied, helping Trenara into a clean robe.

"So, she can summon the wind?"

"Wind? Trenara is now a master of nature, which is rare these days. She could summon the sea itself, if she wished."

Trenara laughed. "Not just yet. I had trouble with my cabin. The wind will be hard enough." Trenara looked down. "I seem to have misplaced my sash. Ena! Where is that girl? Ena!"

"Ma'am?"

Trenara turned with a start and glared up at the girl who had been behind her. "I wish you wouldn't do that!" Before she could answer, Ena's eyes widened in shock, and she took a step away from the guider. "Ena, what is it?"

The girl raised a shaky finger and pointed. "Your... your forehead."

Trenara reached for her face abruptly, but all her fingers felt were a smooth, though somewhat sooty, patch of skin. "I don't feel anything. Joshan, what does she see?"

"I don't know, guider. I can't see a thing. Van? Haiden?" They booth shook their heads.

Ena looked at them in disbelief. "But it's there, I tell you." She looked down awkwardly. "Forgive me, sire. I mean no disrespect, but the symbols are as clear as day."

Joshan took the girl firmly by the shoulders, which only increased her anxiety. "Symbols, did you say? What sort? Can you read them?"

"For heaven's sake," Trenara bellowed. "Won't someone get me a mirror?"

Haiden took off at a sprint and caught a young guard who looked at him strangely, but ran off to do his bidding.

"They are—strange, sire." Ena tried to relax her clenched muscles, but all she succeeded in producing was a grimace. "I've never seen them before, but they are raised like welts and run the length of her forehead." She shuddered and took another step back. "They frighten me."

"Could you draw them for me?" Joshan asked.

"I don't know, sire—I think so."

"Parchment and pen!" Joshan shouted to the guard who had handed Haiden a mirror. The man saluted and ran off again.

"Here, hand me that glass." Trenara scrutinized her brow thoroughly and then clicked her tongue in disgust. "Damn! I can't see a blasted thing." She rubbed her forehead and then lowered the mirror to look at Ena. The girl was pale, beyond what would be expected, unless… "Lass, are you certain you actually see something there. Could it be the soot?"

"No, ma'am. There's writing there." Ena let out a cry. "They're fading."

"Hurry with that parchment!" Joshan said.

At Joshan's gesture, the guard handed the pen and parchment to the girl, and Ena began to draw: one, two, three sets of symbols, spidery in design and intricate with lines and dots. But the fourth came slowly as the symbols began to fade. When they were gone, Ena bit her lip in concentration and tried to draw the fifth. At length she put the pen down as if it were too heavy for her.

"I'm sorry, sire. I can't remember any more." Her voice was dreamy and withdrawn. "I'm so tired."

"That's all right, lass," Trenara said gently, motioning to the guard to come over. She exchanged a knowing look with Joshan. There could be no doubt. The guider eased the parchment from Ena's slack fingers. "You get some rest now. I'm certain if this is important, you've given us all we need. Now, go with…"

Ena's legs gave out, and the guard caught her before she could fall. He lifted her into his arms, and Trenara touched her forehead as Joshan joined her. They both looked down at the beautiful child-like face and smiled.

"Take her to her quarters," Joshan said softly to the guard.

Van scratched his head. "What's wrong with her? She was as chipper as a bird earlier."

Joshan shot him a look. "When you go through what she's just been through, giant, we'd probably have to carry you to bed, too. Assemblage calls it *sight fatigue*. It can take seasons to master."

As Trenara watched after the girl, she handed the parchment to Joshan and shook her head. "I can't make these out. I've seen symbols like these."

"So have I, but I'm not certain where." Joshan searched the lettering carefully. "They are old, certainly, though their origin is difficult to say. Selas, maybe, or possibly…" His voice trailed off as he stared once again after the girl. A shadow crossed his mind briefly and a chill ran through his spine. What was it Trenara had said? *….and I couldn't see her eyes clearly.* He shook off the feeling and stared back at the strange symbols.

"Begging your pardon, but how is it that girl could see them when we couldn't?" Haiden asked.

Trenara looked up from the parchment and shook her head. "I don't know, Haiden. Youth would be my guess. It wouldn't be the first time a child could see something we couldn't."

"Couldn't she just have made them up?" asked Van. "Youth's also got a mighty imagination."

"No," Trenara replied. "I think the *vision* is authentic. Ena knows her letters, but only in common speech." She took the parchment from Joshan. "These are certainly not common, nor Mathismian. They are much older than that. I don't doubt what Ena saw was all too real." She shot Joshan a knowing look. "Interesting that we should find this out now, isn't it?"

"How long, do you think?"

Trenara shrugged. "Hard to say. Two, three seasons, maybe. The odd thing is, I didn't even see it. The signs should have been blaring."

"Unless she is covering them up."

"Maybe. But why would she do that?" She sighed deeply. "She's going to need to be handled, in any event."

"Yes, and soon."

"I'll start tomorrow when she's rested." Trenara rose from the barrel and stretched. "Imagine being without a guider for all that time. She must be scared silly. Poor girl."

"Right now we need to concentrate on speeding this ship," said Joshan. "Guider, if you think you're ready, let's see what we can do about the wind."

"Quite right. However, I do need a good wash and some food before I start. It is going to be a long day and night, and I won't start without either."

Joshan laughed. "You haven't changed a bit."

"Ah, the privilege of age, I imagine."

"I will see to your food myself. They haven't finished the sails yet; there should be plenty of time for both." He took the guider's arm to escort her to the cabins. As she passed, she stopped and gave Van a kiss.

"Meet me for dinner later?" she asked.

"Aye—but we'll have it in my quarters," he said taking her in his arms.

"Oh, right…" Her eyes twinkled as she winked at the giant and then left with Joshan.

Haiden and Van looked after them completely befuddled.

*****

They traveled to Mathisma, a strong wind at their backs, approaching the state of storm, but never quite. The ship clipped along at speeds that should have ripped the sails to shreds, but the new riggings and reinforced sails were strong and reliable.

The next day, Joshan talked to Ena at length, but said nothing about their conversation to Trenara. This irked the guider, who disliked secrets, and when she could get no information from the close-mouthed Joshan, she sought out Ena to question thoroughly. The young woman just shrugged and smiled, saying the emperor had only said he was glad someone could read the symbols.

"He surely said more than that!"

"No, ma'am. He said just that. Then he asked me who my parents were. Of course, I told him I didn't know, being an orphan. That was all he asked. We talked about the orphanage a little." As Ena went back to setting the table for dinner in Vanderlinden's cabin, the guider looked at her sadly.

"Lass?"

"Yes, ma'am?" Ena responded without turning.

"How long have you had the *sight*?" Ena whirled around dropping the silverware she was holding. Trenara raised a brow. "Come now, Ena. It's obvious you've had these experiences before."

Ena paled under her normally ruby complexion, turning numbly to pick up the silver. "I don't know what you mean, ma'am." The girl sat down heavily at the table and examined the floor at her feet. The only light in the room came from the fire that threw shadows across her face. For a moment the guider regretted the question, Ena looked so pained. But after a score of heartbeats, the girl sighed deeply and winced.

"I hoped no one would need to find out. I try hard not to show it, but sometimes it just happens." She looked up. "I can't help it, guider. I almost didn't say anything about the symbols, but I was so certain the others could see them, too. When they didn't, I knew my secret had to come out."

"Why does it frighten you so?" The guider waited a long time before the girl answered.

"Because I hurt someone once. Very badly," she whispered.

Trenara arranged her voice so the words would make Ena relax and tell her the full truth. "Tell me. I think you'd feel better for it."

Ena gave her a sad smile, but her eyes misted at the memory. "I've held it inside for so long, sometimes I feel as if I could burst." She ran a hand through her hair.

"It was a long time ago, probably ten, twelve seasons, when I was at the shelter. There was a boy who used to pick on us younger ones. He was as mean as they come, too, but, well, that doesn't excuse what I did." She knitted her brow and Trenara said nothing.

"One day, I saw him and some of his play fellows push a little girl around until she was dizzy and crying. She was so upset she went running off, hit a wall, and broke her nose. I saw the whole thing, but didn't report it. I had already had my eye blackened once for such a breach.

"The next day, that boy was at the top of the stairs outside the building, talking to some of his friends. I thought how nice it would be if he up and fell down those stairs to get some of his own. No sooner than I thought it, just like someone pushed him, down he went. He almost died," she said in a whisper, "and will never walk again. No one is going to adopt a cripple or take him into service. I doomed that boy to that place for the rest of his life. I swore I would never wish harm on anything as long as I lived, and I would do everything possible to stop this—thing. No one else has been hurt, but I haven't had much success stopping it."

"By the star," Trenara mumbled. "Right under my nose. How old were you then?"

"I'm not sure—six, maybe seven. I can't remember very well."

Six or seven? Trenara was dumbfounded. To have that kind of *power* at that age spoke of a powerful adult. She said nothing about this to Ena, although she would talk to Joshan about it later.

"Can you honestly say a six or seven year old could be entirely responsible for her actions?" Ena did not answer; the guider leaned forward in her chair. "Let me put it this way, lass. Did you know before this you had this ability?"

"No, ma'am. That was the first time anything like that happened."

"Then, how could you know the results?" Ena managed a shrug as Trenara sat back and sipped her wine. "Do me a favor—sing this note for me." A single pure note came from Trenara's throat and Ena just stared at her. "Come on, try it. I don't think I've ever heard you sing."

Ena looked down at her hands, cleared her throat, and began to tremble as she forced the note through her lips. It was very faint and shaky. Trenara sang with her to give the girl courage, and the note solidified into a perfect soprano lilt that made the hair on the back of the guider's neck rise. The guider stopped singing, allowing Ena to find her own strength. Trenara pulled Andelian out of her robes, and the crystal at the top of the scepter sparkled brilliantly, the white glowing like a sun. When the girl saw it, she gasped, and the light faded. Trenara smiled back at her and put Andelian away. "Lass, the only thing that happened, or rather didn't happen, is a guider was never assigned to you."

Ena stood still for a moment without breathing, as if she'd been slapped. She then jumped from her seat and gaped at the guider. "Me? But that isn't possible." She wrung her hands, the implication sinking in. "I mean, it would certainly fit, but I never dreamed." She turned again to the guider. "Do you think so, ma'am? I mean, could I really be a guider, a… starguider?" The pale of earlier was now the flush of excitement.

Trenara laughed. "I'm pretty sure."

The smile broadened. "That would be wonderful! It would explain so much. I didn't have a guider… or anyone to help me. Of course, it wasn't my fault. Well, it was my fault for thinking such horrible things. I didn't have the ability to use the—*power*. I just didn't have someone there to tell me how." She stopped abruptly and her face turned bright red as she looked to Trenara. "I'm sorry, ma'am. I guess I'm babbling."

"You have every right to babble." Trenara finished her wine and handed the glass to Ena. "This changes things, doesn't it?" Ena shot her a fearful look and Trenara laughed. "You certainly can't go on being my servant…"

"Oh, please, ma'am, don't dismiss me."

"Of course I'm not going to dismiss you. If you're going to start your training, you won't have time to look after an old woman. We have quite a bit of work to do. You are nearing *first trial* even now, I'm certain. There's little time." Trenara looked up at the girl, her eyes shining. "Joshan won't need my service as guider, but by the gods, you will." She laughed long and hard. "But I warn you, being my servant is child's play compared to being my student."

Ena's mouth fell open. "You'd be my guider, just like that?"

"Just like that."

She ran to hug the guider and jumped up unable to stay still. "I swear I will work hard. You'll see. I'll do everything you tell me. I'll learn my lessons, I promise you. And I'll…"

"Enough!" Trenara exclaimed, raising a weary hand. "Right now I'm tired to the bone, and the admiral will be here soon. You can't learn everything tonight. Do me one more thing and then we'll begin. I'll need another girl. See what you can do to round one up, will you?" She rose and walked Ena to the door.

"I'll do that, ma'am. The finest I can find on board, and I'll train her myself, even if it takes all night."

Trenara gave her a sideline look as Vanderlinden appeared in the hatch. "I don't think that will be necessary, my girl. Just someone who can turn down my bed and knows the difference between green and blue will suffice. You are going to need some rest tonight as well. Now, off with you." Van wrapped his arms around Trenara as Ena ducked under his arm.

"Yes, ma'am," the young woman exclaimed and bounded out the door.

*****

The following days were full and tiring for Trenara. Between summoning the winds during the day and Ena's lessons at night, the guider was becoming quickly drained of energy.

Ena took quickly to the lessons, demonstrating an adeptness that Trenara found invigorating. Unlike Joshan, who had always hated the necessary repetition of learning, Ena performed each lesson with a vitality the guider had always wished for the young prince. She would listen to Trenara's every word as though each were a wealth of knowledge in itself and often stay with the guider on the deck to watch as she called the wind and moved it through the heavens.

Joshan offered to take some of the burden off the guider during the next day, the fourth since the ship encountered the beast in the sea, but Trenara declined the offer, knowing Joshan was also coming close to his own limits. He would stay up all night with the wind, and most of the day with either paperwork or his books, and got little rest. His eyes had become hollow circles, and his face strained with apprehension as they drew nearer to Mathisma.

Trenara knew they would reach the island soon and hoped that would relieve some of Joshan's anxiety. Not knowing what would greet them took its toll. Each day seemed more anxious than the last, as the mood of the ship shifted from light frivolity to somber anticipation. On top of that, as the days passed, the weather turned unseasonably cold, until the nights were a shrouded misty gloom and the days a gray depression.

All they could do now was wait.

CHAPTER TWENTY-FIVE
A THIEF BY NIGHT

On the eve of the thirteenth day, the guider stood on deck to see the spot of land that had been sighted. Trenara had trouble sleeping the night before, but this night she knew would be impossible. The excitement of being on Mathisma again, coupled with the concern that gnawed at her, was too much.

Dulling the many stars, the red and white moons cast their full brilliance on the sparkling midnight blue water churning below her idle feet, as their light mingled to cast a rosy hue over the world. The icy air, too cold for frail clouds, made the night almost painfully clear. Trenara felt a kind of contentment. The guider didn't forget the brewing terror in the west or the implications to the east, but for the moment, she accepted the temporary peace for what it was—a quiet poised on the edge of the future.

The winds were still now; the ship would reach its destination with time to spare. If Trenara had remembered, she would have known her contentment was due in part to the fact that this was the eve of midseason, the date of her birth, by coincidence, and a time of high festival for the world. She assumed there would be very little celebration this season.

The guider was so caught up in her reflection she didn't notice the figure that stood beside her. For quite some time, he quietly watched the stars with her. "Beautiful, isn't it?"

Trenara jumped. "Sire, you startled me. I didn't hear you come up." She turned again to the east and sighed. "Yes, quite beautiful. I'd almost forgotten. It will be good to get back. I wonder how much it's changed."

"I think I was about six the last time I came here. Mother took me. All I remember is being scared to death." He laughed at the memory. "It should be interesting to see it now, when everything is not so immense." He chewed on a pipe he had recently taken up.

"Come, Trenara. Haiden has invited all of us for a drink, and I think the admiral is already there. We shouldn't insult him by being late."

Trenara sighed and looked again at the night, drinking in what she could before leaving. She allowed Joshan to lead her to the center of the ship and down into the hold. But instead of turning starboard, the way to their cabins, the emperor turned to port and down to the barracks. "Where are we going?"

"We'll go to the cabins presently, guider. I have a quick errand to run at the barracks." They went down the short wooden stairs and came to a large double door.

"Isn't this door usually open this time of night?" Joshan shrugged and pulled the handle. They were greeted by silence and darkness. Trenara put a restraining hand on Joshan's arm. "Sire…"

Before she could finish the lights went up, and standing in front of the completely dumbfounded guider, stood everyone from the ship, singing a heartwarming tune, cheering Trenara and her birthday. As she moved into the room, propelled by a laughing Joshan, someone handed her a drink and seated her at the head of a long table between Vanderlinden and Joshan. After a toast by Joshan—taken gracefully by Trenara who loathed birthdays—the guests began to talk among themselves.

Trenara turned to the giant and regarded him dryly. "This stinks of your conniving, my dear. If so, I'll roast you alive."

Van laughed. "I wish I could take the credit, but our young Joshan here is the one you should roast. Seems the emperor was afraid if me or Haiden was told, we'd tell you for sure." He took a long drink from his mug and wiped his mouth. "I was right hurt to think no one trusted me to keep the secret."

The guider laughed and turned to Joshan, who feigned innocence. "Lad, if you…"

"Me?" he said touching his chest. "Would I be so devious to think of something this diabolical? No, sadly, it was not my idea, though I did lavish it a bit. I'm afraid Ena is the master-mind behind all this. She was the one who said we should have a celebration. I had completely forgotten it was your birthday."

"Humph. Where is that young scamp anyway? I think a good chewing out is in order."

"Now, guider," Haiden slurred. "Don't be too hard on the lass. It was a nice gesture." He rose from his seat and knocked it over. "If you'll excuse me, I think I know where I can find her. I'll be back presently." He tipped his head and then swaggered to the door, looking as if he had started on the ale a little earlier than the rest.

Trenara, despite her adages about birthdays, enjoyed the company very much and soon left Joshan and Vanderlinden when several people called for a song.

After a half hour of jokes, songs, drinking and merrymaking, Vanderlinden noticed Haiden and the girl had not returned. He became uneasy, but said nothing about it, as he didn't want to disturb the festive mood. He rose and excused himself, claiming a need for fresh air. Joshan put a hand on his arm to stop him.

"You stay, Van, I'll see to it," he whispered, gathering the cloak around his shoulders tightly. "Don't let on to the guider there's something amiss. I don't want to spoil this for her." Vanderlinden nodded and took his seat, watching Trenara, as she started on the fourteenth verse of a rather bawdy song about a certain young man from Thrain in very un-guiderlike fashion, which the crowd cheered. The emperor silently slipped away.

He made his way carefully to the lower cabins. The companion way was very dark, which was unusual as lamps were normally lit early in the evening. He created a soft light with his hands so he could continue. At the end of the long hall was his cabin, but now the door stood ajar, the metal twisted and the hinges bent. It would have taken immense strength to break those hinges. He noticed strange footprints on the deck that led to the cabin.

Deinos, Joshan thought in disgust, one of Sirdar's creatures. The deinos were rather large, with a hideous appearance and the brains of a whillen seed. As Joshan stepped into the chamber, a lightning fast blur knocked him over and disappeared down the long hallway. Joshan stood up shaking and went after the intruder, but even as he hit the deck, the blur disappeared over the railing and escaped into the sea, with what appeared to be a bundle over its shoulder.

Joshan ran to the railing, and prepared to cast a bolt at the creature. When he got there, the sea seemed to have swallowed it up without a trace. He flared his hands until bright light shined for many spans in all directions, but he could see nothing around the ship. It was as if the creature had simply vanished. Far off in the distance, barely discernable in the night, he saw the silhouette of a small, black ship with naked masts. It was too far away to reach with his *power*, though he tried. It was moving away so quickly, they would never catch it, even with full winds. Joshan had never seen a ship move like that. After several failed attempts, he hit the railing in frustration with a sparkling fist, inadvertently smashing the wood into kindling.

Joshan put up his hand to give shout when a sharp, muddled cry came from behind. He ran back into the companionway and almost fell over a crawling Haiden who was flailing his arms.

"Haiden, what happened?" Joshan bent down to help him to his feet, but the marshall was gasping and could not answer. He leaned on Joshan and allowed himself to be half carried up the cabin stairs. When they emerged, the emperor called and several guards came at once. He slid down to the deck with his burden.

A lantern was lit, and Joshan swore when he saw the deathly pallor of his friend's face. The right side of his head was bloody, swollen, and bruised. Haiden looked up once from where he lay in Joshan's arms and then fainted.

"Take him to my chambers and wash his wounds," Joshan said urgently. Two guards took Haiden from his arms and went below. "You there, get Vanderlinden. Tell him to meet me in my chamber at once. But be quiet about it. I don't want the whole of the ship in an uproar. Now!"

The guard saluted and went off at a dash. Joshan went back to his cabin and touched the hinges lightly as he entered, narrowing his eyes in concentration. When he realized what had been stolen, he pounded his fist against the metal. It was something abundantly more valuable than jewels or anything else the creature could have taken. Joshan entered his cabin with a curse.

When he arrived at his bed, Haiden had been washed, but blood still oozed from the three claw marks that ran the side of his face, and his cheek was bruised and black. Joshan ordered the guards out and knelt beside the bed. His hands trembled as he placed them on the wound, *feeling* for the extent of the damage. It was bad— very bad—and he thanked the gods it was night. The skull had been crushed above the temple and the cheek. Haiden would not survive the night without immediate assistance.

Joshan held his palm toward the lantern and the crystals caught the light, sending sparkling colors dancing against the wall. The room filled with an amber fire as he placed his radiant palms on Haiden, sang the notes passionately, and then became lost in the healing.

Vanderlinden and Trenara entered the room silently and held each other as they watched the miracle run its course, until Joshan bowed his head and closed his eyes. As the light dwindled to a glow over the unconscious Haiden, the emperor rose, startled to see them. "I told the guard not to disturb you."

"It wasn't the guard's fault, sire," Van whispered. "Trenara knew, same as I did, something was up."

Trenara moved to the side of the bed and knelt. Her face looked broken under the strain of grief, but her eyes were cold and hard as she gently stroked Haiden's forehead. "Will he live?"

"I think so, but we will know more in the morning. I healed the bones, but I have no skill for the brain. Whether it was crushed with the skull, I can't tell. He's too deep into unconsciousness for me to read anything." A wash of sadness went through his eyes. "When I found him, he was still fighting. I only hope that means the damage is not extensive." He took the guider by the arm to help her up and then touched the giant's to lead them to the door. "Haiden will sleep until morning. There is nothing more I can do tonight."

After assigning a guard to keep watch on Haiden, the emperor led the companions to his sitting room where they sank into the chairs in shock. "What happened, lad?" the giant asked. Joshan told them what he found. They both knew of the existence of the deinos, but neither had ever seen one, hearing only of them after the first rise of Sirdar.

"What was it after? The jewels?"

"No." Joshan looked at Trenara staring quietly at the fire. "It was after me."

"You? But he could have had you when you entered the companionway," Van said.

"No, Van. The deinos, though very swift and powerful, has not the intelligence to match. He had already taken someone he thought was me."

"Who?" the giant asked.

"Ena," the guider hissed bitterly and then rose to probe the fire.

Van stared at Trenara in disbelief. "How?"

Joshan rubbed his hands together as if that would dispel the bitter resentment gnawing at his heart. "Because of my carelessness. I sent Ena to my chambers to fetch a gem from my wardrobe for a pouch she was making Trenara. I think the deinos was waiting here for me. Though how he got on board without being seen and then off again, I don't know—some device of Sirdar's, no doubt. When the girl came here, the deinos must have thought it was me. She was heavily cloaked because of the weather. Haiden obviously found him at that point, but you saw what he received for his troubles." Joshan buried his head in his hands. "Why didn't I see this?"

"You are powerful, sire, not omnipotent," the guider responded from the fire.

Vanderlinden rose woodenly. "We'll turn about and find them."

"We can't, Van," Trenara said tightly, her eyes full of tears. "Our problems have just begun.

"When it's discovered the deinos has failed in his mission," Trenara replied, staring at the fire, "Ena may be killed, but I don't think so. She's a powerful girl, and knowing Sirdar as I do, he will try to corrupt that power—before destroying it."

"Then mores the reason."

"Van," Joshan rubbed the stress from his face. "That ship was being propelled by something I've never seen before. I don't think even with full sails that we'd be able to catch it. Besides, if we turn back now to search for Ena, we will never reach Mathisma in time. The consequences of that far outweigh the... loss of Ena. I agree with Trenara; if Ena is delivered to Sirdar, she will be spared—or her life will be, at any rate."

He picked up an empty cup and began to warm it with his hands, the crystals chiming on the glass. "But there are other, more serious implications here. If we walk into Mathisma as we originally planned, the southern spies will know instantly of the deinos's error."

Trenara stood with a grim resolve and brushed the ash from her hands. "So, what do you have in mind?"

Joshan regarded the two for a moment before speaking. "To make everyone believe the deinos did *not* fail in his mission; by changing me into Ena and her into me."

Van returned his look suspiciously. "Can you do that?"

Joshan mulled over the possibilities. "It will be extremely difficult, but I think I can—at least for a few days. Hopefully, enough time to give her a fighting chance."

"What about the guards that saw you? Surely, they will know what's been done," Trenara said.

"Aye," Van replied, "but you can trust my crew to keep their mouths shut. They're not likely to tell anyone."

"That may be true, Van," Joshan said, "but we can take nothing to chance. It's our only way to buy the girl some time before they reach Badain. Your sailors and the guards that saw me tonight will have to have their memories completely blocked, so none of this can go further than the three of us."

Van eyed the emperor and rubbed his chin. "Sire, I've got a world of respect for you, and I'd fight the devil if need be, but my sailors are something else now. I don't take kindly to messing with their minds without their knowledge."

"Yes, I agree," put in Trenara. "It must be their own choice."

"All right." Joshan's voice came out harsh with weariness and grief. "But it must be done tonight, before they can spread the knowledge to others." He reached into a bureau drawer and pulled out several pieces of parchment and a pen. "I'll make you a list of the people who were there. You can find out from them if there were more.

We must take care of this quickly." He looked up at the giant. "Those that decline, however, will have their minds touched as well. Something guided that creature here. I can't trust anyone." But he smoothed the lines in his face. "I say that only as it might pertain, Van. Sirdar has many spies and I can't eliminate anyone, including your sailors."

"Then you better start with me," Van said.

Joshan smiled warmly. "Thank you for that. That's a noble gesture, but I'm going to need you on the island."

"What is it you want me to do?"

"Gather these people and bring them here," he said, continuing to write the names. "Then you and Trenara are going to alert the crew and passengers that the emperor is missing and Haiden's been hurt."

The giant nodded. "What of the girl, sire?"

Joshan gave him a sideline look. "We'll pray, Van, and hope to finish our business quickly, so we can return to the mainland and perhaps stop the beast before he reaches Cortaim. Chances are he'll land on the southern coast of Badain. Other shores will not admit him or kill him on sight. That might give us enough time." He handed the parchment to Van, who bowed and left quickly.

Trenara took the seat across from the emperor and folded her arms. Her face was calm, but inside she was a torrent of fury, confusion, and conviction. Joshan had finished the second parchment and was affixing the royal seal, when the guider spoke up quietly. "If you enter Mathisma as Ena, you will not be allowed to look at the sacred books."

Joshan continued to seal the parchment and started another without looking up. "I know that."

"So?"

"Trenara, I will see the books and accomplish all I have planned on the isle. Beyond this I can't tell you."

"You can't or you won't?"

Joshan just looked up at her and said nothing. Trenara brought down her arms and leaned toward him. "It's about time you told me something. I've been very patient up to this point and have proven you can trust me. Yet you still won't tell me of your full purpose in going to Sanctum."

Joshan looked at her, knowing that he should tell her, but also knowing if he did, he would have another battle to fight before it was done. Although the burden lay heavy on him, he had to do what the purpose required of him. "I wish I could tell you. Believe me, you will be grateful I didn't."

Trenara stood and wrapped her cloak around her shoulders. "Very well, your highness," she said stiffly. "I will do what you ask, but not gladly. With your permission, sire, I will go to prepare the crew." Her formal air was stiff and affected Joshan like a slap in the face. He looked up at Trenara, and the guider melted under the pain in his eyes. "Joshan, I'm sorry. Ena was put in my charge, and I have failed in that trust. I blame myself for this, not you."

"This isn't anyone's fault. I think you told me one time the purpose sometimes takes many roads. Perhaps this is one of those roads. Foresight is better than hindsight, but hindsight can still teach us. Who's to say which way the game will go when not all the rules are known? Neither one of us can." He smiled wanly. "But we try, don't we?"

Trenara returned the look sadly. "Yes, we try."

She threw the hood of her cloak over her head. "I'll be back when the guards are brought, sire. For now, I will need to prepare for your—disappearance." She turned and left.

Joshan ran a hand through his hair thoughtfully and went back to the parchment. His bold strokes penned the most difficult order of all.

I, Joshan Jenhada Thoringale, being of sound mind and body, Emperor of the Eight Provinces and Keeper of Mathisma, do hereby order—

The night approached an inscrutable dawn.

CHAPTER TWENTY-SIX
MASQUERADE

Trenara sat at the desk in Van's cabin and went over Joshan's instructions. The candles had burned down to puddles of wax, and small flames flickered in the early pre-dawn breeze that came through the open port. One more task remained before they reached the island. It would set the stage for the grand masquerade, but she didn't relish it.

Her eyes burned with fatigue and her head ached. At length, when she could keep them open no longer, she slumped into the papers on the desk. The guider woke to someone shaking her gently and the sweet smell of hot cider flowing on the air. She opened her heavy eyelids and shook the sleep from her head. The sun had just begun its climb over the horizon and touched the sky with the silvery gray of dawn.

"It's time, guider," said a young voice above her head.

Trenara furrowed her brow a moment, feeling something was out of place and lifted her head to look into a pair of shining blue eyes. A broad smile creased her face as she clasped the girl in her arms, and tears of joy sparkled at her eyes.

"Ena! By the gods, we thought you were…" But she stopped abruptly and pushed the girl back. She couldn't keep the disappointment out of her voice. "Joshan?"

"Yes, Trenara. I'm sorry."

Trenara rubbed her eyes, looked up, and managed a smile. "You've done an incredible job. The likeness is uncanny." Trenara couldn't stop a pang of loss for her captured aide. Joshan looked so much like her even his expressions were remarkable.

"I can't think of a nicer compliment, guider. Thank you."

Joshan reached into the closet and took out a cloak. "We have assembled the crew. Are you ready?"

Trenara curled her lip and took the cloak. She fastened the catch and picked up a parchment from her desk. "Did Van say when we'd dock?"

"In three hours. There isn't much time."

Trenara shot him an oblique look as she opened the door. "There never is, is there?" The ice in her voice was unmistakable.

The morning promised to be cheerless as a blanket of clouds sailed in with the sun and cast a shroud over the light. The royal colors that generally whisked in the sky now hung wet and crumpled against the mast, while the golden serpent was lowered by half and flickered in the fitful breeze. The mood of the crew as they stood in quiet huddled groups was fearful. Rumors had flown from starboard to aft, but no one knew what to believe. Little was said among them now and that in fleeting whispers.

Bent by grief, Trenara mounted the bridge slowly and held the rails for support with Joshan, masked as Ena, behind her. A haggard look creased Vanderlinden's face as he took the guider's hand and kissed it, escorting her to the center of the platform. Trenara scanned the faces below her and the whispers died down.

"I don't know how much you have been told, but I will try to make this brief." The guider's words came out slowly, hoarse. "The emperor…" It was hard, so very hard to speak. "The emperor was found missing early this morning." Her voice faltered when a vision of Ena came to her mind with the searching tentacles of Sirdar reaching out to overwhelm her. She bowed her head as a tear found its way down her cheek. Joshan put a comforting hand on her arm. Trenara looked up and nodded. The crew and passengers made no sound, but many eyes widened in disbelief.

"From the signs," Trenara continued, "it appears a creature came on board sometime during the night and crept into his chambers. We don't know how, but it wasn't seen by anyone, except Marshall Bails, who was seriously wounded when he tried to stop it. He is now recovering in his quarters and should be up and around soon. We suspect enchantment was used. No blame is put on anyone here for what happened." She stopped to gather her strength when a guard stepped forward from the throng.

"Ma'am, meaning no disrespect, but I don't understand why we make for the isle, then. It seems folly to continue when we should be making all speed to rescue our lord. That is… unless you've already counted him among the dead." The woman gazed at the lowered pendant and many voices were raised in agreement. Van glared at her and stepped forward, but Trenara stopped his rebuttal with a restraining hand.

"No. We don't count the emperor among the dead, but your question is valid. It is Joshan's wish we not turn back." Many questions went up from the group, but Trenara raised her hands in response. "Please. If you allow me to continue, I think you'll understand.

"His majesty may have known something like this would happen. He wrote instructions that were to be read if—if he could not go on. I'd like to read them." She wiped tears from her eyes, broke the seal with shaking fingers, and unrolled the crumpled parchment.

"He writes:

'No matter what sorrows have been thrown at you, do not let tears dissolve the ray of hope that yet remains. The mission to Mathisma must not fail. If it is delayed by grief, then alive or dead, it won't make a difference. We will have lost. In the wake of that, nothing else matters. If you do not continue, our world will have to bow to an enduring enemy that will not stop until he destroys every freedom.' With each word Trenara read, a new strength grew in her heart and filled her with grim determination. *'Don't hesitate in our hour of need because of sorrow. Harden your heart. The path we all follow, whether by choice or fortune, may take many unknown turns. All of them will be difficult. Prepare yourself for that. But this is imperative: do not abandon the fight when it seems hopeless to go on… no matter what the odds, no matter what the strength of the enemy, no matter who falls beside you. This must be remembered: many wars are fought and won—in a single battle. Fight on. Fight now. Win this!'"*

Trenara lifted her eyes to the crowd, and in them glared a fire that Joshan had never seen; resolute and calm, yet grimly fierce. When he looked at the crowd they stood with their shoulders back, their heads held high with a proud spark that burned in their eyes. He marveled at the effect of his words.

"In three hours we dock," Trenara continued. "In the next twenty-four we will demand every ounce of your courage, for this battle—and for Joshan."

As they turned to leave the bridge, a deafening cry went up from the crowd. "Joshan! Joshan! Joshan!" It rolled over and over again. The birds in the sails took wing, the masts shook, and as if set off by the tribute, a gust of wind swept up the emperor's standard and sent the serpent slithering in the breeze.

Trenara's last sight as she left the deck was the giant standing before his sailors with orders. His earlier pallor was gone, and as she watched, seasons of hardship melted away. Trenara hadn't seen that light in Van's eyes since before the first war. She never loved him as much as she did right then. It heartened her more than any words.

When they reached Van's cabin, she closed the door and turned to Joshan. "You never cease to amaze me, Trenara," he said. "I could not have put such power into those words. Thank you." Alone, the enchantment wore away, and Joshan stood before her as himself.

Trenara shook her head and she looked at him with new respect. "I did nothing, sire—except to act the fool. To think I ever doubted *you*."

"Doubted me? You have been my greatest strength."

"I have been a stone around your neck—no, hear me out. I have fought you every step of the way, questioned every action, doubted every move—and like a fool, complained at every request you made of me, while I hid behind my age. I have doubted my own abilities and the gifts that have been given to me. No more. Forgive me, Joshan. Forgive an old fool. I will never doubt you again, I swear."

Joshan put a hand on Trenara's shoulder, but his eyes held an ache she didn't understand. "That you have found your strength at last, I am truly thankful. You have more courage and power than you yet realize. I am absolutely relying on that strength. Embrace it, Trenara, as you have never embraced anything else.

"But listen to me and listen very carefully. Nothing is infallible, least of all me," he said. "Others will bow to me and go blindly where I lead them. That is as it must be; but not you. There's a reason you became my guider of all other Starguiders, Trenara. It's only now I begin to see why. In your own words, your purpose is clear—to guide me through the best and worst of it. You must do that before anything else. Don't be blinded by the glory of the words I hold over others. If you *are* blinded by them, I will be... alone."

The sudden terror in Joshan's face made the guider shudder. "I don't think I could bear that," he continued. "You *must* question. You *must* doubt. If you don't, who will? You'll see this as the days go by. They will bow to me, Trenara—they will do anything I ask them—they will worship me. It's the one thing I can't stop in any of the futures," he whispered as tears formed in his eyes. "Of all those who serve me, it is *you* who must have her eyes wide open, when all others are closed. If you close your eyes to sleep, if you close your eyes when you stumble, if you close your eyes to look away from something you can't bear to look at, I will be blind. You mustn't let that happen. Ever. Do you understand?"

Trenara put a hand on Joshan's and smiled. "I think I'm beginning to. It's a lot to ask a woman to give up all her excuses for failure. I won't even be able to hide in my servitude to you. You ask me to take full responsibility for the outcome of all our deeds, along with you and not under you. Am I right?"

"Yes," he replied seriously. "It could end up being... nearly intolerable. Will you?"

"Gladly, without reservation, if you will have me." She bowed her head to him.

Joshan took the guider in his arms and squeezed her. "For the duration, Trenara," he whispered in her ear.

CHAPTER TWENTY-SEVEN
MATHISMA

Three hours later, Trenara and Joshan disguised as Ena, stood on the deck surveying the crew, as the ship was busily making ready to cast anchor and furl the sails. Vanderlinden was shouting orders from the main deck. The clouds had melted away and the island glistened in the morning light, floating in a mist like an emerald on a cushion of white silk. Though the sun was bright, it did nothing to keep the biting fingers of cold from penetrating heavy cloaks or tainting all that it touched with frost.

Trenara caught her breath, still awed by the island's beauty. Mathisma ran far north, the length of Thrain and Quitain combined, ending in distance. To the south, fifteen hundred spans from Welcome Harbor, the Sanctum Bridge rose high and stone-black, sitting on a cloud of mist as if suspended there. Beyond stood Sanctum itself, with the knowledge of mankind locked in its crystal dome like a mother tortoise hoarding her unborn eggs. The jagged crown of stones behind the dome stood at the heart of the small island and rose majestically toward the sky.

Beyond the wooden docks stood the Assemblage Home. The marble buildings, less majestic than their neighbor, stood in geometrical perfection, man-made tributes to knowledge and art. Directly in front and predominant was the Academy, where *first trial* pre-guiders mastered their use of the *power* and prepared for their calling. On the other side, at precise right angles, stood the immense chambers of the Prelacy.

Trenara stared at the city with deep affection. She had forgotten how lonely a woman could become without communication with her peers. It saddened her to think the reunion was during this time of uncertainty. It had been too long between visits and she regretted it.

The guider turned to gaze at Sanctum. She had learned as a girl that the small island was sacrosanct. It was home to the enigma of mankind. The Crystal of Healing, which she had never seen, lay locked and protected behind its marble walls. Few had entered the sacred halls and only those who were given leave to see the Book of Kerillian or other ancient works from the immense library tucked away in the domed citadel. Only the Provost was allowed to tend the Crystal, and by tradition, he kept this knowledge locked away from all others.

When the emperor stirred at her side, the guise holding even in sunlight, the guider folded her arms and stared up at Sanctum. "It's strange. I feel as if this is the last time I'll see her like this. It gives me a chill." She wrapped the cloak more tightly around her shoulders.

Joshan shot her a look but said nothing and became transfixed on the island before him. A chill ran through him as well, but rather from presence than premonition.

Something shadowed the land. Something only his eyes could see, perhaps, but there it loomed.

When they docked in the cool harbor, a group of guiders was waiting to greet them. They seemed aged and somber, most dressed in blacks and browns. Their faces were what Ena would have called sour, and they didn't seem very pleased to see the ship or its passengers.

"Who are those people, Trenara?"

The guider squinted and scanned the group. "I believe that is the Prelacy, at least most of them. The old guider there, the one with the long staff, is Witen, unless my eyes deceive me. He has been the Prelate for many seasons. Watch him though, sire. He may look very old, but age hasn't dulled his wits any. Witen is as sharp as he ever was. I only hope he has not fallen under Palarine's sway. That would make our mission difficult—and disappointing. With the Provost dead, Witen will be in charge now… until the ceremony." She smiled to herself. "I'll bet he's furious."

Joshan glanced at her. "What do you mean?"

"You would have to know Witen, lad. He hates politics."

"Who is the man standing next to him?"

Trenara squinted again. "That has to be Grandor. He's put on a few seasons—not to mention a few pounds. He's a fine guider and knows more about ancient lore than anyone. Grandor will be the one to talk to about Kerillian. If he doesn't know the answers, he'll know where to find them. I think you've read some of his books. To be honest, if Palarine had not appeared, Grandor would no doubt have been named Provost. He has been studying under Saminee for seasons. I'd be willing to bet there's no love lost between those two. He will be an ally, mark my words. The loss of the appointment must have been heartbreaking for him." She shook her head. "The rest I'm afraid I don't know, but they seem unaccountably young to be members of the Prelacy. It appears things have changed. For as long as I can remember, the Prelacy has always been made up of the oldest guiders."

"It is interesting the Provost Elect is not among them. I thought Palarine would be here to greet us," put in Joshan.

"To be honest, lad, I'm relieved he's not. One step at a time."

A high pitched whistle sounded shrill. Joshan picked up the pack from the deck and strapped it to his back. "Come, guider. That was the admiral's signal."

When the gangplank had grated to a halt on the dock, Vanderlinden, Trenara, and Joshan left the ship and walked to the top of the pier. The people at the docks seemed uneasy to the guider's eyes—or in awe. She guessed the Prelacy rarely ventured from the security of the chambers. The beach was deserted except for an occasional guider or pre-guider, who cast guarded looks toward the ship and then scurried off to finish their business.

When the companions stood before the Prelacy, Trenara held Andelian out formally and bowed her head to the group. "Hail, masters. We beg entrance into the Home of Assemblage to take council and to bring you tidings from the west."

She lowered Andelian and greeted Witen's stern look. The old man was bent with age, but the sparkle in his eyes showed the underlying clarity that lay there. He leaned on his staff and scrutinized the party carefully before speaking. "You are welcome, Trenara, and your friends," he said quietly though the age in his voice was somewhat edged. "We have had grave news, Trenara. Since I don't see the young emperor among your companions, I can only conclude it is true. Is Joshan lost to us, then?"

Trenara was jarred for a moment, wondering at the source of the Prelate's information. "Not lost, Prelate, but feared taken, early this morning. We have just ourselves discovered it. How do you know this?"

"That would be best discussed in council, guider," he replied as if reprimanding an erring child. Trenara bowed her head in assent, but a flash of indignation clouded her face. The old man turned to the disguised Joshan. "Who have we here?" he asked.

"Ena, sir—up until recently my aide. We just discovered she is one of the chosen. I have started her training."

The old man wanly smiled at the young woman, his eyes seeming to penetrate the façade. "Welcome. Are you certain you want to join ranks with us dusty old scholars?" His eyes were ancient, but their sharpness made Joshan uneasy. "I'm certain you'd much rather be exploring the island than listening to the prattle of a lot of old people, hey?"

Joshan managed an innocent smile. "No, sir," he responded wide-eyed. "I mean, sir, begging your pardon, I would very much like to be here. To learn what I can, sir."

The old man's face collapsed into a million wrinkles as he smiled and patted Joshan's ruddy cheek. "Smart girl." He leaned on his staff and turned for the city. "My old bones don't like this snap in the air, and I have been on my corns too long."

They started up a long, twisting road that led to the city proper. Joshan and Vanderlinden brought up the rear and walked a little behind, while Trenara remained with the group to exchange fleeting whispers with Grandor. Joshan looked about in wonder, maintaining the pretense of Ena skillfully. Though he had been there in the past, it was still as enchanting as ever. The domes grew slowly, like granite hills, as they approached. Joshan's thoughts began to turn to Haiden, who would wake soon from his nightmare, to the mission to Sanctum, to the fate of Trenara, to the mystery that was Vanderlinden…

"Lad?" Joshan visibly started out of his reverie. "You're as jumpy as a cat. What's deviling you?" the admiral asked quietly.

Joshan shot him a dark look. "Nothing, Van—everything. I just wish this was over." He increased his steps to catch up with the group.

Van raised an eyebrow and followed, but said nothing more. He decided he would get back to the ship as soon as it was polite. He wanted an end to high matters and the contriving of guiders. He had had enough of both. He found himself wishing he were master of the Village again, and the thought sent a bemused smile across his face.

At length the group walked through a high, finely carved stone archway that led to a large courtyard in front of the Prelacy buildings. Within the yard stood imposing god and goddess statues, rows of sculptured shrubs, and some of the most exotic trees the travelers were ever likely to see. Van noted there had been some additions to the gardens since he had seen it last, making the place seem even more stunning. The only thing lovelier in the garden was Trenara, whose face was for the moment serene as she scanned the additions. Her eyes caught Van's and she smiled, but then turned back to talk to the guider at her right. He sighed and looked back at the garden.

There, in the middle as always, stood the famous stone fountain. It was ugly, lopsided, weather worn by age, with here or there a small bird precariously perched on its knobby rim. It had stood there since Assemblage moved to the island. No stonecutter's chisel could carve it, no guider's wand transform it, to make it more ornate, even though many had tried.

This was the Holding Stone, a fragmented piece of glass that had been burned and fused when it fell from the sky a millennium ago. The Crystal of Healing had been at its heart; Assemblage treasured it far above other precious stones of more sightly beauty. Water placed in the small niche that had once cradled the Crystal, was turned into the precious imaka.

The group turned to take the small, well-worn path to the basin. Each knelt before it in reverence and touched a drop of the liquid to his or her tongue. When Van did the same, he felt wonderfully refreshed. He'd forgotten how good the imaka could make you feel, and this was pure, without dilution. It made his blood race.

When they entered the building, the Prelate ordered servants to take the visitors' belongings to their chambers. "I would have a word with you later in my chambers before the council, Trenara," Witen said, touching the guider's sleeve. "Once you have settled your things."

Trenara bowed. "Of course, Prelate. May I bring the girl, sir? This is her first visit to Mathisma, and an afternoon with you would be a real treat—for both of us."

Witen looked at the disguised youth as Joshan leaned against the balustrade and stared wide-eyed at the wooden staircase that spiraled up the exact middle of the building. Platforms shot out from the stairway like spokes in a giant spinning wheel. Tiers of mezzanines towered high above their heads, crowned by a vivid dome of stained glass. The building was a wonder of art, craft, and brilliant engineering. Joshan could not see Witen, but could feel the old man's eyes bore into his neck.

"Yes, that would be wise," Witen said. "Bring her. What I have to say is for both of you." Trenara looked at him sharply, but the old man merely gave her a faint smile and then hobbled away on his staff without another word.

Trenara followed her companions up the ornate stairs, as the servants trailed behind. When they were well settled in their chambers, three rooms joined by small doorways, Trenara dismissed her servants and knocked on Van's door.

"In a minute, Trenara." The giant's voice was muffled behind the wood.

She turned to summon Joshan, but before she reached the door, the disguised boy came in and sat on the divan. He picked up a brier pipe from the table and began to pack it as Trenara went to the sideboard to pour drinks.

"Isn't that a bit out of character?" Van asked as he came through the door.

Joshan looked at the pipe mournfully, but set it down. "I suppose you're right." The giant laughed and sat across from him.

"What was it Witen whispered to you, Trenara?" Joshan asked.

"That he wanted to see you and me in his chambers before council," she said, setting the drinks down. "Witen has always been an odd sort. I think he suspects something. He is old, but very wise."

"What could he suspect?" Van asked.

Trenara's smile warmed. "Not much gets by Witen. He has been *third trial* for many seasons. At one time, he was offered the Provost seat, but refused it. It would not surprise me if he knew more than he lets on."

"He was your guider, wasn't he?" Joshan asked.

"Yes. He had many students then. I think that's why he turned down the merit. He enjoyed teaching and was never fond of politics. Even as head of the Prelacy he still teaches, I'm told." Trenara drained her drink. "We best get to his chambers to hear what he has to say. I've heard and seen a lot that disturbs me. Perhaps he can enlighten us."

"Aye. It hurts me to see such darkness on the place. There are bad things brewing from the way the servants acted."

"What did they say?" Joshan asked.

Van shrugged. "It wasn't what they said as much as how they said it. They're scared. Something's wrong here. Hell, the way you were talking on the ship, I figured we'd need to come on shore with a fully armed company. It's not that kind of fight, is it?"

Joshan shook his head, the old pain in his eyes looking strangely out of place on the face of Ena. "I wish it were. I'd prefer a good old-fashioned fight to this covert manipulation of minds and loyalties. There may be a real battle soon enough." He looked down at his drink and furrowed his brow. "We play a dangerous game, the political strategies of which will decide many things. I suppose that makes me the king."

Van snorted good-naturedly, "And me the pawn."

Joshan looked up from his reflection. "I didn't mean that, Van."

The admiral laughed; it sounded strange in this place. "Don't apologize, sire. I'm more than willing to be your pawn. Grateful, as a matter of fact. I wouldn't be in your place for a hull stuffed with jewels." He stood up and bowed formally. "So, your majesty, if you'll move me now, I think we can start this game. What next?"

Joshan frowned, feeling the fear of the Assemblage home as a dull ache on his inner *sight*. The giant's laugh had brought to mind what he had felt when he first stepped on the isle. There was no mirth here, no song, no lightness of heart. The feeling left him cold inside.

"Two things," Joshan said, "first, return to the ship, and bring Haiden here. You will find him awake and furious for being left behind. He won't remember much, so tell him quickly, and then return immediately. No one must see you. That's imperative."

"That's easier said than done."

"Not so difficult," Trenara replied, tying her sash. "There's a passage under the dock that leads back into this building. It's not secret, but Grandor told me no one travels that way anymore."

"You mean the one under the pier?"

"You know it?"

"Sure. But it's been seasons. I thought it was blocked up."

Trenara nodded. "It may well be, but I think it will bring you through at least as far as the east wing."

Joshan picked up Ena's cloak. "We will be in Witen's chambers, if you need us. Otherwise, we'll meet you at the bridge as planned."

"You said two things," Van said as he strapped his dagger to his waist.

Joshan paused for a moment to fasten his cloak. "I need the key to Sanctum."

Van's eye widened and he whistled softly. "That's a tall order." He scratched his head. "How am I supposed to do that?"

"The key will be around the neck of the dead Provost. Saminee will be laid out in his chambers. As to how you do it, I leave that entirely up to you and Haiden."

Van shot him a disgruntled look. "Thanks a hell of a lot."

"You'll find him on the fourth floor of this building, east corridor, second door," said Joshan.

Trenara pursed her lips and glanced at him. "I'm not even going to ask how you knew that."

Joshan laughed for the first time since stepping onto the isle and it felt good. "Nothing magical, guider. The servants told me when I asked. I said we wanted to pay our respects." He looked up at the giant. "You'll do fine, Van, but watch yourself. The last thing Palarine wants is for that key to disappear. It will be heavily guarded."

"A guard or two never bothered me much."

Joshan opened his mouth to speak but then simply nodded. "Take your bow," he said.

Van cocked an eyebrow. "Something you're not telling me, lad?"

Joshan shook his head. "Take your bow and quiver. Have Haiden bring his sword. Just a flash of insight, nothing more. You remember the rest of the plan?"

"Aye, that I do. Me and Haiden will meet you on the bridge after council."

"And if we don't make it?"

"Lad, there's no chance of…"

"And if we don't make it there?" Joshan repeated forcefully.

"We're to proceed without you," Van conceded.

"Don't fail me, Van. I'm relying on you." Joshan took the giant's hand and squeezed it warmly, allowing the smile to smooth the lines of his face into a confidence he didn't feel. "Good luck."

"I won't need luck. I always land on my feet, as I've said before." He went to Trenara and took her into his arms. "Don't take any guff from those guiders."

She stood on her tiptoes and kissed him. "Please be careful, Van."

"I'm always careful, my love. We'll see you on the bridge." He kissed her again and disappeared out the door without another word.

Joshan slumped in his chair. This was another alternate future. If Van was swayed now by the poison in his eye, they were lost. All Joshan could do was carry out what was required and hope for the best. He didn't like letting the giant out of his sight and therefore his *power*, until the fragment of *Catalyst* and the threat had been removed, but the alternative was far more devastating. If Trenara noticed his discontent, she made no indication, and Joshan was glad. He adjusted the cloak around the young shoulders and left the chamber with the stride of someone who must face the future, even when that future was uncertain. Trenara followed him like a woman who had no other choice.

CHAPTER TWENY-EIGHT
WITEN'S GIFT

Trenara remained silent as they made their way to Witen's chambers, watching the multitude of guards lining the walls and doorways. What struck her oddly was they reminded her sharply of Vanderlinden, or rather a darker version of him. They were large like the giant, with dark complexions and the eyes to match; shrewd, clear eyes, but they were very thick-boned and had long hair. It wasn't so much their appearance as their manner; rough, earthy speech, and quick tempers. These were not the same breed as the northerners in the Keep during Balinar's treachery. They seemed more intelligent and skilled, if their banter was any indication. More than once, she caught herself staring.

When they turned into a relatively deserted corridor, she whispered to Joshan, "Those guards—certainly not Mathismian."

"I would say we've found the northerners Sark reported. That they are even in this building is not encouraging."

When they arrived at Witen's chambers, they were let in by a very old servant who showed them to a small sitting room. Lunch had been laid and they were invited to eat with an air of dignified pomposity that contrasted the servant's station. Joshan found himself liking the man's arrogant manner and confident certainty. It re-enforced his need to put down his own doubts and ensure his disguise was well done. Witen, the servant told them, would be with them presently, and left with a clipped bow.

"Can we trust Witen?" Joshan asked Trenara.

The guider shook her head. "I hope so. It seems we would have been stopped or hindered long before this, if not. From what I've heard, Palarine's northerners out-number the Assemblage twenty to one. Not that that's a threat to the guiders, Grandor told me, but he was very nervous. I wasn't wrong about him. Before I could so much as open my mouth, he was all on fire to tell me of the Provost Elect's misdeeds." From down the hall they could hear the servant greet his master and the sound of a staff on the hard stone floor.

Witen came in and sat down slowly, dismissing his servant and eying the two sternly. Then all at once, a smile of pure delight creased his face and sparkled in his eyes. "You are looking well, my girl. I'd swear you haven't aged a bit in all these seasons and are every bit as beautiful as you ever were. From what I've gathered, you are still headstrong. Am I wrong?" He patted the guider's knee and Trenara visibly relaxed. Witen sounded again like the man she used to know.

"Why, you old liar, I've aged and you know it. But with you, I do feel young again. It is so good to see you, Witen. I'm afraid for a moment downstairs I thought I had fallen out of your favor."

He smiled at her sadly. "You were always my favorite, Trenara," he said. "Some things never change, thank the gods. For example, you are still drinking the horrid mead, yes?" He stood and tottered to the sideboard. When Trenara rose to help, Witen just lifted a hand. "Sit down, sit down." He poured and handed the glass to Trenara then crossed to settle back in his chair.

"And you are still drinking ale, I take it?" she asked.

"No. Those damn healers and their meddling won't let me near the stuff anymore." He leaned closer. "Though, between you and me, I do sneak a nip or two now and again." He sat back and chuckled. "Only tea these days, mores the pity.

"What brings you to Mathisma, Trenara?" His glance was so keen from beneath the wrinkled brow Trenara had to clear her throat. She fought to keep the quiver out of her voice.

"To bring you news from the mainland, of course. Also, the emperor wished to look at Kerillian's books."

Witen quietly nodded. "Tell me your news."

Trenara shot a glance at Joshan and then back to the old guider. "Wouldn't it be better to relay this to the entire council, when the Prelacy is present?"

The aged guider pursed his lips in thought. "Perhaps, my girl, but indulge an old man, will you?" His eyes looked anything but old right then. "Believe me, there are good reasons why I ask for the news now."

"As you wish, Prelate, but it is a lengthy tale."

"So be it. Make it as short as you can, but leave nothing out."

Trenara relayed all the events of the past several months from the possession of Jenhada to the disappearance of Joshan, leaving out only the truth of the latter and the suspicions of the emperor about the Provost Elect and the cultivated lethargy of Assemblage. During her narrative, Witen made no comment. Indeed, he appeared not to be listening at all, as he had closed his eyes and was breathing deeply. However, Trenara knew Witen hadn't missed a syllable. When she had finished, he opened his eyes and looked at the two companions searchingly.

"I see," he said simply and then poured himself a cup of tea. He sipped at the cup for a long time and stared off into the chamber. At length, he put the cup down and leaned forward in his chair.

"Your news gives me hope, though you have not told me everything, that is, if the emperor has indeed been taken from us." He turned his attention to Joshan, who had remained still for some time. Trenara shot a pleading glance his way, but Joshan continued to regard the old man quietly.

"How long have you known?" Joshan asked.

The old guider sat back and smiled. "Since I saw you on the dock… I didn't know exactly who you were until just now." He bowed his head. "I'm indeed honored, sire. To maintain a disguise of this magnitude is phenomenal; a tribute to your training, I'm certain."

Trenara's look was comically dumbfounded. "But what gave it away?"

"Several things, my girl. I knew the moment you said this girl had been a servant you were lying. I could see it in your face and hers—his. Something in the stature showed me whatever else, she had not led a life of servitude. Of course, the eyes betrayed him most. No student carries such power, although the guise is masterfully done."

Trenara leaned forward. "Prelate, it is imperative…"

"I know, I know," he responded with a wave of his hand. "No one will hear it from me. I know the urgency of what you wish to accomplish, and I will not hinder you. In fact, I brought you here to offer my help."

Joshan dropped the enchantment and regarded the Prelate. Witen finally bowed his head in respect. "Something on your mind, sire?" he asked pointedly.

"Just a question, Prelate. How did you know I was missing?"

"Ah, that." The old guider sat back in his chair with an arrogant smile. "There is much I know that others do not. No, it's not *vision*, though sometimes I wish I still had as much as I once did. Something altogether different. Disguise yourself again and I will show you." Joshan's appearance shimmered and Ena reappeared. Witen shook his head in astonishment as he rang a small bell next to his chair and the servant came in and bowed.

"M'lord?"

"This, ladies, is Acon. Here, open the panel for me, will you?"

Acon looked at his master and then regarded the two strangers narrowly. "The panel, sir? Are you quite certain?"

Witen gave him a wave of his hand and a sour look. "Go on." Acon crossed and removed a small vase from in front of a concealed panel. "You would think after forty seasons the old geezer would have learned a little respect," Witen whispered, and none too quietly. "You just can't find good servants anymore."

Acon snorted and shot a suspicious glance back at the two. Without even a pretense of courtesy, he shifted his body to block the panel from Joshan and Trenara, so they could not see what he was doing. When the servant stepped away, a small opening appeared, with no sign of either latch or hinge. He reached in and pulled out a worn velvet bag.

"Bring it here," Witen ordered. With care and disapproval, the servant carried the object to his master and laid it on his lap. "Thank you, Acon. You may go." The servant opened his mouth to speak, but quickly snapped it shut, and shuffled out of the room.

When Acon was down the corridor, Joshan leaned toward the old guider. "He is marvelous, Witen."

The Prelate curled his lip. "Acon is a royal pain in the ass. Aren't you, you old boot?" he called. There was a rustle in the hallway and then the slow pad of footsteps. Witen smiled to himself smugly. "That will teach him."

"For heaven's sake, Witen, why don't you find yourself another servant?" Trenara asked.

Witen looked at her in horror. "Replace Acon? It's taken me forty seasons just to break him in, though I admit, I'm still working on it. I'm much too old to change my ways now."

The Prelate very carefully opened the pouch and pulled out the object, holding it up for his visitors to see. It was an ancient ornate mirror, surrounded by yellowing ivory, two hands wide. The glass was actually not a mirror at all, but instead a plane of bright gold with veins of silver and opal that ran through it in a chaotic storm, like rain staining a windowpane. There was no reflection, but rather an intricate panoply of colors and designs, like a child's complex kaleidoscope. It was very beautiful.

The carvings surrounding the glass were so detailed they seemed to almost move on their own. The figures were naked deities intertwined in a glorious white dance; the goddesses Ethos, Leukos, Krikos, and Ventus; and the gods Eraze, Pyra, Hydor, and Noscere. They were tangled so intimately, it was difficult to say whether it was dance or orgy as they circled around the glass shamelessly. The artifact was exquisite.

"This, my girl, is the *gazing*," the Prelate whispered, a fine fire in his eyes. Trenara rose from her chair and examined it very carefully, turning the mirror in her hands as if to catch the gods dancing on the other side.

"Where did you… how in the world…"

"Ah, ha. Didn't know it still existed, did you? I found it quite by accident in Sanctum. It fell from some height onto my head and left quite a lump, if truth were known, I don't know from where. So, I guess it found me. How it got there I couldn't imagine."

Trenara became very excited. "Sire, Kerillian speaks of this mirror in his legend. It's said he used it to foresee his prophecies, but it was lost centuries ago. Then you used this to see us on the ship?"

"No, no," Witen exclaimed. "I'm no sneak, for heaven's sake. Quite the contrary. I was trying to locate Sirdar or his armies. How I came upon your ship is as much a mystery to me as it is to you."

Trenara's face hardened. "You mean to say you have been watching Sirdar's movements and didn't report it?"

"Don't get your dander up, my dear Trenara. I haven't been *able* to report anything to anyone. I don't even know whom to trust anymore. Besides, I guess Sirdar figured he was being watched. That's when I came upon your ship. It's been a fortnight since I last saw anything on the mainland. Last night I tried just one last time and there you were, as large as life." He stood slowly, slid the mirror back into the bag, and went to put it in its niche. "Not that I had great pride in the knowledge for long, mind you. This morning, Palarine told *me* the emperor had been taken. I would give my last coin to know how he gets his information before the rest of us."

"Did you tell him what you saw in the *gazing*?" Joshan asked.

"I'm old, sire, but I'm no fool." Witen sealed the panel and returned to his chair. "My offer of help still stands. If you wish to use the mirror, you may. Of course, I only ask you leave it in my keeping until you return to the mainland. I'm afraid I've grown quite fond of it."

Trenara took her seat. "Thank you, Witen, we do appreciate it. But I'm concerned that if you saw through Joshan's disguise, then what of others?"

"I don't think you need to worry. The Provost Elect has many followers—too many. But none of them knows you as I do, Trenara. You have always been a terrible liar, you know."

Joshan's interest sharpened. "Then you know of the deception of the elect."

Witen shrugged. "I know nothing of any deception, but his game is clear enough. That man feeds on obedience like a drug. It's frightening to watch. His stark morality and professed denial of even the simplest of pleasures leeches like a disease on the normal good nature of the young. I don't know what hold he has over them, but whatever it is, it spreads so quickly you can't keep up with it." His voice warmed as he spoke. "He preaches ignorance like a delivering prophet and self-denial like an ancient sage. The young flock to that tripe as if his words alone could sustain them."

He bowed his head and shook it, the anger fading to sadness. "Virtue, he says, lies in *power*—not in knowledge, mind you, but in *power*. As if knowledge and growth were evil. I think he's abandoned the gods; there is no room for divinity in his teachings. He is also careful—he says nothing that could get him accused of heresy—even if he is a heretic. It's very disturbing to watch. I've known for months what he professes is destructive, but I haven't done much to convince anyone else. Oh, there are some of us, one or two old timers for the most part. But these young ones—it's a new age, Trenara. The young just don't seem to have what they used to—they've lost their faith, and with it, their obedience to the old ways. Why just last week, a young first trial, a follower of Palarine's, actually stabbed one of the Prelacy—wounded her quite badly. That's never happened as far as I know, not in our history. Palarine has many followers and his numbers grow daily."

He closed his eyes again and sat back. "At first, I imagined he would eventually destroy himself. His viewpoints were so radically different from our tenets, I thought he would soon be expelled. I completely underestimated his power of persuasion, until it was much too late.

"Then, about a fortnight ago, I had a *vision*. I saw a figure approach me in the dark of my bedchamber. For a moment, I thought it was Acon and told him to go back to bed. The figure kept coming until he stood at my feet. It was a boy—or rather a young man, though I couldn't see him well enough to say how old exactly. He held up his hands and I saw a bright star in each of this palms. You can imagine it took me aback a bit. I sat up to get a closer look, but he closed his hands and said simply, 'Wait for the Sight.' Then he just disappeared.

"That was it. At first, I thought it might be the fish I had for dinner and decided to forget about it. Ha! That *vision* haunted me day and night without letting up. I finally looked into the *gazing* last night and saw your ship." He looked up and regarded the visitors. "You were both in a room with that Vanderlinden fellow and another chap was lying in a bed with a kind of golden glow around him. Then I saw you in another chamber talking about the deinos." He looked down at his knees and grew silent for a long time.

"Sire," he said quietly, "if I might ask, would you show me your hands?"

Joshan looked at Trenara, his body again fading into his own form, and slowly uncurled his fists. The crystals sparkled as he held them up for Witen to see. The old man's eyes widened as he took in a shaky breath. "Then it is true," he whispered.

"What's true, Witen?" Joshan responded.

The Prelate appeared not to have heard him, for he bent his head in prayer with a face that was a study in elation. "Praise Ethos," he said. "Praise the gods you have come to us."

Joshan shot a pleading look at Trenara, but she had eyes only for the old guider. "Witen, I don't understand. What are you talking about?" Trenara asked.

Witen returned her stare bewildered. "You're joking! You mean to say this has been under your eyes all this time and you haven't seen it? My dear, think; The Song of the Prophecy."

Trenara's eyes widened. "My god," she cried, standing with such force she nearly tumbled the chair. "Of course."

The song that came from her was soft and melodic:

The boy, a man, yet not of age,
The man, divine, yet not a sage.
He rises from a veiled match,
He the door, she the latch.

He holds the stars within his hand.
Upon his head a crown does stand.
A serpent's smile, a golden crest,
A heart of passion in his breast.

Be wary, mortals, watch the night
When sunlight's dim and darkness bright,
Worship not the lovely stones
As they will conquer all your thrones.

For in your deeds his future's sealed.
His eyes are blind or yet revealed?
In mortal's foolish hands we give
A choice to die, a chance to live.

So end the war, the hate, the fear,
Close the mouth, unlock the ear,
Before disease jumps sire to son,
Season to season and moon to sun.

For from your curse or noble acts
Will be his strengths or what he lacks.
Upon your wisdom or your might
Fair or foul will be Starsight.

A heavy silence hung in the air for several moments, as Joshan quaked inside. Trenara was shaking her head as she sat. "The haunting of childhood," she mused, but then caught the pallor of Joshan's face. "Lad, what is it?"

I don't want to be a messiah! He wanted to scream at the top of his lungs, but couldn't. He didn't dare speak his deepest doubts—his hidden fears—his terror that he would fail in the end. He owed Trenara more. He owed them all more. Joshan's mind raced for a lie. "It's nothing, Trenara. The verse is a little unsettling." It was feebly weak and unconvincing. To bolster his courage, Joshan unknotted his hands and managed a smile he had to reach down deep to obtain. "Childhood?"

"I had forgotten the verse. That's where I have heard of the stars in the hands and the phrase Starsight. Not from some strange elusive study of ancient lore, but from a rhyme that is taught to every child on Mathisma before she walks."

Joshan sat forward. "I've never heard this verse. It was in none of the books you gave me."

"Nor would it be. Those books are probably still on the nursery shelf where my mother put them." She folded her hands and looked down thoughtfully. "Ironic, isn't it? The verse is quite ambiguous, of course, and I'm not even certain I've quoted it correctly. But it certainly fits. 'The boy, a man, yet not of age.' A perfect metaphor for your transformation. Then the part about the stars in the hands and the crown, not to mention the serpent and the reference to thrones." She shrugged. "Of course, the rest remains to be sorted out."

"Or to occur," Joshan replied involuntarily. "The stone it refers to and the coming of darkness. It could very well mean Sirdar and the wielding of the *Catalyst.*"

"The *Catalyst?*" Witen hissed. He grew pale under the approaching evening light and made a sign against evil. "Is that the power he holds?" His voice was a hoarse whisper.

Joshan shot him a stern look. "You didn't know?"

"Know? How would we know? We've been spending the good part of thirty seasons trying to find out."

Joshan looked at Trenara who mutely shook her head. She had never told Assemblage of her journey to Badain. Joshan closed his eyes over a sudden anger and let out a trembling breath. "I guess you couldn't have known." The ice in Joshan's voice made Trenara uneasy.

"These are ill tiding." Witen's voice seemed genuine with age now. "How can we ever hope to win against such power?"

Joshan placed a hand on the old guider's knee. "If Kerillian's prophecy holds true, then deliverance will come." The effort of his words was only betrayed by the grim light in his eyes. "I don't know if I'm this—Starsight. Nor whether Kerillian was even speaking of a man. Who knows?" *Who knows?* he lied to himself. "I must see his book. You could help me with this, Witen. Say nothing of what has passed here. The rest will happen as it may."

"Sire, you may…" Before he could finish, a loud commotion broke out in the hallway. "What the devil?"

Joshan took on the disguise of Ena again, and they all stood when they heard two sets of running footsteps advancing toward them. Trenara gripped Andelian tightly. Acon came panting into the room. "My lord, forgive me, but the lady…"

Before he could finish, someone pushed him aside and stepped through the entrance. "Wishes an audience," she finished for him.

Joshan's frayed nerves became still, as if the blood in his veins had stopped. He didn't know why, but a lurking premonition flared in the back of his memory that made his ears ring with recognition. However, try as he might, he could not pull it forward. A strange chill ran hotly up his back, as a feeling of ancient rapture seized him. It was as if he had known this woman from the beginning of time, but couldn't place her. A shudder of pleasure flashed through him and for the first time, Joshan knew passion—and was helpless to comprehend it.

The young woman stood a hand shorter than Trenara and had dark auburn hair, the color of craistan nuts in low season, which fell in glorious waves to a thin waist. She had large blue eyes, which sparked with anger at the moment, resting above an almost perfect nose and full, red lips. She wore men's riding clothes, in greens and browns, with her cloak thrown back off her shoulders, and soft leather boots that reached the top of her thighs. About her waist was an ornate green sash that once must have been beautiful, but now was faded with age and stained by long seasons outdoors. Her hands rested on her hips, one fingering an ornate dagger on one side, and the other touching a leather pouch holding a crystal crowned scepter, much like Trenara's Andelian.

Witen was shaking as he sank down into his chair. "Yes, lady, what can I do for you?"

"You'll forgive me for interrupting your conference, Prelate," she began, her voice lyrical yet frightening, "but my business can't wait." She folded her arms and glared at him. "By whose orders was Fiena tethered to the roof?"

"Calm yourself, my lady. It was for the bird's own protection."

Her look was as dry as sand. "She is quite capable of protecting herself."

"That was part of the problem. She killed over five bullions before they could reach her. We didn't want any of the local farmers taking shots at her, lady."

"She is unused to limitation. I will not have her bound like a common eecha."

Witen lowered his head in assent. "As you wish, my dear. The intent was never to harm."

Her eyes flared. "Which brings me to another point—how long do you intend to imprison us here?"

"Imprison you?" Witen's face was aghast. "Why, you may go any time you wish."

"Really?" She leaned menacingly close. "Unfortunately, the guards outside my chambers and around my bird don't agree with you."

"Guards?" he gasped. "I know nothing about guards, but I had hoped you would stay for council."

"The devil take your council, Witen." She stood and tightened her sash. "I came to this accursed island to pay my respects to the dead." A flush of hurt dulled her eyes a moment. "I want nothing more to do with this place." She turned toward the entrance and then back to glare at the Prelate. "I leave within the hour, with or without your precious Provost Elect's permission. You can tell Palarine that."

She glanced at Trenara and Joshan for the first time. Her gaze rested on the figure of Ena/Joshan for a very long moment and she cocked an eyebrow. A cold blue stare seemed to go through his guise like so much mist, but she only nodded and strode out the entrance. Joshan was breathless.

"Oh, dear, oh, dear." Witen wrung his hands as he stood up to follow her. "I really must attend to this immediately. You ladies will have to excuse this unfortunate interruption." He gathered Acon off the floor and headed for the door.

Trenara caught his arm, as he was about to leave. "Who was that?"

Witen gave her a brief smile. "My girl, you have been gone too long. That was Ricilyn." He then teetered out the door with an indignant Acon trotting after him.

"Ricilyn?" Trenara mused to herself. "I *am* getting old."

Joshan had not moved from the moment Ricilyn had entered and only now found his voice. "She's beautiful," he whispered.

"Yes. Much different from the gangling little girl I used to know. She's the late Provost's daughter and left Assemblage seasons ago, due to some kind of disagreement with him. No one knows exactly what it was about, but she swore she'd never return. Obviously she changed her mind." Trenara looked down the hall after them.

"She seems… so familiar to me. Have we met?" Joshan asked.

"I shouldn't think so, sire. As far as I know, she's never been to the provinces. Ricilyn is very hard to forget once you've met her. It's rumored she lives on one of the islands, though no one knows where. She tends the trees in some distant land and flies a giant vulcha she has raised from an egg. I thought that was all fantasy, but obviously not." She nodded toward the hall. "You saw she's *third trial.*"

"She seems so young."

"Very young… the youngest *third trial* guider to be blessed here. This probably accounts for her wildness. The Provost had the devil's own time controlling her, even as a child." Trenara sat back and downed her drink. "We have to prepare for Council. Now that you've met him, do you think Widen can be trusted?"

"I think so, guider. At least to be silent." He squared his shoulders and took on the mannerisms and voice of Ena once more. "We best be going." Trenara nodded and led him down the hall.

Witen was just handing Acon a parchment. "…and do be quick about it. I don't want any more mishaps today." With an agility that belied his age, Acon sprinted off down the corridor. Witen turned to see the companions. "Surely, you're not leaving?" he asked. "There is still so much to discuss."

"I'm afraid we must, Prelate. Council will begin soon," Trenara replied.

"It is getting late, isn't it? After council then." He took Trenara's hand and squeezed it warmly, then raised an aging finger. "I don't want to know what you have planned. I'm too old to be playing dangerous games. I will tell you this; you have many allies here and not all of them Assemblage. Do be careful. You also have many, many enemies." Witen smiled at Joshan with a gleam of hope on his face. "Go with Ethos, my friends."

CHAPTER TWENTY-NINE
THE STOLEN KEY

When Van reached the ship, Joshan hadn't been wrong.

"Where the hell have you been, Vanderlinden?" Haiden cried as Van stepped into the room. He was just getting the bloody clothes changed. "Someone might've woke me, you know. Just like you stinkers to take off for the island and leave me to sleep."

"Pipe down and listen."

After Van told him what had happened, Haiden sank to the bed and scratched his head where the wounds should have been. "Dying you say?"

"Dying, hell—I thought you *were* dead, mate. It'd be just like you to drop on us when we need you most. Now, hurry up and get those boots on. It's damn near time for the council to begin."

They left the ship and edged along the dock in the shadows until they stood under a darkened eave. They had to stay to the side of the pier for some time, waiting for the beach to clear. At one point, a large group of men came down to the dock to haul several crates. At the sight of them, Vanderlinden stiffened and swore under his breath.

"Who is it, Van?"

"Northerners," he hissed.

"The emperor said there'd be northerners. Didn't you hear him?"

"Aye. But hearing ain't seeing—or smelling. I'd know that stink from a hundred leagues off. It turns my stomach."

Haiden scratched his head. "I've never thought of you as a bigoted man."

Van whirled on him. "Bigotry you call it." But he smoothed his face and looked back at the men, suppressing an urge to spit by clenching his fists. "I may well be bigoted where they're concerned."

As soon as the men left, the docks were empty and the companions took the opportunity to scramble down beneath the pier. The entrance to the underground passage was a large gaping cave at the end. Haiden grimaced. "Gods! What a smell. It's like someone heaped a load of fish in there and forgot them."

Van took a deep breath and smiled. "You're daft, man. Why, that's perfume. I've never breathed a sweeter breath."

Haiden curled his lip as he slid down into the entrance. "Well, I have. Come on, let's get on with it. The sooner we're out of this stench, the better."

Once inside, Van stooped in the dirt and drew a sketchy map. "This tunnel leads damn near straight up from here, but it's not bad once you pass the Assemblage outer wall, then it levels off." He drew a fork in the path at this point.

"So, which way to the Provost's room?" asked Haiden.

Van furrowed his brow and looked down at the map thoughtfully. "I haven't a clue, but the building's not that big, we'll find it," he said, lighting the wick of a smoky lantern.

They dug their way through the brambles that clogged the cave mouth and moved into the labyrinth of tunnels running under the buildings. The passage was narrow, and the giant had to duck down most of the way. When they came to the fork in the road, Van stopped and held up the light.

"The right one leads back the way I came last time," Van said, rubbing his chin. "The left… well, from the direction, I'd say to the other wing. Come on." He ducked under the archway and followed the inward curve of the tunnel with Haiden behind him.

They began to notice a steady incline as they plodded along, stooping to keep from hitting the jagged roof above them and cursing when they stumbled blindly against unseen boulders. The climb became steep, until at last they reached the bottom of a long, straight set of stairs cut into the rock. At the top of the broad steps, they could discern a faint light. Van unsheathed his sword as he inspected what he could see of the steps.

"Careful, mate," he whispered. "We're likely to meet one or two of them guards, so watch yourself." Haiden's blade glistened in his hand as Van put out the lantern.

The steps were old and half way up, they began to crumble badly. More than once, Haiden saved the giant from a nasty spill as he stumbled on the slippery rubble. Van was amazed by Haiden's strength. At one point there were no stairs at all, only piles of loose stones. With more than a few curses, they finally scrambled to safety.

When they reached the top, breathless and sweating, they discovered the source of the light and shied behind a boulder to avoid it. A torch was flickering in the cavern air currents, perched outside a wooden door that had a yellow light spilling out from underneath. Van put a finger to his lips and quietly crept forward until he was within a span of it. He stooped in the darkness and listened intently. When he heard voices, he dared a few steps closer and held his breath in anticipation, Haiden a quiet shadow behind him. The voices were faint, but discernable.

"Master," the first one said. "I'm afraid I don't follow you. You want me to kill Trenara?" The voice was loud and deep.

"No, imbecile," snarled a gravelly reply. "I will do that myself. What I want you to do is simple." There was a pause as Van shot Haiden an anxious look. "The ship, you idiot. That shouldn't be too much for your talents, hey?" There was another pause and then the creak of hinges. "Just in case you have trouble, use this."

"What is it?" the first man asked.

"This will destroy that ship. Dive beneath the surface, below the ship's water line. Attach it there, swim out of range, and then use this device to activate it."

There was a shaky edge to the response. "Magic?" he whispered.

A hard chuckle grated against the still air. "Hardly. *After* council. I want nothing to spoil my plans for tonight. Wait until midnight—I have a little display to share with my fellow guiders that should shake them from their complacency. Just make sure you wait until you see the others."

"Others, lord?" the man asked. "What others?"

"You'll see. Watch the Sanctum Bridge for a sign. You won't be able to miss it."

"Yes, sir."

The only reply was the sound of footsteps approaching the door. Haiden and Van scattered back behind the rock in time to see two men leaving. One was a tall northerner, larger than most they had seen, with a long scar on his neck. The other man was thin, with white hair and a long amber robe. He had large baleful eyes, milky green, which glistened in the torchlight, and his back was bent with age. His cheeks were gaunt toward emaciation. The old guider slipped the spotted hands into the sleeves of his robe, scowling, as if his face could hold no other expression. Van's mouth fell open when he recognized the messenger he had seen two seasons before on his ship. It made his blood boil.

"Do not fail me," the older man hissed. "*He* would not be pleased."

The big man stared back and swallowed hard, then bowed. "I will not fail, Master Palarine."

The guider went back into the small room, slamming the door behind him as the northerner grabbed the torch and hurried down the tunnel, leaving Van and Haiden in the dark.

They crept from their hiding place and silently skirted the door. Once out of earshot, they stopped in the darkness. Van surveyed the remainder of the tunnel. "Come on," he said. "We got some work to do before the night is over."

They ran until they came to a wooden door cut into the rock. A single torch cast odd shadows against the two companions, as Van pressed his ear against the wood and motioned Haiden to step back. The giant lifted his sword. Touching the handle lightly, he pulled and the door slid open without a sound.

A brighter light flooded the cavern and Van peered around the corner into the next room. It appeared to be a sitting room with ornate furniture and silken curtains set about with elegant profusion. The place was empty. To one side a long narrow hall led to a small door. They made their way through the room cautiously. Van opened the door a crack and saw the same northerner they had seen with Palarine talking to four other guards in the corridor.

Wasting no time, the companions burst from the room and engaged the five surprised men. These northerners seemed to have much more skill than the ones they had encountered in the Keep. However, there were only five. The giant and Haiden finished them without much fuss, but Haiden had his leg nicked by a chance strike just before he cut down the last one. They hastily stowed the men in a nearby closet and made their way to Saminee's chambers.

They were very cautious as they made their way through the building, but the corridors were surprisingly vacant. That bothered Van, especially after what Joshan had told him. He didn't question his luck. But luck had nothing to do with it; the corridors were empty because Palarine had other plans. When the companions reached the late Provost's chamber, they entered quietly and shut the door behind them.

The room was dark with tightly drawn black curtains and the place reeked of death. While Haiden watched the door, Van stumbled through the darkness until he felt the foot of the bed, and edged his way to the head. He took a deep breath as his eyes grew accustomed to the darkness, and the silhouette of the dead man began to take shape. The skin was icy to the touch and sent chills of disgust through the giant's arms as he groped for the key. When his fingers touched it, he pulled it gently over the stiff, graying head. He was surprised the precious key was held by a simple leather strip, but he put it around his own neck and positioned the old man's head the way it had been.

"Forgive me, father. Our need for the living is greater now," he whispered.

They made their way back the way they had come, and again the halls were empty. Ducking back into tunnel, they slipped into the darkness and disappeared. They were on their way to the Sanctum Bridge, to carry out their part of the plan.

CHAPTER THIRTY
NAMING OF THE PROVOST

A gong struck five times, calling the council to order. The large stone chamber was plain except for the delicate stained glass dome that crowned it. The starguiders mingled among several rows of wooden benches that were arranged in semi-circles around a large dais filled with chairs, a stone lectern at its center. When the guiders were assembled and the doors closed, the murmurs died down and they took their seats as Witen took the podium. *"Kem orderai!"*

The Prelacy sat behind him, six women, and seven men, quiet and dignified as Witen started the tediously long ceremonial proceedings. Having arrived early, Trenara and Joshan sat in the front row of benches, exchanging whispers during the hour or so of formalities. The ceremony was in old Mathismian, began with the roll, and ended with a long dissertation by Witen on the history of the Crystal.

At length, Witen called for a finish to the formalities and introduced Trenara to the guiders. Trenara's speech was short and to the point, but interest increased sharply as she told of the events leading up to their arrival on the isle. The news was greeted with quiet exclamations from the crowd. At the end, Trenara pulled out the documents authored by Joshan and stated they were to be read upon the appointment of the Provost. This news brought some disappointed sighs, as the ceremony surrounding the selection was even more bombastic than the introduction to council.

After another hour, the monotone of the voices finally stopped and the hall remained silent. Witen raised his arms and spoke. "By the power given to me to do the bidding of Ethos, having been agreed upon by the Prelacy and all those who are legally bound by the laws of the Imperium, it is hereby ordered that Palarine of Gorka, be appointed as Provost of Mathisma to take his place as Keeper of the Crystal and Doyen of Assemblage." He scanned the room once briefly. "Let any speak now who would challenge this appointment."

A lone figure rose among the hundreds of starguiders of Assemblage. "I, Trenara of Mathisma, Regent to Joshan Jenhada Thoringale, Emperor of the Eight Provinces and Keeper of Mathisma, ask leave to challenge this appointment." An angry ripple ran through the chambers that began as a murmur and escalated into a loud roar.

"Silence!" Witen bellowed at the growing voice. "I will have silence!" When the crowd grew still, Witen looked at Trenara with a fine sparkle in his eyes, but he kept his face grave. "You are within your rights, Trenara of Mathisma, to challenge the appointment. Please come forth and state your grounds."

As Trenara made her way to the podium, Witen stepped down and covertly touched her arm. "I hope you know what you're doing, my girl," he whispered.

As the Prelate took his seat, Trenara regarded Assemblage grimly. "I know this is… unexpected," she began picking up as many friendly eyes as she could. "These parchments," she said, holding up the scrolls, "contain the orders and last requests of Joshan Jenhada Thoringale. He has asked that they be read as his challenge to this appointment." She removed the first from the bundle, broke the seal before the Prelate, and then unfurled it.

"*I, Joshan Jenhada Thoringale, Emperor of the eight provinces, set forth my last wishes. Since this parchment is being unsealed, I assume I have met my death. Ethos, in her wisdom chooses such fates for her servants.*

"*I am not a man of many words, so I will be brief. The Starguider Palarine of Gorka is a traitor.*"

A roar went up from the crowd and several guiders stood up, some reaching for their *vias*. "Hear me!" Trenara cried with such force the room was struck to stillness. She wondered at the effect, then caught Joshan's eyes as they flashed with *power* briefly. Trenara cleared her throat and lifted the parchment again.

"*You must listen to my challenge, for it is neither lie nor jest. After intense investigation, I regrettably relate the digression of Palarine of Gorka.*

"*After the fall of Sirdar, Palarine traveled to the wastelands and there did wonderful works to help the scattered northerners. What happened is not the fault of the guider or his pupils. Twelve seasons ago, a summons reached Palarine requesting he travel to Badain to see a man who, it was rumored, had attained fourth trial. The man was ill and dying, and a guider was needed to bring him through his sickness. The healers could do nothing for him. Palarine was to come alone and secretly, because of the empirical edict; starguiders were not allowed in Badain. For what reason Palarine did make that journey, only he can say. I would venture he suspected calamity and took it upon himself to see to its undoing. He left a faithful pupil to carry on his work in the north.*

"*The man, though physically weak, was indeed remarkable. Palarine tutored and nurtured him for seasons in the ways of Assemblage, watching him grow stronger every day into the most talented guider he had ever seen. Why he told no one of his discovery showed the subjection was overpowering him even then.*

"*After many seasons, Palarine began to suspect this creature's cruelty, seeing evidence of it in his harsh treatment of people and the strange, twisted bend of his desires. And he began to suspect who this man was. Sirdar was not dead, and Palarine remained silent. I believe by the time he realized the truth, it was too late; blinded by the darkest magic, the old guider could no longer resist. The Mourna bound Palarine to the will of Sirdar, and the guider lost his volition in the span of a moment. No one can say they would not have done the same in his place. He became thoroughly convinced of the goodness of Sirdar and the evil of Assemblage.*

"*Palarine has nurtured our enemy and brought him back to destroy us. His reason has been perverted by the power of the Catalyst. No man escapes that—even by death.*"

At the mention of the *Catalyst*, involuntary breaths were drawn and many cried out. Joshan looked quietly at the accused, who sat serenely in his chair, as though nothing were wrong. He thought that Palarine, once a noble guider, had fallen so far from reason that his twisted mind could only see lies where there was truth. A lump of pity stung his throat, and Joshan was overcome with weariness. Such corruption was unfathomable. He wanted so much to end it.

"*Therefore,*" Trenara continued, "*my claims must be heeded. If they are not, you have doomed the Imperium to disaster. I do not make these claims lightly. Signed, Joshan Jenhada Thoringale.*"

You could have heard a heart beat in the stillness that followed. Trenara looked at the faces in the room and read them mentally to herself. The expressions ranged from outright hostility to wide-eyed horror, but most were shocked, confused, or uncertain. Witen stood to speak, but Trenara held up her hand. "Prelate, there is another document the emperor wished you to read, if you would." Witen raised a bushy brow and turned to face the crowd, taking the parchment from Trenara. He broke the seal and cleared his throat.

"*I, Joshan Jenhada Thoringale, Emperor of the Eight Provinces, Keeper of Mathisma and all lands thereto, do hereby order, as is my right, before Ethos and as laid down by Cessas in his Laws of the Imperium, that Trenara of Mathisma be named with haste as Provost of Mathisma, Keeper of the Crystal and Doyen of Assemblage. This is my wish. This is my right, which by law cannot be challenged. I do so order.*" Neatly inscribed and duly notarized was the signature of Joshan Jenhada Thoringale.

Trenara was stunned, and the turmoil in the hall could not seep into her numb mind as she stared at the empty space where the parchment had been, removed by an angry Palarine. She did not hear the pounding of the gavel, or the order that guards were to be summoned should riot break out. She lifted her eyes to look into the now blue eyes of Joshan. He sat amongst the brawling guiders like an island of quiet with his hands folded before his face where a half-smile touched his mouth, making it appear roguish. The only sound she heard came to the back of her mind as a whisper. *One day you will understand.*

When the turmoil settled, after several of the younger guiders had been removed, Witen finally brought some semblance of order. Trenara numbly returned to her seat next to Joshan and began to feel a strange tingle run through her. Something was coming; the nerves that outlined her *sight* ached with the feeling of an outside presence. She didn't know what it was, so calmed her nerves, and enjoyed the thrill of external power. Softness touched her, a gentleness she had felt before. Trenara knew without thinking, it was the stroke of the gods she felt, working their influence like a game. It didn't disturb her. It made her grateful. She closed her eyes and let Ethos touch her.

"Thank you," Witen was saying. "What the emperor has written is correct as most of you know. There can be no challenge to this." He turned to the quiet Provost Elect. "I'm sorry, Palarine. There's nothing I can do."

The old man smiled benignly with a glint in the green eyes. "It's quite all right, Witen." His voice changed very slowly. "It's not your order, nor your lies." It turned, word by word, into something different. Every ear that heard it suddenly listened very carefully. "I wish to speak, Prelate. If for no other reason than as a man has a right to defend his honor." Joshan looked helplessly around as every guider fell under the voice's charm. The articulation sounded so reasonable, so hurt, a victim of an injustice. "I'm certain no one here would deny my honor has been grossly defamed." His eyes sought out Trenara, but she sat staring up at him, her eyes calm. Witen nodded quietly and took his seat, allowing Palarine to take the podium.

"I will not speak long. There has been too much speech already. Although the emperor says his choice cannot be contested, I disagree. There is an older law—an ancient law. This matter should be decided in another way. Though I am old and not as strong as I once was, honor dictates I demand it now. Let the truth be unveiled by the Trial by Battle. I call for the *makhia.*" An angry cry went up from the crowd.

"Guider," Witen called to Palarine who only had eyes for Trenara. "Are you insane? Neither of you are young anymore. I won't permit this."

Palarine shrugged and put more pressure on the timbre of his voice. "It is the only choice which honor dictates, Witen. I do not withdraw the challenge. Let it stand."

"But the *makhia* is not a challenge for humans. It has never been called by mortals, except in legends."

"Nonetheless, Prelate, that is my demand—unless Trenara would like to confess to the lies. In that event I will withdraw."

Witen turned a pleading look to her. Trenara and Palarine's eyes met. She rose slowly and there was a wistful smile on her face. "Let it stand," was all she said, as she gave her mind wholly to the gods.

"Madness!" Witen's hissed, throwing up his arms. "You've lost your senses, both of you. I will not stop this, but listen to me. This is a challenge for gods, not mortals. What you may release by calling upon it, I pray we don't all regret in the end."

He sank his head as if he couldn't bear the sight of either of them.

CHAPTER THIRTY-ONE
SANCTUM

The figures in the shadow of the bridge leaned carefully against the icy stone pillar and exchanged whispers in the dark, barely heard by one another. The only telltale sign of their speech came in frosty patches of muted white that fell on the cold night air. Vanderlinden peered again around the column to note the position of the guards, while Haiden remained in the shadows and nursed the wound he had received earlier. It wasn't deep, but very painful.

"It's not going to be easy," Van said, silently beating the chill from his shoulders.

"Easy or no, our orders are clear enough, giant." Haiden glanced up at the gelid stars and frowned. "It's this uncommon cold that's got me spooked. If you hadn't told me, I'd swear I'd slept 'til low season. It feels like death out here." A shiver took him as he rubbed his hands.

The giant did not respond, but looked again around the pillar. The two Assemblage guards seemed uneasy and shot frequent glances at the council chambers. They said nothing, but exchanged worried looks from time to time as they paced back and forth along the entrance to the bridge. Van looked up to see the red moon above him, and the white one just beyond, as the stars sparkled brightly in the cold night.

He tightened his belt and felt the tip of his dagger. "You take the one on the left, me the right. That one is at least almost my size. Let's go."

The difficulty they had was not in overcoming their victims—Sanctum guards were more ornament than utilitarian and not usually trained to fight, but the companions would have to navigate thirty spans of well-lit open bridge without raising an alarm. The giant wound a leather strap around his wrist and flexed his hands to limber them, then removed the gigantic bow from his back and fitted a long arrow with blue feathers and gold banding.

Taking a deep breath and expelling it slowly, Van tilted his head up, brought the shaft level with his eye and took careful aim. The arrow left the bow with a soft audible pang and sailed on a wide arch above the torchlight, finally disappearing behind the stone railing on the other side of the bridge. As it hit, the mark true, a roar of tumbling rocks greeted the giant's ears, loud enough for the guards to be alarmed and run toward the sound, but not enough to alert anyone in the buildings many spans from the bridge.

Van and Haiden lost no time in covering the distance and rendering each guard unconscious within seconds. Pulling the guard to the bushes at the end of the bridge, they removed their cloaks and helmets. Van knelt down and administered the drug Trenara had given him earlier. Harmless, the guider had said, but that didn't appease the giant's reluctance to use it. He preferred an honest, open fight to all this sneaking around. Haiden donned the cloak and helmet of the smallest guard and handed the giant the others.

"How long will they be out?"

"Guider said 'til morning." Van quickly threw the cloak around his shoulders and slid the helmet into place. They ran back to the bridge and took up the sentries' march, barely minutes from their hiding.

What seemed like an eternity passed before they heard anything from the great hall. A roar went up from the chamber, piercing the stillness like an unexpected thunder. The two companions stopped and waited for the throng that would certainly pour from the building. When the cry increased, Van made an instinctive move toward the hall, but Haiden stopped him with a touch and gave him a warning look. When nothing appeared, they resumed their march. Van couldn't stop knots of apprehension from cramping his stomach.

A chill wind began to stir from the southwest, and they turned up their collars to ward off the sting of its icy fingers. Aroused by curiosity, points of light began to appear as lanterns were lit in the pre-guider building. Time passed, with the stillness broken only now and again by the wind and the footfalls of the two companions on the graveled ground. Then, without a sound, the huge council chamber doors began to open, sending out a yellow light as two young pre-guiders swung them wide. Once open, the youngsters went to their knees and put their faces in their hands. Haiden and Vanderlinden met at the middle of the bridge and watched.

From the maw of the lighted doorway, two figures emerged bathed in blinding green light. The companions turned their eyes away from the brilliance. The two figures parted and stopped on either side of the courtyard. Each lifted an object to the sky, one long, gnarled, like the branch of an ancient tree; the other short, and sleek, transparent to the eye, but radiant with fire.

A third figure emerged shrouded in white light, seeming to float like a ghost with his head down and his hands clasped behind his back. When he stopped in the middle of the open ground, two separate lines of starguiders issued from the building to form a circle around the three. The melding of white, green, and bright blue was a wonder of color and light, as Van and Haiden witnessed a ritual seen by few mortals.

"It is the *makhia*," said a voice from behind them.

They whirled around to see Joshan watching the guiders intently. He had discarded the disguise of Ena, since all eyes were now on the ritual.

"What's that?" Van asked, looking back at the courtyard.

"The *makhia*—the *Trial by Battle*. It hasn't been done since the Crystal fell here, though Kerillian speaks of it as being the deciding factor for many things—but only among the gods. Between guiders—who knows?" He looked on gravely. "I hadn't expected this, although I knew there would be some kind of challenge. Trenara had no choice but to accept. I'm worried she's too soon from *third trial*. Palarine has been a master of nature for many seasons, not to mention whatever black arts he has learned at the hand of his master." He grew silent as music began to grow from the courtyard. The sound was beautiful, harmonic and reverberated against the air until the windows began to rattle.

"Can you help her, sire?" Haiden asked quietly.

Joshan shook his head, and the sorrow in his eyes went to the heart of the old marshall. "No, Haiden. Assemblage will throw a *shield* around the two, so no outside forces can intervene." He took a deep breath and brushed his hands. "Trenara's fate is in the hands of Ethos now," he said solemnly and turned to cross the long bridge to Sanctum. "Bring the key, giant. We need to hurry."

Van stood with his feet planted firmly and his hands on his hips. "You're not leaving her," the giant said through his teeth. Haiden took a step forward to stop Van, but Joshan held up a restraining hand.

"Do you trust me so little?" Joshan said, his eyes flashing. "Haven't you been listening? Trenara is doing this to give us time to enter Sanctum. This is her choice— and sacrifice, if it comes to that. You're wasting that gift by questioning me. I know you love her, Van. I know you would throw away the entire mission to save her, but you can't. This is not Trenara's death, just her fate. You need to trust me. If it comes to the grips of death, I will risk whatever I must to save her. Is that enough?"

"You don't know how much I love her…"

"Yes, I do. I love her, too." He touched the giant's arm. "I need you to focus on the mission. Can you do that?"

"Aye," he said simply.

"We have to hurry. The battle will begin within the hour and we have a lot to do in that time." He stared up at the fortress in front of him. "Sanctum doesn't welcome intruders easily." Joshan climbed the towering bridge that disappeared into dense mist high above their heads. Haiden and Van followed, the giant sullen and the old guard ill at ease.

Their progress was slow as they crossed, warned by Joshan to walk softly and say nothing. Haiden looked once over the stone railing through a break in the clouds and saw an abyss below his feet that thundered with the crack of breaking waves. The distance was daunting and the sea raged with such force, it converted jagged stones instantly to pebbles, and luckless branches to kindling. He shivered and caught up with the others, but did not look again.

Van thought the need for silence was because of additional guards at the Sanctum gates, but as they emerged from the mist, the gates stood before them unattended. They were much smaller than he imagined.

Joshan led them to the side of the bridge and crouched down to whisper. "Within these gates are the Sanctum Gardens, the first of the barriers. They may appear harmless but don't let them fool you; they can be deadly. When you enter the garden, see to it that your feet do not stray from the path. To do so would be lethal. The grass is laced with Camamarian leeches that will suck you dry before you even hit the ground." Van and Haiden exchanged worried looks.

"Staying on the path will prove much more difficult than you would imagine because of the flowers in the garden. They were brought from the Meridian Gorge and then cultured with *power* to increase their potency. The aroma is… compelling. A master of nature can counteract their scent, thus the order for only third trial guiders to enter the gate. I would do it myself, but we simply haven't the time. I must trust you to stay to the path. To this end, I have brought rope to tie us together. Should one of us falter, the other two can help him." The two companions nodded.

"Beyond the garden is the entrance to the first courtyard of Sanctum. It is this area and the next one that necessitate the need for quiet. Once beyond this gate, don't make a sound, not even a whisper or footpad, until we get into the Sanctum building. The path is soft, but watch your footing. Even the sound of a broken twig would wake it."

"It?" Van asked tentatively.

"The Warder," Joshan replied, unfurling the rope. "She is harmless enough—getting quite old, actually, and barely able to fly anymore. The old creature is more frightening to look at than anything else, but if she is alarmed, her cry could practically wake the dead. Even with the *makhia* in progress, the guiders would stop to investigate.

"So, whatever you do, travel with care, stay close to each other, and above all, no matter what happens, what feelings you may have or things you may see, continue on the path as quickly as possible and make no sound until we've reached the Sanctum Library within the main building. Once passed the Warder and through the Echo Hall, we will be beyond danger. Once in Sanctum we can proceed with our task."

"What is that task, exactly?" Haiden asked, mindful he might have missed something while he lay unconscious.

Joshan looked at the two for a moment. "We haven't time to stay on Mathisma for more than a day. Ena gets farther and farther from us each minute we stay here. The strife in the west grows more horrible by the hour. It would take me days to obtain the knowledge I need by going through the books, days that could mean the difference between life and death for Ena and for countless thousands of our soldiers." Van looked at him sharply and Joshan nodded. "So you see my plight. I will go to the Chamber of Healing and ask the Crystal for the knowledge. I honestly don't know if this is wise or even possible, but something is compelling me to try."

"But, sire," Haiden said, "I've heard tell that people have burned to ash when they touched it. Isn't this risky business you're looking at?"

Joshan looked up at the high spires of Sanctum Gate as he tied the rope to his waist. "Yes, my friend, very risky. That's why the two of you are staying in the library once we get through the Echo Hall. I won't risk your lives along with mine."

"Now wait minute…"

"Peace, giant," Joshan said, raising his hand. "There's no discussion here. That's a direct order admiral." He tightened the rope and gave the giant a half smile. "If it's any consolation, this isn't my time to die. I will survive this—though to what end I can't say." *I dare not say*, he thought grimly. The burden of knowledge made his voice fragile in the cold as he finished tying the knot and handed the rope to Vanderlinden.

"Remember," Joshan said, "complete silence."

Once tied securely, the three went to the gate and Joshan ran his crystalline hands along the hinges. They glowed white for a moment and then went dull. Without a sound, the gates opened a crack to admit them and then silently closed out the rest of the world outside.

Even in the darkness, lighted only by the moons and misty stars, the garden touched the heart and numbed the mind with its magnificence. There were no trees, only row upon row of shining flowers that looked as if springtide had never left them. Sweet yellow dafee with waxy petals and icy stalks; tiny white crested star maidens with sparkling centers of gold; the blazing korfra, crimson three-pronged masters of form and regal in their stiffness; and sunny-pink crown blossoms that shone like little torches in the darkness.

Laced along the ground and tangled among the brush that grew in delightful profusion, ran the playful liesna, purple and white-green, dancing in the moonlight like glorious singing children, while high overhead, in trailing streamers of silver and blue-black hung clusters of breathtaking phoena, guider's bloom, which caught the starlight and threw it back to dazzle the traveler's eyes. Empirical plants were weeds and brambles in comparison.

The companions could not move at first, struck still as the scent lulled their tired minds and brought delights to each of them differently. Vanderlinden smelled the wonderful salt of sea and mist upon a parched and sunburned face, with a light whiff of Trenara's perfume interlaced throughout the air. Haiden smelled the marvelous musk of rich, dark earth and freshly cut wood. Joshan breathed in the redolence of twilight forests, baking bread in the kitchens at the Keep, and another scent altogether—a sweet, clean draught of freedom at the end of a long and painful journey. Each man bathed himself in a luxury of forgetfulness as the blossoms wove their own special magic.

Joshan broke from the trance first and started up the path, the rope pulling a reluctant Vanderlinden and Haiden. They had to move slowly since Joshan had to watch the ground for unseen twigs and rocks. Try as they might, Van and Haiden were quickly losing the battle to stay on the path.

Without warning, Haiden turned, pulling the giant with him. Even as his foot touched the forbidden grass, Joshan grabbed his arm and threw him back. Hundreds of crawling gray worm-like creatures with rows of tiny sharp teeth completely filled the spot where Haiden's foot had been, a writhing mass of snapping jaws in search of blood. Haiden looked up sharply and would have cried out, but Joshan put a hand over his mouth. The old guard shook the enchantment out of his head, the mortification burning brightly on his face as they continued.

Without further incident, they reached the Second Gate. It loomed up above them as the feelings and smells vanished, taking the temporary respite with it. Again, Joshan caressed the hinges to ensure its silent opening. He untied the rope and motioned Van and Haiden to do the same. When the gate opened before them, they stepped back in horror.

The beast was asleep, roosted above the towering Sanctum entrance. It was not a bird exactly, though it could fly well when it was younger. Then again, it wasn't exactly a beast either, though it was covered in fur from head to tail. In some aspects, it was not altogether gruesome as the fur once had a sheen that would have been quite becoming on another animal. It was the three heads that were terrifying.

Joshan looked sadly at the creature in its present state and felt only pity. Where once the pelt had been beautiful and well tended, now lay large patches of scaly skin and tufts of tattered fur. The gnarled heads and necks were unnaturally twisted, and the archaic wings were a frail framework of scarred and spotted leather.

He let Vanderlinden and Haiden rest for a moment while he stepped into the darkness under the gate. The Warder made no sound above a wheezing whisper, and Joshan searched the courtyard for the best way to cross. After the beauty of the garden, the yard seemed harsh and gray. There was nothing living within the fence, only tall frightening statues with soulless granite eyes.

Joshan shivered as he gazed at them, awed by their size and grandeur. To the left, huddled in haphazard groups like secretive children playing, stood the dead Provosts. They were clinging to their *vias*, wisdom written on their gritty brows. Joshan knew few of their names, but wished he had known the guiders, for in those sculptured faces, he saw the answers to many questions—and many reasons why. To the right, and far more commanding, other figures stood tall and stone-cold, blocks of granite ice—the emperors and empresses.

There stood his grandfather, Thoringale, his windy mane of fiery hair now frozen. Kanaine had trumpets at her feet that silently blazed her coming. Beside them stood Mannin the Fair, Woodhale the Kindhearted, Jesper, Evenson, Soreas, and Tham the Unconquered. Then Petaire, Remos, Cartivan, and Dru the Broken.

On and on they went, row after row of solid reminders of the empire's vivid and noble past—and Joshan's legacy. Some stood, some sat, while still others were astride giant stone eechas with banners in their hands and proud soldiers at their feet. All were now gray and unmoving in the misty midnight. For the first time, Joshan gazed upon his forebears, carved in granite by the hearts and loyalty of people who had served them. He wondered briefly about his own statue and the name it would bear, and again about Trenara's, huddled among the silent guiders.

He finally turned his eyes to the figure to his right and tears plucked at his eyes. There in the foreground, the stone freshly chiseled, the statue incomplete, stood Jenhada, the Judicious. Joshan gazed at the portrayal of his father and thought of his own young childhood, when his father had been a pair of strong hands and an echo of gentle words. The sculptor had caught the loving nature of Jenhada's face, the deliberate persistence in the way he stood and the strength of those hands. Joshan bowed his head and grieved for the man whose life was too short—and the child who had never learned to love him. He wiped his eyes against his sleeve and signaled the companions to enter.

Along the north wall was a large awning. Without a sound, they skirted the wall and hid in the shadows, constantly watching the Warder for signs of wakefulness. She was deep in a dream, as her white belly rose and fell slowly, and her breath came out in cloudy wheezing gasps. They had to walk with extreme care, as chalky rubble covered the ground and each step became an agonizing fear of waking the creature.

When they were no more than thirty paces from the entrance, a shrill trumpet call blared from the Assemblage buildings, shattering the tranquil air. The companions threw themselves against the wall and did not breathe as the Warder lifted her heads and scanned the statues sleepily. Her wings flapped twice as she stood up on legs the size of saplings and stretched her necks until they shot out in every direction. As the sound died down, the Warder yawned, one head at a time, and wrapped the bony wings around her body as she settled against the stone arch. Then all six eyes drooped, and the heads nestled back among the spiny warmth of her belly.

How long they stood there amid the warriors of old, mere statues themselves, they could not afterward say, but soon the harsh hiss of the monster's breathing slowed, and they sank their heads in relief. As quickly as they dared, they slipped through the archway and into the Echo Hall before she rose again.

As the door closed, Van began to speak and Joshan jumped to stop him, but too late. No sooner had a single syllable left the giant's lips than the sound echoed repeatedly, so loudly the companions doubled over in pain as it began to crush their eardrums and send their heads spinning toward unconsciousness. Joshan threw his hands in the air at once. When he sang, the *shield* shot down in a brilliant flash of cobalt *power* to engulf them. The sound became a muted throb as the companions sank to their knees and shook their heads.

"Are you all right?" Joshan asked as he stood up and checked the pulsating dome.

"What?" Haiden asked loudly.

Joshan looked at him gravely and shook his head. "Damn! Van, can you hear me?"

"Aye, well enough." Van helped the deaf Haiden to his feet and pounded the lingering noise from his own ears. "What the hell was that?"

Haiden looked around wildly. "I can't hear. Sire, I can't hear."

Joshan took him by the shoulders and slowly mouthed the words, "It will pass—do not panic." Haiden nodded and continued to pound on his head.

"Did I do that?" Van asked.

"Yes," Joshan replied, thoughtfully looking through the glowing dome.

"I'm sorry. I had no idea…"

"It's all right, Van. I suppose my warnings were not strong enough. That could have killed us. The echo hall amplifies sounds to deadly proportions."

"But won't that creature hear it, too?"

"No. The hall keeps sound within its walls."

Van lowered his eyes and ran a hand across his brow. "How long before we can get out?"

"Not long. The sound is dying now, but do be careful. Even a sigh can become quite deafening in this chamber. I do hope Haiden will be all right."

"What?" Haiden asked again.

Joshan smiled at him reassuringly and put a finger to his lips. The hall was not long, and soon they stood inside a massive corridor with richly carved wooden panels and intricate tapestries of the finest silks. They passed through a large door on their left, which opened into a tiered room.

The walls were lined with shelf upon shelf of ancient books, scrolls, and handwritten manuscripts, in all shapes and all sizes, ranging from the most basic child's primer to the ponderous volumes of Cessas and Kerillian. The library was immense, towering many hundreds of spans above their heads. Here rested the wisdom of the ages, in thousands upon thousands of volumes.

In here lay every written work by the hands of man. Centuries of writings ranging from the transcribed stories of blind peasants to the voluminous ponderings of ancient prophets, joined in this room of knowledge. It astounded Joshan. How he wished he had time to search this library, the materials beckoning to him so alluringly.

The library was a huge circular chamber with shelves running completely around the circumference at every level. Large staircases rose up on either side of each to reach the story above it, and beautiful hand carved wooden railings secured each mezzanine. The center of the room was open to the roof. At its heart, and tucked away in each corner, were stately marble pillars that reached all the way to the top of the chamber. The central pillar ended in an intricately carved marble bridge that joined the two highest tiers to one another.

In the ceiling above it, as it was in all other Assemblage structures, was a giant stained glass dome, now dark with night. As beautiful as the chamber was at night, it must have been spectacular in the daylight, and Joshan wished he could see it with the sun shining through that magnificent colored glass.

There were seven tiers of books, tablets, and scrolls, each marked with a different symbol carved into the side of a long wooden marker at each level. He looked at the symbols as he entered, and ran his fingers over one of them. The markings were similar to the symbols Ena had drawn from Trenara's brow. The room was bright with well-kept lamps and immaculately tended. He sighed deeply and turned to his friends.

"Haiden, can you hear me yet?"

"Aye, sire—but faint, like you're far away. I don't ever want to go through that again."

"That makes two of us, mate," Van put in. "Nor that creature. Gods! I'd hate to meet that thing in a dark alley. What was that trumpet call we heard? I thought we were goners down there."

Joshan gave him a cool smile. "Have you been gone from the isle so long, admiral, you don't know the call of the twelfth hour when you hear it?"

"I'll be damned. I forgot all about it."

Joshan frowned. "So did I, and it nearly cost us everything." He shook his head and stared at the symbols. "I really must be more careful."

"What now, sire?" Haiden asked.

Joshan scanned the seven levels until his eyes caught at something on the highest tier. "Come on, I'll show you." Van and Haiden exchanged glances as they followed the emperor up the stairs.

The climb was exhausting, but they made good time. When they reached the last level, perched upon the beautiful marble bridge, were a series of high podiums with a huge volume lying open on top of each. The one at the center of the bridge was set higher than the rest, its yellowed pages scripted in a flowing hand. Joshan studied it for a moment and turned a few pages, then smiled to himself.

"This is wonderfully preserved. Think of it—a thousand seasons old and still useable—and in his own hand. This is a gift beyond measure."

"What is it, sire?" Van asked as he peered over Joshan's shoulder at symbols and words he didn't understand.

Joshan shot him a glance. "My dear friend, this is something few people have seen, the original copy of the Lore of Cessas. It is a millennium old—and there," he walked to another stand, "the Legend of Kerillian. And over there," he pointed to another stand, "if I'm not mistaken, that has to be the Translations—millions of words on every known language since the beginning of time." He shook his head solemnly. "All this knowledge, locked away from mankind with miserly delight. What a waste—no, not a waste, a crime. Yet, here they sit and gather dust, while the guiders dole them out in scrapes and crumbs to the starving masses. I begin to see how Sirdar could rise. Ignorance. Pure, unnecessary ignorance. How could they let it go so far?" He lost himself in thought as Van and Haiden looked on blankly.

"Sire?" Van said quietly. Joshan looked up at the giant. What Van saw in the emperor's eyes the admiral could not fathom, but it struck him to the core like grief.

"I'm sorry," Joshan said. "It's just the more I see of Assemblage, the more I begin to wonder. Here in this room is enough knowledge and wisdom to cure the most formidable of ills. What do they do with it? Do they give it to people so they can use it? No. They lock it away from the world and give it to the few who don't need it, because they have—the Crystal." He shook his head glancing at all the books. "Did I say they don't need it? Perhaps they need it more than anyone else."

Haiden put a gentle hand on his shoulder. "Sire, I've never heard you speak like this. It kind of scares me."

Joshan touched his hand gently. "I've never felt this way, Haiden. I don't mean to frighten you. We would be fools if we thought our leaders had no shortcomings." He wiped a hand across his eyes as if it would hold back the thought of his own. "I'm sorry, gentlemen," he said lightly. "I don't mean to be so gloomy."

He tapped the book and pulled a parchment from his jerkin. "While I'm gone, I need you to find these symbols somewhere in the Book of Translations." He crossed to the book and opened the front cover. "The text is common speech, thanks to the skill of the librarians, so you shouldn't have too much trouble. Start with the languages of Kerillian's time—roughly three thousand seasons ago. When you find them, write them down. Trenara and I will go over them later."

He handed the parchment to Haiden, who looked down at Ena's fine pen strokes. "Shouldn't one of us go with you, sire? Something might happen."

"Something *is* going to happen. Neither you nor the giant would be able to help me. I must do this alone."

Van raised his voice in protest, but Joshan flashed him a warning look. "That isn't a request, admiral."

The giant regarded him a moment, then leaned against a wall and smiled mischievously. "As you wish."

Joshan knew that look. "I'm warning you, Van. If you follow, I will have your head."

Vanderlinden stood up and melted under the coolness of those eyes. He bowed his head in resignation and sighed. "All right," he said nodding and taking the key from around his neck. He pressed it into Joshan's hand and held it for a second. "But you be careful. Trenara would never forgive me if anything happened to you."

"I intend to." He put the key around his neck and took off his cloak. "All right, then," he said, throwing it to Haiden. "I'll be back as soon as I can. Just find those symbols while I'm gone." Without another word, he ran down the stairs and out into the corridor.

Haiden watched after him and then scratched his head. "You think he'll make it?"

"Aye, he'll make it right enough." Van nodded as if he had made a decision and then rubbed his hands together. "We got work to do, mate. You take the Translations book over there, and I'll see what I can find in the indexes." Van went down two tiers and started pouring through several notebooks on a table, while Haiden ran his finger along the finely scripted tabs until he found A.K. 100. He opened the section and smoothed out the parchment. Almost immediately, he found the first symbol.

"Hey!" he cried. "Here's something." When he looked over the railing, Van was gone. "Van?" The library echoed his voice back to him. "Vanderlinden!"

Haiden searched the library from tier to tier, but the giant was nowhere to be found. "Oh, giant." He shook his head and smiled sagely, a twinkle in the old eyes. "I guess you've your own fate to follow now. May the gods be with you, man." He shook his head again and went back to the volumes.

CHAPTER THIRTY-TWO
THE CRYSTAL

Brought up short without warning, Joshan could go no farther. He had followed the long corridor through gloomy double doors, along a dimly lit hallway and then up a long, twisting flight of stairs. The torch he carried was little help, as the stairway had been as dark as pitch and often took odd curves through the heart of Sanctum. He cursed more than once when he stumbled against an unseen railing.

When he finally reached the top of the stairs there was a single door, but it would not open. He tried the Sanctum key and several incantations without success. When he could think of nothing better, he grabbed the doorknob and put his shoulder to it. The door cracked under his weight and shot open, dragging Joshan along with it.

He found himself hanging from the doorknob, dangling over a chasm that dropped into oblivion below his feet. Just as the knob began to give under his weight, Joshan called the *power*. The amber glow blew like a whirlwind around him and lifted him gently back to the doorsill. He fell back into the darkened stairwell and leaned against the wall to catch his breath and slow his heartbeat. When he finally mustered enough courage, he turned to peer out the doorway and saw a sight that made him forget to breathe.

Across the chasm, a luminous crystal dome towered above his head, balanced on a pillar of roughened rock like an opal on a rusty stickpin. Below it was a pit of darkness that disappeared into the core of the island, while above it, a jagged circle of stones framed stars that clustered together in ragged patterns, and a sliver of Whilema that shone brightly to light the blackened sky. The circle of stones rose majestically, hiding the Crystal from the outside world.

The translucent dome sparkled in the moonlight and cast dancing lights along the walls, in colors so vast Joshan could not name them all. As he examined the Chamber of Healing, he marveled at the engineering, construction, and splendor fashioned by the hands of countless people to conceal their most precious treasure. No *vision* prepared him for the sight; no imagining could have done it justice. He felt very small and very mortal.

He wondered how he was going to get to it; there were several hundred spans of open space between Joshan and his goal. Try as he might, he could not call the *power*, and all his songs fell dead on the still air, absorbed by the profound abyss, and devoured by the jagged stone wall. The air became cold, and he shivered when a gust of wind found him huddled and nearly beaten under the barrier. He lowered his head to think. For a long time he did not stir.

His eyes caught a small relief, hidden in the shadows of the doorway, a sculpted four-pointed star. The upper and lower spurs were larger than the other two, obviously cut into the stone by an astute craftsman. Around it were symbols denoting the relief as an emblem of some age; it had to be nearly a thousand seasons old, as old as the Crystal itself.

Within its center, a single jewel stood out from the wall, catching the light and reflecting the dazzling dome in miniature. When Joshan stooped down to examine it, the reflection faded, leaving the gem white and cold. He reached out to touch it, but as his hand approached, a green bolt shot out. He abruptly pulled back and touched his fingers to check for damage. They were whole and unscathed, so he reached again. Once more, the flame leapt at him, but this time he met it.

His fingers became numb as the flame licked them greedily and proceeded up his hand. A sense of warmth and contentment spread through his body. The bolt curlicued around his fingers like a cat rubbing its favorite leg, and Joshan smiled. The light seemed alive, like a sentient fire. He turned his hand over to reveal the crystalline palm and waited for the reaction. It licked the crystals once briefly and then sprang back toward the wall, as though frightened. Joshan smiled again. "I won't hurt you," he said softly.

The flame again advanced toward him, though slowly this time. It encircled the stones and then paused a moment, shimmering and pulsating with life. Joshan's mind suddenly reeled with images; thoughts of recognition and joy he knew could only be coming from this strange light. Before he could say another word, the beam withdrew into the stone. With a quiet hiss, a shining bridge of light shot out from the doorsill to cross the dark chasm and stopped at the crystal dome. Joshan took one final look at the relief and then ran over the bridge. He hastily removed the key from around his neck and gaped at the door before him.

The crystal wall was clear and flawless. Joshan ran his hands over it in wonder, marveling at the artist who must have carved it and the stone it had been taken from. It towered well above his head. The only blemish was a hole carved at the same level as his chest. He held his breath and slid the key in. It turned slowly in his hands; he heard a small click. With a whisper of sound, the door opened. What greeted him was complete darkness as he put the key around his neck. His heart throbbed as he stepped through the door.

After two faltering steps, a sudden wind picked up, quiet at first, then increasing in strength, until it blew Joshan off his feet and sent him several feet forward crashing against a wall. The wind was so strong he had to wait several seconds before he could open his eyes. He fought to stand, but succeeded in simply crawling to the doorway. The sound was deafening when a gust hurled him back again, and the door hissed shut with a shaking thud. He was overwhelmed as pitch blackness clung to his eyes. As quickly as it started, the wind vanished, leaving the chamber so quiet, the silence pulsed against his ears.

Shaking, Joshan stood up and tried to get his bearings. He groped in the darkness to find the door again, but fell against a stone basin, cursing as he rubbed his injured knee and shin. He followed along the basin as it curved away from where he thought the door was. His hands felt a platform that connected the basin to yet another vessel at waist height. His fingertips probed carefully and reached to the center.

The object he touched was cold and then suddenly hot. He furrowed his brow and rested his palms against it. The force of crystal meeting crystal sent sparks flying in all directions, knocking Joshan off his feet. He sat up and shook the daze from his head as a glow began to radiate along the higher platform, and something began to emerge from the shadows.

The Crystal was his first sight, smaller than he imagined, about the size of a man's head. Irregularly shaped, jagged here, and smooth there with bits of darker stone clinging to it at odd angles. It was not the lovely thing he had been led to believe, but rather a lump of rock, cracked and dull with age, and scorched in places. Beneath it, what Joshan had thought to be stone, was dark, glistening gold. The half-light cast from the stone, made the bowl where the Crystal rested glow warmly.

On either side stood two massive basins that crowded the room. Each brimmed with a silver liquid that he knew from his studies had to be *illiminium* or liquid fire, an element brought to Sanctum by the early guiders to help preserve the Crystal. It was highly volatile and could have killed him had he put his hand in either of the basins. A shiver ran through him when he realized how closely he had come to death.

Joshan heard a faint sound like a deep hum that grew as the Crystal brightened. "Who wakes me?" a voice rang out in the hollow stillness of the room. It was deep and feminine, but edged with age. Joshan gaped in wonder, and his heart labored in his chest. "I repeat, who wakes me?" it rang again.

"You speak," Joshan whispered.

"Yes," the voice rippled on the liquid fire, "for those who have ears to listen. Your coming is late, Joshan, and your guider is in grave danger. You risk much in coming to me now."

"It was necessary, Crystal," he said as he got to his knee and bowed his head before it. "Forgive me, if I have disturbed you."

The hum flared against the air as the Crystal brightened in the basin. "Why do you wake me?"

Joshan lifted his eyes. "To seek a favor. I need knowledge and have no time. I came here to seek your wisdom. My quest…"

"I know your quest," the voice broke in. There was a long pause; Joshan remained still. "Twelve answers I will give you, but only twelve. One wish I will grant you, if it is my power to do so. Choose your questions wisely. If the question is incomplete, so shall the answer be. Do you understand?"

Joshan bowed his head, his mind racing with a million questions. "Yes, Crystal, I understand." He only hoped he did. Joshan cleared the uncertainty from his throat and took a deep breath to relax his knotted muscles. "How can Sirdar be destroyed?"

There was a pause, as the hum grew louder for a moment and then died down. "He cannot."

Joshan looked up in disbelief. "What?" he exclaimed, but then stopped himself quickly. "No, Crystal, I'm sorry. That wasn't a question."

"Ask again."

"If we can't destroy Sirdar," he began slowly, "how can we stop him from destroying us?"

Again, the hum flared and died. "Neutralize the stones."

The *Catalyst*, Joshan thought, as he pondered the next question. "Crystal, how do I neutralize the stones?"

The room became brighter as the Crystal pulsated with light. "You must bury the stones with a sacrifice."

Joshan bowed his head and admonished himself for not asking a better question. He had no idea what the Crystal was saying, but finally he stirred. "How do we bury the stones? What sacrifice shall be given?"

"That is two questions. Which shall I answer?"

Joshan lifted his head in frustration and tried desperately to clear his mind. "Forgive me, Crystal. I shall ask another." He took a deep breath to calm himself. "By what means do we bury the stones?"

This time there was a very long pause, and the hum seemed to chime on the air for an eternity before the Crystal answered. "Unknown. You are granted another question."

Joshan's brow began to glisten in the strange half-light. Perhaps another direction was better. Had he asked three or four questions? He didn't know. "Crystal, how can I find the answer to my last question?"

This time the answer was almost immediate. "You must seek the *Obet*."

Joshan frowned. "What is the *Obet*?"

"The *Obet* will decide the future of your race and your world."

"But who is it?"

Again, there was a long pause. "Unknown. You are granted another question."

He cursed under his breath and searched the floor at his feet. "Where do I find him?"

"You will find the *Obet* on the Isle of Dru."

Then several questions came out in succession before Joshan could think to stop them.

"Will he help me?"

"Unknown."

"Will he be able to tell me how to bury the *Catalyst*?"

"Unknown."

"Will the gods help us?"

"Unknown."

He stopped himself. This was getting him nowhere. He was quickly running out of time and questions. How many now remained? "Crystal," he said in desperation, "what steps should I take to save my world?"

This time the hum was very loud, and Joshan flinched from the high pitched grating on his ears. The Crystal began to glow brightly, and the shadows in the room melted under the brilliant amber. At length it spoke, but the words hammered against his ears.

"You must take up the given sword and bring forth its light, so that all others are blind. You must merge with the *Obet* and guard the wise one's future with your life. You must seek the fallen soul and part the flesh when the moira has touched it. Then you must allow the sacrifice. When all these things are done, then you will have the strength to bury the stones.

"You needn't go alone. This much I will advise you; take those whom you trust and are willing to serve you. There will be few these days, but you have found many already… you will find more. Keep them close to you, but utilize their strengths— and be wary. They are valuable coins and should be spent wisely. Heed these words, Joshan, for this is the measure of loyalty. A man may be trusted to stand by your side in any flight or any fight, but may not obey you in orders that could mean your destruction or the end of those things for which you both fight. The man who stands behind you now can attest to this."

Joshan spun around to see Van standing in the shadows gaping at the Crystal in wonder. "I told you not to follow," the emperor grated through his teeth.

Van's lips trembled so violently Joshan felt only pity for the giant. "Forgive me, sire. I wish I hadn't," he blurted out. Joshan smiled at him and then turned back to the Crystal.

"Lodged in the giant's eye is a piece of the *Catalyst*. How can I remove it?"

"Upon my left side you will find a break in the stone," the Crystal said. "Place your hand on it and the other on the giant's eye. Then evoke the healing." The Crystal took on a blue hue, then green, then blinding amber. "Quickly, now, place your hand."

Joshan crossed to the basin and rubbed his hands in anticipation before placing the right one on the stone. When the crystals met, he threw back his head in shock as energy shot up his arm and exploded in his head. An unseen force lifted Van off his feet and carried him toward Joshan. As he was set down, the patch dissolved in a twinkling, leaving a hideous blood-red mutilation that puckered the eye closed and ran in a jagged scar to his beard.

When Joshan opened his eyes, Van stepped back, watching as they blazed with golden light, without pupil or iris. Joshan touched the giant's face and Van found himself lost in the light. He swayed back and forth, as it lulled him to conscious sleep.

Music began to pulsate against the air, and the world became a hazy dream. In Joshan's mind, he could see an ancient Kerillian standing on a mountain gazing deeply into an abyss beneath his feet, singing the same song. The old man swayed to the rhythm of the melody and gazed into Joshan's heart, strengthening his magic. Joshan did not understand the *vision*, but he felt the notes swell to a howl as his voice rose in pitch and his ears rang with the sound. His eyes burned and sweat poured from him.

The emperor could sense the splinter now; a miniscule mote, no larger than a dust particle, lodged deep within the eye. Even that small thing pulsated with darkness. Joshan felt the scars begin to melt beneath his hand until only faint red lines remained. He concentrated on the tissue around the eye itself. This began to heal immediately, leaving the socket intact.

When it came to the eye, however, Joshan hesitated. The thought of touching the *Catalyst* repulsed him. Tears began to streak his face as he pushed the *power* on and forced down the fear. Gradually the mote began to move—grudgingly at first, as though another will held it fast. He focused his thoughts. The mote began to quiver as two forces fought for dominance. All at once, the sliver erupted from the eye and lodged itself in Joshan's hand with such force he almost let go of Van's face. Searing pain ripped through Joshan's body and he threw back his head screaming.

"Hold!" the Crystal demanded and the light intensified to blinding proportions.

In a flash of red fire, the sliver vanished and the pain was gone. Joshan felt Van's eye now, and with his last lingering strands of strength, healed it. The giant would see again.

A flash of something else, something dangerous lingered in Van's subconscious. Joshan could feel it as an ache in his heart. "Crystal, there is a darkness within the giant's mind. Can you tell me what it is?"

"It is the curse of Sirdar. It cannot be healed away, Joshan. There is no cure for such a malediction."

Joshan knew Van was weakening from the touch of *power*. "Crystal, will Vanderlinden betray again because of this curse?"

"Unknown."

"How, then, do I remove this threat?"

"There is only one way to remove it. You must make the execration your own." Joshan looked at the Crystal in horror. "Think wisely, for if you accept this, you may mar the future and change events. Are you willing to take that risk?"

"Yes," Joshan whispered. "I am willing to risk it." However, the conviction of his words seemed to weigh him down heavily as he closed his eyes.

"Prepare yourself."

The searing pain was intolerable, and Joshan cried out as the curse spread through his body and mind like a sickness. He could hear the voice of Sirdar inside his head. It made his ears ring and his stomach churn violently. *Lost hopes—shattered dreams.* Joshan wept as his mind darkened.

"It is done," the Crystal said.

Just as the darkness grew in Joshan's heart, Van's began to lighten. His thoughts, his secrets, dammed up fears, hopes, dreams gushed into Joshan's mind unabated until the emperor reeled back in dismay and sank to his knees on the stones.

The illumination faded to a misty glow as Van shook the enchantment from his head and slid down to the floor holding the basin for support. He trembled uncontrollably, overwhelmed by emotion, and then slowly reached for his eye. When he touched his face, he could feel no scars and light was slowly coming. It was still hazy, but he could see. His first full sight was Joshan, pale and mystified, staring back at him.

"Joshan?" he said hoarsely.

Joshan looked up at the giant and scowled. "Let me see your shoulder," he demanded.

"What?"

"Open your tunic and let me see your left shoulder, Vanderlinden."

Van looked at him in horror, but then looked down and closed his eyes. His fingers trembled as he unbuttoned the tunic and slipped the fabric off his shoulder. There on his arm was the imperial crest, the red and black tattoo blazing in the soft glow of the Crystal's light. It was identical to Joshan's own.

Joshan looked back at the man in wonder. "You are first born of Thoringale, the heir to the throne of the Imperium." The giant opened his mouth to speak, but couldn't and sank his head in pain, shrugging back into his tunic. "Why didn't you tell me? You are Thoringale's first son—my father's brother."

"Yes," Van grated quietly. "Thoringale was my father." His face looked strained in the dim light and his words dark and quiet. He did not speak for a very long time.

"Van," Joshan urged, "you must tell me. This knowledge is so deeply buried, so painful, I can't see it fully in your mind, though other things I see clearly. Please."

Van looked up and gained some measure of comfort from Joshan's eyes. "I'll tell you," he said, shaking his head slowly. "You have trusted me beyond what I have earned, and I should have told you long before this." When he spoke, it was barely a whisper. "What knowledge do you have of Thoringale's first bride?"

Joshan shrugged. "Little is known by anyone. Her name was Ninia and she came from western Thrain, as I remember. During the Northern War, she was captured and slain. That's all I know."

"Slain?" Van looked at him grimly. "If only it were as simple as that." The Crystal glowed softly, and the stones were silent shadows for a long moment before he could continue.

"Did you know Thoringale had a son by her?"

"No," Joshan answer simply.

"Nor did he—not at first. Six seasons passed before word finally reached him, and too late by then. But I begin in the middle of the story.

"When the Northern Wars began to reach their climax, Thoringale marched to meet it. Ninia was sent away from Thrain for her own protection. Their parting was very bitter—more painful than any ballads could say. They both knew it would be many seasons before they would see each other again—if at all. My mother was expecting me when they parted, but did not know it then.

"She waited long seasons for her love to return from Calisae, his northern fortress of snow and ice. No news could be sent to the fortress or returned to the provinces, as all messengers died before reaching the battlefields. They couldn't even tell Thoringale he had a son…"

CHAPTER THIRTY-THREE
VORIUS

Ninia was only seventeen, as she stood on her balcony of her parent's estate in Silverland, looking over the lush green hills of the Border Mounds and the endless Great Forest to her left. The beauty of the landscape was lost on the consort, as her heart ached for her sire, Thoringale. She touched her massive exposed belly absent-mindedly, cooing softly at the baby that grew there and didn't hear the woman who had entered behind her.

"We're ready, lady," the Elite guard said quietly.

The consort didn't look at the young woman at her back. "You kept it quiet? You told no one—not even your husband?"

"As you ordered, my lady. There is a carriage waiting for you and a squad of reliable guards I have gathered, per your instructions. Please, ma'am, won't you change your mind? This journey is extremely dangerous."

"No. I must find him. I have no other choice." As she turned to leave, a sharp pain suddenly broke in her abdomen and she looked down at the quivering belly. "No!" she screamed. "Not now!" But it was too late. Her child was early, and there was nothing she could do as her water splattered against the stone floor. Ninia's unborn son had betrayed her.

Two weeks later, her secret was broken and those who had sworn loyalty to her plot were caught, reprimanded, and reassigned. Her personal guard was disbanded and new escorts were put in their place—people devoted to her parents and sworn to protect her and her son. The lady's faithful Elite were sent back to the Keep; Ninia hadn't even been allowed to say goodbye.

For a long time they forced her to remain there, only her son filling the painful hole left in her soul by her missing husband, now at war for five seasons. It had become at times almost tolerable, but the ache had never completely healed. Sometimes, on long, cold nights, her loneliness would drive Ninia mad, and she would scream well into the night. When this happened, the child was taken by his nurse to stay with his grandparents, and ladies were called to soothe the consort. But nothing could quiet her heart, and it would take the guider hours to calm her.

At the beginning of the sixth season, Ninia again began her campaign to see her husband; but this time, in secret, with an entirely different group of people.

Vorius sat at his mother's feet one morning drawing stick figures and sketchy mountains, as rain came down in great torrents outside the portico. His mother was staring out at the storm when an aide came in and handed her a parchment. She rose from her chair and stood to read it in the gray light from the window. As she read, the child saw her eyes grow in wonder and then agony, until her face became a mask of pain.

"Thoringale," she whispered and then looked down at her son. "No," she said to him and then shook her head. "No, I will not believe it. It's a lie!" She angrily crumpled the parchment and threw it across the room. Her mother hurriedly entered and went to her daughter, but Ninia would not be comforted when the old woman tried to take her in her arms.

"I'm so sorry, Ninia," her mother pleaded, ringing her hands.

"Sorry?" she asked. "About what, mother?"

The old woman took a step back and looked at her daughter as if she had lost her mind. "Your husband, child—they say he is dead."

Ninia looked into her mother's eyes and there was actually a small smile dusting her lips. "They lie, mother," she said. "My husband is not dead."

"But the dispatch…" The consort did not answer her mother, but instead, swept up her son and went straight to her quarters, shutting out the love and despair of her parents. They tried everything they could to coax her from her room—her state of mind—but she remained silent and would not answer their pleas. As each day passed, they became more anxious; the consort accepted neither food nor drink and would not answer anyone.

On the morning of the third day, in desperation her parents ordered the doors broken down. When they rushed in with an escort of guards, the room was empty. The consort and her son were gone, taken to the wilderness by shady men who could be bought by any coin. Ninia had left to find her husband.

Vorius found the initial journey an adventure. He had never traveled beyond the confine of his grandparents' stone home in Silverland, so being in a wagon with his mother traveling through the great Northern Woods was very exciting for the boy. The men would allow him to run along the road following their eechas and they laughed at his childish antics. Vorius was very bright and learned everything they would teach him.

As each day became shorter, and the road became more difficult, the men began to change. It frightened the boy when they went from being kind to angry men who yelled at him. He watched his mother become more and more frightened as they traveled deeper into the cold mountains.

Their leader was more courteous than the others, but even he began to treat her differently the farther they went into the north. Ten days into their journey, when she began to suspect danger, Ninia told him she had made a mistake and wanted to be returned to Silverland.

The leader looked at her a long time, his dark eyes gleaming brightly in the firelight. Though rugged and worn, he held himself nobly, and his face was one of compassion and wisdom. "Unfortunately, lady," he said, taking a drink of water, "I have made… other plans."

She looked up at him confused. "I don't… understand." She couldn't keep the tremor from her voice. "I paid you in advance—I will give you whatever you wish. If it's a matter of money, I have…"

The man just smiled at her. "It isn't a matter of money, lady." He looked down at his hands almost embarrassed. "It is a matter of loyalty. You are going to help me win a war."

"What?"

He reached into his jerkin and pulled out a wrinkled duplicate of the "dispatch" that had announced her husband's death in Silverland. She glanced through it quickly, and realization flowed through her face as a deep blush. "You sent that notice…"

He nodded softly. "We knew it would shake you from your roost."

"Why?" she screamed as tears filled her eyes.

"You should never trust anyone, Ninia, least of all someone who says he can give you your dreams. There are no dreams to be had in this world," he said softly. "I am sorry I have misled you. It was necessary, and I'd do it again." He stopped and bowed his head low. "I should introduce myself. I am Prince Nocine. My father is Norsk, King of the Northern Alliance."

Ninia gathered her son in her arms. "No!"

"I'm sorry, lady."

"What will you do with us?" The consort was no stranger to war; this one had been waged all her life and six hundred seasons before that. Hostages were commonplace; it was why Thoringale had removed her to Tola, to keep her safe. Without thinking, Ninia had purposefully walked into the hands of her husband's enemies. She knew her position was impossible. This man would no more let her go than he would betray his own country. Her desperate bid to find her husband had failed, and she had fallen into a trap. Ninia knew she was lost and with her, her only son. If the consort did not play this perfectly, they would both die.

Nocine threw a piece of wood into the fire and stared at the growing sparks. "I have no wish to harm you, lady," he said. "In fact, I've been trying to figure out a way to keep you and your son safe. I just don't know how." When he turned to her, she saw something that frightened her more than his allegiance. In his eyes, she saw his lust. At that moment, the only thing that became important was the life of her child. Ninia would do what she had to, to protect him.

"Vorius," she said to the boy. "It's late. I want you to go to the wagon and sleep. Be a good boy, all right?"

"Yes, mama," the child said and rose to give his mother a kiss on the cheek, but it was wet. "Mama? Why are you crying?"

She smiled gently through her tears. "Go to bed. I'll see you in the morning." The boy nodded and looked again at his mother, not knowing what was wrong with her. As he crawled into the wagon, he heard his mother crying as he tried to fall asleep.

"Prince," Ninia whispered, "I will do anything you wish, but you must promise me…"

"Lady, I don't need to promise anything. You are my captive and know what that means."

"Please, I beg you. Swear to me you will spare my child. I don't care what you do to me, but he is not part of this war. His death will not further your cause. Promise me you will do whatever it takes to spare him and I will do anything you ask…" It was difficult to get the words out. "…willingly. If you swear this, I have information that could help you… to defeat my husband. Please."

There in the firelight, Nocine had never seen anything more beautiful than those splendid eyes. He wanted her the first moment he saw her. Ninia's willingness only made this triumph sweeter. The prince knew he could take what he wanted, but the victory would not be as great without her surrender. He could afford to be magnanimous. Besides, he liked the boy and she was right; he would not win this war with the blood of a child. He gently took her hands and kissed them. "If it is in my power, lady, I will see that the boy is spared. Now, tell me your secret."

She looked up into this man's eyes and forced herself to betray her country for the life of her son. "There are hundreds of ships headed to my husband's castle at Calisae, with hundreds of thousands of soldiers to fight for him. They will be there within a fortnight. It is said these troops are highly skilled and have been training for seasons for this last attack against the north. You will not survive them. There are too many. They have but one mission—to kill every northerner standing."

Nocine thought for a moment she was lying, and then saw the spark of loathing in those sad eyes. He knew she was fighting for the life of her child and could not take sides. "Thank you, lady. If we survive, I swear I will protect your boy."

Tears streaked her cheeks as he took her shoulders in his hands. "Thank you," she whispered. Nocine pulled her into his arms and forced his first kiss from the consort.

Two weeks later, when they reached the vast northern armies on the field before Calisae, Vorius was overwhelmed by the thousands of soldiers spread before the massive white castle that loomed high above them. His mother held him tightly in the wagon as they approached, Prince Nocine riding a black eecha before them, waving to his soldiers who cheered his return.

Ninia had lost so much weight during the journey that her eyes were sunken, hollowed circles, and her body had wasted into a maddened scarecrow. Those vacant black eyes now peered at the thousand of enemies who jeered and whistled at her. Vorius was trembling as he clung to his mother.

An older man came to the wagon on a large silver eecha and hugged Nocine tenderly. "Son," he said taking the man's hand.

"My liege," said Nocine, "I have returned with the bastard's wife and child. Today, we win this war and march on the provinces. I also bring news, father, which you must hear immediately. We must prepare…"

"That can wait until later. Come to my tent where we can talk." King Norsk then turned to the two huddled in the wagon and gently lifted Ninia's face. She pushed her son behind her to protect him as the old man glared down into her terrified eyes.

"You, madam, have an appointment with your husband. When he sees you, he will come to me and die on my blade. You will pull him from his hiding. If he does not march, you will die on the field before him."

Without warning, he slapped her hard across the face sending her sprawling in the wagon. His eyes shone greedily as he stared down at the woman. Nocine shot an angry glance at his father, but said nothing.

"Lady," the king continued, smiling, "if your husband does what we wish, you may soon join him. If he doesn't, then you and your son will die." He threw back his head and laughed. "Welcome to the north!" He pulled his reins away from the wagon. "Take her to a holding tent next to the royal colors and make certain she stays there," he ordered his men as he rode off with his son.

The soldiers led the wagon out of the crowd and into a clearing surrounding the king's camp. There, the woman and child were roughly pulled from the wagon and forced into a small tent put up on the hard cold ground. Ninia gathered her son into her arms and waited. Vorius did not know what else to do, so he held onto his mother, praying that he would be warm soon, as he shivered in the darkness. He finally fell asleep in her arms.

Late that night, when the noise of the camp had quieted, Nocine entered their tent. "Ninia, wake up," he said shaking her. She came out of her exhaustive sleep to look up at him, but the sadness in his eyes shone in the flickering torchlight. Ninia's last vestige of sanity began to slip away.

"I can't save you," the prince said desperately. "I told my father that ships were coming, but he won't listen to me. I tried to convince him to send you back to your husband as a sign of good faith, so we could live to fight again. It's too late, Ninia," he said shaking her. "He has sent a locket of your hair and your wedding wrist band to the castle. Thoringale stands upon the parapet. I can't save you!"

Outside could be heard the sound of hundreds of angry voices. Ninia looked out of the tent flap and began to cry. Nocine took her in his arms and held her tightly for a moment. "I can't help you, lady… you must give me your son," he whispered gently.

She pushed back on him violently and scrambled to take Vorius into her arms, going as far as she could to the back of the tent. "No!" she screamed, her eyes mad with fright.

"Lady," he whispered desperately, "let me take your son to safety before they kill him. It's the only way."

Ninia's face was pathetic as she looked up at him panting in the darkness, pawing at her son like an animal. Her mind shattered as the boy began to struggle against his mother's deadly embrace. With the strength of a madwoman, she began to squeeze the life out of her only son. Nocine knew it was too late to be gentle. He crossed to them in the dark and took what he could of the boy into his arm. "Forgive me, lady."

With his free hand, he hit her hard across the face. Ninia hit the tent wall almost tipping the delicate fabric, and Nocine fell back with the boy in his arms. Without losing any time, he threw his cloak over the screaming child and muffled his voice with his hand. Quickly crawling to the entrance, he rushed outside just as torches began to appear before the king's tent, only a span away.

He caught a glimpse of his father coming out of the entrance to talk to the crowd, but did not stay to watch. As fast as he could, he stealthily made his way to the back of the camp and into the surrounding forest. When he stopped to catch his breath and to check on his charge, he could hear a sudden heart-breaking scream from Ninia as guards forced her from the tent.

Nocine watched in horror as they dragged the poor woman by her hair to stand before the king. In the torchlight, he saw his father mount his silver steed and brutally pull the young woman up before him, laying her across the saddle, belly down, kicking and screaming. Norsk struck her on the back of the head with the hilt of his knife, and she collapsed. Then he kicked the beast and sprinted off toward the front lines before the castle.

Nocine jumped to his mount, throwing the bewildered child before him. He looked down at the youngster and shook him. "You must listen to me, Vorius. I cannot save your mother, but I can save you. If you make a sound, you will die. Do you understand?" He did not have the time to make this threat anything but very real to the frightened child. Vorius looked up at the angry man and began to cry, struggling to be free. "Stop it!" Nocine yelled, shaking him fiercely. "If you make any sound, you will die! Do you understand me?"

Out of sheer terror, Vorius halted his cries and raised large black-brown eyes to his captor. He nodded once and then lowered his head. Nocine lifted and turned the boy around. Digging heavy spurs into the eecha, making it scream in the darkness, the prince raced for the front line, concealing himself well inside the trees.

When Nocine arrived, he dismounted and quickly found a hillock to get a better vantage point, pulling the small child with him and standing behind a tree. From there he could see the castle wall and the entire front line of the northern alliance. His father was almost directly below him. He wanted desperately to save Ninia as well, and thought an opportunity would present itself. It was a desperate hope, but he had to try. When he turned to look up at the castle, he lost hope.

There on the parapet, standing motionless in the cold pre-dawn night stood the emperor, Thoringale Kanaine Evenson. Nocine was too far away to see the expression on the emperor's face, but Thoringale stood completely still, as if he were stone. The only movement was the blaze of fiery hair that flowed unchecked on the wind. Over his head, the ram banner blew frantically in a high gust that whistled up from the wintry bay behind the castle. The inlet was blackened by night now, but the sun would soon rise beyond it. Around Thoringale stood hundreds of soldiers, each armed with a bow or lance. But the Emperor and his troops did not move. They stood like statues in the black pre-dawn.

Nocine heard Ninia's cries as she was thrown from his father's eecha and lay weeping in a ball of agony on the hard, cold ground. "Thoringale!" cried the king up to the high walls of the white castle. His voice was echoed defiantly by his followers. "Come out, you coward, and save your whore!" He jumped from his eecha and pulled Ninia up by the hair to face her husband.

"Come to me, you bastard and show us you are not a coward! As the gods are my witness, I swear her blood will flow if you do not. Come out of your stinking hole and fight me as a man or she dies!" He waited a long time for a response from the emperor, but Thoringale stood unmoving on the parapet overlooking the siege troops. They screamed, shot arrows, and threw rocks at the wall, but there was no response, no movement.

Finally, King Norsk turned Ninia around to face him. She was a screaming fury of swinging blows as she tried to fight him, but her tiny fists had no impact. He struck her hard across the face, and she fell to her knees. "Your bitch is on her knees before me, Thoringale, where she belongs! Come out of your hiding, oh great emperor and join her!" He shook his fist up at the castle, but the men did not move on the wall.

Norsk became mad with fury. Lifting her up by her tunic front, he screamed as he ripped it open exposing her breasts. He turned her sadistically around to face her husband half naked in the frozen morning. The king held her arms behind her back with one large hand and looked up at Thoringale as if he were possessed. "I will show you what we will do to your provinces when we conquer!" he screamed and then pulled a long knife from his belt.

Nocine threw a hand over the child's eyes turning him away. A piecing scream came from Ninia, and even the soldiers surrounding their liege stepped away from him in horror. The prince held Vorius close to his chest as he glanced back at the scene. The king was still holding the woman, but her entire front was covered with blood, the cut deep and bloody across her breast. Laughing like a madman, Norsk cut her again and again, until she lay unconscious, folded over his arm. His eyes were consumed by a mad red fire as he stared at the silent, unmoving Thoringale.

"You bastard!" Prince Nocine screamed at Thoringale, his eyes blazing, unheard above the roaring northern crowd. "Save her, you bastard! Kill him!"

"For the north!" King Norsk finally screamed and threw Ninia to the ground. He pulled a long sword from the scabbard at his side, lifted it high above his head, and cut the woman's head from her shoulders with one great stroke. The strike hit the ground with such force, the blade buried itself several inches.

Vorius broke away from the prince and turned to see his mother's broken body, her head several spans away, the face in the bloody mud. He screamed and fought the strong hands holding him. As Vorius watched, his childhood slipped away. His mother was gone, and the stranger who was his father had watched her die. For the first time Vorius felt an unforgiving, all-consuming hatred. It would be seasons before he could cry again.

The sun broke over the horizon beyond the bay and spilled a brilliant ray of yellow light on Ninia's lifeless body. As the northern alliance looked up from the field, each man or woman screaming for blood, what greeted their angry eyes were hundreds of blackened sails silhouetted against the rising sun. The ships were charging into the bay, and thousands upon thousands of provincial soldiers screamed back at them from their decks. A wave of blazing arrows, so vast, they darkened the sun for an instant, showered down upon the northerners, killing hundreds in the first volley.

King Norsk fell back in horror as he gazed upon the ships and the soldiers, his sword still dripping with Ninia's blood. His lieutenants screamed to their legions to form the line, but it was much too late. The ships slammed against the docks, and a hundred thousand soldiers charged, a heaving wave of death. At the same moment, the castle gates flew open and thousands of troops poured from the fortress, swarming angrily to kill the northerners, Thoringale like a vengeful god at their head.

King Norsk fell back before the hoards, knowing he was outnumbered a hundred to one. He and his men would all die on the field that morning.

Nocine quickly gathered the boy and mounted his eecha, torturing the animal to go faster toward the back of the field. When he arrived at a tent, he jumped off the eecha dragging the boy with him and screamed, "Where are you?" An old woman came out of the tent and looked from the man to the boy.

"My lord?" she said bowing.

Nocine handed her the child and the reins of the beast. "Take the boy and head up the northern coast. Go, now!"

"Lord? Your father, he will want the boy…"

"Do as I say!" he screamed, showing her the back of his hand. "My father is a fool! If we're fortunate, we can use the child to try to save something of our nation before this war is over. Take him up the coast to my village and keep him safe until I come. Do you understand me? Do it now."

"Yes, my liege." With trembling hands, she quickly reached into the tent, grabbed a pack, and then mounted the eecha. Nocine lifted Vorius to sit behind her.

Vorius looked at him in terror; the prince managed a smile. "Don't worry, lad. She will see you are not harmed. I will come, I promise." With that, he smacked the animal's rump, and it went sprinting down the back road toward the northern coast. Vorius watched as Nocine disappeared behind him.

But it went ill for the northerners that day, and none returned from the field. Thoringale butchered them all without thought of mercy. Prince Nocine died along side his father on the bloody cold ground and never fulfilled his promise to the child.

After the Great Battle of Calisae, try as they might, the northerners could not bargain. Thoringale gave no quarter in his fury and ordered any killed that would try to approach them. Requests for parley did not even reach the emperor's ears. Those few that survived Thoringale's wrath were driven even farther north and east, their ranks broken, their people scattered.

In the end, Thoringale returned to the provinces victorious, but the road he traveled was wide and bloody. He would return to Thrain to fulfill his grief. It was along this road that he finally learned he had a son, but they told him the child had died at the hands of the northerners, as had his wife. This added to the fire of his pain. He never knew to look for his son.

Bitter, cold seasons passed for Vorius, the pitiable slave of the northern remnants. They remembered their defeat on the field of Calisae and struck back at the ram through his son. Vanderlinden they named him, son of the goat in their tongue, and the name of Vorius Thoringale Kanaine was forgotten at the stroke of an angry whip, the constant beatings, and the endless days of hard labor. Often they wanted to kill him; often he begged for death. But each day became more painful than the last as they let him live, this, their cruelest torture.

When Van was fifteen, a giant of a man now and strong from the long labor he had endured, he strangled the life out of his master and escaped into the south to search for Thoringale. For seven long seasons, he wandered the north: stealing, murdering, and sneaking like a thief with bands of men who were little better than the curs they ran with. Van came at last to the borders of Thrain to kill Thoringale, as he was certain the bastard had killed his mother.

One night, well into Meridian after he had finalized his strategy for his assault on the Keep, he fell asleep under a tree and had a strange dream. In it, the goddess Krikos came to him and whispered into his ear, "Vorius, in the woods you will find a man who stands at death's door. In his hands lies your future. Heal him, protect him, listen to him, and he will give you your heart's desire."

The next morning Van woke and shook the dream from his head, thinking how real it had been. He didn't believe in the gods and laughed at himself as he made his way into the woods to hunt.

Several hours into the hunt, Van was cursing his luck when he saw a beautiful buck in the brush and ran after it. As he leapt over a log, he tripped over something on the other side and fell heavily into the duff. When he turned around, he saw a man sprawled under the log. The man was very badly injured, his leg broken, a white bone sticking out of his shin. He stared up at the giant weakly and smiled.

"Bless you, man," the stranger whispered. "If you could just cut my throat, you would be doing me a great service." He screamed in agony, digging his splayed fingers into the dirt on the forest floor. Van looked back at the man as if he were a ghost. His dream had been real, and it frightened the hell out of him. The man looked up from the ground with pleading eyes. "Kill me… please," he whispered so quietly it could barely be heard.

Van squatted down next to the stranger's head and smiled. "Not today." As Van started digging to free him, the man screamed again and fainted.

Over the next week, Van nursed the unconscious man day and night to save his life. He had set up a camp next to a stream and killed only nearby prey to stay close.

He set the broken leg the first day, but it had already turned gangrenous where the bone had broken the skin. The giant boiled water and cleaned the wound, then used his knife from the hot coals to cauterize the flesh. The stranger stopped breathing twice, and both times Van pounded on his chest to get his heart going again. He supplemented what few medicines he carried with herbs from the forest, and used up the few garments he owned to wrap the leg and splint it, but nothing seemed to help. The man was slowly dying. Finally, when he took a turn for the worse, Van stole into a nearby village in the middle of the night to take medicines from the healer there. When he administered them, the man at last began to improve.

Seven days after he found the stranger, as he cooked a broth of rodent meat and tubers, the man finally woke. "You didn't kill me." His voice was hoarse, unused to speaking.

Van glanced at him over the fire, but did not get up. "No," he said, stirring the broth.

"Why?"

Van poured some of the soup into a cup. "Don't know."

"Well, I guess I'm grateful. What day is it?"

"Fifth of Cessian. You've been out for about a week."

"By the gods," the man swore, staring up at the boughs over his head. "Who are you?"

"Name's Vanderlinden," the giant said as he crossed to the wounded man. He put his arm around his back and helped him to sit. Van knew the man must be in excruciating pain, but he didn't let out a peep.

"Mine's Jen. Nice to meet you." Van just nodded and handed him the cup. Jen sipped at the hot broth, and then downed it hungrily.

"More?" Van asked.

"Please."

When Jen finally had enough, he looked up at the giant and nodded. "Thank you for saving me. I was certain I would die in these woods." He smiled roguishly. "I must have a goddess watching over me."

Van laughed long and hard at that; Jen just looked on confused. "You could say that, mate."

He sat next to Jen and talk to him solemnly. "I've got to tell you—I'm a wanted man. I can't go for help. I'm sorry."

Jen just looked up at the giant. "Thanks to you, I think I'll be up and around soon. If you can take me as far as the road when I'm able to stand, I'll take it from there."

Van took his outstretched hand and shook it. "That's a deal." After the meal, the man collapsed in exhaustion. Van took the opportunity to hunt for larger game to sustain them.

During the convalescence, the two men became fast friends. They found they had very much in common, even though they were from completely different backgrounds. Van found it easy to talk to this man and became very fond of his quick wit, intelligence, generosity, and understanding. Without knowing why, Van told Jen all about his past, who he was, what his hopes were. Even what he most desired—the death of the man who had allowed his mother to die. Jen would listen gravely, but said little about himself.

Once he was on his feet, Van taught Jen to hunt, to fight, to read the trail, and smell the signs of danger. Jen didn't seem to be in any hurry to return to his old life, and as the weeks passed, Van began to wonder why. Jen taught Van his letters and how to judge a man. Finally, six weeks after he could walk, Jen announced that he would have to return to his life. That night, they ate before the fire, both unusually quiet.

"Van," Jen said, staring into the flames, "I can't tell you how grateful I am, and not just for saving my life. You have given me something that I thought I would never have."

"What's that?"

Jen just looked up at him and smiled. "I'll tell you one day. Right now, I am going to grant you your fondest wish."

Van scowled at him over the fire. "What wish?"

"I'll give you a password that will work at all the gates in the Keep." Jen's voice was hushed and serious. "It will give you access to the marshalling yard just outside the castle. You will find the barracks there. You will need to wait until six bells when the buildings are clear and the troops have gone to dine. In three days at that hour, I will see to it that the field is open. You will need to move very swiftly and go to barracks twelve. On the first floor, along the southern wall, you will find a secret entrance at the back of the last bunk on your right. Push hard at the top of the panel and the door will open. Inside you will find a torch and two tunnels. Light the torch and take the tunnel to your right. This leads to the East Hall of the castle. The emperor's room is directly across the passageway outside that hall. Is that clear?"

Van just stared at him incredulously. "You're joking."

Jen shook his head very slowly. "No, giant."

"How the hell would you know about that?" Van asked, but he couldn't keep the excitement out of his voice. Again, the goddess's message echoed behind his ears.

"You need to trust me. Do you?"

Van's heart labored in his chest as he looked back at him, knowing Jen was handing him his dream. But trust didn't come easily to the man who had been betrayed from the beginning of his life. "Why are you doing this?"

"Because I owe you my life."

Van thought for a long time. "All right," he said looking down at his hands. "But, if this is some kind of joke…"

"It's not," Jen said. He made Van repeat the instructions until they were flawless. The next day, Jen shook the giant's hand and limped off down the forest road using the cane Van had made for him, a cane he used for the rest of his life.

Van's day of vengeance came. What Jen had told him was absolutely true. In the dark night, he found himself suddenly outside the emperor's chambers without seeing anyone on the way. When he went to turn the handle of the chamber door, he found it unlocked and his hands trembled in anticipation. He crept to Thoringale's bed, a knife in the dark for his heart.

However, when Van finally saw his father after all those seasons of sorrow, the knife fell from his hand unused. The man in the bed was old, beyond his seasons, and sick beyond repair. Van could only feel pity for the creature that lay there, desiccated by life's horrors, a shriveled trembling shade of a human being. As he looked down at his father, the old eyes opened and he smiled up at the giant.

"Vorius?" His voice was no more than a dry whisper as bony hands and stick arms reached out in the darkness. Van took a step back and looked at the frail old man helplessly. "My son… my son. Please, forgive me. Please." Thoringale fell back into the bed, the effort exhausting him into sleep. Van stepped to the bed and looked down at his father. The hatred was gone. He reached down, took the tiny withered hand into his own, and held it to his cheek.

"He says that same thing every night," said a voice from the shadows. Jen quietly stepped into the light as Van sat next to his father and brushed the hair from the old face. "For twenty seasons he has been in this room and every night at this hour, he cries out for his son or his wife, begging them to forgive him."

Van looked up at Jen with tears in his eyes for the first time since he was a young child. "Who are you?"

Jen smiled down at him and placed a hand on his shoulder. "Don't you know, Vorius? I am Jenhada Thoringale Kanaine, your brother."

Then Jen spoke quickly, urgently, and for a very long time. He wanted Van to come to Thoringale, to see him as he was, so his passion for blood could be cooled. In that hour, as their father's life faded, Jen told him of Thoringale's long sorrow for the woman he loved above all else. He explained how he watched that cold morning while the northerners ripped his heart from him.

Thoringale couldn't go to her. The Elite had tied him to the parapet so he would not run to help her, as he desperately desired. They would have restrained him in his rooms and they tried, but he would not leave the parapet, so they tied him there. If Thoringale had gone to her, the war would have been lost.

For twenty agonizing seasons, Thoringale carried that sorrow and it ate away at him. He had married and sired Jenhada out of duty to the Imperium, then left the Elite and the councils to raise his son and rule his nation, while he wasted away, locked in his chamber season after season. Jen's mother and then later Jen himself ran the empire, only in secret. The credit all went to Thoringale. The ballads sang his name, and his statues showed the triumphant emperor as they all wished to see him. He would go down in the annals of history as the conqueror of the north.

Just as Jenhada's story ended, so did the life of Thoringale and the brothers wept in each other's arms through the night. Van's life changed that night, the promise of the goddess fulfilled. Finally, after seasons of hatred and pain, Vanderlinden finally knew the desire of his heart—to be reunited with his life.

*****

"Jen was to become emperor," Van continued as Joshan's eyes shone in the muted light from the Crystal, "and a better one I couldn't choose. Yet, after all this, when father died, Jen offered the seat to me without hesitation, saying it was my right. I couldn't take it then, sire, no more than I could take it now. Not after all I've been and done. I abdicated gladly in favor of my half-brother, begging him to never tell anyone of my past—a past I was never proud of." Van's voice stopped and he ran a hand across his eyes. "Do you understand?"

Joshan looked deeply into his eyes and nodded. "Yes, I understand many things… uncle." He put a hand on the giant's shoulder and Van embraced him. The Crystal began to hum loudly and the color brightened.

"The *makhia* begins, Joshan. You must hurry now."

Joshan stood up slowly and turned to the Crystal.

"Crystal, where do I find the *given sword*?"

The room became suddenly black and Joshan did not move. There was a brilliant flash of amber light and before him, like a shining ray of sunlight through black clouds, he saw a sword where the Crystal had been. It was the brightest gold with intricate symbols, patterns and forms carved along the edge as it stood upon its point and glowed with golden magnificence.

Down the center of the blade shone hundreds of fine crystals, so similar to the ones in Joshan's palms, he took in a startled breath. The blade was long and sleek with a slight curve, razor sharp, and the hilt was an elaborate web of crystal jewels and gold, intertwined until it was hard to tell where one began and the other ended. The sword was so perfectly sculpted it shamed any other.

"Here is the *given sword*." Joshan's eyes widened in wonder and Van could do no more than sink to his knees.

"Before you take it up, Joshan," the Crystal's voice echoed through the chamber, "one question you must answer. But take care—if your answer is false and you touch the blade, it will destroy you. Do you understand?"

Joshan nodded solemnly, swallowing past the lump of panic rising in his throat. "I do," he whispered.

The hum increased in intensity. "Who are you?"

When it came to Joshan, he stepped back from the basin. *No, it isn't possible,* he thought. *It isn't fair. I don't want to be a messiah.*

"Who are you?"

"I am…" The words stopped in his throat as emotions surged through him begging him not to answer. "I am…" His eyes misted and his face contorted in pain. "I can't," he whispered.

"Who are you?" the Crystal demanded.

"I am—Starsight." His voice could barely be heard.

"Take up the *given sword,* Starsight."

Joshan hesitated as fear reverberated in his ears and burned the back of his neck. *Am I?*

Van whispered behind him, an echo of his own doubt. "Sire, what if you're wrong?"

Joshan stared at the sword and surrendered to his fate. "Then the quest will end here, giant."

With that, he closed his eyes and slowly wrapped his fingers around the hilt of the sword. The *power* that filled him was overwhelming. Life, death, growth, destruction… all of it lay in his hand now. All the futures and all the pasts merged together within his grasp, as a golden arch spilled across his shoulders and around his head like a crown, filling his eyes once again with an amber light. As he held the blade up, Vanderlinden shook and buried his face in his hands. Joshan gazed at the blade and knew at once he was Starsight, but trembled at the power he held in his hands and what it would mean for his world.

"Crystal," he whispered, "will I win?"

The voice that came from the blade was now very small and quiet. "All the answers have been given. I can give you no more. When I leave this chamber, I will not speak again. No starguider will be able to use the *power,* except you, but only at greatest need. Have you the courage?"

"I have," Joshan replied with more conviction than he felt.

"Very well." The Crystal's light began to fade. "A wish you have been granted. You must take it now before the light is gone."

"Then here is my wish, Crystal. Place the knowledge of the library in my mind, the knowledge that Cessas and Kerillian have found throughout the ages of existence, and I will be content."

The Crystal paused and hummed in his hand. "Knowledge is a dangerous thing. With it comes responsibility. Will you have the strength, I wonder. Time alone will tell. I will grant your wish with this condition—the knowledge will not be yours until you have succeeded in your task. If you fail, the knowledge will fail with you. Do you accept?"

Joshan nodded grimly. "If this is the only way, then I do."

Without a sound, Joshan could feel his mind being ripped opened creating a chasm in his consciousness. Knowledge poured in like a raging river. But not just the books of Cessas and Kerillian; all the volumes of all of the books in the library, the experiences of three millennium and millions of people were suddenly his. Joshan's face contorted painfully as the volumes flowed into his memory in less than a heartbeat. He fell to his knees from the impact, and a piercing scream filled the room. When it was done, he fell to the ground, sobbing.

The Crystal's voice was no more than a whisper in the now dark room. "Trenara is in grave danger. The *makhia* will take her if you do not hurry."

The door to the chamber burst open and cracked against the crystal wall, making the dome tremble. Van jumped to his feet and grabbed Joshan, pulling him and the golden sword through it.

Joshan looked once into the chamber, but all was black within.

CHAPTER THIRTY-FOUR
TRIAL BY BATTLE

Darkness. Tangible, touchable darkness. And silence. No… lack of sound, lack of light. No smell, no touch. Nothingness or perhaps beingness. Could one *be* without the physical universe? Trenara swung on the edge of consciousness, teetering back and forth between abstract and reality. Her first conscious awareness came starkly, yet dream-like. She felt as if she flew above the crowd of singing guiders.

Free. Incredibly free.

She became aware of the sailing moons, the cold, frosty night, the companions at Sanctum disappearing through tall gates, and the crowds which began to appear at windows and shyly at doors, watching the *makhia* with fear or doubt or wonder. She became aware of yet another presence. There, high in the night sky, flying her trusted Fiena back to their forest home, stopping only long enough to spare a fleeting glance at her former life—Ricilyn on the wind.

Trenara let herself drift along the trees and hills that were Mathisma, seeing through a void of blurry delight. She found that wherever her mind wandered, there she would be. Time seemed strange here, outside, as if the more she moved the earlier it became. It was very disconcerting, but she decided to let the goddess take her where she would. Trenara knew there was something Ethos was trying to show her.

She sailed across the vastness of the Ethosian Sea in a split second and saw the further shore. Here was the Keep, lighted now against early night, its small torches making it sparkle like a star-lit sky. Thiels walked the parapets with his Elite, watching the sea expectantly for signs of the emperor's return, but his eyes turned constantly to the south. Trenara finally allowed her mind to wander there as well.

As she flew across the provinces, she perceived only fires here and there where a camp had been hastily put together, and people hunched before the glow, to warm frozen hands. As she drew nearer to the heart of Palimar, the lights became fires, blazing across dying grasses and stampeding beasts. The plains were aflame and it sickened her heart.

There was Sark, standing in the stirrups of a foaming eecha, his blade naked and stained with blood as he drove his legions through the night toward a massive wave of enemies. Trenara did not idle there, but drifted past the infernos and the raging tide of war as it crept ever north and east. Her mind cringed at the memory, now thirty seasons old, of a similar sight. She knew there would be more.

Gorka came and went with signs of fighting everywhere, bruising the once beautiful land. But here it was day, and the light blazed against the smoldering buildings as they burned in the sunlight. She saw far southern Palimar: sad, dark and smoking, annihilated by a sudden violent attack. Survivors scratched through the dust and rubble to find someone they once loved. Again, it was earlier, dawn creeping up on the destruction. It had to be the day before last by her distorted reckoning.

Badain still sweltered even in the early morning sun, stripped of trees and green. No animals roamed there anymore; no people dared from their homes. Where forests had stood, strong and green, now were foundries, belching smoke and vomiting wastes from their metal bowels. Where villages had nestled in mountain recluse, now fortresses stood, black and menacing, manned with powerful weapons sooner left unmanned. The land was bleak and desolate.

Trenara stopped in her flight for a moment, pondering her next move. Could she confront Sirdar, only in spirit? Her mind reeled at the thought of seeing him again. She hesitated a long time. But she trusted the touch of Ethos and forced herself to continue, pushing back the crippling fear. The guider allowed her mind to search for Balinar, her only link to Sirdar. She found him almost instantly.

He cringed and sniveled, pawing at the knee of his master like a starving cur for a favor. Trenara could just hear what was being said. She couldn't see the master through the shadows that surrounded him, but she could see the other, a groveling, twisted shape before a golden throne.

"You dare come to me without results?" Sirdar's voice was deep and chillingly familiar. She had to force herself to listen; it took every ounce of her courage to keep herself from fleeing.

"Yes, master… I mean, no, master. You asked for report. I thought best to bring it myself. I have news—wonderful news. I pray you will consider it in judging me."

"So?" Sirdar boomed testily.

"We have the emperor, sire. I sent the deinos to capture him. He has succeeded."

Sirdar paused and lifted a gloved hand to the cowl that covered his face where it disappeared inside. "How do you know you succeeded?"

"Spies on Mathisma have sent word this morning. The emperor is gone and the sailors say he was taken from the ship in the night."

The devil sat back and folded his long fingers. "Where is the deinos now?"

"Sailing back, lord. I provided him with a swift craft," Balinar replied calmly, taking the quiet in his master's voice to mean approval.

"Idiot!" Sirdar leaned forward and Balinar screamed in his shadow. "A ship that will take weeks to arrive?"

"Forgive me, master," Balinar whined. "But you have taken my *power*, and…"

"Double idiot!" Sirdar cursed. "Now we will have to find that ship, and that in itself could take weeks." He stopped, and a chilling laugh floated through the air. "I will give you a chance for retribution, Balinar," he said slyly. "Since you saw fit to take it upon yourself to catch Joshan, I will let you complete your task. Take Dornarth and fetch the boy here to me."

Balinar looked up in horror. "You stripped my *power* from me. The Mourna might…"

"Afraid of a little bird, Balinar?" he taunted nastily. "You will take Dornarth and fetch me that boy." Then he paused and pondered. "Before you do that, I have another task for you." He laughed until the air ached with the sound. "Yes, that would serve the purpose better, and what ironic justice." He leaned toward Balinar who trembled at his words.

"*You* will fly to the isle and retrieve the Crystal. I was going to send the daligon, but this amuses me more. Palarine will keep the guiders occupied, and Dornarth knows what to do."

"The Crystal? But, sire, the last time it…"

"Enough," Sirdar hissed and Balinar fell to the ground. "You would be wise not to remind me of that idiocy." Balinar wept as Sirdar sat back and caressed the gold beneath his hands. "When you succeed, we will see about giving you back your sniveling *power.*"

"Yes, sire. Thank you, sire." Balinar rose and bowed low.

Sirdar's body began to crackle with power as the room filled with red iridescence. Balinar writhed in pain and doubled over, falling back to his knees. "I warn you—if you fail me this time, you will wish you had never existed. This I promise you."

Trenara became aware of a dark presence at his side. Daligon. She saw nothing in the room save the guards and one or two of Sirdar's slaves, who were allowed to serve him. The presence moved to be close to Sirdar and he sat up alert, releasing Balinar from his pain.

"Where?" Sirdar hissed, standing up from the throne.

The air began to hiss as the guider felt an uncomfortable blackness start to impinge on her awareness, seeking her identity. The cowled head moved from side to side, like a scavenger on the scent of food. "I know you are here… Assemblage." All those in the chamber fell to their faces and trembled as he began to glow with red fire. "Trenara… my beloved." Sirdar's voice was a hiss that burned the air with a mad fire and sent a flush of panic through the guider… and a deep familiar desire.

Trenara did not stay, but put her attention back on the isle and the *makhia* still in progress. As she traveled in that split second, she felt an immense power touch the periphery of her awareness. The sensation was like catching her foot on a snag while running, a sudden stop in progress, urging her to return to Sirdar. Suddenly a deep overpowering longing welled up inside her, irresistibly compelling her to return to her lover. Even though she was far away now, it took all her strength to break loose from the spell before it could get a better grip.

She snapped back into her body with such force it staggered her and made her head pound. Tremors shook Trenara for several minutes before she could calm herself. She recovered by putting her attention on the group around her.

The guiders were in such a state of communion the *shield* they formed was a bright translucent blue with an occasional flash of white or green. It covered nearly half a league in all directions. No one could enter and no one could leave.

I must get to Joshan immediately, but how? If Balinar had left that morning, she knew he would be there soon and could destroy everything if they didn't prepare. Trenara would have to wait for the completion of the *makhia*—and she would have to win. The thought was unsettling as she looked up to see Palarine staring back at her sagely, as if he knew her thoughts.

The glint in the old guider's eyes was not evil, just infuriatingly self-assured. Did Palarine have some device Trenara didn't know about? She couldn't guess and refused to reflect on the possibility. The man had spoken of honor. Would he indeed be honorable in this battle? Trenara didn't doubt it at first, but now she wondered. The old guider was still a tool of Sirdar and therefore an extension of his will. Trenara shivered with cold and apprehension.

Her attention was drawn to Witen as he raised his arms to the heavens. "The *makhia* has been called. Let no one interfere." He struck his staff against the ground once and bowed his head gravely.

Before Witen was ever fully out of the circle, there was a shrill hiss as Palarine threw the first bolt of *power*. The force of the blast knocked the Prelate to the ground and flashed toward Trenara. But it was white and relatively harmless. When Trenara held Andelian up, the light fizzled to nothing when a blue beam hit it. Trenara turned to Palarine and gave him a half-crooked smile.

"You will have to do better than that." She pivoted on her heel and released a showering pinwheel of *power*. There was nothing Palarine could fire on, as it was too swift and irregular in its advance. He rolled out of the way, allowing it to explode against the *shield*. The earth shook violently, but they both stayed on their feet.

"Enough of these childish fireworks, Trenara," Palarine shouted from across the ground. "Have you the courage to fight me hand to hand?" He drew his staff sideways and whirled it once where it blurred in his hands. When it stopped, he held a huge broadsword that sparked with energy.

"You choose your weapon well, Palarine," Trenara shouted above the din. "If you indeed wish to fight 'hand to hand' then I say we rule ourselves to one weapon each."

"The *makhia* has no such rules, save no interference from outside."

"Honor has rules," Trenara said, narrowing her eyes at him.

"Indeed." Palarine smiled. "So be it. One weapon each, of our choice. This sword has served me well before now. I will let it serve me again." He swung it back and forth; it whistled a sweet song. "What for you, my friend? Certainly, a sword would be too heavy a burden for your frail form. The south has hardened me, but Thrain has made you soft, I fear."

Trenara smiled back at him. "Perhaps you're right, Palarine. A sword has never been my forte. I think something lighter would be more fitting."

She pulled her scepter up delicately and flicked it once. The *via* began to lengthen, losing its rigidity in Trenara's hand and snaking out before her until a whip sparkled like a luminous serpent at her feet. Palarine lost his smile. The guider lifted the crop above her head and sent the whip sailing in a flaming green circle. The wind created from the movement howled around their ears and blew their robes against their bodies. When she flicked the lash, *power* snapped in a cascading array of fire, making the ground shake and sending sparks to smolder in the grass.

When the noise stopped, Palarine recovered himself and chuckled dryly. "Very impressive, Trenara, but hardly a proper weapon."

Trenara regarded him darkly. "When you go to tame the devil's cur you bring the proper equipment... traitor."

There was a long pause while Trenara rolled the whip around her hand. They both began to move. The guiders circled within the domed *shield* and studied each other's movements. Palarine was disadvantaged in that he could only use his sword at close range, while Trenara could bide her time, waiting for Palarine to step close enough for the deadly sting of the whip.

Twice Palarine charged at Trenara, his sword blazing, only to be sent back by the roar of the snapping lash. The second time the whip snaked close to the side of his head, nicking him badly and deafening his ear. He stumbled back in furious pain. They circled again, Trenara always keeping her distance, knowing the advantage it gave, but Palarine suddenly stopped and reached behind his head. The bolt was thrown so quickly, Trenara had little time to dive out of its path. She fell awkwardly, and the whip was wrenched from her hand as she hit the ground. In a flash Palarine was nearly on her, holding the sword in both hands to pinion Trenara to the ground where she lay.

When the sword came down, Trenara twisted and it landed in the ground with a hiss, burying itself several inches. Trenara jumped to her feet. Thanking her training with Haiden and without the least guilt, she lifted her robes in a very un-guider-like fashion and sent a rounded kick that caught Palarine directly across the face, sending him sprawling. Trenara quickly recovered her whip and dodged out of range just as Palarine rose and pulled the sword free.

He was furious, which made him careless and Trenara was ready. As soon as Palarine turned, Trenara made an expert pivot with the whip, encircling his blade several times. She jerked the lash back, pulling the sword from Palarine's hands and sent it sailing across the arena. The two starguiders faced each other, one armed, and the other helpless.

"Have done!" Palarine screamed, wiping blood from his face and sinking to his knees.

Trenara's eyes blazed with passion. All the anger, hate, and seasons of grief at the hands of this man and men like him rose in her blood. Suddenly, it was not Palarine who stood before her, but the young Sirdar, the handsome Leogan, the man who had stolen her love, her life, her innocence, and the monster who had nearly convinced her to betray her world.

Hate consumed Trenara's heart as she raised the crop above her head to strike him down. But she hesitated, as an odd sensation turned her blood to ice, and she stood frozen in the middle of the hushed crowd that surrounded them. It felt as if she were lifted from her body and set above the arena to watch. What happened next, Trenara swears she had nothing to do with. She would have killed the traitor out of hand.

"Kill me!" cried Palarine.

"No." The voice echoing from Trenara's mouth was an unfamiliar contralto that rang with the roar of storms. "You have been deceived, Palarine. Sirdar is not the deliverer you thought. Therefore, you are spared." Palarine trembled in rage, but could not speak. "The *makhia* shall never again be called by mortal man. We will see to this. Your life is spared, but only from this ordeal... not from the hardships that lay before you. You have much to account for, Palarine of Gorka, and a house to clean before you join the ranks of the wise. Therefore..."

The figure raised her hand to the *via* where it lay on the ground. Palarine could not move except to clench his fists futilely. A strong wind blew from the east, lifting the staff from the ground and carrying it high into the air. There it glowed like a lost star, but only briefly. A flash of lightning split the sky, followed seconds later by a crashing peel of thunder. The staff exploded into a fine dust that rained down to disintegrate on the shining *shield*.

"Your *power* is purged, Palarine," the figure said. "One day you may earn it back."

Tears streaked the old guider's face as he sank to his knees in ruin. "Who are you?"

The figure looked down at the guider, her eyes sparkling with a golden fire. "I am Ventus, Goddess of the Winds. I have come to stop this desecration and to bring a message from Ethos to the keeper of the stones."

"But the *makhia* is to be fought without interference!" Palarine cried, as a mad light began to burn in his eyes. He stood on the brink of sanity as his world crumbled beneath him.

"Mortal, I made this game. Do not tell me its rules."

Palarine shook and closed his eyes. "But he said you did not exist... none of you. He said there were no gods, only humans and *power* and mortal fools."

Ventus looked at him sadly. "Sirdar told you this? I pity you, for you have listened to the voice of deceit, and all his words are lies."

Palarine screamed and fell to the ground weeping. Ventus bowed her head a moment, and all Assemblage sank to their knees before her, the *shield* fading as they did. When the goddess looked up again, tears welled in her eyes like jewels. "I cannot stay. Even now I feel this flesh failing as I possess it. Prepare yourselves. Ethos comes." With that, the golden hue faded and Trenara could feel the same lifting sensation as she was brought back to her body.

Trenara fell to the ground, feverish, exhausted, and faint. She had to fight to stay alert. *I must reach Joshan*, she thought.

The guiders moved to help her, but Palarine held them back. In his hand, a bloody fire had materialized, pulsating with life and glowing bright red. It lit his face with a hideous light as he rose, and burned into his flesh until he screamed in madness. Trenara was too weak to stand, but struggled to her knees as the guiders moved back in revulsion. She reached out to them, but they would not move.

Palarine turned to face Trenara. "Look at it, magician," he whispered. "Look at the power it holds. Within my hands lies the future. Your future." He sent the rock flying through the air toward the weakened guider. Trenara was too weak to stay on her knees and could do nothing more than sink back, bow her head, and close her eyes.

Without warning, a whirlwind rose from the ground that swept the rock up before it reached her. It spun the glowing stone until it was a blur of crimson light, and then released it. Palarine hadn't even time to shout before it struck his heart and burst with a deafening thunder. Trenara was knocked to the ground by the force of the blast and stunned.

When she forced open her eyes, Joshan, Haiden, and Vanderlinden were looking down at her gravely. Joshan leaned close as Trenara grabbed his sleeve and fought to keep conscious.

"Balinar," she whispered as her eyelids began to flicker. "On his way with…" But she said no more. Joshan examined her face with a scowl.

"Sire, is she going to be all right?" Van asked as he picked up her hand and kissed it.

Joshan nodded. "I think so, but something has happened to her."

"What was it she said?" Haiden asked watching as the giant lifted her into his arms.

"Something about Balinar." He looked thoughtful for a moment and then shook his head. "I couldn't hear her clearly." Then he opened his mouth in sudden understanding. "Sanctum!" He whirled to the guiders. "Quickly, all of you…"

Just then, there was an earsplitting explosion, and a cascade of flying rocks showered over the guiders. Joshan was hit and went down with a bloody gash on the side of this head. Then a roaring thunder shook the ground as a pillar of fire rose in front of the Sanctum Bridge and cascaded down again. When it hit, the bridge exploded.

Mortar and stone flew everywhere, hitting many of the guiders and shattering hundreds of windows in the buildings. The bridge seemed to undulate in a slow dance as it heaved up and then down. Piece by piece, it fell into the abyss below, until it was gone. Northerners scurried in all directions after setting the charge, but many were shot down by their own sabotage.

The next sound was a penetrating cry like a screaming wind. The Warder's trumpet call pierced the air, sounding the alarm. The guiders ran to the open wound where the bridge had been.

"The *power* bridge!" Witen cried holding up his staff.

Vias went into the air and the song was loud and swift, but nothing happened.

They tried over and over again, but there was no more *power*. All they produced was silence. The starguiders looked up at Sanctum horrified. There above the tower, black against the midnight sky, a giant bird soared. They fell back from the sight.

"Mourna," Witen hissed.

The bird floated in a circle high above the small island, like a scavenger above carrion, coming lower and lower with each pass. From the ground, another figure rose into the air to meet it. Old and tired, the ancient Warder flew. Up and up she climbed, her three heads strained against her necks, her wings thumping against the sky as she rose. Again, her cry shrieked against the air and the guiders watched as she flew to kill the violator of her charge. She opened her taloned feet to rend the giant Mourna.

As brave as she was, they all knew it was pointless. As the old creature attacked, the giant Mourna brought his massive claws across the Warder's belly and opened her wide. She screamed her last breath and pummeled through the air toward Sanctum.

When she disappeared into the circle of jagged rocks, there was a rolling crash and then, to the amazement of all who watched, a massive fountain of fire shot from the heart of Sanctum, red and golden in the pre-dawn light. The Warder's fall had broken the Chamber of Healing, and the vats of *illiminium* had been spilled and combined.

The pillar soared into the sky and scorched the Mourna as he darted out of its path. Up and up it rose, growing brighter and stronger as it went. In a moment of silence, it hung in the air suspended by time. Then it began to fall. It tumbled from the sky, gathering speed as it descended and grew to a vast fireball. In an earthshaking explosion, it hit Sanctum in a blaze of destruction, kindled by thousands upon thousands of books.

The guiders clung helplessly to the ground as it rose and fell in solid waves. Chasms opened, and buildings began to crumble. A giant piece of cliff broke off and fell into the sea far below, carrying many guiders with it.

And Sanctum fell.

As they watched, she broke apart and crashed into the ocean until there was nothing left but rubble and debris. In the stillness that followed, when the earth settled and the only sounds were moans of anguish, a piercing cry was heard on the wind. Like a spear, the Mourna dove from the sky to kill. The guiders could not move, frozen where they were, as the creature's voice touched their essence and solidified their blood.

But it did not come for them.

It swooped over their astonished heads and charged for another, as though shot from a deadly arbalest. The human eyes were a fire of passion as it rushed for the figures before it. One was down and bleeding, while the other stood above him with a naked sword in his hand, his eyes grim and full of death. The Mourna folded his wings and stretched his neck, a figure clinging to its back like a deformity.

So it was that Haiden beheld the bird as he stood above Joshan and waited for it to strike. He brought his sword up, and planted his stout legs firmly on the ground, as sweat poured from his brow and his hands began to tremble. All he could see was a thousand pounds of feathers and death soaring toward him with talons he knew could cut him in two with one sweep.

Just as the bird swooped within a span of his victims, the Mourna veered suddenly and screamed in pain, a blue feathered arrow, banded in gold, protruding from its heart. Van stood on a rise just behind Haiden with the giant bow still singing in his hands. The Mourna flew back into the air and tried to reach the sea before it died, but failed even as it left the cliffs. As it plunged earthward, a figure leapt from its back and barely caught himself on the edge of the cliff, his feet dangling above the abyss. The Mourna bounced off the cliff, then fell into the sea and died.

*****

Haiden knelt down to Joshan and touched his brow. As he did, Joshan's eyes fluttered open and he smiled up at the guard. Haiden was overcome with joy. "Thank the gods. I thought you were dead."

"Haiden, what's happened?" The old guard helped Joshan to his feet, but he didn't need to answer, even if he could.

Joshan looked at the destruction and gaped in dismay. Massive rends were torn into the earth and dusty chasms steamed in the early morning light. All the Assemblage buildings, all the uncounted seasons of labor, all the hardships, and broken backs that went into their construction were tumbled, scattered, and broken beyond repair.

Where the council chambers had been, now lay a pile of crushed stone. The pre-guider building had collapsed with many of the young students still inside. People were furiously trying to move the rubble in a desperate attempt to save the children, but the effort would prove daunting. Many wounded and dead lay on the ground while others helped them—or mourned.

Joshan lifted his eyes to the golden isle of Sanctum and then sank to his knees in despair. "The books," he whispered. The sea boiled where the isle had been, but everything else was gone.

*****

Van stood on the high cliff top and gazed down at the figure clinging at his feet. Balinar looked back in terror. "Help me. Please, giant, help me. Sirdar enchanted me. It wasn't my fault. You must believe me." Balinar glanced down at the ragged rocks and raging sea beneath his feet. "Please, help me." The stones began to crumble under his bloody fingers. Vanderlinden remained as silent as death.

Haiden and Joshan ran up behind the giant, but could not reach Balinar as Van blocked their way. The hate in his eyes made Joshan hesitate before he spoke. "Van," he said softly. "You must not give into this. Don't kill in hate as our enemy would. Let me bring him to justice as the law prescribes. You mustn't do this."

The giant grimly shook his head and stared down at the terrified traitor. "Forgive me, sire," he said softly. With that, he kicked Balinar in the face and watched as the man smashed repeatedly against the rocks and crashed into the sea, dead before he hit the water.

The giant sank his head and wept as Joshan placed a hand on his shoulder and led him away.

*****

When they joined the guiders, they helped them with the wounded and buried the dead. Long hours of toil passed before any of them could rest. The death toll was staggering and all mourned the loss. The few healers among them could only use what little knowledge they had gleaned from their studies, but there were too few, and they couldn't reach all the wounded before they died.

The guiders buried the dead and built tents for the wounded, but without the *power*, there was nothing more they could do. Joshan tried many times to call the healing, the *power,* but it was useless. It became as dormant in him as it was in the others. He swore at the gods many times that morning, furious with their capricious nature, as he watched people die. Late that afternoon, when there was nothing more they could do, Van and Haiden went to the ship to sleep, with Joshan's assurances he would join them soon.

The day was bright, the sun a pale yellow disc on the western sky. It looked out of place against the dust of destruction that turned everything gray or black, the monochrome eerie against the blue sky and vivid sunlight. Joshan scanned the makeshift camp a moment, gathering strength to enter the tent behind him. There, Witen lay dying. He fell as Sanctum did, during the first conflagration. The old guider did not know the island was gone.

Joshan knelt beside the Prelate and placed his hand upon his brow, but could do nothing more for him now. Witen would be dead before nightfall. Joshan wished Trenara were here with him, but the guider still lay unconscious on the ship and would not awake until the next morning. It would be a bitter thing to tell her.

Witen opened his eyes and gave Joshan a weak smile. "I knew you would come."

"Lay still now, Witen. You must let the wound heal."

"It will never heal, sire. But I have had a good life and no regrets. I am very grateful I met you before I died." A fit of coughing took him, turning his face red and then deathly pale. "Sire, do one thing for me, will you?"

Joshan's eyes misted. "Anything."

"The books," he rasped. "Get them to the people where they belong. I tried. For seasons I tried, but never succeeded. You must carry on for me now. Do that for me, lad." Witen did not know the books, like Sanctum, were gone. Joshan didn't have the heart to tell him.

"I will," he said.

Witen was taken by another fit of coughing and blood dripped from the corners of his mouth leaving a trail to his ear. "It is a good world," he whispered at length as his eyes drooped. "Don't give up on it, my boy."

"I won't," Joshan said, but Witen didn't hear him. Joshan sank his head and sobbed.

A figure came from the shadows, an object clenched in his arms. He was pale and drawn and his arms shook as he knelt next to Joshan. "Is he gone, sire?" Acon whispered. Joshan looked up and placed a hand on his shoulder.

"I'm so sorry."

The servant closed his old eyes against grief and sighed deeply. "It's all right, sire. He knew he was going—told me so himself." Acon looked down at the package in his hands. "He said you were to have this." He handed the *gazing* to Joshan, who took it from his trembling fingers. "He said to tell you not to gaze too deeply or too long within it."

"Thank you. I know you loved him." Joshan put the bundle into his pack and rose to go. "Will you come with us to the mainland?" he asked quietly, already knowing the answer.

The old man picked up his master's hand and put it on his chest. "No. I will stay with him for a while. I don't think I could serve anyone else." Joshan touched his shoulder and then turned to the entrance. Before he left, he heard Acon begin to sob.

When Joshan emerged from the tent, a crowd of guiders had gathered before it. They looked up at him in anticipation, but he merely shook his head. Many wept. One guider came forward and knelt before Joshan. "Sire, what will we do? Without the Crystal, we are beaten."

"The Crystal?" he spat viciously. "Is that what you think is gone? By the gods!" Joshan tightened his fists until they paled. "You have no idea what you have lost." He reached into his belt and held the golden sword over his head. It caught the sunlight to dazzle in his hands as the guiders gazed in wonder and fell to their knees before him.

"Here is the Crystal. Here is your power, your magic! Gaze upon it. Relish it. Worship it. But hear me… all of you. It is because you listened to the voice of deceit that now a few brave souls must fight for our existence. The Crystal travels south with me, to undo what you have done. While we are gone, think hard about the blood that must be spilled, and the good people who have to die because of it. Think well! And, if any of you have a shade of honor left or a thought you can call your own, consider this while they are dying. It is the hands of heroes that shape the world. It is fools that tear it down!"

Joshan strode to the ship without another word.

APPENDIX A
GLOSSARY

Bullion Beast - A domestic animal bred for its meat and milk. The bullion is very large and docile, living mainly in the Palimar Plains where it roams freely. It looks similar to a giant, hairy tick with a large bloated body, small head, legs, and large feet. It is not very swift, but hardy and prolific as it delivers litters of several offspring two to three times a season. Bullions are "harvested" throughout the year from the plains.

Camamara - A small island to the far west of the provinces off the western shore of Selas.

Catalyst – The power source of Sirdar. Red stones similar to the Crystal of Healing.

Clurichaune - A small people living chiefly in the woods and on one or two islands. They have a charm about them, but are very rare since few females are born to the race. They tend to the trees and forests and are very reclusive.

Craistan Nuts – Similar to English chestnuts.

Crystal of Healing - A stone made of white crystal, which is the source of *power* for Assemblage. It is from this stone that the starguider's via acquires the *power*. It rests in the secluded Sanctum on the Isle of Mathisma.

Da – A Tolan slang term for father.

Detachment - A serious depression that affects pre-guiders after first trial. In extreme cases, it can cause delusion, deep depression, and eventually madness. Suicide is very common with the disease. Some symptoms of the disease are manifested in all pre-guiders. This madness is rare in modern times, but was quite common in the beginnings of Assemblage. Guiders are rigorously trained to help the student avoid detachment.

Dispersion - Usually occurs in pre-guiders where they have sporadic control over the power, often causing some very unfortunate and often interesting "accidents" involving the *power*, but usually not fatally.

Eecha - An animal used for transportation, hauling, and pulling wagons (larger varieties). They are similar to the horse as they are hoofed with very long legs; however, they have some characteristics similar to camels as well. Eechas are bred to be very swift runners and have great endurance (about double that of a common horse). They have flat faces with wide nostrils, very long fine hair (usually two to four inches) that covers most of their body, long pointed ears, and short stubby tails. Their eyes are very large and are usually either very dark brown or green. Their night vision is excellent. They come in a variety of coats from very long (common) to some short hairs ranging in color from white to brown to black and a variety of coat patterns in many combinations of colors (again, depending on where they were bred). Though very hearty in most situations, they spook easily at danger (unless specifically bred otherwise. Mathismian eechas are bred for their intelligence and ability to suppress their startle reflexes).

Elite Guard - The emperor's personal guard. They see to the protection of the imperial family and the security of the Keep. They handle most of the duties for running the Keep on a daily basis. Only the most experienced guards are promoted to the Elite and only by the hand of the emperor.

Ethos, The Star - Largest star in the Imperium solar system. The belief is Ethos, the Goddess, inhabits this star and channels power down to the Crystal of Healing on the Isle of Mathisma in Sanctum.

Ethosian - Roughly December

Eventide - Roughly September

Figin Fruit - A yellow sweet fruit with a hard outer shell and mushy fruit inside.

Fireweed and Fratellas - A type of salad with red leafed fireweed that is very spicy and orange rinds of fratellas, a hard tuber root vegetable.

First Prince or Princess - First born of the emperor or empress and heir to the throne of the Imperium.

First Trial or Coming to Power - When novice starguiders have their first confrontation with the *power*. When they can control it, they are capable of the first level of guidance. This is actually the most dangerous of all levels because of the unpredictable nature of the *power*. Young pre-guiders can easily die at first trial or go mad from the touch of the *power*.

First, Second, Third and Fourth Trial - The differing levels attained by the guider as he or she progresses through the training. Assemblage discovered the *power* had varying degrees of strength, and each was denoted by a differing color. White was the simplest and most common and came with *first trial* or the *coming to power*. Blue denoted the *second trial* or the *coming to knowledge*, which enables one to learn quickly. It is at this stage you begin to develop your *sight*. Green denotes the *coming to nature* and gives you power over trees, grass, wind, rain, etc., helping them to be—well, more than they are. There is also a *fourth trial*, but it is very rare and is thought to be a combination of the first three levels.

Fourth Trial – See First Trial

Goddesses – Ethos, Goddess of Ethics, Rule & Government, Leader of the Gods; Leuko, Goddess of Light and the moons; Krikos, Goddess of Life; Ventus, Goddess of the Air, Wind and Weather.

Gods - Eraze, God of the Earth; Pyra, God of Fire and the Sun; Hydor, God of Water, the Sea and the Rains; Noscere, God of Knowledge, Learning and Wisdom; Lughati, formerly, The God of Liberty, but became the God of Lies, Deceit, the Fallen One.

Guider or Starguider - A member of Assemblage whose duty it is to teach and guide a young student through First Trial and beyond as necessary.

Guider's Sense - Not exactly prescience, but rather a guider's ability to "feel" there is something wrong or when there is pending risk. They can sense when someone is in danger, hurt, or even alive, when there is doubt. They can usually also sense someone else's emotions, especially strong emotions like hate, fear, anxiety, or even love. Guider's Sense usually comes only after Second Trial and gets stronger as the guider does.

The Hold - The prison located in the lower three levels of the Keep on the eastern side toward the sea.

Imaka - A liquid medicinal that helps with pain and fatigue, usually administered by a starguider. Made from water that is placed in the niche in the Holding Stone where the Crystal of Healing had been when it came to the Imperium.

Immunity Sanction – Security clearance.

Imperium - A number of provinces and the religious sanctuary of Mathisma, a large island to the east of the mainland provinces, both ruled by a combined supreme authority, the Empire on the one side and Assemblage on the other. Governance of the provinces and Mathisma is split into two ruling bodies. The provinces are chiefly run by the Emperor/Empress who oversees the Councils of Trade & Justice, which administer trade, security, and law. Mathisma is chiefly run by Assemblage, which governs religion, the arts, and education. The Northern Wastes and several smaller islands are not incorporated or protected by the Imperium.

Kerillian the Prophet - A man who traveled throughout the disperse tribes of humans scattered through the ancient provinces. He brought knowledge to those tribes he felt were deserving. "The Legend of Kerillian" is possibly the first written record of the Imperium history that covers his journeys and his prophecies of coming events. Many of his tenets are still strictly followed by the modern Assemblage. They used his writings as a basis for setting up the Imperium.

Knoshkin – A type of hard sweet pastry, usually toasted, made of whillen wheat.

Laminia – Creatures who live on the blood of the young and weak. They were associated with Sirdar during his first reign.

Last Defense - The trial of an accused criminal where he or she is allowed to offer their last defense against accusations and present evidence before sentence is carried out. Somewhat like our appeal process. Usually, before anyone is accused and brought before Last Defense; investigations, interviews, and evidence are meticulously gathered and evaluated by the Council of Justice. If someone is innocent, he or she is usually found so during this part of the process. If someone makes it to Last Defense, usually this is the last ditch effort to fight for their innocence.

League - The Imperium common unit of distance roughly one-half mile.

Locare - A very rare gift among guiders. Those who have mastered the art of locare can find people, things, and places using their *vias* and this sense. Some with this ability can even pick up an object and gain a very accurate insight into anyone who has held it, similar to psychic readers.

Low Season- Roughly winter

Makhia - A legendary trial by battle fought between the gods to settle matters of great importance. These were usually fought so wars could be avoided and usually ended when one would concede. There are legends that the makhia was also sometimes fought by ancient kings and to the death. The winner would usually inherit the lands of the loser.

Marshall of the Guard - Commander of the Elite, the Council, and the Gate Guards.

Mathisma, The Isle of - Home of Assemblage and the Crystal of Healing in the far east of the Ethosian Sea.

Mourna - A creature of Sirdar, a giant bird, similar to an eagle but much larger with black feathers and human eyes. Its voice sends out a sound that enchants a starguider so he or she falls under its master's sway. The creature's voice, however, has no effect on non-Assemblage. Also called Assemblage Bane.

Meridian Season – Roughly Fall

Power - That energy which emanates through a series of three points, forming a rough triangle. The belief is it starts from the star Ethos, then through the Crystal of Healing on Mathisma and then into a *via* held by a starguider. It is amplified by the resonance of musical notes sung by starguiders trained to control the intensity, direction, and wavelength of the *power*. It is known to incinerate on contact anyone not trained in its use. It is strongest at night when Ethos is high in the sky.

Pre-Guider - A student who has gone through first trial, but has not been ordained as a starguider yet. Many years of education and training are required before a pre-guider receives his or her via and are granted the rank of guider.

Prelacy – A group of starguiders who advise the Provost headed by the Prelate.

Prelate - The starguider who is the speaker of the prelacy. He or she officiates at meetings and acts as liaison to the Provost.

Provost - Leader of Assemblage, in essence the second most powerful leader in the world after the emperor. The Provost has almost limitless power and is aided by the prelacy, a committee of starguiders who advise. The prelacy is chaired by the prelate who acts as liaison to the Provost.

Redwyn - A large red moon, largest of the two that orbit the planet. It rises first followed by Whilema about half an hour later.

Salminian - A large bass-like fish found throughout the provinces in fresh water streams and lakes.

Sanctum - The structure that houses the knowledge of mankind in a great library and the Crystal of Healing. It is located on a very small island bridged to Mathisma and is tended by the Provost and the Keeper of the Books.

Sea Scalards - Large bright blue and black sea birds, a common shore bird throughout the Imperium.

Season - A full rotation around the Imperium sun roughly approximating our earth year.

Second Trial – See First Trial.

See – See Vision.

Shoalfish - Largest fish in the Ethosian Sea. It is larger than our blue whales, but very timid and scarce. Despite its name, they usually only appear in the deep ocean.

Sight – See Vision.

Span - The Imperium common unit of measure - roughly six feet.

Springtide – Roughly Spring

Staking or The Stake - Brutal form of execution where the condemned are stripped and bound to a large stake, their hands, and necks stretched and tied to the top, and the ankles and legs stretched and tied to the bottom. The stake is lifted up and then quickly thrown into a hole where it is tapped down. When the stake hits the hole usually the prisoner's neck, shoulders, and hips come out of their sockets. If lucky, it will break the neck immediately and kill the person. If not, they will leave them there until the prisoner dies in excruciating pain the entire time.

Starguider or Guider - A member of Assemblage whose duty it is to teach and guide a young student through First Trial and beyond as necessary. All members of Assemblage are commonly called guiders.

Starmoths - Small points of light that are summoned by the *power*. They "dance" in the air merrily and let off a soft tinkling sound, like suspended glass in the wind, which to most, is quite enjoyable. Their main attribute is that they detect evil that lies in others. The latter can be seen by their reaction to the one being tested. Despite their airy countenance, they can be quite terrifying if aroused by evil thoughts or lies.

Tavelson - A Tolan acid used to clean rust from tools and dissolve iron.

Third Trial – See First Trial.

Via - An instrument of varying sizes and shapea, which contains a piece of crystal that allows a guider to channel the power. It is usually an object that can be held in the hand such as a scepter or staff. However, many guiders have *vias* in the shape of a ring or pendant. The original *vias* were made from the Crystal of Healing, however, another source of crystal was found in the Imperium that worked as well, thus causing a quick early expansion of Assemblage.

Vision or Sight - Precognition experienced by many guiders, usually occurring during one of the trials and sometimes in dreams. Occasionally guiders can experience a vision even when awake.

Vulcha - A very large predatory bird with black and red feathers, bare head, and neck. They can grow to be around ten feet tall.

Whilema - Smaller of two moons that circle the Imperium. It rises after the larger Redwyn.

Whillen – A staple grain of the Imperium. Grown and harvested everywhere in the provinces, it is used for most of their staple foods and their beer.

APPENDIX B
SEASON/CALENDAR NOTES

COMMON SPEECH	*MATHISMIAN SEASONS*	*APPROX. ENGLISH*
Springtide	*Vernal*	*Spring*
High Season	*Estival*	*Summer*
Meridian	*Autumnal*	*Fall*
Low Season	*Gloaming*	*Winter*

COMMON SPEECH	CORRESPONDING SEASON	APPROX. ENGLISH
Prima	Springtide/Vernal	April
Seconda	Springtide/Vernal	May
Tertian	Springtide/Vernal	June
Cessian	High Season/Estival	July
Felon	High Season/Estival	August
Eventide	High Season/Estival	September
Gleaning	Meridian/Autumnal	October
Cordomber	Meridian/Autumnal	November
Ethosian	Meridian/Autumnal	December
Watembra	Low Season/Gloaming	January
Corma	Low Season/Gloaming	February
Equin	Low Season/Gloaming	March

* Unlike an English year, the Thrain calendar has only 360 days. The week is seven days long and there are thirty days to each month. The two times of equinox are rarely celebrated on the same day, but within five days of the dates given. Common speech is used most often for the names of the seasons, the Mathismian words only as needed for ceremony and by some diehards among Assemblage. The names of the months are the same in Mathismian and common speech.

APPENDIX C
HIERARCHY OF EMPIRE AND ASSEMBLAGE

The Imperium is broken down into two sections, the Emperor and his Councils and Assemblage. Below is a brief description of how each is broken into a chain of command:

EMPEROR/EMPRESS	ASSEMBLAGE
<u>(Imperial Guards & Fleet*)</u>	_____
<u>Councils of Trade & Justice</u>	Provost
Province Baron	Prelacy
Province Regent	Prelate
	Starguider - 1st, 2nd & 3rd Trial
	Pre-Guider

Both Councils have twelve members each. They can only over-rule the Emperor's decision by unanimous vote, and only as relates to rulings regarding their respective responsibilities (justice and trade). In contrast to this, the Provost can only over-rule the Prelacy in matters where they are deadlocked on a decision. The Prelate merely acts as an emissary between the Provost and the Prelacy, and has very little power beyond his or her status as a member of the Prelacy. The Prelacy has twelve members as well.

The Emperor/Empress or the Councils can only make decisions on laws governing secular matters; the Assemblage only on matters of religion, education, or ethics. Assemblage, by long standing law, did not get involved in the imperial wars or military actions, except as advisors. However, should an attack occur against the Assemblage itself, they would engage in retaliatory activities in conjunction with the emperor, such as the first war with Sirdar. *Note: The Imperial Fleet and the Guard are directly under the Emperor during times of war. At all other times they are technically under the Councils. However, both the fleet and the guard are fairly independent.

The hierarchy had remained as above for approximately 950 seasons until the Starsight reorganized the government during his reign.

APPENDIX D
HISTORY OF THE CRYSTAL OF HEALING
As told by Trenara of Mathisma at a lecture for pre-guiders before the coming of Starsight

"The origin—there are many differing ideas about that. The most popular and certainly the most enduring, is based on the old ballads that were handed down at the time. You have heard the story of Goddess Ethos descending from the heavens and entrusting the Crystal of Healing to us for safekeeping, until she returns to retrieve it and place it back in its rightful place among the stars. To be honest, I think that and all other embellishment of it are a lot of rot, though there are those who would ask my immediate expulsion for saying so. Personally, I'm more of the opinion that the crystal did come from the heavens, but by a much more conventional route, simply falling from the sky when it came close to our world. Many of the scholars are now studying the heavens and have theorized that there are many such stones floating in the heavens. Not perhaps as the crystal is, nor radiating such force, but they have found other plainer stones in odd places that could only have gotten there in that way. But I won't pursue that. I have never had much interest in rocks from the heavens, except the crystal, so I can't elaborate.

"But however the stone came here, the fathers found it and discovered its great power, though in rather a hard way. It is said that many people died from its touch the first few seasons it was here—thus the forming of Assemblage by the first Provost, Cessas, nearly a millennium ago. Unbelievably, the crystal was thought by most to be evil, a blight to the world. The first Assemblage guiders were considered demons or madmen. But Cessas had a great curiosity and many think he was a genius for his time.

"Of course, back then the world was quite barbaric, being for the most part several small countries that were in essence no larger than villages that bickered and warred among themselves. Cessas gathered what people he could and took the stone to where Thrain is now. There he began a methodical study of the crystal and its amazing properties.

"It is said that he discovered its healing powers quite by accident—his own, I'm afraid. He had received a great injury and was laid in the same room with the stone. When his servants came to check on him the next morning, he was completely healed. He had gained a great measure of knowledge concerning the stone and Ethos after that. He began to teach its uses to his disciples and sent them out to find others that were special in the way they were; thus the custom of search each season. They grew in numbers rapidly, extending well beyond the borders of Thrain into the other provinces.

"Soon Ethos and the Crystal of Healing were thought of as gifts from the gods.

Certainly, crops and people fared better when a starguider was present with his or her *vias*, which were made of the actual crystal in those days, rather than fabricated from other stones as they are now.

"The land began to have purpose and unity. Some seasons later, Thrain was looked on as the ruling province, and more and more the Assemblage was looked at as being the law. It's no small wonder Cessas in the last seasons of his life, conceived of the idea of the Imperium, a world governed by two bodies, the empire on the one hand to govern the provinces, and Assemblage on the other to promote the religion of Ethos and provide knowledge to the world. He had always wanted to study and learn, increasing his knowledge and that of Assemblage. He felt that was the purpose of the group. But more and more the people turned to Assemblage for leadership and the guiders became judges, administrators, and the like, until there was little time left for study.

"It wasn't until after Cessas' death that the Imperium began, when Felos was blessed as the first emperor. The empire began to run the land, and Assemblage retired into study. However, Felos was killed soon into his reign, assassinated by the king of the north's guard. This sparked the Great Northern Wars, and the northerners attacked the still embryonic empire, nearly destroying everything Assemblage had built.

"That war lasted nearly sixty seasons, but finally Assemblage succeeded in driving the northerners back to their land on the other side of the mountains and dispersing them. Of course, the war continued for over six hundred seasons after that, but during this brief respite, they built the Keep to protect the young empire from attack, so they could find a more suitable place to continue their work. It is said that many of the corner stones in the Keep were placed there by the starpower, although I half wonder if that is not some fanciful tale spun by minstrels of the time. In any event, the Keep was built, much to the relief of the growing Assemblage. Once the empire could stand alone, they removed themselves to Mathisma, where they finally built their schools and temples. They took the Solemn Vow never to interfere in the affairs of the empire, except as advisors. The Imperium was at last complete."

Watch for the next exciting volume of Starsight by Minnette Meador coming in 2008 from StoneGarden.net Publishing

STARSIGHT – VOLUME II
BOOK III – THE SIGHT
by Minnette Meador

CHAPTER ONE
THE ENEMY'S MOVE

The Mourna stretched her wings in the dead night and honed her beak against the ancient stones for what must have been the hundredth time. Nissa stood on the central tower and craned her neck to see beyond the horizon. Initially all that greeted her almost human eyes was the black night in a clear eastern sky and faint icy stars. Had there been anything left of her heart, it would have broken. Crippling loneliness had turned her emotions to stone long ago, so that now all she could feel was a kind of soft pain and a thud of emptiness.

Where is Dornarth? Why hasn't he returned? She scanned the horizon with those odd eyes and took a deep breath. *If Dornarth dies, there will be only one of our kind left—me.* The thought sparked something deep within her like satisfaction. *Perhaps it's better that way.*

The Mourna had flown to the tower because of the starling dreams. She had dreamt she was a child again, a human child. Dewy grass had cooled her tiny pink feet, and a garland of wild korfra had crowned her golden hair like jewels. It was a happy time, a time of innocence, a springtide of youth.

How did it happen? How did I become this monster? Oh, yes, now I remember. It was an attack by night, the screams of her mother and father, the sudden silence—the blood. And then he came. Sirdar, the madman, surrounded by his servants, the giant ebony sasarans with their shining black horns, the laminia with their hideous mouths, and a shadow of fear, the daligon. How old had she been? Six? Seven? Nissa didn't know or care anymore. All she had known then was fear, then later pain, and still later complete degradation when she woke one morning forever encased in the body of a grim and deadly bird.

Nissa looked at the wings where hands and arms had been and the taloned claws that were once running feet—human feet. How she hated him. How she loathed him for the creature he had made her—and yet, how faithfully the Mourna had served him, as they all had. Her mother and father who had died early, her brother who had gone mad and thrown himself from this very ledge, the villagers and royalty of

Cortaim, each tortured, broken, and then enslaved by the touch of the *Catalyst* and Sirdar's compelling persuasion.

Only the most worthy, so Sirdar said, would be privileged and given strength. Twenty-five were thus honored with the nightmarish existence as the black Mournas. The horrors had been created in the far north, waiting only for a human spirit to be forced into their feathered forms to release the deadly cry of their voice, fill the blank eyes with human fire, and bring to life the lump of ice that served as a heart.

Yes, they had all served him—and hated him.

Then he had fallen, had died under the mountain, and they were free from his corrupt touch. Their joy was short-lived. People hunted them like the atrocities they had become. They knew no better. One by one, the Mournas fell to the blades of revenge, until deep beneath the blackened waste of Mt. Cortaim, starved, weak, and beaten, the final six hid from sight.

Season after season passed, and over the long torment, four more died. When the master returned, only two remained; Dornarth the Warrior and his mate, Nissa the Weaver of Enchantment. When Sirdar came before them with renewed strength and demands, they tried to rail against him—tried to fight the words, the voice, the compelling command of the red fire—but they could no longer resist his will. Again, they served him.

Nissa could not decide, even now, whom she hated more—Sirdar or herself. She had wanted to live, even if it meant a half-life in the shell of a perversion. *No*, she thought again, *I hate him more*. It was the only thing that kept her alive.

"Do you despise me so much, my pet? Have I not been kind to you?"

Nissa bowed her head low and closed her eyes to the shadow that had appeared at her back, terror seizing her heart. "Forgive me, master. I did not hear you approach. What is your command?" It was everything she could do to keep the spite from her voice.

"You can answer my question, Mourna." He spoke in such a way Nissa cried out in pain. "Do you hate me so much?"

The Mourna cursed herself for not guarding her thoughts. "Hate you, sire?" She did not lift her eyes for fear they would betray her. "You are my lord, my master. How could I hate you?"

"It is well to remember that, my pet." Sirdar then chuckled. "Keep your hate, Nissa. It will serve me, as all things do, in the end." He crossed to the stone railing and leaned toward the east. "You seek news of Dornarth, yes?"

The bird lifted her head and regarded the demon's back. "I was wondering when he would return, my lord."

Sirdar folded his hands. "He won't return. But you already knew that, didn't you?"

The Mourna stared at the dark sea, her voice as fragile as ice. "Yes, sire. I suppose I've always known."

There was a sadistic glower in the eyes that sparkled from beneath the cowl. "Does it bother you?"

Nissa tilted her head and blinked, trying desperately to dig up some emotion from deep within her numbed existence. She knew there should be sadness or loss or at least hopelessness, but those feelings were as foreign to her now as dewy grass on naked human feet. There was nothing left in her—only hate. "No," she answered flatly. Sirdar's laugh rolled harshly on the air. "Has he failed in his mission, lord?"

"No, my pet, he has succeeded; he and Balinar both. They will fall as planned. Joshan will come to me now, and Sanctum will also fall. The starguiders will be helpless without their *power*. It will be your turn soon."

Nissa's eyes sparked with hope. Would the master release her from life as well? Had she dared, she would have begged it. "Will I be expended like Dornarth, sire?" She couldn't keep her voice from breaking.

"No, Nissa. I have something entirely different planned for you." He turned to regard her. "How would you like to have your human form back?"

A faint light akin to interest sparkled in her eyes for the first time in many seasons, but it was quickly replaced by suspicion. "The lord teases me," she replied dryly, ruffling her feathers.

"No, Mourna, I do not tease you." His voice was suddenly smooth and kind, making Nissa cringe at its sweetness. She had learned long ago not to trust that voice, although she would obey it without hesitation. "Come, if you do not believe me. I will show you." There was a murmur of red power, and the air blackened around them. "Watch."

A faint luminosity irised slowly from within the darkness. Like a midnight flower opening, the light began to take on form, hazy at first, then suddenly very clear. There appeared an elongated bed of crystal, covered by a transparent dome. Within the glass, shrouded by mist from head to foot, reclined a naked human. The woman had long golden tresses cascading over her shoulders and around her breasts to end in fine silky curls at her hips. Her lifeless eyes were radiant blue-green as she stared up without blinking and her form was slight, but without flaw. Nissa stepped back from the vision in shock, and Sirdar laughed cruelly.

"Yes, Nissa, it is you, if you had been allowed to keep the human body." He turned to regard the vision and let a faint lusty breath escape his teeth. "Beautiful, isn't she? She is almost my greatest achievement. The body has life and breath; she grows and matures. But her life is small. You could give it more, Nissa. You could give it passion and fire again. All you have to do…"

His voice stopped abruptly, and he staggered back. It was the first time she had ever seen fear in those blazing red eyes, and it terrified her. "Quickly, Nissa, take me to the Tower," he gasped harshly. He jumped to her back and clung to the feathers until her eyes watered as she leapt into the air and took him high above the castle.

When they landed, he stumbled to the railing like a drunkard and stared out at the sea with trembling hands. The daligon appeared as a shadow behind them and crossed to the master quickly. "Master!" the shadow hissed in an urgent whisper. "I felt…"

"Silence!"

Sirdar leaned against the railing and watched the horizon intently. He spoke under his breath viciously in a language Nissa did not know. Then, for a long time he stood very still. A small breeze gusted from the east. As it picked up speed, Sirdar began to sway. In a startling movement, he brought a black gloved fist hard against the stone railing that shattered the ancient granite.

"No! I'm not ready!" Sirdar said. He put a finger to his lips and thought for a long time. He finally whirled on the shadow at his back. "What strength have we left in reserve?" he spat at the daligon.

"Nearly three-quarters, my lord," the shadow whispered. "They prepare for the final attack."

Sirdar stared at the stars. "How is our progress on the field?"

The daligon moved closer to Sirdar. "Would you have me speak truthfully, lord?"

Sirdar's eyes flashed brightly. "Do you imply the reports are false, demon?"

The shadow lowered before the hooded Sirdar. "Not false, sire. However, your generals are perhaps more optimistic than the facts warrant. The troops move the humans back, yes, though slowly, mere inches in days rather than leagues, as they should. There's a captain among them, a westerner named Sark DeMontaire. He drives his people with hope and fills them with such strength of will, everywhere he appears the humans sing and laugh as they fight. The idiot laminia flee from his bright eyes and many southern humans have deserted our ranks to join the Thrain scum. Wherever he rides, he cries the emperor's name, and his soldiers take up the challenge until the field rings with the noise.

"Lord," he continued urgently in that dark whisper. "If I could have your leave, I would take half of those that yet remain and march them against this cur from the west. We will trample him under our beasts' hooves to capture Thrain. I would deem it a personal honor, my lord, to rid the Palimar Plains of this menace Sark, whom I'm certain would flee like a frightened mongrel at my approach."

"You think so, daligon?" Sirdar said quietly. "Then you don't know this mercenary or the master he serves so well."

"You know him, my lord?"

"It is the breed I know; the hero who fights for what he thinks is right, then finds in the end it is all for nothing, save the vile taste of honor." Sirdar's words were so bitter, so full of rage, both creatures had to turn away from him. He regarded the daligon a long time. "We have little time, watchman. I will give you what you wish, indeed, more. Release *all* that remain tonight and smash them down!"

"All, lord?" the daligon hissed. "That would leave Cortaim without protection."

"It will matter little, daligon. You will do as I say."

The shadow bowed low. "Immediately, my lord."

"Now," Sirdar said to the shadow, but regarded Nissa, "that boy, the one Balinar said the deinos captured. Where is he?"

"We still haven't been able to locate him," the daligon replied. "We suspect he must be somewhere east of Dru. I can send the tarsian out again to search if you wish, sire."

"No," Sirdar replied thoughtfully. "I will attend to it personally. How long will it take the soldiers to reach the Palimar Plains?"

The daligon remained silent as he calculated. "From here, lord, a fortnight, perhaps a day or two longer."

Sirdar shot him an angry look. "You have fifteen days, no more, watchman. Do you understand?"

Again, the daligon bowed. "Yes, my lord, fifteen days. With your permission, I must make haste to the camps." Sirdar nodded as the daligon rushed down the wide ramp and disappeared into the night.

Nissa returned her master's look and then lowered her head. "What is your command, lord?"

Sirdar ran a gloved hand along her neck seductively, sending a repugnant chill through her spine. "A special task for you, my sweet, to prove your loyalty." She looked down at him and those eyes smiled back. "No, I do not trust you, but I don't need to. After you take me on a small errand, you will fly to the Isle of Dru. If you succeed, we will reunite you with your lost humanity. What would you do for that?"

The Mourna's eyes sparkled with desire. "Anything, my lord," she whispered.

Sirdar pointed to the east. "You are about to witness the end of many things. After you have watched, then give me your answer."

On the horizon, looking like the rosy haze of sunrise, a faint light began to shine. But the hour was too soon for dawn. She suddenly realized what it was, a pillar of fire rising in the sky.

"You witness the fall of Sanctum, Nissa, the fall of wisdom, knowledge, and the last hope of peace for these people. You also witness the destruction of Dornarth your lover, Balinar the Heretic, and Palarine the old fool. An era has passed, my pet, and a new world is about to emerge. The Sight is born tonight," he whispered passionately. "Watch well. For a power has awoken in the world you will never see again. Trenara will be mine—all of creation will be mine—and Joshan will fall to darkness, as the island has. Light will be gone from the universe forever. Such is my revenge.

"I now ask you again, Mourna. What would you do to become human again, faced with only eternal darkness?" Great tears formed in her cold, almost-human eyes for the first time in twenty seasons, but she did not speak. "What will you do, Nissa?" he breathed into her ear.

"Anything, my master," she whispered.

Sirdar's voice was as cold as death. "Then this is what I command…"

As the light faded, a great rolling thunder of drums echoed across the valley floor beyond Cortaim, heralding the troops that would march to crush the empire.

Visit StoneGarden.net Publishing Online!

You can find us at: www.stonegarden.net.

News and Upcoming Titles

New titles and reader favorites are featured each month, along with information on our upcoming titles.

Author Info

Author bios, blogs and links to their personal websites.

Contests and Other Fun Stuff

Web forum to keep in touch with your favorite authors, autographed copies and more!

From Dean Chalmers
The Key of Oberkion
(1-60076-039-2 -$14.95 US)

On the placid Isle of Briars, young clerk Ralley Quenn is troubled by dreams of a golden-eyed princess held captive in a strange desert land on another world--a place where war is fought with flying battle machines, and the searing white energy called ambia can destroy the mightiest of defenses.

Plunging through an ancient gate between worlds on their quest to save the princess, Ralley and his soldier friend Jack Chestire find themselves caught up in a battle with a bloodthirsty general who has declared war on all of human civilization.

Soon, the war spreads across the world-gate, threatening Ralley's homeland as well. The two heroes must survive sword-clashes, aerial dogfights, and battles of wits; the outcome of their struggles will determine the future of both worlds ... and the destiny of humanity itself.

StoneGarden.Net Publishing
3851 Cottonwood Dr., Danville, CA   94506

Please send me the StoneGarden.net Publishing book I have checked above. I am enclosing $_____ (check, money order for US residents only, VISA and Mastercard accepted—no currency or COD's). Please include the list price plus $3 per order to cover handling costs ($5 outside of the US). Prices and numbers are subject to change without notice. (Prices slightly higher in Canada.)

Name:_____
Address:_____
City:_____State:_____Zip:_____Country:_____
VISA/Mastercard:_____
Exp. Date and CVS Code:_____ /_____
Please allow 4-6 weeks for delivery.

LaVergne, TN USA
03 August 2010
191900LV00005B/30/P